D1487360

UNFALLEN

Book 1: Exile

JULIET Y. MARK

ISBN: 1478285540
ISBN 13: 9781478285540
Library of Congress Control Number: 2012914221
Createspace, North Charleston, SC

To my dad, Charles B. Mark, Sr.,
who was rarely serious and made life fun.

I have so many memories of times we laughed until we cried.
If laughter were the best medicine, you would have lived forever.
I wish the news of your death had been a bad joke.
It was the first and last time you made me cry in grief.

I knew you were not kidding when you said
I should write a book.
Here it is. :)

*Immense and boundless gratitude to the following,
for the following:*

To my daughters, Rose and Kate, who incessantly fuel me
with motivation to finish what I start.

To S. Guy Giumento, Rachel La Porta, Beth Lane, Chip Mark,
John Mark, Gloria Emerald Mark, Mary Jane Masiulionis,
and Andrea Peek for reading rough drafts and
providing encouragement and/or insights.

Again, to Rachel La Porta, my volunteer editor, who received
high praise for polishing the grammar of the roughest draft.

To Marlene Gaffney and Jeannie Odell, my proofreaders.

To Rebecca Jewell who perfectly captured Ava's pathos
outside the wall in the cover photo.

To the best sounding board a writer could ever ask for: Gary Sage.
You gave my voice back to me in more ways than I can count.

Last, but not least, to my entire CreateSpace team.
Using the priceless advice and talents of my service repre-
sentatives, my Editorial Evaluators, Janet A. my copy editor, my
Interior Layout team, etc., it took me less than a year to polish
and finalize the novel I began six years ago.

TABLE OF CONTENTS

PROLOGUE

At the dawn of time, the serpent tempted Eve, and she chose to eat the fruit of the tree of the knowledge of good and evil. Though Eve had tried every wile she possessed, she was not able to persuade Adam to eat also. He remained stalwart in his resolve and true to the command of his Maker not to eat the fruit of the forbidden tree.

When God came to visit, Eve was ashamed, and hid. Adam met Him innocently, concerned about his mate. The Lord told Adam He must talk to the woman alone. When the Master returned, Adam learned that Eve had been banished from the Garden. Adam never knew that when Eve was cast out of the Garden, she was pregnant.

ADAM'S SIDE/EVE'S SIDE

*A*va, the youngest daughter of Adam and Aurora, perched on the end of a branch high above Paradise and sang happily. She had arranged her brown, waist-length hair to cover her body and was pretending to be a bird with hair, not feathers. To complete the illusion, she had carefully pulled her arms beneath her hair and used them to hug her knees tightly to her chest, so only her lean, oval face was visible. Her bare feet were the sole part of her that made contact with the rough bark of the branch. Ava maintained her balance effortlessly, as her brown eyes vigilantly swept the distant landscape of the Garden of Eden below her.

Ava was centuries old and perpetually young. She had the same innocence and joy that every member of her family possessed, and the same brilliant mind. Her only problem, as she saw it, was that as the youngest of her eleven brothers and sisters, she was still treated like a baby. Her family acknowledged her superior performing skills and her verbal abilities, but she had never been able to beat her entire family in the physical games they played. Ava was fiercely competitive. Over the centuries, her obsession to excel at everything had become an affectionate joke among them. Ava was determined that today would be the day she would win her first tracking game and put an end to the jokes. She blushed to think

1

how proud everyone would be of her, especially Seth, as they realized she was no longer a baby, but an equal member of the group. Only the praise of the Creator, who walked among them sometimes, meant more to her than the respect of her family.

Ava was well schooled in the two rules of Eden. The first was not to eat of the fruit of the tree of the knowledge of good and evil. Even Ava recognized the desperation in Adam's voice when he exhorted them never to eat the fruit of that tree. Ava had considered hiding in its branches, but if her trail led the best tracker among them to the center of the Garden, she would surely be discovered, because that tree stood alone. It was a solitary reminder of one mysterious tragedy.

The second rule was not to cross the Wall that separated their homeland from whatever lay beyond it. Almost three hundred years ago, when Ava was still a child of five, she had seen the Wall for the first time. She remembered it perfectly, because in Paradise there was never any breakdown of the pathways of the neurons in the brain.

Ava stopped singing as she recalled every detail of that day. Her mother, Aurora, had thought of a way they could harness water for power. The family was engaged in the last stage of her project, which involved attaching the wooden paddles that would be turned by the river. Aurora was enthusiastic about the project and did not have time to entertain Ava. There was no way a five-year-old could contribute to this stage of the process. Everyone in the family was engaged in Aurora's project except for Adam, but he would not play with his daughter because he was deep in thought. Ava was lying on her stomach in the hot sun watching some ants on the ground as they worked on a project of their own. She glanced up and saw her father walk away.

She got up and followed him stealthily, making a game of it. They traveled for hours until Adam reached the great Wall. Adam stood facing the Wall and placed his hands against it. His shoulders began to shake and a strange noise emanated from him. Ava was overwhelmed by curiosity and approached him.

"Father, what are you doing?" Ava asked.

Adam turned to her. Ava was surprised to see that his face had water on it. She looked up to the sky to see if it had begun to rain and she hadn't felt any droplets yet.

"Ava! What are you doing here?"

Ava examined her father's face more closely.

"Everyone is busy and I wanted to play," she said. "I followed you because it was fun. What is the water that runs from your eyes?"

"I don't have a name for it. It only happens here, at the Wall," Adam said. He challenged her. "Here, Ava, stand at the Wall and see if water flows from your eyes." Adam resumed his stance and Ava imitated him.

"No, Father, it does not happen to me," she reported. "Perhaps it only comes with great age and great wisdom. You are the oldest one of us, right?"

"A wonderful hypothesis, young one!" he said with a laugh. "Yes, I am the oldest, and you are the youngest. Someday you will be able to test your theory."

"When, Papa? When will I be as old as you are and have the water flow from my eyes?"

"I will not tell you how very old I am!" Adam said. "Your mother is a baby compared to me. I will not have her fuss over me as she did over Seth when he had the accident on the mountain and broke half the bones in his body. How old I am will remain my secret!"

Adam took her hand in his, and they walked back to the work site together.

As Ava thought about that day, she remembered the happiness she felt at having the companionship of her father all to herself. He loved to carve wood, and he always smelled of wood dust, and pleasant scents of pine and cedar. They had taken turns talking.

Adam had told her it refreshed him to hear her speak of the wonders of the world as she saw them through her young eyes, and he had patiently answered her many questions, especially her favorite one: "Why?"

That day had led indirectly to this one. Every few years she returned to the Wall to test her theory. Though she imitated Adam precisely, her eyes never watered the way his had done when he touched the Wall. It was on one of her pilgrimages that she had the brilliant idea of hiding in the branches of the tree that she was perched in now. It grew outside of the Wall, but its branches breached her homeland. She believed she was the first in the family to think of this hiding place, and they would never know that she traveled to it by climbing a Garden tree and swinging from limb to limb, like a monkey, across the trees until she reached the branches of the not-Eden tree.

Abruptly, Ava put her hands on the bark and leaned forward. The branch drooped slightly as she shifted her weight. She watched a tiny figure in the distance cross a stream where she had been early this morning. She had never thought to hide where she could observe the others tracking her. She had never realized how good they were at following the signs of her path. Ava lost sight of her pursuer, a speck on the landscape, as he or she followed the trail Ava had inadvertently left into a valley.

Ava was worried. The game would end when the sun kissed the horizon. Someone was closing in on her, but she might still win if sunset came before she was found. Her hiding place was daring. A small hope kept her quiet and still.

She heard a rustling in the tree behind her. Ava looked back toward not-Eden. On the same branch that she sat on, but much closer to the trunk of the tree, was a creature she had never seen before. It was long, dark, and tube-like. It had no legs that she could see from her position, but it moved in an unusual side-to-side motion on the wide limb. Ava could think of nothing but the novelty of the strange beast. Long ago, her father had named all the creatures of the earth. Ava wondered what he would call this one. How amazed he would be that she had found a new species! She forgot about the tracking game.

Enthralled, Ava held her breath. She sat motionless and willed the creature to come closer. It inched cautiously toward her but stopped abruptly, as if there was an invisible barrier between them. For a moment, the black eyes of the creature, eyes set on top of a triangular head, looked directly into hers. Its tongue flicked in and out of its mouth. It did not speak, but made a hissing sound and dropped its head out of sight into the foliage below. The length of it followed in a slithery motion. Captivated by the strange movement and bursting with curiosity, Adam's youngest daughter turned and followed. She crossed the boundary between Eden and the rest of the world with a vague feeling that she had forgotten something important.

The creature moved much faster than she expected. She was not able to keep it in sight once her feet hit the earth outside the Garden. She searched, hoping to find it, or at least find some clues about its habits so that she could tell her family about her adventure. She was disappointed that she could not find anything. Ava noticed the sun was almost at the horizon. She remembered the game and was consoled to know that she had not been found.

With an unerring sense of direction, she began her return trip to the Garden. When she was close enough to see the Wall, she saw a figure standing near it. Anxious to be back with the people she loved, she ran.

She recognized a familiar form, the one Michael the Archangel most often took, and felt relief. A few paces closer she could see the expression on his face. Ava slowed. Michael did not look happy. She recalled how her father looked that way sometimes. He would never explain his expression, no matter how much her mother, Aurora, begged him to tell her what troubled him.

She stopped, uncertain of her reception. She had disobeyed. The Master taught them to love cause and effect, to learn from it, and to embrace it. But she hadn't meant any harm, and there was nothing here that wasn't in Eden except for the creature. She shuddered for a reason she could not understand. Surely, she would go back to the Garden to face her consequence.

Michael had not shown any sign that he had seen her. He stood, as if on guard, with the inexplicable look on his face. Ava changed her course to pass by him. She hid behind foliage and trees, and made her way sideways, always keeping the top of the Wall in sight. Whenever she peered out, no matter how much progress she made, Michael was there at the Wall directly ahead of her. It was as if he was guarding Paradise from her.

It was a preposterous thought! She had every right to go home. She belonged to the Master, heart and soul; and besides, how would the family get on without her? It would break their hearts, especially her mother's. Aurora reviewed the two rules of the Garden with her children frequently. Her father would get those sad moods more often. She was certain of it. Recalling her father's dark moods took on an ominous portent. As if he could read her thoughts, Michael, who had not seemed to notice her, called her name.

Ava left her hiding place and went forward, trembling. Michael's look softened. She spoke before he could.

"Michael, I was playing the tracking game. I didn't mean to go over the Wall. I only wanted to hide in the branch of a tree that breached our garden. I saw a creature I'd never seen before. Without thinking, I followed it. I'd like to go home now, even if I'm disqualified from the game. I'll accept whatever punishment the Master has for me. I'm sorry, Michael, truly sorry."

"I am sorry, too," Michael said. "To disobey our Master and leave the Garden of Eden is to leave forever."

The enormity of what she had done hit her. In response to an unfamiliar pain in her heart, water leaked from her eyes. She made the connection instantly.

"No, Michael, no! Oh, I am not the only one to break a rule of Paradise, am I?" she asked.

"No, precious one," he answered gently. "You are not the first. Because you are not, you won't have to live in the land outside the Garden alone. You have relatives there, less than a thousand-day walking distance from the Garden."

As surprising as this revelation was, Ava was not interested in leaving her family. She had an idea.

"Michael, what if I wrestle you to get back into the Garden? If I win, I get to return to my home; if I lose, I will accept banishment."

She smiled innocently as she said the words. She was the second best fighter of her father's children, having six brothers and five sisters to out-maneuver to get her way. She was shocked by Michael's reaction.

He seemed to gain size, and his look of pity was replaced by anger, which frightened her. Fear was new to her. She took several steps away from Michael, but stood her ground as he spoke.

"If you try to return to the Garden, I have been commanded to use the power the Almighty has given me to kill you."

"Kill? What is kill?" she asked.

"To kill is to bring death. Death is what comes to the leaves in the fall, to the flowers after they bloom, to fire when it has burned its last ember. You would not draw breath, or have thoughts, feelings, or movement. Your body would lay still and cold, uninhabited. Death comes to humans this side of the Garden, while it cannot touch your family in Eden."

"Michael, I do not wish to die. Will this death come to me?" Ava trembled.

He still looked fierce.

"I do not know. It is not for me to determine. This moment you are immortal. You did not intend to break the rule when you followed the serpent. Your error was carelessness. Our Master has not ordered your death or appeared to you Himself to deliver your punishment as He did to the other one. I believe there is hope for you.

"Whether you will remain immortal when you are faced with the temptations of this land, I cannot say. You do not have the advantage of your stepbrothers and stepsisters who possess knowledge of good and evil. However, you know the Master well. If you choose to act as He would act, and live as He has taught you to, someday you will be reunited with your family.

"If you oppose the will of the Master on purpose, you will surely, eventually, face death. For now, I have been ordered to keep you out of the Garden. I will obey our Creator, even if I must kill you, though I love you."

Michael smiled at Ava.

"My advice to you, dear one," he said gently, "is to travel to where your stepsiblings dwell so that you will not be here alone, pining with misery just outside the Wall. Life is a gift; gather from it what joy you can."

"Joy?" asked Ava incredulously. "I have just lost everything I know, everything that I love. How can you speak to me of joy? I will go because I must. I do not wish to pine at the Wall, and I do not wish this death. I will try to serve the Master well so that I can return someday."

"You have the Almighty's permission to ask me three questions about life on this side of the Wall. Choose your questions wisely."

Ava thought carefully. Questions came to her easily, but she wasn't sure which three she should choose. Her mind raced, and then she made her decision. "These are the three questions I would like for you to answer, Michael: Where did these relatives come from, what should I fear most, and will I meet the Master there?"

Michael nodded, pleased with her choices. "I will answer your questions, and as I do so, we will walk. Soon, the signs you left behind as you marked your trail will lead Seth and the others to the Wall. Since I do not want any more residents to leave Eden, I will remove the temptation for you to call to them."

"And if I refuse to walk with you?"

Michael looked stern again. "Child of Adam and Aurora, search your heart. Do you wish any of your loved ones to share your fate?"

Ava made her decision instantly. As her answer, she turned and quickly walked away from the Wall.

"What of my family?" she asked the empty air around her. "To not know what has happened to me will grieve them. They will come looking for me here when they do not find me in the Garden."

Michael appeared at her side, as she had known he would.

"The Master will give them the news. They must accept it, or go into exile."

She paled.

"Michael, can you take them a message from me?"

"Give me the message, and I will ask the Almighty."

"Tell them I am sorry. Tell them not to come after me. Tell them instead to petition the Master to help me to obey Him. Assure them I will do everything in my power to serve the Master on this side faithfully so that I may rejoin them someday."

He nodded.

"It will be permitted. Now I will answer your three questions. After that, you must travel on, alone."

They walked together, and Michael talked until the sun was three-quarters past the horizon.

"Ava, I must leave you now," said Michael. "The Almighty is with your family at present, and has summoned me to His side."

Michael disappeared, but his voice continued.

"Follow the star your father named Aviva, and you will find your stepsiblings. I wish you a good journey and a happy life."

9

"Will I ever see you again?" she whispered the words.

"You will see me if the Master wills it." Michael's disembodied voice sounded in her head.

Ava realized that if she had been in Eden, the Archangel's words would have been an answer. The Master's will was always known in the Garden. In this new place, she could not say for certain what His will was.

Ava began her thousand-day journey. Though she could not see Aviva, she knew where it hung in the horizon, washed out by the dwindling light of the sun. What had begun as another of a series of endless days of beauty, purpose, and belonging had ended in separation, uncertainty, and exile.

As Ava took the first steps of her journey away from Paradise, the ruler of the Queendom of Evlantis stood alone on the roof of the People's Palace and looked out over the bustling city of six thousand women. Rachel had ruled as High Queen of Evlantis for nearly twenty years. Her eyes constantly scanned the roads leading to the palace for any sign that her daughters were en route to their meeting.

Movement caught her eye, and Rachel squinted. On the fast lane of the main road that divided the Queendom in half, she could see a speck traveling quickly. Rachel gripped the guardrail of the roof tightly with both hands and watched as the speck grew bigger. A smile lit her features as it became clear that the horse was the white stallion that belonged to her daughter Rebekkah. The rider was bent over the horse's neck, spurring it on, but long, brown hair streamed out behind her. Rachel wished Rebekkah would not ride Baezus because the stallion was only half-tame, but her daughter stubbornly insisted it was the only horse worthy of her. Rachel kept her eyes fixed on the young woman riding in at a break-neck pace, and she willed her to make it safely to the palace. If Rachel had still been searching, she would have seen her daughter Arrival riding her horse Stealth on the road leading to the palace from the Soldier Sector.

Rebekkah arrived at the great open doorway of the People's Palace. Rachel watched as her daughter dismounted with one graceful movement, threw the reins of Baezus to a slave, and ran into the Palace. Rebekkah never once glanced up to see if Rachel was waiting for her. Something important must have happened. Rachel turned and waited, her eyes fixed on the opening to the roof, which they had chosen as their meeting place because it was one of the few places where they could talk in private. In the Queendom, power and gossip were one and the same. They would not be overheard here as long as they kept a watchful eye on the only entrance to the one flat area on the third story of the Palace.

It did not take long for Rebekkah to come bounding through it. Rebekkah's chest heaved with deep breaths, and her body dripped with sweat. Rebekkah ran to Rachel and flung herself into her mother's arms.

"Mother, I did it! I finally did it!" Rebekkah was elated.

"My goddess!" said Rachel, crinkling her nose. "What did you do? You smell horrible! Take three steps back! Better yet, stand downwind!" Rachel gave Rebekkah an extra loving squeeze before she let go and playfully pushed her away. "What was so important that you couldn't wash quickly before your audience with the High Queen?"

"Is Arrival here?" asked Rebekkah. She grinned and looked around. "I want to tell you both!"

"Not yet. She is rarely late. Give her a minute or two."

"I can't wait! I'll tell you what was so important. Today I figured out how to escape confinement from the Sacrificial Tree!"

"I thought we talked about your volunteering to be the spring sacrifice and decided that plan was far too dangerous."

"You decided it was too dangerous. I decided to keep working on it. Do you want to encourage the women to begin a sister
city, or not? The old biddies that rule the Sectors always veto
your proposal to expand. We need to wake them up and shake
the Queendom to the core. What better way than to set me up as
the spring sacrificial victim and have me survive? After I return
triumphantly to the city, we will be able to pass any law we want
in the aftermath. This city clings stupidly to too many ancient
traditions."

"I couldn't agree more," said Rachel, "but your plan is too risky.
The expansion is not worth risking your life over. I will not be able
to pass any laws if you die."

Rebekkah had an argument ready, but a figure appeared in
the doorway. She stopped speaking until it was obvious it was
Arrival.

"Sister-second!" said Rebekkah with another grin. "Second
in birth order, second in command, and second at the meeting.
Always following me. Mother should have named you Shadow."

Arrival grinned. Rachel watched as her daughters hugged.
Rebekkah was older than the twenty-some years she looked. She
was very pretty, with long, thick auburn hair that hung to her waist.
Her face was an oval, with high cheekbones and alert brown eyes.
Arrival was slightly taller, but she was the more beautiful of the
two. She kept her hair short, as most of the soldiers did. She had
strong features, high cheekbones, and beautiful eyes. Her skin was
dark. Both women were thin and muscular.

The family resemblance between the sisters was there, but not
as strong as between Rebekkah and Rachel, which was as it should
be. Arrival was actually the only child of a distant cousin of hers.
Her cousin had died in childbirth, and Rachel had taken Arrival
into her household, raising her as a daughter. In truth, it was
Rebekkah, only six years older than Arrival, who had done most of
the day-to-day tasks of mothering Arrival.

Etiquette demanded that Rachel get the first hug, but when the three of them were alone, they never followed protocol. Rachel knew Arrival preferred Rebekkah's company to her own. Even as a baby, Arrival would wriggle and try to get out of her arms as soon as Rebekkah entered the room.

"At least I smell better," Arrival retorted with a good-natured smile. Arrival turned for a quick embrace with the High Queen.

"Mother," she said in greeting.

"Daughter," Rachel replied. "Your sister has not forgotten about the ridiculous scheme she brought up a year ago. Help me talk her out of it!"

"Not the plan where she offers to be the spring sacrifice and miraculously survives?" asked Arrival.

"You are not as dumb as you look, kiddo," said Rebekkah. "Today I freed myself. It was the only fly in the honey keeping me from my sweet reward."

"That's where you were while I was left to run drills and fight slaves?" asked Arrival. "Climbing trees? Give me a break! I had to fight number 293326 today in your place. He almost beat me."

"If a man can beat you in a fight, you don't deserve to be second in command. Quit whining and improve your techniques."

"Girls! Stop arguing!" said Rachel. "Arrival, for goddess's sake, take my side against hers and tell her she is out of her mind to think of risking her life like that."

"I'm not sure it is such a terrible idea," Arrival said slowly, contemplating the idea. "The spring sacrifice is a stupid, pointless religious ritual. If Rebekkah is sure that she will succeed, we should at least talk more about it." Arrival turned to Rebekkah as Rachel threw up her hands in frustration. "Would you do this next spring?"

"No, not next spring," answered Rebekkah. Arrival watched Rebekkah touch her belly lightly. Rebekkah noticed Arrival's glance and moved her hand up to finger-comb her tousled hair. "This fall I will leave on another exploratory expedition."

"How long do you plan to be gone this time?" asked Arrival.

"At least until planting season next year. I need to see what the winter season is like in the area I have mapped out. We are going to need a lot of information to convince women to leave their home hearths in Evlantis, even after we pass legislation allowing us to leave. Do you think you can manage my Sector all that time? Or are you afraid a slave will beat you in practice combat? Maybe I should promote Diana. She never complains about fighting slaves."

"I don't know if you've noticed, but while you were out on your mysterious vacations, exploring no-woman's land, I've been doing all the real work of ruling the Sector. I will be fine without you, just like always."

"As long as you stay away from number 293326—but maybe you'd like him to beat you!" The tone of Rebekkah's voice was suggestive.

Both Rachel and Arrival looked shocked. Arrival held up two fists, ready to fight.

"Take that filthy thing you said back!" she yelled. Her face was red with anger.

"For goddess's sake, Rebekkah!" said Rachel. "What is wrong with you? Did you fall on your head out of the tree? Take it back, now!"

Before Rebekkah could apologize, Arrival leaped at her and began to pummel her with her fists. Uncharacteristically, Rebekkah dropped to the ground and covered herself with her arms.

"Sister, I'm sorry!" Rebekkah said. "I know you've never looked upon a slave with an illegal thought in your head. Forgive me! It was a stupid joke!"

"Yes, you had better be sorry. How could you say such a thing to your sister?" asked Rachel of Rebekkah.

Arrival stopped fighting and looked in surprise at Rachel. Rachel almost never took her side. Arrival missed the intent scrutiny Rebekkah directed at their mother as she answered.

"Mom, I wasn't thinking. It was a schoolgirls' taunt. It just slipped out. I rely on Arrival to run things while I am gone. I was worried she couldn't handle the responsibility. What's the big deal?"

"You know what the big deal is," answered Rachel. "Men are barely huwoman, and for a woman to debase herself by consorting with a slave outside of the Quickening Chamber is disgraceful. You were both present when Eriad and number 35241 were burned at the stake.

"Rebekkah, you took it with the strength of your foremothers, but Arrival, you vomited for hours afterward. To jest about such a thing is not funny. Especially since I am High Queen. If my enemies suspected that either one of you was consorting with a slave, it could ruin us. You know everything we have worked for. Think of the Queendom, and don't ever make such a rude comment again. And, if you can't do it for the Queendom, do it for me. It would break my heart to watch either one of you suffer the death penalty on a trumped-up charge."

"Eriad wouldn't have died if she hadn't confessed to the crime," said Rebekkah. "No one could make me confess to an illegal relationship. She was stupid."

"Rebekkah!" said Rachel.

"Fine. Edict 243 on how to be the perfect daughter of a High Queen noted and filed. Now, can we move on? Arrival, do you forgive me?"

"I forgive you. Get up. Let's get back to business. If you are not going to risk your sorry life this spring, then when are you?"

"In three years' time, the same year Mother is up for re-election. It will ensure a landslide victory. We can use the momentum to successfully push our agenda to begin a new settlement. It is the perfect plan."

"Perfect?" asked Arrival, "I disagree. Two more innocent women will have to die in the stupid rite. Show me how to get down from the tree and I will do it sooner."

Rachel nodded her head while Rebekkah shook hers.

"No, Sister, this is my plan. I did the work. I will get all the glory. As your Commander, your Queen, and your sister, I forbid you."

"As your mother and as High Queen, I am changing the subject. Now, I called you up here to talk about politics. Ariana, the niece of Eriad, is running for the office of Low Queen of the Livestock Sector. Polls show she is likely to win. I want to make sure she is firmly on our side, and that if she wins, she will not use her position to redact retribution for the just sentencing of her aunt."

"Mother, that was over a decade ago," said Rebekkah. "Why would she harbor a grudge that long? She seems very nice."

"Being pleasant does not preclude you from the banquet of revenge," said Rachel. "Arrival, I want you to befriend the young queen. Make sure she is on our side. As Rebekkah mentioned, three short years from now my seven-year term is up, and the women must vote to keep me in power. My sources tell me Sephora will run against me again, and that she is willing to risk everything to win."

"Risk everything? What exactly does that mean?" asked Arrival.

"It means the rumors we hear about how she tortures and murders her own people and does whatever she likes with the slaves in her Sector are true," said Rebekkah.

"Nonsense," said the High Queen. "Those stories are too horrible to be true. No woman is capable of the atrocities recounted in the rumors. When I was young, women spread terrible rumors about me. It took so many years for me to become pregnant that women were saying I was preventing pregnancies on purpose, just so I could visit the Quickening Chamber every month." Rachel shuddered. "I hated quickening duty. I wanted to be a mother so badly I was willing to endure whatever I had to," she said, looking at Rebekkah with love, "and I was rewarded for my suffering beyond my wildest expectation."

"What made the rumors stop?" asked Arrival. "I've never heard anyone so much as breathe a word about you having the least bit of treasonous desire."

"My first pregnancy, and stillbirth, silenced the rumors."

Arrival nodded. "Whenever I hear women talking about your youth, they speak of your perseverance, not perversion."

"Mother, I have a question for you," said Rebekkah, changing the subject. "Have you decided if you are going to tell Low Queen Sephora about the secret panels behind the Throne Room and the Royal Dressing Room?"

Long ago, frustrated by women who would blatantly lie about what happened behind closed doors, Rachel had made it a policy to include witnesses to every transaction. When she learned the hard way that witnesses could be paid to tell falsehoods, she came up with an ingenious idea. She placed key witnesses behind secret viewing areas she had installed in public areas of the Palace. Tapestries covered wood panels that could be removed to allow witnesses behind them to see and hear everything. At first, she had only one panel installed. Soon, she found it helpful to build more. The viewing areas were highly guarded secrets. Rachel had gone so far as to have the slaves who had built the areas behind the walls killed.

"No," said the High Queen. "I am only revealing their existence to my allies. I have never been exactly sure where I stood with Sephora. I think it would be prudent to keep them from her, at least for now."

"I agree," said Rebekkah and Arrival in unison. They laughed.

"I am getting chilly up here on the roof," said the High Queen. "We can talk about the rest of my business in the comfort of my Palace quarters. Arrival has accepted the assignment to befriend Ariana so that we can infiltrate her faction. That was the only item I needed to conduct in secret.

"Rebekkah, you can get cleaned up. I will send for dinner. We can reconvene in half an hour in my quarters and dine together. Let's go."

Arrival and Rebekkah recognized Rachel's tone for what it was: a command rather than suggestion. They walked together to the opening of the roof. As usual, Rebekkah was in the middle, talking gaily to Rachel and Arrival. As usual, the conversation became most animated between Rebekkah and her mother. After a while, Arrival fell behind.

Rebekkah was giddy with joy. An opponent had boxed her into a very uncomfortable position. She was being blackmailed into living a double life, and she was forced to keep secrets from the people she loved the most. She now had a viable plan to turn the table on her enemy, Urthmata. It all hinged on the trick she had mastered today.

Rachel had forbidden Rebekkah to move forward with her plan, but Rebekkah's intelligence system was far more intricate than either Arrival or Rachel guessed. Rebekkah and Sephora were always engaged in a complex dance with agents and double agents. Using her agents to drop a word here and a word there, over the next three years, Rebekkah would manipulate Sephora, her mother, and the entire Queendom so that she could have freedom from her blackmailer. Three years was a long time, but the wait would be worth it to have everything she dreamed of. The women must leave Evlantis to colonize the world. Rebekkah's happiness depended on it. She hoped freedom from the demands of Urthmata would not alienate her own mother. Rebekkah glanced back at Arrival, who trailed behind her. Rebekkah smiled at her sister, certain that Arrival would love her, no matter what.

Arrival returned Rebekkah's smile. She was aware that women wondered if she was jealous, always coming second to Rebekkah. The truth was she was the happiest woman in the Queendom. There was no one's company she loved more than her sister's. Arrival had the perks and benefits of being a princess without the constant scrutiny of the High Queen that Rebekkah lived with. Arrival had the challenge of running the Soldier Sector in Rebekkah's frequent absences without having the responsibility of the difficult decisions that Rebekkah insisted on making. Arrival walked behind Rachel and Rebekkah, listening to their conversation, feeling profound peace and happiness.

JOURNEY'S END

Ava was lonely. The three-year period she had traveled was nothing compared to the hundreds of years she had lived in Eden, but without companionship, time dragged. She had often cried, but in spite of a pervasive desire to sleep, she kept moving because she had been promised she would find people to live with. She had passed through three distinctly different terrains during her journey: first a desert, then a mountain range, and finally, a forest. She had lived on whatever edible fruit, plant parts, and fish she had found as she traveled. Whenever she found rivers flowing in the direction Aviva led her, she swam or floated down them.

Ava stood at the edge of a meadow, hoping she would not be alone for much longer. In the distance, she could see the end of a much smaller mountain range than the one she had crossed previously. Her long hair was bound in a tight braid and knotted in a thick bun at the back of her head. Her body was muscular and fit. She had left the Garden with nothing, but over the years, she had found it necessary to create tools and carry them with her. She had not always worn clothing, but she had found it helpful to cover herself against the temperature changes, which were much more extreme out here than they were in Eden. She had dressed herself in pieces of animal skins she had found along the way and sewn together with a bone needle and strong twine she made of natural fibers. She had learned to keep food and water with her in a pack she had fashioned. To keep her mind active, she had studied everything around her along the way. She had made up songs and stories about the wonderful sights she had seen. Though she saw the Maker's hand everywhere in the wonders of His creation, she had not seen His beloved face or heard His beautiful voice anywhere. The grief of leaving Paradise was always with her, but so was the hope that she could live a good life among her stepsiblings and return to her family.

Ava heard hoof beats. She turned her head and watched in wonder as a stallion approached her. It was pure white, and the biggest, most powerful horse she had ever seen. It seemed to recognize her. It stopped, snorting and pawing at the ground nervously. Ava spoke to the horse in the language her family used to talk to the horses in Eden. So far, none of the animals she had come across had known any of the hundreds of dialects the Edenites used to communicate with other species. Neither did this horse, though it twitched its ears. Slowly, Ava took some wild strawberries from her pack and held them out to the beautiful creature. The horse sniffed, then ate. Ava switched from the horse dialect to the language she had learned from her family.

"I am looking for people. Do you know where I can find them? I was told it would be a thousand-day journey, so I must be almost there. Do you know where the humans are?"

She had the animal's full attention now. Ava felt excitement. This animal had heard words spoken before.

"Will you take me to them?"

She did not know if the horse understood, but he whinnied. Without hesitation, Ava moved to his side, reached up to his back, and used her strong arms to lift her legs up and over its back so that she was sitting astride the stallion.

"Take me to your people," Ava commanded.

The horse galloped back the way it had come, toward the smallest and last mountain in the range. When the white stallion reached the base of the mountain, it reared. Ava slid off his back, and as she landed on the ground, she felt a sharp pain in her ankle. She cried out and the horse galloped away.

"Wait," Ava called to the horse. "Wait! Come back!"

The stallion never looked back. Ava did not know that the horse had been turned out of his home because his owner had received a death sentence. The horse was frightened. He only knew that his beloved mistress was in danger, but every time he tried to go to her aid, he was driven away.

Ava watched it retreat with dismay. She examined the broken bone in her ankle with her fingers and grimaced in pain as she determined where it was fractured. She held the bone tightly together. She had been hurt many times during her journey, and she knew from experience the break would take less than an hour to heal. Still excited at the knowledge that the horse recognized language, she chose her next course of action. Instead of skirting the mountain range as she had planned, she would climb the small mountain that rose up before her and search for signs of life below. She had worried the entire trip about missing a small pocket of people in the world, which, she was learning, was immense.

The hour ended and Ava jumped up fully healed. She started up the mountain eagerly. If the climb went well, she would be at its peak by mid-afternoon.

The sun was almost at its zenith when Ava reached the top. She yelled joyfully at the first signs of civilization she found there. Ava discovered a great carved stone, its top ground flat enough to serve as a table.

Beyond the table, there were wooden benches, dozens of rows of them with a space down the middle. Ava walked slowly down the center aisle trying to guess what purpose the place served. She could not imagine why so many seats were required. Her family only consisted of fourteen people, and they had been on the earth for as long as her stepsiblings had. Ava noted that on the outskirts of the benches were rock sculptures, all vaguely female in shape.

The terrain before her was clear and free of trees that would have obstructed the view before her, which slowly materialized as she walked. Her paradise-perfect eyes took in a vast ocean. More steps carried her to a place where she could see rough-hewn, long wooden buildings on the edge of a bay. Ava ran forward eagerly and then stopped abruptly. She felt dizzy as she took in the scene below her. She sat until the dizziness passed, but then her view of the scene spread before her was limited, so she crawled on her hands and knees until it was visible again.

Along the concave edge of a wide bay, thousands of buildings peppered an area large enough to house almost ten thousand people. Though the city below was huge, it was crude. She mentally compared it to the beautiful complex of buildings in the Garden of Eden and found it lacking. Each structure of the home she had left behind her had blended into its surroundings. Each room had function and beauty. This place was haphazardly put together, as if the buildings had been piled onto the landscape by a clumsy hand.

The city was laid out in a rough semi-circle at the edge of the ocean, with six distinct pie-shaped pieces jutting from a complex at its focal point. The long, low, wooden buildings she had first seen were a different style than the six pie-shaped structures. Those sections were separated from each other by wide partitions. A wall surrounded the entire city. Outside the wall and to the right of the city were immense gardens. To the left, large herds of livestock roamed.

When Ava no longer felt dizzy, she stood. Her heart pounded in her chest. There was a clear path down the mountainside. Ava thought she might be able to reach the city by nightfall if she hurried. Her journey was close to its end. Her great loneliness would be assuaged. She stopped only once where the path led her to a small bridge that spanned a stream. She unbound her hair and bathed there. She wanted to look her best when she finally met her stepsiblings.

The long wooden buildings Ava had first seen were barracks that housed the men, all of whom were enslaved by the women of the city. A slave wearing a brown hooded robe was sitting cross-legged outside the door of one of the barracks, which were supposed to be empty at that hour of the day. He had pulled the hood of his cloak up and over his face to mask his identity. He reclined against the wall to give the impression he had chosen to nap through the lunch period. He was not sleeping, though; he was guarding the room where Servus, the self-proclaimed King of Slaves, met with his most trusted advisors, Justus and Kiertus.

Servus was a handsome man. His dark hair and chiseled features had made more than one woman catch her breath when he was in his youth. He might have become a favorite in the Quickening Chamber had he not been so restless and distant to women when he had served that duty. Servus possessed a hatred for man's subservient position in society, and he had a talent for leadership. The city leaders had long ago identified him as a threat. Experience had taught women not to martyr firebrands such as Servus, but to control them through hard work and frequent punishments. The hardship Servus suffered only strengthened his resolve to change the system. His body had become muscular and powerful. He had rallied the men behind him and had risen within the hierarchy of the men to appoint himself King of Slaves. Servus had sought kingship for one reason: His goal was to begin the rebellion that would end slavery forever. He longed to see his brothers enjoy the same rights that the humblest women in the city of Evlantis had. He would gladly sacrifice his own life if his brothers could live in freedom.

"What did you call us here for, Servus?" asked Kiertus. "If we are caught, the punishment will be severe."

Kiertus was a favorite delivery slave in the Queendom. He had black hair, sloped eyes, and a quick wit. His tie to Servus was known to only a few, yet his contributions to the cause were innumerable. He had unerring diplomacy, steadfastness of purpose, and a cheerful disposition. Everyone respected him, including the women. Servus counted himself lucky to have recruited Kiertus.

In contrast, Justus was everything Kiertus was not. Justus was an older man with a dark complexion and a shaved head. Servus and Justus had been friends since Servus had left the boys' barracks. Justus was quiet, but when he spoke, truth was heard, whether it was welcomed or not. Instead of resenting Kiertus's presence among them, he had welcomed the young man and had mentored him.

"I have called you here because we have to increase training and weapon making," Servus answered. "In as little as three months' time we must be prepared to fight."

Justus and Kiertus exchanged a glance.

"Permission to speak freely," said Kiertus.

"We don't have time for anything less," said Servus. "Speak, and quickly, Kiertus."

"We have been planning to start the war for our freedom seven years from now. We do not have enough weapons, and most men don't want to fight. Under High Queen Rachel's rule, they have become complacent. She believes men to be inferior, a necessary evil to be endured, but her love for the city keeps her vision clear. The grain bins must be kept full, and the livestock must be kept healthy. The walls and buildings must be maintained. The complex irrigation system that feeds the farmlands on the southeastern side of the city must be kept in good working order. Any man who gives an honest day's work is treated well. If we meet our quotas, Rachel even allows us to practice our ancient religion openly, and she encourages the recreational games we love. How will you rouse the men's interest in rebellion when things are going well and there is so much to do? What has made you change your mind?"

"The work to incite the men to war will be done for us," said Servus. "Even though I have been certain that Rachel would be High Queen for the next seven years, this is the third day of the spring sacrifice, and Commander Rebekkah still swings from the sacrificial tree. My spies have told me someone high up in the government of the Arts Sector is bragging Sephora will be High Queen after the upcoming election. I've been thinking about what will happen if Rebekkah never returns.

"Of all the queens, Sephora, Low Queen of the Arts Sector, is the most oppressive to slaves. While we have not been able to rouse the men's fighting spirit under Rachel's rule, Sephora will soon have our brothers begging to wage war for freedom. Also, with Rebekkah dead, the Soldier Sector will be divided as they choose a new Low Queen. We must use these events to our advantage. We must be ready to fight!" Servus pounded his right fist into his left hand for emphasis.

"How can you be sure this will be the time?" Kiertus asked. "Isn't it foolish to risk what we have painstakingly prepared on a rumor? In seven years we will have more than enough trained men and weapons."

"Our rebellions have failed because of the unexpected," Servus answered. "I believe success will hinge on using the unexpected to our advantage. I need both of you to be as passionate and committed as I am. Justus, what is your opinion?"

"I agree with you, Servus," Justus said. "We must be ready. Kiertus, I will give you the highlights of two slave uprisings that have happened in the past. These stories have been handed down in the oral tradition from generation to generation.

"The slave riot of Corria the Somnolent's rule failed only because Corria's maidservant began her menses unexpectedly and returned to her quarters to rest. It was her quarters that our leaders had chosen as the gathering place to launch our war. They had intended to murder the ruling family, leaving the city's government in chaos. The maidservant was killed, but not before her shrieking cries alerted the soldiers in the hall. The women, with their superior communication system, were organized instantly. The battle was bloody but quick. Many good men were executed. Corria the Somnolent's rule came to an end at the next election. Terreza the Quick, who managed the slaves with great brutality, replaced her. Instead of freedom, we experienced decades of suffering, all because of the unexpected return of a maid to her room.

"Another instance was ironic. Ferrata the Vain was undeniably the cruelest ruler this city has ever known. While the slaves could not hope to gain freedom by her assassination, any ruler was preferable to her. The exact moment of the assassination attempt, Ferrata noticed a toe ring off-center and bent to straighten it. The poisoned blow dart, which would have killed her, hit the slave attending her. The slave in attendance had the presence of mind to extract the dart and swallow it, so there were no repercussions to the rest of the men. He died within the hour, and because we are so insignificant and easily replaceable to the women, they never questioned his death. Ferrata the Vain lived well into old age, but her vanity drained the resources of the city. For a long time afterward, the lot of the slaves improved because the women needed the sweat and labor of mankind to bring prosperity back."

Justus paused. When he spoke again, there was bitterness in his voice.

"We can be certain that if Sephora becomes High Queen," he continued, "our lives will become hell. The only incentive I need to back Servus is the knowledge that starting a war will save men's lives. Since Sephora has been elected Low Queen of the Arts Sector, scores of men have gone into her Sector to serve and have not been seen or heard from again."

Kiertus looked grim. His duties took him to the Arts Sector frequently, and he heard rumors about the missing men that made his skin crawl. He voiced his last objection.

"Servus, if we go to war, we will have to fight our daughters, and the mothers of our daughters."

"It will never be otherwise," the king said with great sadness. "We have no other choice but war. If we wish to know our daughters and sons and to be respected by them, we will have to kill for our freedom.

"At the end of our war, if I live, I may discover that all those who I have fathered have died. Even if I lose those whom I fight for, I must fight to restore the ancient rights and responsibilities of manhood. The gift of freedom and family that my sacrifice bequeaths to your offspring is worth any price I must pay."

Kiertus sighed.

"You are right, Servus," he said. "It is just that in my work, I have grown fond of many of the women and consider them friends. But I know that if I lost my value to them, they would give less thought to killing me than the pets they keep in their homes. I must...."

Kiertus stopped speaking as the door opened and the sentry wearing the brown robe entered.

"A soldier is coming. Hurry!" he said. He took off the brown cloak, threw it at Kiertus, and retreated to the sleeping section of the barracks to hide. Kiertus donned the robe, stepped out of the barracks, and stretched.

Left alone with Servus, Justus turned to his king and whispered.

"You should tell Kiertus that war is not as easy for you as you make it sound; after all, you may lose what you hold most dear."

"Justus, I see no point. I cannot lose what I do not have."

"Servus, as your advisor I am telling you not to keep this secret from him."

"My secret is personal. I will not let it affect my decisions. If I did, how could I risk her death in a war?"

"What will you do if she remains Commander?"

"She is not a soldier of Rebekkah's caliber. She will be replaced by another."

"What if she isn't?"

"It won't change my decision. I cannot give up my life's ambition when it is attainable simply because the woman I have loved since we were children, a woman who has never once looked my way, has become the leader of my enemy. Furthermore, I am certain someone will replace her. I am grateful you have accepted Kiertus, but I prefer not to talk about my feelings with him."

Justus nodded. He would not push Servus, whom he had carefully groomed for leadership since he was a young boy. He was torn between his loyalty to Servus and his love for Kiertus. A decade ago, Justus had decided not to let the women rob him of the role of father. He might never know if he had a biological son among the men, but he could choose a man and treat him as he longed to treat a son. Kiertus was that man. Kiertus had secrets of his own. Justus would not interfere.

Once he was outside, Kiertus sauntered away from the barracks as casually as possible. He hoped the soldier he had seen approaching would take no interest in him, but she called to him.

"Stop, slave! Come here!"

Kiertus had no choice. He turned and walked back to her. Kiertus recognized Partouche. She was a new resident of the Soldier Sector. Servus and his men suspected she was a double agent, whose loyalty belonged to Sephora, the Low Queen of the Arts Sector. As women went, she was an especially dangerous enemy.

"Do you think you can fool me so easily? Do you think I am as stupid as a man is? Lower your hood! Show me your number!"

Kiertus faked a confident smile as he followed orders. He pushed the sleeve of his cloak up his arm until the numbers branded on the skin of his forearm were revealed.

"Kiertus!" Partouche recognized him, too. "What are you doing here at the barracks of Servus?" she asked suspiciously.

Kiertus looked behind himself nervously before he replied in a whisper.

"Did you not see me sitting outside as you approached? I have been asked by a woman, whose name I cannot reveal, to spy on Servus. I went in for a moment because I did not recognize the voice of the man he was talking to."

"Who was inside with Servus?"

"An older man I did not recognize."

"I will see who is in there myself, but what were they saying?"

"The usual—how bad slavery is, blah, blah, blah. I don't think it is so bad. I get to travel the Queendom all day and spend my time in the company of beautiful women. He should quit complaining. He only makes it harder on himself." Kiertus winked at Partouche.

She laughed.

"You speak truly, Kiertus. You are a decent sort, for a man. I wouldn't trade my favorite horse to own you, but I can see why some say they would! Now get to work before I change my mind and put you on the punishment list."

Kiertus turned to go and Partouche slapped his rump. Kiertus felt the familiar anger rise inside him. He left quickly so that Partouche could not see his fury at being woman-handled.

Partouche entered the barracks where she found Servus and Justus sitting quietly, each with a cup of goat milk.

"What do we have here? The prince of poop with his second in command! I don't like finding the two of you alone together in the middle of the afternoon. Servus, you will work on the palace grounds for three extra hours today. At dusk, you and Justus will report to the dungeon to receive twenty lashes. Don't let me find you alone together again, or next time I will double the punishment. Now, follow me, and hurry."

Ava followed the path down the mountain. This was the easi-est part of what had been a difficult three-year journey. She had discovered early on that the world looked the same as Eden, but it was starkly different. For one thing, the animals were dumb, poor shadows of the creatures that lived where she came from.

In Eden, the animals were sentient beings. Even the lions were as tame as kittens. Ava remembered a day she had napped with a sleeping lion while holding a baby lamb in her arms. The ani-mals did not speak, but they communicated with their eyes, their gestures, and with clicks of the tongue or other noises they could make. She and her family tended to their needs, studied them, and enjoyed their companionship. From the mighty elephant to the tiniest fish, all creatures were cherished. Sometimes, with their permission, their energies were harnessed to accomplish projects planned by her family.

One of the first differences Ava had noticed in not-Eden was that the animals were skittish and fearful of her. She had not understood until the day the tiger died. She saw it running toward her, and she went merrily to greet it. It sprang upon her, and she welcomed it with open arms. It began to bite and claw her flesh with a viciousness she had never seen in an animal. She defended herself and retreated, but the creature stalked her and tried to attack again. She spoke to it in its language until the truth dawned on her. There was no intelligence behind its eyes, just instinct. In order to proceed, she had to engage it in a fight. She jumped on its back and used a technique she had developed to defend herself when wrestling with her brothers. She held its head in a lock. The tiger struggled violently. She tightened her hold until she heard a snap. She had broken its neck.

"Now you've done it. That injury is difficult and painful to heal," she had told it in a series of tiger snarls. The tiger had made no response. She began an examination and was shocked to find its heart had stopped. She tended to the tiger for hours, trying everything she knew to cure it, but she could not restart the heart. The tiger was now flesh only. The essence of the tiger—the life—was gone.

Remembering the tiger tinged her excitement with apprehension. What if all her stepsiblings were dead? There were so many dangers in this part of the world. The buildings she had seen from the top of the mountain might be as deserted as the shrine she had left behind.

Her stomach grumbled. Ava had skipped lunch, but it was not quite time for dinner. Ava stopped and took some deep breaths. She forced herself to finish the strawberries in her pack. As she ate, her optimism returned. She would find people. The flags, the vast well-tended gardens, the animals grazing in the fields—these were all signs of order and human activity. Ava continued to make her way down the mountain.

At the dinner hour, in the chambers of the High Queen, plates heaped with food went untouched. Two women, whose faces were usually calm, were contorted in anger. Rachel and acting Low Queen Arrival argued.

"Three years ago you forbid Rebekkah from this stupid venture. What possessed you to change your mind? Do you think you are charmed? Do you really think you are immune from losing what you love most?" asked Arrival. "You have ruled the Queendom for over twenty years, and even though she has excelled at everything she has ever tried, you are deluding yourself if you think she cannot fail—or that she will not be killed! You think the goddesses smile upon you! I am telling you there are things at work here you do not know. We must get her from the clearing soon, or it will be too late!"

The High Queen tolerated Arrival's disrespect only because Arrival loved Rebekkah as much as she did.

"Too late?" said Rachel. "It is never too late with Rebekkah! I was told it was too late for me to conceive her and I did! I was told it was too late when she was three and she was dying of a disease that killed a sixth of our people, but I found a way to save her! I was told it was too late when she was pulled unconscious from the water when she was nine, do you remember that? You must have been three. Do you remember, Arrival, when she drowned?"

"Of course I remember! I was there when her body was carried from the ocean," Arrival said. "She looked like a rag doll, her limbs loose, swinging back and forth, her head lolling back. I ran to her, I took her hand, and I would not let go. Women tried to separate us, and I ignored them. They laid her on the sand and women crowded around her. There was silence, then weeping."

"I was hearing cases in court that day," said Rachel. "A runner came to me and told me Rebekkah had been pulled from the water unconscious. I did not know if she was dead or alive when I ran to the Palace Beach. When I got to her, you were trying to wake her up."

"I don't remember that. I remember that when you arrived, a woman told you she was gone. I could not understand what they meant, for she was right there before us. You examined her and then you put your mouth on hers. I thought you were hurting her," Arrival recalled.

"Yes, you attacked me! You never let go of her hand with your left, but with your right, you made a fist and pummeled me with it, just as you attack me now with your angry words! Yet, I barely noticed. I had discovered Rebekkah had a heartbeat, but no breath. I thought that if I could give her my breath—my life—she would live. I had fought disease and won. I would not let mere water take her from me."

Arrival continued the story, called up from where it had been submerged in her memory.

"When she coughed and threw up, I thought you had made her sick, but I was happy you stopped smothering her. She was no longer a rag doll."

"You would not leave her side," said Rachel, "not for the days she recuperated, and not for weeks afterwards. I think she was annoyed at times, but she was patient with you, especially at night when you woke up screaming."

"She was always patient with me." Arrival wanted to be angry with Rebekkah, but could not be. The situation they found themselves in was not Rebekkah's fault. "Why do you bring this up now?"

"Because I know she will come back to us. I see how worried you are. Think of the many times she has cheated death. This time is not different," Rachel said.

"This time is different. I can feel it. I have the gift of intuition. Remember how my teachers begged me to enter the priesesshood?"

"Yes, and you followed your sister into the Soldier Sector. You did not develop your gift. Your gift is clouded by your love for her and your fear that she will not return. You know you cannot fill her shoes."

"Those are harsh words, Mother."

High Queen Rachel studied her adopted daughter for a minute before speaking again. Arrival seemed unaware of her regal beauty and that many women yearned to be her partner. When she had taken up residence in the Soldier Sector, one of two Sectors where its occupants took oaths of celibacy, many women had cried themselves to sleep after the ceremony. Arrival was an amazing woman in her own right. Rachel felt guilt for a moment that so much of herself was poured into the Queendom and Rebekkah. Rachel put aside her own worry and attempted to comfort Arrival.

"I'm sorry I hurt you. I only meant to show you that your intuition deceives you. She will come back to us. We have almost lost her many times. Your sister has not escaped injury in her life as a soldier. I nursed her back to health each time.

"The choice Rebekkah made to become a soldier made me sad, for in addition to the risks of the job, she will never have grand-daughters. Even so, I encouraged Rebekkah to choose her own path in life. Rebekkah is strong, determined, and able. She is pre-pared. Trust your sister as I trust my daughter. Trust me, even as I proved myself trustworthy that day at the ocean shore."

"Mother, Mother, this is not the same at all." Arrival's anger was temporarily replaced by despair. "I am not a child. You are not at her side. No one lives forever, not even Rebekkah. I have followed her all of my life. I love her every bit as much as you do. I too helped nurse her back to health each time, though perhaps you never noticed I was there. There are more reasons for my fear than just the situation she has put herself in. True, I have not fully developed my gift of intuition, but it is real. Why won't you listen to me?"

"Arrival, is there more than intuition that guides you? Do you have information I do not have?" asked Rachel.

"Mother and Queen, my intuition should be enough for you. But, as it happens, I do know more than I have told you. Rebekkah bound me to keep a secret I am to reveal to you if she dies. What woman, who is sure she will live, entrusts a grave-secret to another? As acting Low Queen, I have the power to break the bond of secrecy if I feel the secret interferes with affairs of state. This one does. If she does not come back in the next few hours, I must tell it to you and we must take action."

Rachel looked horrified.

"Arrival, to reveal a grave-secret is to tempt fate. I forbid you to tell me this secret. There is nothing in the Queendom that is not known to me."

Arrival opened her mouth to speak. Rachel covered her ears like a child.

"No! I will not listen! Obey your sister and keep this secret until the day she dies. I pray I die first and never hear it."

Arrival grabbed Rachel's arms and pulled her hands off her ears.

"Mother, she is in great danger! I would not break my oath lightly! Rebekkah thought this was the only way to solve her problem, but this is too risky. If I tell you, you may think of another way out of her dilemma. We can get her from the clearing and end this madness."

"Arrival, I will not hear a grave-secret!" Rachel was furious. "I am aware of Rebekkah's purpose in being the sacrificial victim. I have faith in her abilities. She will be the only woman who has ever survived the sacrifice. She is not a young, barren outcast but the highest-ranking soldier of the land. Not only will this end the brutal spring sacrifice, it will clinch my re-election and ensure we win the next vote to begin a new colony. I support Rebekkah."

"No, Mother. You are not supporting Rebekkah. You are supporting Sephora." Arrival tried a different tactic. "It was Sephora's suggestion that Rebekkah become the spring sacrifice."

"Don't be absurd. It was not a coincidence that Sephora suggested Rebekkah be the victim at this year's meeting. Somehow your sister manipulated her into thinking it was her idea."

"You had the right to refuse. Why didn't you, as you did years ago?"

"Because Rebekkah came to me ahead of time to inform me about Sephora's proposal. She swore to me that she was ready for any ambush Sephora had planned."

"Because you can never say no to her." Arrival muttered.

"What did you say?" asked Rachel.

"Nothing I am going to repeat, Mother. You must disregard anything she said to convince you to agree. She would have said anything to gain your cooperation. Rebekkah's agenda in this matter is complicated. Take my counsel. Time is running out. Get her from the clearing now. It is the only way to save her."

"Are you saying Rebekkah lied to me?"

35

"If hiding the truth is lying, yes. First Rebekkah manipulated you and now Sephora is manipulating you. Use your head! Rebekkah swings from the sacrificial tree! That is insane! Send me, in your name, with a contingent of soldiers to bring her back from the clearing. Do it now, before it is too late." Even before her mother spoke, Arrival could see she had gone too far. Rachel shook with rage.

"You have overstepped your authority, Arrival! You have been Low Queen for two days, and you think there is only one way, your way, for Rebekkah to survive? Rebekkah has far more wisdom and experience than you have. She is a volunteer not a victim. We must trust that she will return to us, just as she always has. I will not tempt the death-goddess further by having you in my presence. Get out!"

Arrival sighed. She would have blurted out Rebekkah's secret then if she could have been sure Rachel would side with Rebekkah and not the law of the land. Rachel had been a Queen for more years of her life than she had not. Arrival could not be certain of her reaction, just as Rebekkah had not been certain. What would be a source of shame before her death would be a source of comfort afterwards.

"I go, High Queen. If you come to your senses, send a messenger for me. I will be on the wall, watching for Rebekkah to return, until intuition tells me it is too late."

"I forbid you to wait on the wall! It is a position far below your rank! I would be there myself if it were not such a demeaning task. You are the Low Queen of the Soldier Sector until Rebekkah returns. You must think of your image."

"Is it my image you are thinking of, or hers? She's the one you've always thought of first. I will do any task I assign the least of my soldiers to do. If you wish to stop me, you must arrest me."

Arrival pulled herself to her full height and walked with queenly grandeur from the room. Rachel's anger dissipated as she watched Arrival retreat. She wanted to call her back, to tell her she needed her company, and admit that she too had doubts about the wisdom of the plan. Rachel's pride in her own ability to heal others kept her silent. Rachel had nursed Rebekkah back to health so many times that people now said of her, "Most mothers give life once to their daughters. Rachel gives it over and over."

Eventually the phrase took on a different meaning. Rachel had the gift of healing. She originally came from the Agriculture Sector and had a profound understanding of the powers of healing plants. Coupled with common sense and a quick mind, she was given credit for saving the lives of hundreds of the sick and dying in her city. Physicians were sent for first. If the doctors said there was no hope, families petitioned the High Queen to come to them. Sometimes Rachel knew she could do nothing. In those cases, she would sit with the family until their loved one passed away. It was the least she could do in their time of suffering. She was always mindful that it could have been her in their place. She considered herself a mother to every woman of the Queendom.

Rachel looked at the uneaten meals on the table and sighed heavily. After dinner, during the spring sacrifice, it was her custom to go to the Temple to pray. Usually, when she grew weary of praying, she retired to the Great Library in the Religion Sector and read in the forbidden room until she fell asleep. No one would disturb her there, for only the High Queen and the High Priestess had access to those documents of the Queendom. Rachel knew High Priestess Caliphus never went into the forbidden room because she wished to keep her heart from blasphemous ideas. Rachel did not really believe in the existence of goddesses, but she thought she just might stay in the temple and pray all night anyway. She would pray her daughter would return soon, and if not on her own, at least in good enough shape for Rachel to rescue her from the grasp of death once more.

Arrival walked out of the palace, her thoughts still preoccupied with Rebekkah's secret. In the matriarchal society of Evlantis, the primary relationship was between mother and daughter, with the secondary being the relationship between sister and sister. Occasionally women paired up in relationships that lasted a lifetime, but most partnerships were temporary and based on convenience and sexual need. Arrival had never felt a sexual attraction for another woman, and her relationship with Rachel had been polite at best. But her relationship with Rebekkah consumed her life.

Arrival had never questioned the precepts of their society until a few days ago when Rebekkah had entrusted Arrival with her grave-secret. Rebekkah had explained to her how a woman named Urthmata had managed to blackmail her. Arrival hurriedly walked the garden path, preoccupied with forbidden images begotten by her sister's revelation. She was deep in thought when she stumbled over the leg of a slave who was kneeling, intent on weeding flowers at the edge of the path.

"What are you doing here? Slaves are not scheduled to work the gardens at this hour!" Arrival demanded in a gruff tone.

The slave, still kneeling, pivoted. His face remained toward the ground. He was shirtless, and dozens of scars covered his powerful, sweaty back. He could be one of a dozen men, and not the one she had just been thinking of. She noticed chains shackled his legs. It explained why a guard was not present.

"A soldier has sentenced me to work late, and then receive a beating," he answered.

"What was your crime?" Arrival asked.

"I had a cup of goat milk with a friend at the noon hour."

She could barely hear him. She wanted to see his face.

"This is ridiculous," she said. "Stand and face me while you talk so that I may hear you clearly." Arrival shook her head, disgusted with herself.

She caught her breath as he rose to face her. They were equal in height. Scars covered his chest. A few peppered his face, but he was still beautiful. She longed to reach out and trace the pathways they made with her fingertips. Her heart beat faster and she cursed the feelings that had overtaken her.

"Servus." Her voice was a whisper. She prayed none of the emotion his presence evoked could be heard in her voice.

"You know my name." He looked as puzzled as he felt at this unusual exchange.

"Everyone knows your name." She felt relief as she found her voice was under her own command.

He smiled. "I doubt that."

"Everyone in the upper echelon of the Soldier Sector does."

"You flatter me, Commander." He could not believe he was face to face with her, talking with her, as if they were equals.

"Do not call me that. Rebekkah is Commander."

"You do not wish to lead the Soldier Sector?" He looked at her intently.

"I want my sister back. I want my life back. I have to go." She had already broken tradition by allowing a slave to stand while talking with a Low Queen. She took one step and stopped. She might as well break a few more rules.

"Servus, I see no harm in allowing you to have a cup of milk with a fellow slave. You have already been punished with extra work. I countermand the order for the beating of you and your friend."

"I accept—not for me, because I can withstand such hardship, but on behalf of my friend, who is older than I am. Thank you, Princess Arrival." He knelt on the ground before her, as was proper. He felt relief. He enjoyed facing her, but he did not want her to get in trouble. She must be worried senseless about her sister to disregard protocol in such a flagrant manner.

She left him quickly, eager to get away from the feelings he aroused in her. Servus watched her retreat. One thing was certain to him after their brief interview. She had so little desire to lead she would never be able to hang on to the Queenship of the Soldier Sector if Rebekkah did not return.

Arrival walked quickly to the stables. She mounted Stealth and rode him at a gallop to the great wall at the outskirts of the city. She half expected to hear hoofbeats behind her and half expected Rachel to arrest her, but she made it to the wall without incident. She tethered Stealth and climbed the ladder to the top of the wall.

Diana, second in command of the Soldier Sector until Rebekkah returned, stood on the wall looking toward Mount Great Mother. It was an unusual position for a Soldier, since they normally guarded the wall to keep the citizens within the confines of the city. She had heard the horse and rider approach, but did not turn around.

"Any sign of the Low Queen Rebekkah?" asked Arrival.

"None, Commander." Diana was professional. She recognized Arrival's voice and turned to face her, though she kept her eyes averted. Diana's face betrayed nothing of the fear she felt. Surely, Arrival must have come to dismiss her from her post.

Arrival answered the question Diana had not asked.

"I will keep watch with you on the wall."

"I thought…I'm sorry Commander, I misspoke."

Arrival knew what Diana had left unsaid. "You thought the High Queen, my mother, desired me to lead the Sector from the city— that to stand watch on the wall was beneath my station."

"Yes, Commander. Forgive me."

"I acknowledge your petition for forgiveness and grant it. As Commander of the Soldier Sector, I have decreed that two of us will keep watch out of respect for the greatest soldier who has ever lived."

Diana permitted herself to look at Arrival.

"Permission to speak freely."

"Granted."

"What does your second sight tell you?"

Arrival thought carefully about her reply before she spoke. Diana's support might be critical in the coming days.

"My second sight is clouded. There is trouble coming, so much that I cannot make out where the greatest danger lies. I do not see the imminent return of our Commander."

"Let me go to her, I beg you, before it is too late. I will protect her."

"No. I cannot allow it. I see clearly that Rebekkah will die if her mother the High Queen does not win the reelection of her post. If news were to get out that anyone gave aid to Rebekkah, Sephora would win the election easily."

Diana could tell Arrival was being evasive.

"What is it you know? What did she tell you? You were alone together for hours on the eve before the Sacrifice. Your manner has been distant and preoccupied ever since."

"Is it not enough that the sister I worshipped since birth may die? I think you are jealous she did not spend those hours with you."

"Commander! I have been true to my post and celibate, as our oath requires. What you suggest is not polite to speak of, especially now."

"Diana, we both love her, though in different ways. I don't begrudge what you feel for her, though you have challenged me many times for the second-in-command post so you could be closer to her. If you and I had followed Rebekkah into any other Sector in the city, we would probably be sisters-in-law. I may need allies in the days ahead. Can I count on you for the sake of our bond with Rebekkah?"

Diana's face revealed nothing. It sounded to her as if Arrival thought Rebekkah would not return. If Rebekkah died, Diana would want to rule the Sector, if only to live in the same quarters Rebekkah had lived in, not to mention sleep in the bed she had longed for, but had never been permitted to enter. Diana answered Arrival's question carefully.

"I do not know, Arrival. I cannot understand why you will not let me protect her. If she dies, I will hold you responsible. What would you do if you were in my position?"

Arrival looked at Diana intently. She could see the pain this woman was in. It was clear that she loved Rebekkah. Arrival spoke gently to her.

"Diana, she entrusted me with a grave-secret. I am sworn to reveal it to Rachel first. Afterwards, I will reveal it to you if you will help me. It will change your life and bring you comfort if Rebekkah does not return. Until her secret is revealed, may I have your support?"

"Why do you keep talking as if she will die? Why aren't you doing more to protect her?" Diana longed to beat the secret out of Arrival, but just like Rachel, she did not want to tempt the death goddess.

Arrival looked more closely at Diana and saw more than hurt in her eyes. She saw hatred. Arrival sighed.

"If my sister does not return to us, can I at least count on your support until I carry out her wishes?"

"Until she returns, and especially if she does not, you may count on nothing more than my job requires." Diana turned her face toward the forest.

"If that is what you wish, Diana, I cannot change it. Permission given to speak freely is rescinded. We will wait in silence and pray she comes back to us."

Adam's daughter Ava discovered a clearing at the base of Mount Great Mother at dusk. She was thrilled to find her desire for human companionship satisfied at last. The immortal watched, delighted, as a woman hanging from a tree grasped a leather thong that bound her to a branch and began to swing back and forth. Soon she was swinging high enough to catch the branch to which she was tethered with her feet. She shimmied her legs up and over the branch. Her muscular thighs grasped the branch, and after that, most of the woman's body was obscured from Ava's view for a few moments. Her purpose in such an exercise became clear at once, as her hands appeared free. She spread her arms, released her legs, rotated in mid-air, and dropped to the ground, landing lightly on her feet.

Ava laughed, clapped her hands, and went forward happily to greet the first person she had seen in years. Rebekkah looked surprised to see her at first, but then looked at ease.

"Hello, stranger! You think that was a good trick? It was nothing!" she said. The elaborate, pleated ceremonial robe she had worn during the rite was folded at the base of the tree. Rebekkah donned it to warm herself against the chilly night air and reached for her spear that rested against the trunk of the tree. "The real trick is getting back up! With any luck, the beast will show tonight and…whoa, take care! Behind you!"

Ava turned, but it was too late to get away. An enraged brown beast covered in fur, and standing two feet taller than Ava, charged. It roared and slashed at her with its claws. Ava threw up her arms to protect her face. Rebekkah's spear whistled past her with deadly accuracy and struck the beast in its throat. Rebekkah ran across the clearing and hurled herself at it. The force of the impact knocked the beast off its feet. It lashed out, but Rebekkah wrestled to keep it down. Ava, ignoring the pain from the claw wounds on her arms, joined Rebekkah, and together they subdued it so that it could not harm them as it drew its last breaths. When it was dead, Ava threw her arms around Rebekkah.

"Oh, thank you for protecting me! If you had not stopped the bear, I would have sustained injuries that would have taken weeks to heal! It is so good to see you! I have been looking for you for over a thousand days. Oh, and what a great trick that was, falling from the tree like that. I am going to try it now; watch me!"

Ava ran across the clearing and climbed the sacrificial tree.

Rebekkah was stunned. She could understand the meaning of the words the girl babbled, but that wasn't what caused her such shock. The truly amazing thing was that looking at the girl was like looking into a mirror in a darkened room. They could be womb-born sisters. Under certain circumstances, they would easily be mistaken for each another. Rebekkah was intrigued. Though she had planned to return to the city in triumph immediately after slaying the beast, she decided instead to spend some time with the stranger. First, she must stop the girl from killing herself by jumping out of the tree.

"Come down from there before you hurt yourself…" Rebekkah's words trailed off as she watched the agile stranger climb to a branch higher than the one she had freed herself from. The girl dropped from the branch the way Rebekkah had, except she made two revolutions in the air. Ava landed gracefully and laughed happily.

"Beat that!" Ava said. "I looked, and there is another branch higher up that I think we could make three flips off of. I'll let you go first if you want to!" She stood underneath the tree, her hands outstretched in an invitation to play.

Though the girl looked like Rebekkah, she was childlike; she almost seemed like a simpleton. Rebekkah suspected that she had been cast out from her people, and had somehow survived. It was a shame, but Rebekkah decided she could still use her as a body double in situations where the young woman was not required to speak. Rebekkah crossed the clearing, speaking purposefully to this girl-woman with every step.

"I am Low Queen Rebekkah, Commander of the Armed forces of Evlantis. I welcome you, stranger, to the outskirts of the Ancient City. I have a different kind of game I would like to play with you.

"You and I look alike. Come with me, and I will let you live in secret at the palace. You will live in luxury. All you have to do is pretend to be me from time to time. I will take good care of you, and you will not have to live alone in the forest any longer. Would you like that?"

Rebekkah took Ava's face in her hands and turned it side to side in the waning light, examining it.

"Amazing! Who are you? Who is your mother?" For a moment, Rebekkah wondered if one of her mother's many stillborn children had lived after all.

"I am Ava, youngest daughter of Adam and Aurora. What is a queen?"

Rebekkah laughed.

"A queen is a ruler. A queen has power and privilege. A queen shapes the lives of many. There is no higher rank than that of Queen, and the High Queen rules everyone. I will be High Queen after my mother is tired of ruling, especially with your help. If you don't have to speak, do you think you could do it?"

"Wait here, just for a minute!" Ava said. "I will be right back."

Ava skipped back to the other side of the clearing. Rebekkah watched, puzzled, as Ava pulled grass up from the ground and drew some dirt from below it. She rubbed the dirt below her cheekbones and under her chin. She stood, shifted her posture, and began to walk across the clearing. As she walked, she repeated, verbatim, the words Rebekkah had spoken.

Rebekkah's eyes grew large. In the dusky light, she was certain she was watching herself walk the clearing. Goosebumps pricked her skin. The words were pronounced flawlessly; all traces of the girl's speech impediment were gone. Ava took Rebekkah's face in her hands when she reached her. The contact broke the surreal quality of the moment.

"Do you think I can do it?" Ava asked. All trace of her Edenite accent was gone as she mimicked Rebekkah.

"Yes, I do. Where do you come from?" Rebekkah said.

"I come from the Garden of Eden, a thousand days' journey from here."

Rebekkah's eyes twinkled in amusement. She was entertained and curious.

"A thousand days! Even I have never been that far from Evlantis. The women of my city believe they are the only inhabitants of the world. Tell me, please, what brings you here?"

Ava looked sad.

"I broke a cardinal rule of my homeland and now I am an exile. I was sent to find your people so that I would not have to live alone. Tell me about the buildings I saw from the top of the mountain. You have so many. Why?"

They made themselves comfortable on a fallen log close to where the slain beast lay. Rebekkah began the task of cleaning the beast's claw wounds on Ava's arms as best she could with cloth she tore from the bottom of her ceremonial sacrificial robe.

"You came from the top of this mountain, here?" Rebekkah asked. She motioned with her chin.

Ava nodded and Rebekkah spoke again.

"What you saw as you looked down from the top of Mount Great Mother is the city of Evlantis. The city is almost two thousand years old. It was founded by the Mother of all Womankind, but it was abandoned when the area was depleted of game and drought descended upon the land. For hundreds of years afterwards, women and men lived as nomads, ruled by the Great Mother."

Rebekkah's voice took on a singsong quality as she told the legend just as it was taught to the children of Evlantis.

"It is said the Great Mother lived a very long life. In her final years, she expressed a wish to return to the city she founded. Upon returning to the ruins of the abandoned city, her people found the area rich with game and fresh water plentiful. Structures were patched and re-built upon early foundations. The Mother of all

Womankind died, surrounded by her people, in the place she loved most on earth.

"Many myths explain how the Great Mother of All came to walk upon the earth alone and pregnant. It is commonly believed the goddesses created her in their image and afterwards created a man to impregnate her. That man abandoned her, not realizing that it was woman who was superior and the bearer of life. There was nothing but loneliness and death for him. His name is not even recorded in the ancient scrolls that tell the story of our people.

"Yet the goddesses had not been kind to the abandoned Eve. The Mother of All bore the curse of twin sons. In bitterness, she ruled them both with an iron hand until the day when one slew the other in a fit of jealous rage for a favor she had justly shown. This was the first recorded death, the death of her son Abulus. Eve's grief transformed her bitterness toward mankind into hatred. She taught her female descendants to see men as treacherous beings that were inferior to women. She counseled her daughters and many generations of granddaughters never to give their hearts to men.

"Women had never enjoyed the nomadic life. The leaders who ruled after Great Mother Eve made improvements to the city. Women made discoveries in the fields of farming, medical science, animal husbandry, and the art of subduing mankind, which allowed them to stay at their home hearths instead of roaming in search of food and shelter. The city flourished, and six sectors evolved: the Government Sector, the Agriculture Sector, the Religion Sector, the Arts Sector, the Livestock Sector, and the Soldier Sector. Six Low Queens rule the Sectors, with a High Queen to oversee them all."

Rebekkah would have gone on, but Ava stopped her.

"Rebekkah, I know the name Eve! I know of your Great Mother! When Michael sent me away from my homeland, I was allowed to ask three questions! My first one was how other people came to be on earth. Eve was my father Adam's first wife. She broke a rule of the Garden and was cast out, just as I was. My father never knew she was pregnant. If he had, I know he would have never left her side. He only took a second wife, a woman named Aurora, who is my mother, after he learned of Eve's death."

"You know your father? That cannot be possible. We are talking about ancient herstory!"

"In the Garden of Eden we do not grow old or die. If I choose wisely, I will not die here, either."

"Don't be ridiculous! You say your people do not die? I do not believe it!"

Ava pulled away from Rebekkah's ministrations.

"Watch," Ava said. From her pack, she pulled a coconut shell she used to transport water. She removed the pieces of twig she had used to stop up the holes in it and poured water over one of her wounds. Ava held the edges of torn skin together with her hands. She and Rebekkah watched as the bleeding stopped and the flesh knit itself together.

"This is some kind of trick," said Rebekkah.

Ava took the strip of cloth from around the deepest wound. The ends had healed, but the center part of the wound was still open.

"Put your finger in the wound. Show yourself it is real. Then pour the water over and hold the edges together. Then tell me it is a trick."

Rebekkah did as she was asked. They waited in silence.

AMBUSH

*I*n the gloom of the falling night, Sephora, Low Queen of the Arts Sector, arrived at a spot twenty minutes walking distance from the sacrificial clearing. Two slaves followed her. In spite of the darkness, she wore a black hooded cloak. She was astonishingly beautiful. With her shiny black hair, tan complexion, and emerald eyes, she was one of the most easily recognized women in the city of Evlantis. It was vital she remain undetected tonight.

"I will not go further," Sephora said to her slaves. "Do not kneel! Stay on your feet! I need you to continue on to the clearing. Kill Rebekkah. Take her Ring of Power and dispose of her body in the Great Ravine. Leave no sign you were there. Then return to me with the Ring as proof you followed my orders. Be careful. I do not expect you to find her bound to the tree. She would not have accepted my challenge to become the spring sacrifice unless she had some trick to return to the city victorious."

"My glorious Queen and Master, how will two lowly slaves be able to kill Rebekkah?" asked Tiburnus. "If she is loose, she has her spear. I don't care about my own life, which is yours, but only that you be glorified and not condemned. Everyone knows me. I have belonged to you all of my life."

"Oh, Tiburnus, good and faithful servant, I have plotted the High Queen's downfall for decades. Rebekkah's death will guarantee my victory in the upcoming election. Of course, I don't expect you to do this with your bare hands; no man is capable of that. Take these and hide them in your tunics." Sephora gave Tiburnus and Baraus each a dagger. "Wait until she throws her spear at one of you. The other should attack when she is unarmed."

"Master, you could be sentenced to death for giving us arms," said Tiburnus.

She reached out with one hand and stroked his cheek affectionately while she spoke.

"See how much trust I have in you, Tiburnus? Why, I am not even armed myself!" Sephora said, smiling through her lie. She felt the weight of the broadsword holstered and strapped to her back under her cloak. She removed her hand from Tiburnus's face. Unconsciously she closed it into an angry fist as she continued.

"Rachel is fifteen years older than I and not as beautiful, fertile, or bright, yet it is Rachel who is elected every seven years by the citizens to rule Evlantis. Those fools preferred that plodding old workhorse to me! I will show them! They will regret they made me wait for what is due me."

"And you two, Tiburnus and Baraus, you will be at my side as my royal consorts. You cannot imagine the rewards I have in store for you. They start as soon as you return to me with your task complete." Sephora smiled suggestively, first at Tiburnus and then at Baraus.

Tiburnus felt his knees go weak. To his fellow slave he said, "Baraus, let's go now, and do the Queen's bidding," and then he turned to the Queen and said, "We will return soon, great Master. You are like a goddess to me. Send us with your blessing."

"You have it slaves, goddess speed to you." Sephora watched until she could no longer see them. She leaned against a tree to wait. She wanted to kill Rebekkah herself, but it was too risky. She would vent her lust for blood when her slaves returned with their task complete.

Rebekkah stared at her bloody finger, the one she had put into Ava's wound. A quarter of an hour passed in silence as the flesh healed.

"You would be either a powerful ally or an unbeatable enemy. Will you support me?" Rebekkah asked Ava.

"I like you, but I must choose wisely," Ava answered.

"What do you mean, choose wisely?"

"I have been wondering about that myself. I asked Michael what I should fear most outside of Eden. This is what he said."

Ava imitated the voice of Michael as best she could as she spoke the words he had used verbatim: "'What you should fear most in this world is the choosing of evil. Though you do not have the knowledge of good and evil, you are free to choose it, as you were free to go over the Wall. You can do real damage to your soul if you choose evil, so beware. As long as you remain immortal, your body will repair itself of any injury it sustains. If your soul rots from within, there is no balm, or salve, or work, or petition to the Creator, that will fix it, and the decay of your body will follow. Not every choice is good or evil; many choices carry no moral weight. Beware of alternatives that will unquestionably bring pain, chaos, and disorder for no foreseeable benefit. Alternatives must be assessed very carefully, and the Master will judge what is in your heart when you make your choice. I must also warn you that there will be times when inaction, or refusing to make a choice, is evil. It will not be easy for you. Some choices will be obvious, and some will not be clear at all. I can only tell you of my own observations and experiences of the mortals. Sometimes my work for the Almighty requires me to walk among them.

"'They have had none of the advantages you have had living in the Garden. Chaos is the natural order of things in their part of the world, yet there are those who choose to rise above it. Despite the hardships life here presents to them, they develop their potential, and some of them achieve greatness. Many show courage in adversity and appreciate the gift of life. Others choose to propagate chaos. They do not care if they cause harm to others, and only think of their own comfort and needs. Some even take pleasure in seeing or spreading misery and pain. In determining good from evil, it may help you to remember how it felt to be with the Master and in His care. Then you will know what to strive for, what to share with those you choose to call family on this side of the Wall, and what to deny those who cannot appreciate who you are. Do not waste your talents and care on those who would abuse them. Do not be afraid to fight for what is good and right, and to destroy evil when you find it. I advise you to always remember that life is a gift. Never doubt, even if despair should touch your heart, that our Master can salvage good out of evil in His own way and in His own time. Trust in Him always. Again I say to you, if you serve the Master well, you will someday be allowed to rejoin your family.'"

"I have to disagree with your Michael," said Rebekkah. "There is no hardship in Evlantis! We live in prosperity and comfort, especially since my mother became High Queen. Our culture thrives, and most of our people are content."

Ava looked sad.

"What is wrong?" asked Rebekkah.

"I miss my mother and the rest of my family," Ava answered.

"I understand," Rebekkah said, as she took Ava's hands in hers. "In Evlantis, family is everything. My mother is an amazing woman. Losing her love would be the worst thing ever."

"Is it something you worry about?" asked Ava. "Could you be sent away from Evlantis, as I was sent away from Eden?"

"Or were you?" Ava added, as she realized how far the city was from the clearing they were in.

Rebekkah looked troubled. She squeezed Ava's hands.

"You are intuitive, aren't you? I will answer your questions, but not tonight. Out of curiosity, Ava, I must ask, what was your third question and the answer Michael gave you?"

"My third question," answered Ava, "was whether I would see the Creator on this side of the Eden-Wall. The answer was, 'both yes and no. The Master cannot walk among those who oppose His will. You know Him. He is pure. He is love. He is perfect will and perfect knowledge. But you may catch a hint of Him here or there, in the birth of a newborn, in the sunset or sunrise, in a thought, in a whisper of a breeze. The Creator's presence is everywhere, and you will find Him in places you never dreamed you would.' So far, though, it only feels as if I have left Him far behind me."

A tear rolled down Ava's face.

Rebekkah picked up one of the unused strips of cloth she had ripped from the bottom of her ceremonial robe. She used it to wipe the tear from Ava's face, and as she did, she heard twigs snapping in the brush behind them. She had been expecting an ambush and was ready. Ava, too, was aware that others were approaching them. She thought nothing of it until Tiburnus took a chance and leapt to attack Rebekkah. Rebekkah jumped up, spun, and sent him sprawling. He was on his feet instantly.

"Help me, Baraus, do not let either of them get away!" Tiburnus called to his partner.

Baraus left the shelter of the trees and joined Tiburnus. The two men circled Rebekkah and Ava. It was clear they would not let the women leave.

"My goddess, Tiburnus! Which one of these women is Rebekkah?" Baraus asked.

"A game!" Ava clapped her hands and jumped to her feet, eager to play.

"I would say it is the other one," Tiburnus said dryly, "the one wearing the ceremonial robe."

"Tiburnus!" Rebekkah said, "I know you. I know which Low Queen you call mistress. As head of the army, it is my business to hear the rumors, and I have heard your mistress Sephora is boasting she will be elected High Queen. Since that will happen only if I am not here to prevent it, you must have been sent to kill me."

Ava remembered the word kill. The smile left her face. She glanced at Rebekkah, who was calm and in control.

"As you say, princess," said Tiburnus, "you know who I serve. You have named her. Now we must kill your companion, too."

Rebekkah laughed.

"No one is dead yet! And besides, how could you murder me in front of her and let her live? Do not try to blame any failed attempt at murdering anyone on me. Make no mistake. You will fail. This woman and I killed the great Beast together. You have no hope of beating the two of us. And why should you try?"

"There is another alternative. Do either of you recognize this woman with me? I tell you, you cannot. Neither can anyone else from Evlantis. We have thought ourselves to be alone in the world, but there are others. You can go free. I will tell you how to travel to them."

Ava would have objected, but the look Rebekkah gave her silenced her.

"You lie!" Tiburnus hardened his heart. He had served Sephora a long time, and he was looking forward to his reward. "Do not listen to her, Baraus. This woman is most likely from the Religion Sector. It is the only way the Low Queen can be sure we have not seen her before. No one lives outside Evlantis. Everyone knows we are the only people on earth. You will see the goddess of death bless our mission!"

It was the signal the men had agreed upon. Both men reached inside their tunics and brought out the daggers they had concealed there. Ava noted Rebekkah seemed surprised.

Ava decided she must help her friend. Baraus was near her. She slipped easily past him and went to the beast. Baraus followed.

Ava pulled Rebekkah's spear from the dead beast's neck. She broke it in two across her knee, hailed Rebekkah, and threw the pointy-end half to her. It was an accurate throw, and Rebekkah caught it easily. Ava kept the stick end and wielded it like a sword. The four of them engaged in an intense battle, with Tiburnus and Baraus fighting to kill.

"Sephora armed you!" said Rebekkah as they fought. "She will lose her throne, perhaps even her life, for that. My mother will win the election easily once I report this.

"I don't know what Sephora promised you, but I can give you more. Lay down your arms and we will talk. You do not need to die with your mistress. I give you my word of honor I will not kill you. I will let you go free."

"Don't pay any attention to her! Keep fighting! She is trying to distract us!" said Tiburnus to Baraus. The men fought hard, but they were outmatched. Rebekkah was the best soldier in Evlantis. Yet, as legendary as Rebekkah's skills were, it was Ava who out-fought them all. Though Baraus had a dagger and Ava a spear shaft, Baraus was constantly on the defensive, parrying her intricate moves.

"Where did you learn to fight like that?" Rebekkah asked Ava, with admiration in her tone.

Ava answered, laughing.

"I have six older brothers and five older sisters. I had to learn to defend myself among them!"

In Evlantis, the population was strictly controlled and women were rarely allowed to give birth to more than one girl child. The Evlantians paused for an instant, in shock, at her revelation. Ava followed through with a stroke of the broken spear shaft that Baraus was not prepared for. Her blow knocked him off balance and he tripped over his own feet. His head hit a rock on the ground. His eyes rolled back in his head, and he lay still.

The split second of surprise passed, and fighting between Rebekkah and Tiburnus resumed. Ava knelt by Baraus and was relieved to find he was still breathing. Ava jumped up and ran to Rebekkah to fight beside her.

Tiburnus panicked. To fail Sephora was not an option, but he could not win against both women. He took a desperate gamble. He threw the dagger he held at Rebekkah. If he missed he would be unarmed, a miserable failure.

The dagger struck Rebekkah in the upper arm as her arm was drawn back to strike at him. As she completed the forward movement of her arm, the handle of the blade caught in an ornamental pleat at the side of the breast of the ceremonial robe she wore, where it lodged. The blade sliced through more flesh. What should have been nothing more than a flesh wound became deadly as the blade severed the artery beneath the skin. Rebekkah looked down in surprise at her robe, which turned crimson as the wound wept blood. She sat down in shock.

"I am no longer armed; do not harm me. I surrender," Tiburnus said. He could not believe his good luck. He knelt on the ground.

Ava threw the spear shaft away and examined Rebekkah. Ava carefully removed the blade. Blood poured from the gaping wound in Rebekkah's upper arm. Ava could see the pierced artery. She wished she could sew it together, but settled for pinching the edges of the wound with one hand. With her free hand, she unwound one of the bandages on her own arm and used it to bind the wound on Rebekkah's upper arm. Rebekkah had seen wounds like this before and knew her fate was sealed. Ava's efforts were futile.

"Ava," Rebekkah said, "take my Ring of Power and put it on your finger. Escort the slaves into the city and find my mother, High Queen Rachel. My ring should protect you from harm. Tell her what happened here. Tell her and her alone where you are from, what type of person you are. Trust no one else. She will know what to do."

"Hush! Let me fix you!" said Ava. "You need to drink water so that your body can make more blood. Tiburnus, at the edge of the wood, where the beast lies dead, you'll find my travel pack. Please, bring it to me."

Rebekkah was interfering with Ava's ministration by trying to force her to take the ring. Ava took the ring and put it on her finger to calm Rebekkah.

Rebekkah spoke weakly.

"I have cheated death often. If you hurry and get my mother, I may cheat death again." Rebekkah shivered. "I am cold."

Ava watched as the color drained from Rebekkah's face and her lips began to turn a pale shade of blue.

"Hurry with the water!" Ava said to Tiburnus.

"I have so much to do...so much more...." Rebekkah's voice was a whisper. Her tone was urgent. "Listen to me, for you hold the future of Evlantis in your hands. Carry on what I have begun. Promise me."

"What have you begun? What is there to carry on?"

"So weak...so sleepy. You must go...get my mother. Promise me."

"You must have water. You must begin the healing sleep."

Ava scooped Rebekkah off the ground and cradled her in her arms, trying to warm her. Ava was alarmed by the way Rebekkah's body temperature had begun to drop. The subtle difference was easy for her to detect. Tiburnus brought the water to Ava, wondering about the strange container she stored it in. He began to think Rebekkah had told the truth when she said the woman was not from Evlantis.

Rebekkah longed to close her eyes and sleep, but there was something she had to do. She had to make the girl promise to help her. She had others to think of.

"Drink," Ava said. "Drink and live."

"I will not drink until you promise me," said Rebekkah. "Promise to help me."

"I promise, I promise!" said Ava. "I will find your mother, and I will carry on what you have started. Now drink!"

Ava's promise calmed Rebekkah. Ava held the coconut to her lips. Rebekkah drank the last of the water, and then she closed her eyes and seemed to fall asleep.

Ava sighed in relief. She laid Rebekkah gently on the ground.

"Tiburnus, give me your outer covering."

Tiburnus obeyed. Ava took his cloak and laid it over Rebekkah to keep her warm.

"Where is the nearest source of water?" Ava asked. "If we can wake her and get her to drink, she will live."

Tiburnus decided, as Rebekkah originally had, that Ava was an imbecile. Tiburnus was relieved. He was certain he could finish his mission successfully. The girl could outfight him, but she could not outwit him.

Tiburnus stood and walked to where Baraus lay unconscious on the ground.

"This man knows where water is. If we wake him, he and I can carry Queen Rebekkah to it, and then take her to see her mother. Forgive me for my action against her. I lied when I said I wanted to kill her. I truly only wanted to frighten her so I could capture her and take her to my master." His eyes scanned the grass for the blade Baraus had dropped. The girl had not thought to recover it.

"Wake him up and ask him. Hurry! We don't have much time. She needs help now."

Ava monitored the pulse in Rebekkah's neck. As the pulse became weaker, Ava's concern increased.

Tiburnus had located the knife. He knelt with it between his knees and pretended to try to awaken Baraus.

"I cannot rouse him. Can you assist me? I have none of the healing arts women have. I am only a foolish slave."

For the second time, Ava was puzzled over the word slave, but she went to where Baraus lay prostrate and knelt opposite Tiburnus.

Without hesitation, Tiburnus freed the knife from its hiding place, and with a mighty yell, heaved himself at her chest.

The blade lodged in Ava's heart. Ava fell back, shocked as much by the deception as by the injury. Tiburnus lost his balance and used his hands and arms to catch himself, one arm on each side of Ava's prone body. He looked down at her from the position of a lover. He balanced himself on one arm and withdrew the dagger from her heart. Tiburnus watched with satisfaction as blood pooled on her chest.

Ava sensed she was gravely injured. She lay very still and hoped Tiburnus would not attack again. It was not difficult, for though she remained conscious, her body began to shut down all peripheral functions so the powerful healing agents within her could begin to knit the torn heart muscle together. Ava willed her eyes to stay open so she could observe Tiburnus. She must find a way to help Rebekkah.

Tiburnus was elated. He had killed the Commander of the Armed forces of Evlantis and her accomplice! He would share the glory of this night's work with no man. He pushed himself back to a kneeling position and used the knife he was holding to slit the throat of Baraus. Ava was shocked by his brutality.

Tiburnus had work to do before he returned to Sephora. He had to dispose of the bodies and all evidence of treachery. He had been told to bring the Ring of Power from Rebekkah's hand back to his master, as proof of her death. Tiburnus remembered that Rebekkah had given the ring to Ava.

Tiburnus returned to Ava and tried to slip the ring off her finger. The ring would not come free. He used the dagger to sever the finger from her hand.

Ava watched in horror as Tiburnus cut through her flesh, but mercifully felt no sensation. Her central nervous system had blocked the pain receptors, channeling every function of her body to repair her heart muscle. Tiburnus put the ring in a cloth pouch tied around his waist. He gathered Ava's travel pack, dropped the finger and empty coconut shell into it, and secured it around her waist. He could leave no evidence of Ava's presence at the clearing. He lifted her body and threw it over his shoulder. She remained limp as he carried her to the lip of a ravine nearby and threw her down the bank. She rolled until the earth of the ravine dropped away. She fell fifteen feet and came to rest on a rock shelf next to a riverbed.

Her back was broken on impact. Pain flooded her senses as the neurons in her brain opened themselves to feedback from the nervous system to evaluate the new injuries. There was pain in her back, which was excruciating, but she could not feel her legs, which frightened her. Her chest burned where Tiburnus had pierced it. There was a dull ache where her left ring finger had been. She knew her injuries must heal before she could keep her promise to Rebekkah. She found she could use her arms. She used her good hand to open her bag and find her severed finger. She held it to the open wound on her hand where it belonged.

Ava heard another body roll down the ravine. She turned her head in time to see the body of Rebekkah land a mere twenty feet from her. Ava was thankful Tiburnus had at least delivered Rebekkah to her.

"Rebekkah! There is water here! Crawl over and drink, and you will live!"

Rebekkah did not answer her.

"Rebekkah! I cannot come to you; there is too much damage to my body to walk, and soon I will enter a healing sleep whether I want to or not. I saw this happen to my brother, Seth, who fell from the side of a mountain. It took him months to heal. Rebekkah, show me some sign that you can hear me, that you will drink! As soon as I am well, I will find your mother. I will keep my promise…."

Ava could no longer fight the need of her body to shut down and repair itself. Her voice trailed off in exhaustion. Her mind did not register the sound waves generated by the body of Baraus as it fell down the steep edges of the ravine and came to rest not far from Rebekkah.

Progress continued on the repair to her heart. Flesh and bone on her hand began to knit together. The repairs to her spinal cord would begin later, but her immune system began to produce antibodies to combat the hosts of foreign bodies that had entered through her open wounds. Though her body was immortal, healing took time. Ava slept, and as she did, she dreamed of Eden.

Tiburnus, his work finished, came through the trees, breathing heavily, intent on making it back to where Sephora waited for him. He came to the huge elm that had a V at the base and a fallen limb that made a makeshift bench. He scrutinized the area around him carefully, but did not see Sephora. He sat and waited for the Low Queen as he collected his thoughts. He was disturbed that things had not gone quite as his master had planned. She would not be pleased at his news of the strange woman he'd found with Rebekkah, and Rebekkah's claim that there were others who lived beyond Evlantis, but he must tell her. He now wished he had saved the stranger's coat or travel pack as evidence of his encounter with her in the clearing.

Sephora appeared before him as if his thoughts had summoned her. She stood with both hands behind her back. She had taken off her cloak, and Tiburnus could see that she was wearing a loose, white sheath. Even though she was dressed simply, her posture and beauty bore testimony to her leadership and strength. He felt a shiver of fear go up his spine, and he dropped to his knees as etiquette demanded. He was a lowly slave in the presence of a great Queen.

Sephora spoke immediately.

"Is it done?"

"Yes, Queen Sephora."

"Where is your companion?"

"There was a fight. Baraus was killed."

Sephora was disappointed. She had thought she would be able to vent her blood lust on two slaves this evening. Killing Tiburnus alone would present no challenge at all. He remained with his head bowed down and did not see the look on her face.

"How did you dispose of the bodies?" Sephora asked him.

He wondered if it was the right time to tell her, but he thought he would appease her with the ring before giving her the news.

"I carried them to the Great Ravine as you commanded and threw them in." He omitted the fact that there had been three bodies.

"Excellent. Did you remember to get the ring?"

"Yes, my Queen, here is the token you asked me to bring. I give you Rebekkah's Ring of Power with my undying loyalty and affection."

He reached into the pouch at his waist and from it took the ring. He handed it to his master and waited while she examined the beautifully wrought token of power Rebekkah had worn since taking the oath of office to lead the great army of Evlantis.

"This ring is a bloody mess. Weren't the two of you able to surprise her and kill her instantly?" she asked. She sounded angry.

He swallowed hard. He wasn't ready to risk her displeasure.

"No, my Queen, she defeated the beast as you predicted. Baraus was just about to strike a killing blow from behind when...."

He faltered, but Sephora finished for him.

"I know, the uncanny bitch wheeled and dealt a killing blow. I swear she had eyes in the back of her head. Well, that is why I sent two of you. So you attacked and killed her."

"There is more, good Queen, but first you should know her death was not easy. She suffered. I cut the ring from her finger while she lived," he said. An outright lie, but it had the effect he had been waiting for. Sephora crowed with joy. Her voice rang loudly, obscenely so, into the night.

He had to tell her now. He looked up at her, ready to tell her the whole story, and stared in shock. She held an unsheathed sword above her head, ready to strike.

"No, my Queen, there is more...."

Sephora never hesitated. His words trailed off as the blow cut through the meat where his jaw met his neck. Blood sprayed as she severed most of his head from his neck. Her white shift was speckled and streaked crimson. Sephora smiled.

The meeting place she had chosen was near an ancient well that had serviced a nomadic settlement before the founding of Evlantis. It had been left as it was, since most women were terrified of the forest, and few roamed the dangerous woods at night. Sephora feared nothing and knew her way around the forest as well as the city. She dragged the body by its feet to the well, not caring if her minion had finished dying or not, and pushed it in at a spot where the stones had crumbled inward. It was easy work because she kept herself in excellent physical shape. She was covered in blood, but before she bathed, she wanted to see the Sacrificial Clearing with her own eyes.

Sephora made her way there in the cover of darkness. There lay the beast, dead, with Rebekkah's broken spear lying near it. It did not surprise her.

In the moonlight, she could see a pool of blood. It must have been some fight. Rebekkah was ferocious, the best warrior in the written herstory of Evlantis. Now she was gone. Next Sephora would get rid of her mother.

Sephora wanted to keep the Ring of Power to spite Rachel, but leaving the Ring would work in her favor. It was an old custom for a mortally wounded soldier to leave her ring at the site of her last battle and venture out alone to meet the goddesses. It ensured that the woman would be remembered in her glory and prime, not as one who had been defeated. Sephora stood still, lingering in uncharacteristic indecision. Finally, reluctantly, Sephora planted the Ring of Power in plain sight on the forehead of the beast.

She slunk away to bathe in the stream of the goddess Ephrea, giver of life. She had hidden clothing and a towel nearby earlier in the week. When she was finished, she made her way back to the well where she had dumped Tiburnus, and she threw her bloody clothes down into the hole with the body. She then made her way back to the city and waited for the inevitable events she had set in motion to occur.

On the wall, standing in silence with Diana, Arrival felt the cord inside her that bound her to Rebekkah snap. She would shed her tears in private.

"Wait until the morning light, and then go to her," said Arrival. "I will wait in her chambers. If she is alive, bring her home. If she is dead, report to me at once, that I may not bear the burden of her grave-secret for one second longer than I must."

Arrival strode away, her back straight, her heart breaking. Intuition reverberated within her. Her inner eye tried to show her there was worse to come. Arrival dismissed it as fancy. There could be nothing worse than losing Rebekkah.

DENIAL

By the light of a spectacular dawn, Caliphus, who was the High Priestess and the Low Queen of the Religion Sector, discovered the grim scene in the Sacrificial Clearing. It was her annual task to inspect the site each morning of the spring sacrificial season. There were messages from the goddesses in the remains of the victim for her to interpret. It was not one of her favorite duties.

Servus was one of the first people in the Queendom to hear the news. A white-faced slave boy sought him out as he was eating gruel by the fire in the center of the slave compound.

"Servus, help me," whispered the slave urgently. "My master is dead. Oh, goddess, I wish I were Baezus. Her horse gets to run free, while I will be killed. Please, sir, is there anything you can do to help me?"

The soldiers only used slaves to tend to their horses. This boy served Rebekkah. Servus glanced at the People's Palace and the palace of the Soldier Sector. Rebekkah's flag still flew from both buildings.

"How did you come by this information?" asked Servus.

"You know they drove Baezus away on the first day of the sacrifice. Since then, I have spent every minute I wasn't required for other duties in the horse barn at the Great Wall, waiting for news about my master. This morning, I was lucky. There was a highway detail nearby, and I pretended to be part of it when High Priestess Caliphus returned from the clearing. General Diana was waiting for her. They began to talk.

"I moved close enough to hear the news. Diana even looked right at me, but you know how it is—though she has seen me a hundred times, she didn't recognize me. It is as if we are invisible to them, unless they want something." The boy spoke bitterly.

Servus nodded. He had excellent sources of intelligence because the women talked so freely in front of their slaves. That fact would be of no comfort to the boy.

"I believe you," Servus said. "What did they say?"

"The beast is dead. Rebekkah is missing, but her ring was found at the Sacrificial Clearing. Sir, my master would never have left her ring behind. What will I do if they say she is dead? I don't want to die."

"You will be killed only if the new Commander does not want your service."

"Arrival has never let a slave tend Stealth. Why would she start now?"

"Because you are going to ask her to allow you to have the honor of doing that job," said Servus, remembering how she had remanded the beating Partouche had ordered. "Is there anything else you overheard? Something that might be useful to Arrival?"

The boy furrowed his brow.

"Yes! I heard Diana ask one of the priestesses attending Caliphus to offer up incense to the goddess Marsa for her, because she is going to challenge Arrival for leadership of the Soldier Sector right away."

Servus was incredulous. This was great news. If Rebekkah was dead, and he would wager she was, this was excellent news for their cause. He did not want to begin his war with Arrival in charge of the armed forces, for both personal and tactical reasons. Servus hoped Diana would win the challenge. With an inexperienced Commander in charge of the armed forces, they might be able to win their freedom quickly. He turned his attention back to the boy.

"Go; take her the news about her sister. Warn her about Diana, and beg her to spare your life. It is your only hope. Hurry."

Servus watched the boy run toward the Soldier Sector Palace, a simple three-story structure on the border of the Soldier Sector and the slave grounds. He took a chance in forewarning Arrival, but it might help her decide to spare the boy. When the boy disappeared, running at full speed into the glorified barracks of the soldiers, Servus sighed and turned back to the fire. If Arrival ordered the boy's death, it would be much easier to face her in battle if she did win the challenge.

As Rebekkah's personal horse slave, the boy slave had full access to Rebekkah's quarters, which adjoined Arrival's rooms. He ran right into his master's quarters and slammed the door behind him, intending to knock respectfully on the connecting door to Arrival's rooms.

"Goddess of Flame!" said Arrival, sitting up and rubbing her eyes. She had been sleeping on the couch in her sister's room. "What is your hurry, slave?" Her tone was gruff.

The boy fell to his knees, weeping.

"I did not know you would be here in her rooms. Forgive me," said the boy through his sobs.

"On your feet, boy." For the second day in a row, she ordered a slave to stand in her presence. "Who gave you the right to enter my sister's quarters so brazenly?"

The boy stood, all hope gone.

"My goddess!" Arrival exclaimed. "Aren't you the boy that tended to Baezus? Did Rebekkah send you?" For a moment, Arrival felt hope that she'd been wrong in sensing Rebekkah's death. Perhaps Rachel was right, and Arrival's gift of intuition was not as reliable as she herself thought it was.

"No, Servus sent me," the slave replied deferentially. "He said I should beg you for my life. I was coming to find you. I did not think you would be in the rooms of my master. I apologize."

"Beg for your life? Why?" Arrival felt as though her heart plummeted into her stomach. Rebekkah was gone forever.

"I was at the gate when Caliphus returned."

Arrival looked at the boy. He could not be much older than nine. It must have taken great courage for him to come and face her.

"Tell me everything," she said.

Arrival listened in fascination. She realized Servus had sent the boy to warn her. Was his motivation simply to spare the life of one boy, or was there more to it than that? She was deep in thought when the boy finished his narrative with a question.

"What did you say?" asked Arrival. "Repeat yourself."

"Please, may I serve you?" he asked again.

"What is your name?" asked Arrival.

"Number 429011," replied the boy.

"Not your number; I can see the number on your arm. What do you call yourself? What do the men call you?"

The boy looked at Arrival as if she had grown six pairs of arms.

"J-J-Jed," stammered the boy.

"This is not a simple matter. If Caliphus proclaims Rebekkah dead, I will spare your life and allow you to tend Stealth, though I will have to train you. I am the only one who has tended to him since he was a young foal. If I claim you before the death notice, it will look like I am trying to usurp my sister's throne."

Jed understood at once. "Anything could happen once Commander Rebekkah's death is public knowledge. I could be killed before you could save me. There is no hope for me."

"You believe she is dead, then?"

"She would never have left her Ring of Power behind." He began to weep again.

Arrival realized the boy was not only courageous; he was intelligent and intuitive.

"Jed," said Arrival, making up her mind, "I do have the authority in this situation to reassign you. I have a friend, Low Queen Ariana of the Livestock Sector, who could use your services until this matter is decided. I will recommend she give you duties away from the public eye until it is prudent for me to come and claim your services."

The boy wiped away his tears. He looked at her in wonder and adoration. She was as kind as she was beautiful.

"Why are you helping me?" he asked. "Your sister never cared if I lived or died, and I served her faithfully for years."

Arrival thought of the grave-secret Rebekkah had shared with her only days ago. She could not explain to Jed how profoundly it had changed her. She chose not to answer him.

"Jed, I must get to Rachel before Caliphus does. Did you ever assist my sister with her armor?"

"Yes, many times."

"Help me now. I can't send you to get Stealth, as it would send the wrong message. I'll have someone else do that. Help me get ready to fight Diana, then hide here for me until I can give you a personal escort to Ariana's Sector."

"Whatever you order, I will do. Thank you, most gracious and generous Queen. I may not be your slave in word, but in deed I will be always."

As they hurried to Arrival's chambers, she realized she had saddled herself with the burden of the life of Rebekkah's slave. She felt more weighted down by the baggage of her sister than ever before.

High Priestess Caliphus hesitated outside Rachel's chambers. She knew this would be a very difficult interview. After speaking to Diana at the main gate of the city, she had made a quick visit to her apartment at the People's Palace to change into her most formidable and impressive vestments.

"Caliphus!"

Caliphus heard her name and turned to see Arrival coming toward her dressed in full body armor. They sized each other up. Arrival had not seen Caliphus dressed in such splendor since her childhood, when the city had experienced its last drought. Caliphus was a striking figure when she chose to be. She was a few years younger than Rachel and a little taller. Rachel's shape had become rounder through the years, but Caliphus had become gaunter. The formal green gown Caliphus wore was embroidered with intricate pictures of Mother Eve, one portrait on the front and the other on the back, and it hung loosely on her. Arrival remembered that when Caliphus was younger, she had an annoying habit of tapping her feet constantly, but years of meditation and self-discipline had cured her of it. Caliphus stood straight and still. She looked grim.

"Caliphus!" Arrival was relieved she had gotten there before Caliphus entered. "Please, let me enter first. I have business with my mother to conduct in private. I will not be more than one or two minutes."

Caliphus was not looking forward to her audience with the High Queen.

"Certainly, Princess. Go with my blessing. I will wait here."

Before Arrival could knock, the door opened, and Rachel stood before them.

"Two of you out here!" the High Queen said. "I saw Caliphus approaching on the main road. I wondered why you did not come to me right away. I was just coming to find you. Come in, come in!"

"High Queen," said Caliphus, "Low Queen Arrival would like a word with you in private first."

"Caliphus, I see you both are dressed in official regalia. It can only mean one thing. Don't deny me both your comfort as I hear the news. I will talk to Arrival alone afterwards. Come in, both of you. Don't delay."

Rachel pulled them both into the room. She lowered herself into a chair. Rachel could not imagine what could have gone wrong, but the news must be bad, or they would not both have come dressed so formally. She didn't wait for Caliphus to say the words she dreaded to hear.

"Where have you taken her body?" Rachel asked. "I will sit here a minute to gather strength and then go to her. Where is it? I must see it."

"High Queen," said Caliphus, "I have been to the clearing. I found the beast there, slain. I have examined the signs. I have asked the goddesses about the fate of your daughter. I have, here in my hand, your daughter's Ring of Power, which I found on the head of the mighty beast. All the signs and portents are clear. Rebekkah is dead. You have my sympathy."

"Her body, Caliphus," said Rachel. "Where have you taken it?"

"Her body was not at the clearing. Only the ring was there, which clearly proves that she left it behind."

Caliphus walked to where Rachel sat and handed the ring to her. Rachel examined it closely.

"This is definitely her ring," said Rachel. She had sat in anticipation of grief, but now she stood in denial. "And so, I know she is alive. Rebekkah would have never left her Ring of Power and gone off alone to die. Without her body, there can be no funeral. Rebekkah would never deny me the comfort that a lavish State Funeral would bring. The abandoned ring is not evidence of her death. It is evidence of treachery. Four short weeks remain before the election of High Queen. Who benefits most by my daughter's disappearance? Use your head, Caliphus."

"I presume you mean your opponent, Sephora. Her where-abouts have been accounted for every minute of the past three days. Last night I saw her myself, dressed in veils at the temple, all her minions around her, praying for the safe return of your daughter. My priestesses reported that she did not move from her spot all evening. Do you think either Arrival or I would have allowed Sephora or her henchwomen out of our sight?

"The omens in the clearing were unmistakable. She is dead. She could not bear for you to feel the guilt that finding her body would bring, and she left. I must obey the law and follow proto-col. I have declared a one-month waiting period, the maximum allowed, because it will benefit your effort in the election and gar-ner you sympathy."

Caliphus could see by the look on Rachel's face that she had chosen the wrong words. It didn't help that a commotion began outside.

"Arrival! Arrival! Come down from the Palace! I challenge you for the title of Commander and Chief of the Armed forces!"

"My goddess!" said Rachel. "Rebekkah is missing and vultures are already presuming the meal has been served. Arrival, go down and put whoever that is in their place."

"It is not that simple, Mother," said Arrival. "My first order of business is with you. I must talk to you alone as soon as possible."

"Arrival," said Rachel, "nothing has changed since last night. I will not hear what you have to say. I will not allow you to defy your sister's wishes."

"Rachel," said Caliphus. "Rebekkah is not going to return. You should listen to whatever Arrival has to say to you. I will go."

"No!" Rachel yelled the word, clearly not in control of herself. "Rebekkah is not dead! I am her mother! I would know! Don't you think I would know? From this point on I will not be alone with Arrival until Rebekkah returns."

Arrival began to pace, thinking. Her mother had the motivation and the means to prevent her from telling the grave-secret. Arrival doubted Rachel would believe her now, anyway. In addition, Diana waited below. Arrival must decide quickly what to do. Every minute she delayed the challenge she looked less like a Queen. Arrival damned the stubbornness of Rachel. She had never needed her mother more, and Rachel could only think of Rebekkah.

Arrival sighed and walked to the window. Below her, Diana waited with a few supporters around a freshly drawn challenge circle she had chalked out in the grass in front of the People's Palace. Arrival guessed correctly that the news was spreading, because the roads leading to the palace were congested for this time of the morning.

She glanced down the road to the Soldier Sector. A large contingent of troops was on its way. Arrival began to pace again. This would be a very public challenge unless she chose not to fight. If she did not fight, she would lose her privileges as Low Queen and would have no access to Rachel. The advantage of abdicating was that she could use her time to find her sister's body. Then Rachel would have to listen to her, but if she abdicated, it might weaken Rachel's efforts to win re-election. If she remained Commander, she would have to continue to defend her position against challengers. Arrival had never really wanted to rule, but if she did, her duties would bring her in contact with Rachel. There might yet be a way to tell her mother Rebekkah's secret.

"Rachel," Caliphus said gently, "Rebekkah is dead. You must do what is best for the Queendom. I need you to remember your six thousand daughters and put them ahead of your womb-born one. If Sephora wins the election, Rebekkah will have sacrificed herself in vain."

"Caliphus," Rachel was calmer now. "Rebekkah would have kept the Ring of Power on her finger and died crawling back to Evlantis rather than abandon it. There is no way to know for certain the blood at the clearing was hers. Help me, Caliphus. Make a declaration that she survived the sacrifice and will return to us."

"Rachel, the goddesses left signs. They took her. She is not among us anymore. I cannot betray my office. I serve the goddesses first, the people second, and the High Queen third. My duty to all of you aligns in this case. I will delay the news of Rebekkah's death until just before the election. By law, it is the longest I can delay. You must concentrate on winning as a way to honor Rebekkah's sacrifice."

Rachel and Caliphus stared at each other in stony silence. Arrival had half heard the words they had spoken, and she felt torn by the decision she had to make. To rule or to abdicate—she must decide now. She was not certain she had what it took to lead in Rebekkah's stead. Compounded with the weight of the grave-secret, Arrival was conflicted.

"Arrival! Arrival, you coward!" The voice of Diana could be heard clearly. "I can see you in your mother's room. Quit hiding behind her skirts and get down here!"

Arrival stopped pacing abruptly. A trance overtook her. Words Rebekkah had spoken to her many years ago poured into her consciousness. The memory of the beloved voice became the focus of all her senses.

"You lose another challenge and come to me for comfort?" Rebekkah had said to her. "You make yourself look ridiculous! What came easily for me you had to work for, and you worked damn hard. Yet you compare yourself to me and find yourself lacking. If you would stop telling yourself that you are not good enough to win, you would win. It is as simple as that. No one has worked harder than you have to master the art of combat, yet you move up through the ranks slowly. Know your opponents better than your own imaginary weaknesses, trust in your gifts, and you will win. I will stop insulting you now, for I watch you practice on the battlefield, and I am no longer positive that I could beat you. Leave me. Come back when I can see a warrior in you, and not a child. You did not overcome all the opposition set before you to follow me into the Soldier Sector to remain in my shadow forever. I need you as my Second in Command. Go! Get the job done!"

As the voice faded, Arrival returned to the present moment with her decision made. Rebekkah was not here, but her sister still needed her. She drew herself to her full height. Her entire being emanated power. She left the room without saying a word to Caliphus or Rachel. Her bearing reminded Caliphus and Rachel they were Queens, not ordinary women. Caliphus broke the silence.

"Sephora is causing trouble, resurrecting old rivalries among the powerful and the rich in an attempt to divide the votes among them. You know this. Some of your staunchest supporters have died mysteriously in the last year.

"This is a pivotal point in our herstory. I have seen it in the stars. For goddess's sake, Rachel, think of something besides your own grief. You are behaving like a desperate mother. That was your right for all of ten minutes, but now it is time to behave like the High Queen. Obey the oath you swore and put the needs of your subjects first."

"You are right, and you are wrong," said the High Queen. "I will behave as High Queen, but I am not grieving, because Rebekkah is not dead.

"You heard Arrival; Rebekkah was keeping something from me. She must have a reason for staying away. She must have left the Ring behind as a message to me to trust her. I will heed your advice and pour my energies into winning the election. Rebekkah must have a plan, and I must trust her. She will appear before the election; I am sure of it."

Rachel was certain Rebekkah must have gone to one of the camps she had made when she went on her long Warrior Retreats. There she would have shelter and provisions to help her recuperate. Rachel would have to wait patiently. In the meantime, she would rebuff her younger daughter's attempts to reveal Rebekkah's grave-secret. It was the only way she could think of to even the odds in her daughter's favor since she could not tend to her now.

Outside, Arrival, looking powerful and confident, made an impromptu speech on the steps of the People's Palace to the large group of women who had gathered there, many of whom were soldiers.

"These are troubled times. Rebekkah is missing. Sephora challenges Rachel for the throne of High Queen. I ask each and every soldier present to give her full loyalty and service to me until after the election. Then I will accept challenges for title of commander. We need to concentrate on keeping peace in the Queendom. I am the best soldier for that job. Diana, will you agree to withdraw your challenge for the good of the Queendom?"

"I will not withdraw," said Diana. "You say you are the best to rule. Prove it."

"You have all heard what Diana says. She would choose discord and change instead of a united front. But, I accept her challenge. Though it is my right to choose the weapon, I will let her do so. Not only will I beat her fairly, but I will do so in less than two minutes so that I may demonstrate to every one of you how certain I am that I am the right leader for these times. When I win, I expect the support of every soldier in our Sector until after the election. Then the challenges may begin in earnest, for I do not seek to change our way of life, but only to unite our Sector as one fighting force."

"If you lose?" asked Diana. "How will we be any better off if you choose to challenge me for the leadership again?"

"You will not win, Diana, but if you do by some slim chance, you will lead the Sector and I will retire from service. By show of spear, whose support do I have on these terms?"

Rebekkah had been a demanding Commander. Many had preferred life under Arrival when Rebekkah went on her long retreats outside the city. The soldiers who would like to rise through the ranks would happily accept Arrival's temporary leadership if she could beat Diana in two minutes. No one wanted to see Sephora as High Queen. The majority of soldiers in the crowd raised their spears.

"Now, do you accept my terms, Diana?"

"I do." Diana could not believe how easy Arrival was making this for her.

Arrival wasted no time.

"Weapon of choice?" she asked Diana.

"Staff."

Arrival snapped her fingers and one of the soldiers attending her placed a staff in her hand.

"Review the terms," said Arrival.

"First woman forced out of the circle loses." The soldier who had placed the staff in Arrival's hand called out the terms. "First woman down for ten counts loses. First woman unable to continue fighting loses. To forfeit, a soldier must kneel with her head to the ground. Winner becomes Low Queen and Commander of the Soldier Sector."

"Acceptable. Begin timing when the challenger enters the circle."

Arrival stepped into the circle and ran to the center.

Diana entered the circle and ran at Arrival swinging her staff.

Arrival defended against a series of blows. Diana was furious and spoke the words that drove her to challenge Arrival.

"She would be alive now if you had let me go to her. It is your fault she is gone."

Arrival did not answer. She had less than two minutes to win. She planned to use a trick the children used to win their circle games. She controlled the fight, though she made it look as if Diana was forcing her to the edge of the circle. Six inches from the edge of the circle, just as Diana thought to force Arrival out, Arrival dropped to the ground. Diana fell over her, landing with her head and arms outside of the circle. In a flash, Arrival was up with Diana's legs in her arms. She threw them outside the circle to the cheers of her supporters. She put her staff on Diana's chest to keep her down. Arrival bent over and whispered in her ear.

"If I had let you go to her, you might both be dead. If you had followed orders, I would be relieved of the burden I carry and you would have comfort. Now, according to the terms of our agreement, you must serve me until the election is over, but I hope not as my second in command. Be ready to defend your position."

Arrival turned and spoke to the cheering crowd of soldiers.

"I have won the challenge fairly using a child's trick against my second in command. Her post is open for challenge. Now, we have work to do. We must keep the women of the Queendom safe during the frenzy of these last few weeks of the campaign. We must keep the slaves in line, for our sentries report unrest among them as well. Most of all, we must keep the High Queen safe from treachery. For the glory of Evlantis!"

"For the glory of Evlantis!" The soldiers cheered.

Arrival was hoisted upon the shoulders of the women who served her, and they paraded around the grounds of the People's Palace and the Soldier Sector in celebration of their unity and as an expression of their loyalty.

Servus was being led out of the Slave Sector in a contingent to work on the Palace grounds. When he saw that Arrival had won, his heart sank. He knew he must put aside his concern for her and make the decision that was best for the men.

Kiertus walked cautiously through the old tunnel, the secret entrance to the home that once belonged to Eriad, Ariana's aunt. Eriad's accusers had not discovered it when they gathered evidence against her. Besides the caution that was always necessary for clandestine meetings, his feet moved slowly because his heart was heavy. Servus was right. Conditions were perfect to begin their war. He must tell his lover that it was far too dangerous for him to continue to see her. This would be their last private rendezvous.

The panel to the room ahead stood open. She must be waiting for him. He squeezed through the hole in the wall and she approached him, one hand on her pregnant belly and one outstretched to him. He wistfully remembered the days she ran to him holding both arms open. They had met in the Quickening Chamber and had fallen in love. He knew that Ariana wondered if her aberrant attraction to him was a flaw that she had inherited. Kiertus constantly assured her it was the law that was wrong, not their hearts.

He gathered her in his arms.

"It took so long," Ariana said. "I was afraid you weren't coming."

Kiertus sighed. "I'm sorry. There are more people on the roads than usual this morning. I had to be extra careful."

"Is there news about Rebekkah?"

"If there is, I have not yet heard it. Ariana, we must talk. I need you to understand that I cannot keep seeing you. It is far too dangerous. I can't risk losing you and our unborn daughter or son."

"No, Kiertus," she said. "We've talked about this before. You mean more to me than the child I carry. I cannot live without you. You are my life."

"You say that now, but when our child, quickened in love, is placed in your arms, it will sooth the pain of our parting. You will forget me."

She stepped back and looked at him.

"You are serious about this."

"Yes, I am."

"Why? Why now when we have risked our lives for months?"

Kiertus could not tell her about the coming war. If he was ever to have any chance of a future with his lover and his child, the men had to win their freedom. Kiertus was not sure he could trust her with the truth. He stayed silent.

"Are you rejecting me because I will have to give the child up if it is a boy?" she asked. It was one of the few things they had argued about. She had sought a position of leadership in her Sector because she wanted to make the lives of the slaves easier. It was something she had promised her beloved aunt before her death. Ariana had never expected to fall in love with a slave. She finally understood why her aunt had risked everything, and why she had gone to the stake so peacefully. Eriad had tried to explain to her how she could not live without her lover, and that they believed they would be in the afterlife together, but Ariana had been young. She had not understood then, but now she did. She would rather die than lose Kiertus.

"Ariana, I am not rejecting you," Kiertus said, but he was, and they both knew it. "No one knows what will happen in the next few weeks, and our baby is due at the end of the summer. For now, it is too risky to continue our affair."

"Later then?" asked Ariana, hopefully.

"When it is safe for us to be together, then yes. Nothing will keep me from you."

"I will die without you," Ariana said, beginning to cry. Kiertus pulled her into his arms, feeling damned. He had chosen to put her life at risk every time he agreed to meet her. Now he was choosing to give his loyalty to Servus, which made her the enemy. He wanted to tell her, but he did not know if she would choose to be loyal to the women or if she would help the men.

"And I would give my life to save yours," said Kiertus. "I'm asking you to put our child first, for now. Please." Kiertus knew the memory of Eriad was always with her. "It is what your aunt would have wanted."

"Oh, Kiertus, of course you are right. What was I thinking? That the laws would change and we could be together to raise our child? If my mother found out, it would kill her. It is bad enough living with the suspense of whether I am carrying a girl or a boy. The sex of our child makes such a difference to our family status."

Kiertus closed his eyes so she would not see his pain. Ariana belonged to the women, not to him. He had made the right decision.

QUEEN'S FALL

Exactly one month to the day that Ava had met Rebekkah, Ava awoke, refreshed. She could vaguely recall waking up in pain several times to drink from the river. Ava drew in a deep breath, grateful to find the pain from the wound in her finger and heart was manageable. Then she remembered Rebekkah.

Ava sat up abruptly and looked around. Rebekkah was nowhere in sight. She could be anywhere.

Ava called out, "Rebekkah, are you well? Did you make it to the river to drink? Rebekkah…Rebekkah!"

But the only response was silence.

Ava remembered Rebekkah saying she needed to get back to the city. Perhaps she had already gone. The immortal tried to wiggle her toes and was delighted to see and feel them move. Very carefully, she got to her feet and stretched, feeling joy in the movement. It was then she noticed Rebekkah's robe on the rock shelf not far from her. Puzzled, Ava walked toward the cloth. A bit of white caught her eye. She knelt by the cloth and then gagged as she realized there was nothing left of Rebekkah but the bones of her body. Sadness filled Ava's heart and tears flowed from her eyes. The pain in her heart at the death of Rebekkah was worse than the pain from the knife wound.

Ava pulled the outer cloak away from the remains of Rebekkah and gently arranged the skeleton into a position of rest. Out of respect for her friend, Ava gathered rocks from around the rock shelf and piled them around the remains. Ava had to rest often because she became tired very quickly. On her search for rocks, she found the remains of Baraus. She deliberated, and then covered his remains too.

Ava was exhausted. The summer night faded. Ava knew she had to go to Evlantis and find Rebekkah's mother, but she was not sure she had the strength to climb out of the steep ravine.

In Evlantis, the residents of the city assembled outside the west balcony of the Palace to hear the final speeches of the candidates the day before the election. The women had a creative way for citizens to attend the presentations of the candidates so that they could hear every word. Written copies of the speeches, carefully guarded by each candidate until the day before the election, were handed out to official Readers at key points in the crowd. Each candidate would dole out their speech one paragraph at a time, and then wait to continue until the Readers finished repeating that paragraph of the speech. A supporter of each candidate was stationed with each Reader to ensure the speeches were read verbatim.

Speeches of minor candidates began at first light. Early in the day, no Readers were needed. The small crowd that assembled directly below the second story balcony could hear every word. As the day wore on, the crowd grew and more Readers were added.

Every elected official ruled for seven years. During an election year for the office of High Queen, the speeches given by the incumbent High Queen and her opponent were the last scheduled. On this day, they were scheduled to take place after the dinner hour. However, a record number of citizens showed up. There was a delay while more copies of Rachel and Sephora's speeches were transcribed and new Readers were sworn in. Tradition dictated that the challenger go first. An hour before last light, Sephora was led from the anteroom to the balcony where Rachel presided as the incumbent Queen.

As soon as Rachel saw Sephora, she knew something was coming that she hadn't anticipated. For the first time in her recollection, Sephora was dressed conservatively. Sephora took great pride in her looks, and for her to be covered head to toe in priestessly green instead of a revealing, beaded shift was unheard of. Sephora had even pulled her long black hair into a tight ponytail so that her head resembled the shaved and closely cropped hair of those high in the ranks of the Religion Sector. As Rachel listened to Sephora's speech, her astonishment grew.

"Beloved citizens of Evlantis," Sephora began with a loving smile, "I come to you today as a humble supplicant, asking you to make me your High Queen. As you well know, this is the third time I have come to you asking you to allow me to lead you. The first time I was a mere girl with high hopes. The second time I was more experienced, but not so much as my opponent, High Queen Rachel. This third time, I come to you well seasoned, and as you will see, I am the only real choice.

"I could speak to you of my plans. As with my other campaigns, I promise to open the granaries to the poorest among you. I promise to reverse my opponent's softness on slaves. They must be handled with much more discipline to have as much work squeezed from them as any other animal of burden. Everyone here knows my platform. I am consistent. I have not changed except for one detail.

"What has changed is this: I am the woman you should vote for because I am the Queen the goddesses themselves have chosen to sit on the High Throne."

Sephora waited for the buzz to die down before continuing. Rachel sat in disbelief. Sephora was known to be irreverent and a casual follower of religion at best.

"It was I who suggested that Low Queen Rebekkah be sacrificed to the Beast. The goddesses were so pleased with the offering of Rebekkah that they allowed the Beast to be slain. From now on, we are free of the spring blood ritual. It is because of my efforts we no longer need to live in fear of the Beast."

The crowd stirred, but Sephora continued.

"There is more. The Goddess Ephrea herself came to me the night after Rebekkah's Ring of Power had been found."

Sephora paused as the crowd reacted in the familiar ripple pattern from front to back as Readers repeated her audacious claim. No one had ever seen Ephrea. No one but Mother Eve had spoken of her. The claim was preposterous, but Sephora stood before them calm, self-confident, and looking far more impressive in her priestessly gown than Caliphus, the High Priestess who stood upon the balcony and stared at Sephora with her mouth hanging open in shock. Sephora waited patiently, a radiant smile on her face. When it was silent again, she continued.

"The goddess thanked me for the simple courtesy of offering the very best the Queendom had to offer up to the goddesses. Then she said she had a message she wished me to give to you. She said, and I quote, 'Mortal woman, it is one such as you who should rule my children. It is your insight that my legion of goddesses and I will bless in the coming years. Whether you remain Queen of the Arts, or whether you are elected High Queen, I will pour daughters like water from the ocean into the wombs of the women you rule. I will make the slaves docile and productive. I will bless the crops so that the bins overflow. The winters will be gentle and the summers long. All this and more will I do to thank you for the courtesy of respecting the mother of all goddesses. Go and tell my children that they may exercise their right to vote wisely. Do not be afraid of condemnation, for I will punish those who doubt me.'

"There is more," said Sephora, when she could continue. "Not only do I have the blessing of the goddesses, but I am the only candidate who meets our constitutional requirements to lead the people. The candidate for High Queen must be a mother."

On cue, Sephora's firstborn daughter stepped onto the balcony to stand beside her mother.

"I have not one," said Sephora, as her second daughter came and stood beside her sister.

"Not two," she continued, as a third daughter joined her sisters, "but three daughters."

Sephora stretched out her arm toward her girls in a dramatic gesture of presentation, and there was thunderous applause.

In a city where bearing daughters was a woman's reason for living, having three daughters was rare and considered a true blessing. The population was strictly controlled by the Quickening Committee, which determined with a census count that there could be no more than one thousand women per Sector. If a woman visited the Chamber and produced a son, she was not allowed back in. High-ranking women were allowed two daughters.

After birthing two daughters, Sephora had, fifteen years ago, bribed the committee to allow her to conceive a third child. She had been lucky enough to be one rare woman to have given birth to three daughters and no sons. She ruled her girls with an iron hand, and she allowed no room for them to express their own personalities. She followed an ancient custom, long out of practice, of numbering her daughters instead of naming them. They were known as First, Second, and Third Sephora. They were beautiful girls, all in their teenage years. First Sephora in particular resembled her mother, both in looks and temperament. Second Sephora was chronically restless and unhappy, and Third Sephora was merry, but spoiled and indulged. Standing beside their mother in their finest raiment, they were a strong testament to the bloodline of Sephora. After the applause trailed off, Sephora continued.

"However, while I am mother to three daughters, my opponent, sadly, is childless. Ephrea told me herself that Rebekkah has gone to the land of deceased warriors. Caliphus has been in league with High Queen Rachel to deceive you. Some of you may think Commander Arrival is Rachel's daughter, but it is no secret she is adopted. Arrival is the womb-born daughter of Rachel's cousin, who died during childbirth."

It was a fact known to most women in the crowd. The amount of head nodding that occurred when Sephora mentioned it was confirmation for those who did not.

"So, beloved citizens, I am the only woman running for the office of High Queen who meets all the qualifications to rule you, and I have received a mandate from the goddesses to rule you. Do what is right, and vote for me to be your High Queen. Allow the goddesses to shower blessings down, not only upon the Arts Sector, but upon the entire city so that Evlantis may reach new heights of glory!"

Sephora raised her arms and looked up to the heavens as if she could see the face of Ephrea there. There was thunderous applause, which began in her Sector of the Arts. Many women there felt they would be better off without her as their Low Queen. Their applause was genuine. Everyone else was caught up in the moment. Sephora's speech was like nothing they had ever heard before.

There was nothing wrong with Rachel's speech, which because of the Reader system, she was forced to give as she had written. Unfortunately, none of it countered the atrocious platform Sephora had just taken. Rachel was adept at finding options when everyone thought there were none. When the applause finally died down, she rose smiling. She looked confident and calm. She had to if she wished to stay in power, and to find Rebekkah and bring her home again. She changed just one word of her speech—the third word. As she said it, she made the gesture for the word she changed so that those too far away to hear could see it. That word changed the outcome of the vote from a landslide to a very close margin.

"My beloved daughters," she said, and then continued reading the speech she had written word for word. Her eyes scanned the crowd anxiously for any sign of Rebekkah's return. It would be just like Rebekkah to make a dramatic return during her speech. But Rebekkah did not come.

Rachel's first act the next morning, as the election began, was to strike from law the qualification that the High Queen must be a mother. The law, which would have met with violent opposition the day before Sephora's speech, passed quickly with five of the six Low Queens voting for it.

Word spread quickly, but not in enough time to overturn the women's bias against the motherless. Voter turnout was a record high. Two full days passed before all ballots were counted. A simple majority decided the election. Though the vote was close, it favored Sephora.

Before the Crowning Ceremony, Sephora met with her daughters briefly in her suite at the People's Palace. Her agenda was well planned. She shared a little of it with her offspring minutes before the traditional Escort of Royal Children knocked on the door to escort her to the Royal Dressing Room.

"Now that I am about to be crowned High Queen, I am able to share my plans for the Queendom with you. Everything hinged on my winning the election. With that done, my throne in the Arts Sector will be vacant. An election will be held to fill the position. I will appoint Third Sephora temporary regent, and we must work together to see that she wins the election in the Sector by any means necessary. We will start by intimidating or removing those who would run against Third Sephora."

"What about me, Mother?" asked First Sephora. "I would have thought you would appoint me Queen."

"You are the best fighter of my offspring," Sephora answered. "You will be Queen, but you must work for it. I am counting on you to beat Arrival in a contest to become Queen of the Soldier Sector."

"But I am not a soldier!"

"I am High Queen now. Just as Rachel removed the restriction for a childless woman to become Queen, I will remove the restriction that presently makes you ineligible to be Low Queen of the Soldier Sector because of your citizenship in the Arts Sector. Give me a day or two. The Low Queens will vote for whatever law I propose. I guarantee it!" Sephora laughed unpleasantly.

"Then I will only need to put Second Sephora on a throne, and I will control all Queendom policy. Once we achieve that, I will propose a vote to make me dictator for life. I plan to change the city from a democracy to a monarchy, and after I am done playing Queen, I will pass the city on to one of you to rule.

"Go to the throne room. Greet the Royals waiting there in my name and then dismiss them. I will be along shortly with Rachel, and then the fun will begin!"

"Mother," said Second Sephora, "the Royals are not going to want to see us; they want to see you. Tradition dictates you visit with them while the Royals say goodbye to the outgoing Queen. Then the outgoing Queen comes to brief you."

"The election is over, stupid," said Third Sephora to her sister. "We can do whatever we want. What the Royals want does not matter. Weren't you listening to Mother? We will never have to campaign again! She has come up with the perfect plan, and I am thrilled to be part of it!"

"Oh, you good girl!" Sephora said to Third Sephora. "You treasure of a child! Mother can always count on you to understand." She gave her youngest daughter a hug, and bestowed upon Second Sephora a look of scorn.

Sephora kept the rest of her agenda to herself. Her daughters were never privy to her most private thoughts. Those she shared with her poison mistress, Pirna, and Pirna alone. First Sephora would settle old scores. The first score would be settled minutes after the symbol of power was placed on her head. Rachel thought she would be passing on her wisdom to Sephora. Rachel would soon learn it was the other way around.

Rachel waited in awkward silence in the Royal Dressing Room with the five Low Queens. There were many closets and mirrors. Shelves lined the walls. Hundreds of crowns were displayed as well as centuries' worth of precious jewelry, and tables were covered with pots and jars of the newest and best beauty products. There was a selection of comfortable furniture in the middle of the room, but no one sat. The mood was starkly different from the joyous laughter and gossip that usually occurred when the Queens were assembled in this room to prepare for a royal event.

Arrival stood patiently at Rachel's side. It was just a matter of time now until Arrival would be alone with her mother. Stripped of her power, Rachel would not be able to avoid being alone with her. Then Arrival could reveal the grave-secret and be at peace. It was not good that Sephora had won, but Arrival was confident the Soldier Sector could handle any challenge Sephora presented.

The other four Queens—Questar of Government, Dawna of Agriculture, Caliphus of Religion, and Ariana of Livestock—were visibly nervous. No one had foreseen that Sephora would win. Everyone realized that, for better or for worse, big changes were coming.

Rachel was numb. She was discouraged that her citizens had been swayed by the preposterous fabrication Sephora told during her final campaign speech. Now Rachel would have to beg Sephora to search for Rebekkah. There was a good chance Sephora would refuse. If she had to, Rachel would look for Rebekkah by herself. At least she would have plenty of free time to find her daughter.

There was a knock at the door. Questar walked to the door and opened it. Lots had been drawn among the eligible children of the Queendom to be in the Procession, which had started at Sephora's chambers. The child in the lead of the procession was a twelve-year old Royal. She had one line to say. The rest of the ceremony took place in silence. Despite the gloom, there was comfort in the solemn tradition.

"The children of Evlantis present their Queen to be crowned with all haste so that she may take up her sacred duties and lead us."

Questar bowed. The girl returned the bow and turned to the child behind her, who was one year younger. The elder girl took the younger girl's hands and pulled her to the entrance of the door, then stepped aside. Questar then bowed to the eleven-year-old girl. The eleven-year-old girl turned to the ten-year-old who stood behind her and pulled her forward. Sephora was clearly visible, standing at the end of the line. Sephora was dressed in a white-sequined sheath that hugged her frame tightly. She looked down demurely at the head of the five-year-old child who would soon take her by the hand and pull her to the door. Sephora savored the moments until she stood in front of Questar, who bowed and stepped aside so that she could enter the room. As soon as Sephora stepped into the room, Questar closed the door.

"It is time," Questar said.

Rachel took the crown from her head. She did not wear one often, but when she did, she was partial to the simple circlet of gold embedded with chips of polished jade. She never thought she would miss such an accoutrement of power, but as she took it off her head and set it on the black cloth on the shelf of honor, which held the favorite crowns of the women who had ruled before her, she felt a stab of pain.

Woodenly, she walked to the table where the crown that Sephora had chosen the night before sat. It was undeniably one of the most valuable crowns in the collection because it was made of polished silver and encrusted with precious stones. Rachel had thought it gaudy and had never worn it.

Rachel remembered to smile as she placed the crown on the head of Sephora in the presence of the five Low Queens. No words were required, so she did not speak. The Low Queens bowed in silent homage to their new High Queen.

"There will be no small talk today," Sephora said. "You have had twenty-one years with this woman as High Queen. That was enough time to say what you needed to say to her. I am going to start my Reign of Glory immediately. My daughters have greeted the Royals in my name and have dismissed them. You may stay here if you like, or go join in the celebrations I have commissioned. Rachel comes with me."

Arrival sensed it was imperative to keep Rachel with them. She challenged Sephora.

"High Queen Sephora, tradition must be followed. I have things to say to my mother that the hectic pace of the election would not allow."

"Commander Arrival, you were an infant when the last High Queen had to step down, yet you presume to tell me about tradition? The law of the land dictates tradition must bend to the will of the High Queen. I wish to be briefed immediately, and I will be. If you have a problem with that, you are welcome to step down from power."

Arrival opened her mouth to object again, but Low Queen Questar of the Government Sector put a hand on Arrival's arm.

"High Queen Sephora is right. She has every right to be briefed immediately. We can exchange pleasantries with Queen Rachel afterward."

Arrival looked to Low Queen Ariana to help her. Ariana said nothing but shrugged her shoulders listlessly as if to ask, *What does it matter?* Arrival had noticed Ariana seemed downcast for the last few weeks, but Arrival had been too busy to find out why.

With the hair on the back of her neck rising, Arrival remained silent and watched Rachel leave with Sephora. She could not ignore the warning she felt, not even to find out what was bothering Ariana. Within moments of the door closing, Arrival strode to a different exit.

"Where are you going?" asked Ariana. "Aren't you going to wait for Rachel to return?"

"No, Ariana, I am not going to wait here. I will assign a soldier to find me when she comes back," said Arrival. "You heard Sephora. We can go about our business. I have something I must attend to immediately." Arrival hurried out the door. There were times, she knew, when intuition needed help.

Sephora's daughters applauded when she entered the throne room. Sephora headed straight to the throne and, with obvious enjoyment, she sat down with deliberate, regal precision. Rachel followed and would have sat in a chair to the right of the throne, but Sephora forbade her.

"Do not make yourself comfortable," Sephora said to Rachel. "You will not be here long."

Third Sephora giggled as if the disrespect her mother showed to Rachel was funny.

Rachel opened her mouth to object, but Sephora continued. The Three Sephoras listened in silence to the exchange between their mother and Rachel.

"There is no need for you to waste your time briefing me on the state of the Queendom," said Sephora. "I have been looking over your shoulder for the last twenty years in preparation for this day."

"Why, then, did you call me away from the Low Queens?" asked Rachel, puzzled.

"It was out of concern for you, Rachel. I did not wish to embarrass you in front of them."

"Embarrass me in what way?"

"Like it or not, we have to face the facts. You are now daughterless, and as such, your status has been reduced to that of a barren woman. You cannot own property. You must work to earn your keep. Yesterday, you were royalty. You are now reduced to mundane status."

"I object to being called daughterless!" Rachel interrupted. "I have Arrival, and for over twenty years I have been mother to the citizens of our city. Also, while Rebekkah has been presumed dead, her body has not been recovered. She may return to us."

"You can take your complaint to the courts if you wish," said Sephora, "but remember, I am now the sole judge of our people. You will lose your case. I hate to rub salt in a wound, but you had one—only one—womb-born child. Both you and I know the only thing that would have kept Rebekkah away from the city during election time is death. My spies in the Religion Sector tell me Caliphus has drawn up the death certificate with yesterday's date on it. This is something you need to deal with. The sooner you begin living your new status, the better it will be for you. To help you begin the healing process, I found a family in the Arts Sector who will be your temporary benefactor. You will provide them with whatever services they require until I find a permanent job suitable for you.

"Don't think your tie with Arrival will save you. Arrival is not your womb-born child. She will not even retain Low Queen status for much longer. I plan to replace her with First Sephora as soon as I remove the law that prevents a non-Soldier Sector combatant from challenging the Low Queen of that Sector. I am confident First Sephora will be able to beat Arrival. If by accident Arrival should die in that fight, you would not even have the weak claim of your motherhood of Arrival in your favor."

"Are you threatening me?" asked Rachel. "Are you saying if I resist you stripping me of my rights that the death of Arrival will be the consequence?"

"Really, Rachel, I hadn't thought you to be as dense as you appear," answered Sephora. "I will elucidate. Arrival will be challenged, and she will be killed in that challenge, or soon there-after. You saw her disrespect to me in the Dressing Room. I cannot tolerate such insubordination."

Rachel strode toward the exit.

"Where do you think you are going?" asked Sephora.

"I am going to get my things together. Then I will move in with one of my cousins in the Agriculture Sector. On my way, I will warn Arrival of your plans."

Rachel swung the door of the throne room open and came face to face with Pirna, Sephora's poison mistress, accompanied by a dozen of Sephora's secret policewomen.

"I anticipated you might be reticent to accept the hospitality of the Arts Sector so I invited an escort here to persuade you take advantage of my generous offer," said Sephora. "If you refuse to go with them, Pirna will very graciously give you a sedative. She has a potent dose of sage oil just for this occasion. I can understand how upsetting it must be losing the election and having your only daughter declared dead in the same week. A long rest would be of great benefit to you."

The expression on Rachel's face never changed despite her having just come up with a plan—half a plan. However, she did not know where it would lead. If Sephora planned to kill Arrival, then surely she was next. Rachel knew she was both Arrival and Rebekkah's only hope. Rachel closed the door of the throne room, leaving Pirna and the guards outside, and turned back to Sephora.

"Permit me to beg you for mercy. Will you not allow me to at least gather a few of my personal items and say good bye to Arrival?" Rachel asked.

"No," said Sephora. "You have been leeching off of the citizens for the last two decades. This is the People's Palace, and everything you own belongs, by right, to the people. As for Arrival, you will not see her alive again."

Rachel had not been sure if she would tell Sephora about the special viewing areas behind the throne room and the dressing room. Her mind was now made up that Sephora would not hear about them from her. Rachel turned away from the door and walked to the special tapestry in the throne room. The tapestry showed Mother Eve with one hand clasped to her heart and the other extended as if in greeting to the one who gazed upon her. Rachel was famous for standing before the icon and touching the outstretched hand of Eve when deep in thought. To her relief, when she touched the hand of Eve now, she felt the block behind it being pulled away and the pressure of a hand against hers from behind the cloth.

"This is your way of making sure I cannot warn Arrival," said Rachel.

Rachel was expecting a light tap on her palm, a sign that whoever was listening would warn Arrival. Instead, the symbol for Arrival was traced on her hand. Rachel met the eyes of the portrait, unable to see Arrival's eyes but knowing she was there. All Sephora and her daughters could see was Rachel's back as she stared up at the portrait. *Trust me*, she mouthed to the face on the cloth. In response, she felt a gentle tap on her palm.

"This is merely another way I can make you miserable," said Sephora. "You stood in my way for far too long. I should have been High Queen years ago."

Rachel turned around.

"I will go with your guards peacefully," she said, "if you promise to show mercy to Arrival. She has done you no harm."

"I will consider it," Sephora lied. She was delighted, for she had not thought confining Rachel in the Arts Sector would be so easy.

Sephora walked to the throne room door and opened it.

"Guards, escort Rachel to her new residence."

Sephora watched with obvious pleasure as her secret police surrounded Rachel and escorted her from the room. Sephora did not shut the door again until Rachel and the escorts made a turn in the corridor and walked out of her sight.

"Second Sephora," Sephora said as she turned to her middle daughter, "go to the Low Queens and say that Rachel has decided she is exhausted and will retire after the briefing. Then meet your sisters and me in the Record Room. There is information there I was not privy to as a Low Queen that I wish to examine immediately."

"Yes, Mama." The girl did as she was told.

Arrival replaced the wooden panels and made certain they were secure. She left the secret viewing area. She should have no difficulty getting back to the Dressing Room before Second Sephora, but she hurried all the same. As to Sephora's threat on her life, she vowed to hang on to her position and her life, at least until she had found a way to deliver Rebekkah's last message to their mother. Sephora had no idea of the power of the secret Arrival was keeping.

In the throne room, Sephora walked to the portrait of Mother Eve and stood before it deep in thought. She duplicated Rachel's moves obeying an instinct she did not understand. She felt nothing as she touched the hand of Eve but the threads of the tapestry and the hard wood of the wall behind it. She looked into Eve's eyes and saw nothing there that would ever make her quit fighting for what she wanted. She shrugged and left the throne room with First and Third Sephora trailing behind her.

The second morning after the election, a few hundred women who had not imbibed at the celebrations the previous night gathered in the Palace Hall to see their new High Queen. The hall was centuries old, rectangular in shape and large enough to seat fifteen hundred people comfortably. The ancient hall, built using the knowledge of the Golden Mean, conjoined the Palace structure. It was the preferred gathering place because the acoustics were excellent. Seats were arranged in six sections, with the Royals and upper class of each sector grouped together. The lower classes could wait on the steps outside the hall or look through windows that lined the hall at regular intervals.

Sephora kept the session brief. She named Third Sephora temporary Regent of the Arts Sector until a formal election could be held in a month. She insisted that in order to find the best fighter among them to rule the Soldier Sector, the leadership positions in that Sector must be open to every woman in the Queendom. Queen Questar of the Government Sector, Dawna of the Agriculture Sector, and Third Sephora voted in favor of Sephora's proposal. High Priestess Caliphus, Queen Ariana of the Livestock Sector, and Queen Arrival voted against it. Sephora broke the tie, and it was accomplished. She dismissed the people so the real work of the day could begin. Women were confused about the brevity of the session until they left the hall.

First Sephora waited outside in full body armor. Before Arrival descended the last step of the exit to the Great Hall, First Sephora spoke.

"I, First Sephora of Sephora of the Arts, challenge Arrival for the Low Queenship of the Soldier Sector."

"I accept your challenge," Arrival said confidently. She was ready. "I name staff as weapon. Since I have chosen the weapon, you may have the advantage of circle-center."

Arrival did not care if she won or not. Rachel had lost the election. Arrival only wished to find her mother and deliver her sister's grave-secret. She named the staff as weapon only because it was the least lethal, and she wanted to be in good health after this fight. She would not relinquish command of her Sector willingly to First Sephora, but if she lost, she knew others would challenge First Sephora. Arrival stood at the perimeter, staff in hand, with her eyes closed to focus her energy before the fight.

A crowd gathered quickly, as Sephora had known they would. She watched from the rear balcony of the Great Hall with Second and Third Sephora beside her.

Diana was pleased. The election was over, and she had the right to challenge the Low Queen for the leadership of their Sector. Diana fought for a spot around the perimeter of the circle so she could challenge the winner of this fight for leadership of the Soldier Sector the minute this fight ended.

Servus also found himself at the perimeter of the circle. He had been among a contingent of slaves working nearby on a new building in the palace petting zoo. Justus, who was the head carpenter, was among them. The soldiers guarding the slaves heard about the challenge and brought them along. Servus could not believe how lucky he was to be present at this challenge. If Arrival lost, he could begin his war without reservation. With unrest in the Soldier Sector, the men would be certain of victory. He watched as Arrival opened her eyes and entered the circle.

First Sephora smiled confidently and took her place at the center. She was the best fighter of her mother's secret police, who were known for brutality and ruthlessness when they engaged in combat. Arrival lived by the Warrior's Code. First Sephora did not.

Arrival danced lightly on her feet. She circled First Sephora, holding her staff in both hands before her. First Sephora turned as Arrival circled, keeping Arrival before her, her own staff held in the same traditional position. When Arrival was within range, First Sephora swung her staff at Arrival's feet in an illegal move that Arrival wasn't quite prepared for. Arrival stumbled, but used her own staff to keep herself upright. The crowd roared. "That is an illegal move, First Sephora," said Diana. "Step down! I will continue the challenge in your place."

"I will not step down," First Sephora answered. "I challenge the old wisdom. The leaders of today must challenge tradition to move the city forward. Check with the High Queen, who stands at the window, to see if she agrees with me."

No one doubted whom Sephora would support, but some looked up at the window to see her nod in approval.

"Let the fight continue," Arrival said. "I will beat her fairly, though she uses illegal tactics."

The soldiers in the crowd cheered. Diana watched in frustration as the challenge continued. First Sephora was fighting dirty, but Arrival remained on her feet, though she was taking quite a beating and would be black and blue later. Arrival engaged in a series of dancing steps again to find her feet. She darted back and forth toward First Sephora and defended herself as best she could against legal and illegal blows. On her forward darts, Arrival began to make successful hits upon First Sephora. It was obvious First could not take the beating Arrival was enduring and keep fighting. Diana decided Arrival would be the winner. She looked forward to challenging her when the fight was over. Arrival would be exhausted and Diana would win easily.

First Sephora let go of her staff with her right hand for a moment to make an adjustment to her chest armor. Only Servus, Justus, and Diana saw the small dagger First Sephora pulled out of its hiding place. She surreptitiously held the dagger against the staff with her right hand. It was clear to them that First Sephora intended to kill Arrival. Servus opened his mouth without thinking to warn Arrival, who was dancing toward First Sephora again. Justus covered Servus's mouth with his hand.

"Help me get him out of here," Justus ordered the slaves with him. "The guards are not paying attention and we must get out. First intends to kill Arrival. If she does, Servus will be an obvious target. You know how Sephora and her brood hate us. Servus would stay and fight, but now is not the time. Help me get him out; he will thank you later."

The slaves obeyed Justus. Servus was unable to warn Arrival. He struggled with his men, but Justus prevailed, and he and his men got Servus out of the area safely without being noticed.

Diana evaluated her options. If Arrival was killed, she could easily beat First Sephora for leadership of the Sector, but she would never know Rebekkah's secret, the one Arrival promised would bring her comfort. If Arrival lived, Diana would have to protect her, for if First Sephora failed, Sephora would send others to finish what her eldest daughter had started. Diana reluctantly became the Commander's ally.

"Arrival, beware!" Diana said loudly. "First Sephora has a dagger in her right hand."

Women gasped in horror. It was bad enough that Rachel had been taken into Sephora's custody after the Crowning Ceremony. Now it was evident Sephora sanctioned the death of Arrival. Voting for Sephora had already led to more change than they had bargained for.

"The fighting must stop!" said Caliphus, who had remained on the Hall steps with the other Low Queens to watch the challenge. She interceded on behalf of Arrival. "The blood contests were banned a century ago, and the ban must be enforced."

Arrival herself objected.

"I will not have anyone say I was unable to beat First Sephora in a fight, fair or dirty. Throw away your staff and arm yourself with two daggers. Let me prove before all who is most fit to rule the Soldiers."

First Sephora snarled.

"I take no orders from a want-to-be. The days your family ruled have ended. My reign will begin with the anointing of my brow with your blood."

She charged Arrival, and again she swept her staff behind Arrival's legs. This time, Arrival fell backwards and First Sephora fell upon her, intending to slit her throat.

The grave-secret motivated Arrival to show strength no one suspected. Arrival's staff was still in her hands, pinioned across her chest. With a battle cry, she pushed it up from her with such force that First Sephora flew backwards. Arrival was instantly on her feet. She threw away her staff and flung herself on top of First. She jockeyed for position and straddled First Sephora's chest, holding her down with the weight of her body. There was a struggle as First hacked at Arrival with the dagger, inflicting flesh wounds, while Arrival tried to catch her wrist. Once Arrival had captured First's wrist, she slammed her hand repeatedly into the ground until First Sephora let go of the dagger. Arrival pinioned each of First wrists beneath her knees and pummeled First Sephora with her fists.

"There is blood for your brow, you sneaky, cheating daughter of a bitch," said Arrival.

"My mother is High Queen, you fool," said First Sephora. "She will punish you for this. Kill me, or let me up. I will fight you another day."

"You will not fight me again," said Arrival. "I have proven my superiority. I will not stoop so low as to repeat the mistake of accepting you as a worthy challenger. I will not kill you, though you would have killed me, because I will not have the blood of a coward on my hands. Get up and run to your mother."

Arrival stood up, grabbed First by an arm, and pulled her to her feet. Arrival escorted her to the edge of the circle where she ceremoniously insulted First Sephora by kicking her out of the circle by planting her foot upon her butt. Women tried not to laugh, for the High Queen was watching, but snickers broke the silence.

"Escort this loser to her mother," Arrival commanded the soldiers standing at attention nearby. "I command my soldiers to keep First Sephora thirty paces out of my reach for her own protection. Now, I will take any and all challengers for the throne of my Sector in fair fights, as I promised my Sector before the election. Does anyone wish to challenge me?"

Arrival looked at Diana.

Diana walked to Arrival in silence. She knelt before her.

"You are my rightful Queen. I will serve you as I served your sister. Your enemies are my enemies from this day forward."

"Rise, Diana, Second in Command of the Soldier Sector. I thank you for your fealty. Do I have any other challengers?"

No one stepped forward. Arrival's show of strength, courage, and skill had amazed them all.

"Fine. I will be in my Sector tending to my duties."

Arrival, bloody and bruised, walked slowly out of the circle, her head held high, every inch a queen. She had won this round. The people cheered her.

Arrival knew there would be more challengers. Diana was beside her, but Arrival did not trust her. Though the people clearly loved Arrival, she felt isolated. Her mind's eye recalled the face of a slave. Moments before Diana had warned her about the dagger, she had caught sight of his ashen face at ringside. He had looked worried, as if he had been concerned for her safety. Arrival looked for him, but he was not here now. She must have imagined it. Damn Rebekkah and her life-altering secret.

Back at the construction site, Servus paced frantically and cursed Justus under his breath. It seemed like forever to him until the soldiers returned. The soldiers, relieved to find the slaves they were supervising back at the work site, decided not to punish them. They chattered about the fight and Arrival's victory. The relief Servus felt when it was clear Arrival had survived and his men would not be punished was short-lived. Servus realized that Arrival would be the Commander of the Army his men would face in their war for freedom.

At the dinner hour of the third day after Sephora's crowning, Servus knelt on the floor in Sephora's private dining area dressed in nothing but a loincloth. Sephora and her daughters ate leisurely. Servus was hungry. He had been preparing for his meal when armed soldiers appeared to escort him to the High Queen.

Sephora did not acknowledge his presence until after she finished her dinner. Then she pushed her plate away from her and stretched. Her daughters immediately pushed their plates away, too.

"Boy," Sephora said to slave who served them, "clear the table and leave us."

Only when the slave had finished his task and shut the door behind him did Sephora speak to Servus.

"Rise, Servus, self-proclaimed King of Slaves."

Servus rose unsteadily, with his hands still bound, from the kneeling position he had maintained for the duration of the meal. He kept his eyes straight ahead and his expression neutral. She circled him, eyeing him as the herders eyed the animals. She poked and prodded him as slave buyers did in the marketplace. She was looking to start the interview off by belittling him, and he knew it. He kept his thoughts calm and his wits about him.

"Servus...King Servus." Sephora laughed. "What an honor the King of Slaves could take time out of his busy schedule to visit with the High Queen of all Womankind! I have audiences with the Chancellor of the Goats and the Prince of the Pigs next!"

Servus held his tongue. Sephora continued.

"I have heard a lot about you," said Sephora as she continued her examination of him. "It is said you rule the animals called men well. It is said that if you say jump, the men ask how high. Tell me, King, do you enjoy living?"

Servus again was silent. If she meant to kill him, he meant to die with his dignity intact.

"I, Queen of all Womankind, give you, animal Servus, permission to speak. Indeed, I demand it, unless you wish to lose your tongue."

A blade flashed in her hand. He felt a flicker of fear, but he answered calmly.

"I enjoy living, High Queen, but I will not beg you for my life. If you intend to kill me, do it."

The High Queen stopped circling him and stood face to face with him. She pressed the blade of the dagger against his chest. Servus looked her straight in the eye and leaned against the blade so it pricked his skin. A bead of blood pearled at its tip.

Sephora's laugh rang out as she stepped away from him and walked to a table across the room.

"Animal, today is not your day to be slaughtered. I will not martyr the King of Beasts my first week in office. Though I promise you, your death will come at my hand. My plan is to make you the most hated man in all of herstory. Your own men will draw lots to decide who will kill you when you sleep. Your death will be applauded. One of my pets will be proclaimed King of Slaves in your place, and everything you have worked for will have been in vain."

Servus willed himself to show no emotion.

"Servus," said Sephora, "do not try so hard to suppress your feelings. It must be taxing for a beast to compose its features into anything but the basest emotions. Let's speak of something more pleasant. Join me at this table." It was an order.

Servus shuffled slowly across the room to join her. Sephora's daughters remained at the dinner table behind them. Servus heard one of the girls laugh nervously.

Sephora spoke as he reached her.

"Do you know what lies in front of me, Servus?"

Servus saw many papers laid out on the table before him. They were filled with diagrams and markings. Since it was illegal for men to read, the marks meant nothing to him. Servus shook his head.

"You are so stupid," said Sephora. "You are looking at one of the most coveted things men desire. This is the genealogy of the slaves."

Servus gasped. There were long nights of debate in the slave barracks about whether the women, who kept meticulous records of women's genealogies, had bothered recording anything of the men's.

Sephora could see she had struck home.

"My foremothers considered the parentage of slaves to be at the least insignificant, at most, a danger. They reasoned that if slaves knew of their relationship to one another, or worse, to their mothers and daughters, they would be harder to control because they would fancy themselves capable of loyalty—to be responsible to and for one another. I think my foremothers were foolish. What better hold can one have over a slave than to control what he desires most? This is your name here." Sephora stuck the blade she had been holding into a spot in the middle of one of the papers.

Though he could not read, Servus saw that the symbols pierced by the blade matched the marks seared into the flesh of his forearm. His heart began to beat faster. From the mark that was his identification number there was a branch leading up, with two marks near it and three branches below it, with marks on each. It had been a long time since he had been allowed to do quickening duty, but he had had his day. The marks below his name must mean he had three offspring! Whether sons or daughters, dead or alive, he could not tell. Two separate marks above his must indicate his parents were recorded too. As he studied the marks on the paper, trying to commit them to memory, Sephora attacked. She knocked his knees out from under him. Servus fell backwards onto his bound hands. His eyes watered and he desperately tried to draw the breath that had been knocked out of him back into his lungs. As Servus stared at the ceiling, Sephora put a foot in his groin. The pain was intense.

"Second Sephora, bring me my chair," she commanded. "First, Second, and Third Sephora will witness as the High Queen spells out for this King of Beasts his new duties." She removed her foot and reclined in the chair Second Sephora had brought for her.

"You may stay where you are instead of kneeling while I speak."

Servus lay painfully on his bound hands and listened in growing horror to her plan. He carefully kept his features free from reaction.

"I am going to double the quotas required of the slaves. I will reduce the sleeping time to one-half of what it is now to give the men more time to meet their quotas. I have opened the granaries to the poorest of women, so I must cut slave rations in half. The life of a slave is now worth less than nothing. If I catch one slave complaining or shirking his duties, then he, along with you, will be called before my oldest daughter and given the names of two of his relatives. It will be at her discretion which two will be revealed—father, uncles, brother, sons. Then, Servus, you will choose which of the three will be punished. The punishment will be random, and again, it will be at the discretion of First Sephora. It will be as mild as a beating or as severe as death. Should you refuse to choose, all three will be punished." Sephora laughed.

"In time, the men will come to hate you. I intend to strip you of every vestige of power you have. You leave here with your life today, Servus, but your days are numbered, and your legacy will be one of hatred and failure."

Servus said nothing, which seemed to anger her more, for then she kicked him.

"Did you not hear what I said?" asked Sephora. "I intend to ruin you, Servus."

Servus lay still, but his mind worked furiously to understand what seemed to be her inexplicable rage. He could not think of anything he had done that would anger her this much. He had barely had any contact with her at all over the years, though he often worked on the Palace grounds.

"Perhaps the King of Slaves would like to beg me now for an easy death? Speak, Servus," Sephora said.

"Your will is my command." He responded with the formal reply to an order given by a slave master. She bent over him with the knife, but this time he felt no fear. He was sure she wished to carry out her original plan. Sephora stood abruptly.

"Get on your feet, king of beasts!" she commanded.

Servus was too proud to ask for assistance. He rolled onto his belly and used sheer lower body strength to rise to his feet. Sephora was not satisfied. He had shown no emotion and she wanted to see him suffer.

"Look at me!"

Servus, who had been looking at the floor as slaves were required to do, looked directly into her face. He finally realized what she wanted from him. She was looking for a reaction. If he gave her one, perhaps she would let him go. He desperately wanted this interview to be over.

"First Sephora," she called to her eldest, "go to the animal husbandry records and read out loud the name of the mother of Servus."

They all heard First's exclamation of surprise the second before she spoke.

"Sepheera of the Arts Sector is the mother of Servus."

Even if Servus had been trying to control his features, he would have been hard pressed to do so. Sephora finally got the reaction she had been baiting him for. He looked stunned for a moment and then horrified.

Sepheera was Sephora's mother. He was standing before his sister and nieces. Servus realized Sephora's interest in seeing him debased and broken had little to do with his position of power among the slaves. Women distanced themselves in all possible ways from the men. He knew they thought of themselves as far superior, even a different species. Ancient names such as father, son, brother, and uncle were obsolete in their culture. Only in the men's religion were such words said in secret. Servus felt a rare wave of discouragement. His days among the breathing were indeed limited, and Sephora would make the last days of his life hell. Her victimization of him was personal. They shared a mother, and knowledge of it was a death sentence.

The sound of a gong rang out. Servus had been so lost in thought he had not seen the signal Sephora had given to her middle child to ring it. Soldiers entered to escort him back to the slave barracks. On his way out of the Palace, Servus overheard groups of women talking about the hot topic of the day, which was who, if anyone, would dare run against Third Sephora for the throne of the Arts Sector. Servus smiled grimly to himself as he thought, for the first time in his life, that it was better to be a slave than to be the woman who challenged Third Sephora in her run for the Arts Sector throne.

Hannah of the Arts, daughter of Nebo of the Arts, chatted gaily with the girls in her sewing circle. Hannah was in her late teens. She had flaxen hair and wide blue eyes. Her skin was fair. She had always been heralded as one of the most attractive young women in the Arts Sector. Hannah was the first daughter of one of the most royal families in Sephora's sector of the city. Hannah had lived a pampered life for sixteen years until she was declared barren. Her mother, who had not cared for childbearing, had never used her rank to apply to have a second child until Hannah greatly disappointed her by not conceiving. If there was no female heir, their status would be reduced and their family line would die with Hannah. Nebo loved the benefits of royalty. There was still time for her to conceive. She reluctantly made the proper applications, which were approved.

Nebo soon found herself pregnant, but she resented having to bear a second child. Hannah's pampered life eroded after the birth of her younger sister, Tilda. Hannah loved Tilda, but all the attention that had been Hannah's was now transferred to her sister, as the family hopes centered on her. It wasn't overnight, but in time, Hannah found herself to be little more than a servant in the household, barely tolerated by her mother, until the day Nebo found Hannah a respectable job as a costume decorator in the Theater of the Arts. It was a job that required many tedious hours of sewing tiny beads and sequins onto elaborate stage costumes for plays. Most importantly, it got Hannah out of their palatial home.

What no one counted on, least of all Hannah, was that she would love her job. What most found monotonous and painstakingly boring, she found rewarding. She loved turning plain cloth into shimmering rainbows for the actresses to wear. She loved the hectic pace of the theater, the people, and the dramas that went on daily—on stage and off. Hannah resumed goddess worship. She had stopped going to the temples in the Religion Sector when her impassioned cries to become fertile and bear a child went unanswered. Now she went regularly to give thanks to the goddesses for her fulfilling and exciting life.

Hannah had a sunny disposition. She would try any task put to her, and she found many ways to be useful at the theater. She was a popular person, both in the Arts and the Religion Sector where she divided her time. She spent as little time as possible at the palace of her mother, which was why the news that was brought by an out-of-breath co-worker was a shock to her.

"Long live Queen Hannah of the Arts!" said the newcomer, who giggled and bowed to Hannah.

"Get up, you goose!" said Hannah. "Third Sephora is running unopposed in the election. Only a fool would challenge her, and I am not that fool."

"Oh, but you are! Your mother has hired seers to determine your chances of winning. The word is that the citizens of our Sector prefer you two-to-one to Third Sephora. Everyone knows Third is a spoiled brat and would be a puppet queen, while you are well known and well loved in two Sectors. I'm voting for you, Hannah." The girl turned to the others who had gathered around and asked, "How about the rest of you?"

The chatter around Hannah increased. Everyone had something to say except Hannah. She sat in shock. Why had Nebo done it? Did her mother hate her that much?

The girl nearest Hannah noticed her look of dismay and made the others hush.

"Hannah, what is the matter? You don't look happy. You would make a wonderful Queen. What is wrong?"

"Sephora will never allow anyone who could beat her daughter to enter the race," Hannah said. "My mother has as good as signed my death warrant. Look at what Low Queen Arrival has endured in the past twenty-four hours. It is only a matter of time until she joins Rebekkah in the land of the dead."

The laughter stopped immediately. Since her fight with First Sephora, Arrival had fought two more challenges from Sephora's minions. Arrival had won both challenges, but no one believed she would last much longer. There were high wagers among the gaming community on which day Arrival would fall.

"Just refuse to run," said the youngest among them.

Someone else answered for Hannah.

"She can't. If Nebo gets enough support, Hannah's name will be put on the ballot whether she wants it there or not."

Hannah shivered.

"My name will not be on the ballot. Sephora will see to it. How she will manage it, I do not know. Do not endanger your own lives by speaking of me being Low Queen. It will not be. I was happy here at the theater. It is all I ever wanted for the rest of my life. You have been wonderful friends. I love you all."

"You speak as if you are leaving us, Hannah! Stop it—you are scaring me!" the youngest spoke again.

Hannah turned merry for the sake of the others.

"I am sorry. I will stop my dire predictions at once. I am here with you now. Let's get back to our work. Please, someone tell me the latest scandal."

The girls grew merry again. Hannah kept her promise and kept her fears to herself. She had no hope that she could outfight an attacker as Low Queen Arrival had been doing. Hannah hoped her death would be quick and painless.

DISCOVERY

Two months had passed since the election. Servus trudged behind Partouche, who was leading the work detail he was part of, to the People's Palace dungeon for cleanup detail. It was his least favorite work, removing the dead and carrying them to the outer limits of the city where their remains were cremated. During Rachel's rule, there were few dead, and the work mostly involved cleaning out cells. Sephora had seen no need to keep jail cells clean, and the conditions in the dungeon were deplorable. The bodies they transported for cremation bore evidence of appalling torture.

Servus reflected on all the changes that had taken place under High Queen Sephora. Life was much harder for the slaves. Punishments were dealt randomly. Death was commonplace. Even the boys were tortured on a whim. The men were afraid. Even he himself ate each meal wondering if it were his last. Men fell ill and sometimes died after eating. It was rumored Sephora was having poisons tested on the slaves. They could think of no explanation why they were served from a common dish, but only one or two men died.

Paradoxically, since the day of his audience with Sephora, Servus's power among the men had increased, for he had given them the news that their genealogies existed. Servus made it clear that those who broke Sephora's rules did so at their own risk. Some men committed infractions on purpose just to learn the precious names of those they were related to. For the first time in their lives, they had the means to learn of their kinship with one another. The secret army of Servus grew as men volunteered to join the rebellion.

Servus told no one, not even Justus, that he and Sephora were brother and sister. He knew it was only a matter of time before she killed him, and he was certain she would kill anyone who discovered that she was related to a slave. He thought the death Sephora had promised him waited in every dark corner and in every plate of food. He would die knowing rebellion would come. His hope did not entirely fade away. There was always the unexpected. He remained ready for it.

Arrival spent as much time as possible in the reflection room. It was called such for two reasons. First, the reflection room was a peaceful place where the soldiers could meditate and center themselves. The Army of Women required its soldiers to be strong emotionally as well as physically. Maintaining peace in the city meant using brawn and brain to subdue the men, and psychological tactics to keep peace among the women.

The second reason for the name was literal. Many highly polished pieces of metal adorned the walls, and the room was filled with greenery, fountains, and huge rocks to sit upon to invoke an atmosphere of mediation. The polished pieces of metal reflected light and revealed movement. It was impossible to be ambushed in the reflection room.

In the weeks since the election, Arrival had clung to her Low Throne steadfastly. She had bested all Sephora's challengers, showing them mercy, though they would have shown her none. Now,

Arrival knew Sephora had no recourse but to replace her by murdering her. Arrival stayed on guard all the time. She surrounded herself with soldiers she trusted, and when not in the reflection room, she stayed on the move.

Arrival felt she had a duty to live, for she had not been able to deliver Rebekkah's last message to Rachel. She had not had a chance to find the body of her sister. The duties of her new Command position had taken up all her time. Arrival felt the heavy weight of guilt. Had she shared the news sooner, perhaps her foster mother might not have descended into madness.

Arrival had still not found a way to see her alone, but it was common knowledge that Rachel had experienced a break with reality. After the election, Rachel had made daily pilgrimages to stand on the wall of the city, where she paced and shouted to her dead daughter as if they were conversing. Six weeks ago, her mother had petitioned High Queen Sephora to allow her to search the woods for her daughter. Sephora had convinced the Low Queens and the Royals it was the compassionate thing to do. Arrival's vote was the one dissenting vote cast. Now Rachel was out of Arrival's reach both physically and mentally.

Arrival wished she had at least one ally. There were some discontented soldiers under Sephora's rule, but Arrival was not convinced there were enough to win a civil war. The other Low Queens had their hands full with their own problems. Sephora stirred up as much strife as possible and had raised taxes in all except her former sector.

On top of all of this, there were the slaves to worry about. Servus was a strong leader, and it was not a secret that he hated slavery. Rebekkah had made surveillance of Servus a priority. Arrival had followed her Commander's example in this regard. Not long after Sephora became High Queen, Arrival read in the reports that Sephora had held a private audience with Servus.

Arrival burned to know what had happened at that meeting. She knew she could not bring down Sephora alone, but with help, she could do it. Never before had soldiers joined forces with the slaves, but then, never before had there been a need.

Arrival noticed the light had begun to wane. She sighed heavily. It was almost time for the riskiest part of her day. Each day at sundown, when Rachel returned to the city limits, Arrival chose to be there. It was the time she was most vulnerable to her enemies. Sephora had replaced Arrival's guards at that gate with her own lackeys. Though she was essentially in enemy territory, it was the only time of day she could catch a glimpse of her mother. So far, no opportunity presented itself for her to have contact with Rachel before Sephora's guards took her into custody for the night, but Arrival would not give up trying. Intuition, and the guilt that weighed her down, told Arrival it was worth the risk she took. She must divest herself of her sister's secret, and sooner was better than later.

Hannah trudged through the forest behind the mad former High Queen from first light to last every day, a routine she had followed for six weeks. Sephora had indeed found a way to keep her from running against Third Sephora in the special election for Low Queen of the Arts Sector. Hannah had been assigned to accompany Rachel on her search of the forest, which made her ineligible to run. Third Sephora had run unopposed and had been crowned Low Queen of the Arts Sector. Hannah was grateful to be alive, but the forest was dark and dangerous, full of biting insects, strange sounds, and wild animals. She still lived every day in fear.

Though she had reason to hate Rachel, Hannah felt nothing but sympathy for the mad former High Queen. Rachel was now like Hannah—a daughterless woman; a nobody in their society. She had lost her womb-born daughter, her throne, her home, and everything that was dear to her.

Hannah rarely talked to Rachel, or Rachel to Hannah. It made it easier on Hannah, because when they returned to the city she was quizzed at great length about where Rachel went, what she did, and what she said. Hannah suspected Rachel knew and was silent to protect her.

Hannah wasn't entirely certain that Rachel was mad. Everyone said she was crazy with grief. Rachel had good reason to grieve, and grief was stamped on her every look and gesture, yet her search was thorough, and as soon as she was a safe distance from the city, her endless, mumbled, nonsensical conversations with her dead daughter ceased.

Rachel had dictated where and how they would search. She and Hannah had begun at the ceremonial grounds. Each day after that, Rachel methodically searched every inch of a new section of the forest surrounding the city. Hannah carried a paint pot, and as they made their way into the forest, she marked the trees carefully using a different color and symbol each day at Rachel's request.

It was unseasonably hot on this day of trudging through the nightmarish forest, and Rachel's pace had been faster than usual. Hannah had a stitch in her side that caused her pain when she breathed.

"Former High Queen Rachel," she said. "Please, could we stop for a moment? My side hurts."

Rachel could count on one hand the number of times Hannah had complained in the last six weeks. Rachel knew Hannah was with her for three reasons: one, to report to Sephora everything Rachel said and did; two, in the city Hannah had been a threat to Sephora's plans; and three, because she was expendable. Rachel knew that when Sephora was done playing cat and mouse with her, she would send henchwomen to kill both of them and blame their deaths on an accident or a wild animal. Rachel wondered if Hannah knew. She would do her best to protect Hannah when the time came. Though the girl had reason to resent Rachel, she had chosen to serve her with efficient wordless kindnesses.

Rachel had been lost in thought and hadn't realized how fast she had been walking. She had been thinking about how she had let herself go. She had ruled in the city of Evlantis for almost thirty years. She had always believed her purpose as High Queen was to serve the people. The people's needs were never ending. For the first decade of her rule, she had worked hard at maintaining her appearance. The women of the city ran the gamut as far as personal maintenance was concerned. The soldiers believed physical fitness was the measure of beauty. The women of the Arts sector believed the beauty of face and form was what mattered. The women of the Religion and Agriculture Sectors believed true beauty was the development of goodness within the soul, and mere appearance meant nothing. The women of the Government and Livestock Sectors believed self-fulfillment, personal achievement, and happiness were marks of beauty. For the first ten years of her rule, Rachel tried to be all things to all women, and she spent a great deal of time on her appearance and fitness.

In the last ten years, she had been so busy with the needs of the people of her Queendom that she neglected her own needs. She hated turning down the hospitality of women she visited in times of trouble or joy, and she ate and drank everything she was offered. She seldom got enough sleep. She used to exercise an hour a day, but duty nibbled away at her fitness regimen until it was nonexistent. In the end, her Agriculture Sector upbringing won out. She tried only to be a good mother and a good ruler and let the practices of the other Sectors fall by the wayside.

She had been happy. She had loved ruling. She never regretted growing older, stouter, and a little frumpy. When she first feigned madness, she purposefully neglected even basic hygiene routines, and now when she looked at herself in a mirror, she was shocked. The unkempt hair, the care-worn face, and the haunted eyes that stared back at her showed she was a shadow of the woman she had been. The only good thing was the past few months of walking through the forest had returned her to physical fitness, though the baggy clothes she wore hid the transformation.

As an answer to Hannah, Rachel mumbled, "I can't stop searching. Rebekkah needs me. I must find Rebekkah. I hear her calling me." But Rachel, grateful for the care Hannah took of her, and mindful of what the girl would lose because of her, slowed her pace.

For the rest of her life, Rachel would wonder what would have happened if Hannah hadn't asked her to stop. It was then the miracle happened. She glanced around out of habit and glimpsed flesh, just barely visible, beneath a leafy fern to her right. Rachel knew if she had kept up her frenzied pace, lost in her thoughts, she would have missed it.

There was a body hidden beneath the lush canopy of low ferns and a fallen tree trunk. Rachel stopped short. Hannah, thinking Rachel had decided to honor her plea to stop after all, began to take deep breaths to control the pain in her side. Rachel stood very still, staring and thinking.

Rachel was done with denial. She knew she would not find Rebekkah alive. Rachel's plea to go searching for her was just a way to get out of the city, to think, to grieve in private, and to buy time. Rachel had not poured out her life ruling this great city of women wisely to see Sephora, with her crafty wiles and cruelty, undo everything good she and others before her had built up. Rachel had feigned madness, and Sephora had gone along for reasons of her own.

Rachel ran options through her mind. She was certain Hannah had not seen the body. They were on their way back, most likely three leisurely hours of walking from the city and from sunset, which was the curfew Sephora had imposed upon her.

Rachel came up with a daring plan. Finding her daughter's body would bring her peace, and it might help her save the Queendom from Sephora. She needed to first draw Hannah's attention to Rebekkah's body and then send her back to the city so that Rachel could claim she had found her daughter alive.

Rachel could pretend Rebekkah confessed with her dying breath that she had been attacked by Sephora's henchwoman and left to die. Rachel could then bring a charge of murder against Sephora. She thought she could get a majority of the six Low Queens to back her. Whether she regained her crown or not was secondary to removing Sephora from power. Indeed, perhaps she was better off retiring and mourning in private.

Hannah felt much better. She surveyed the forest for the easiest path back along the trees she had marked. Rachel startled her when she whooped in joy and yelled.

"Rebekkah! I hear you! I have come to help you!"

Hannah had heard nothing out of the ordinary and felt chills run up and down her spine. Hannah turned slowly and watched as Rachel ran several yards away and knelt at a section of ferns and brush near a fallen tree.

"Hannah, come help me with Rebekkah!" Rachel said.

Hannah cautiously made her way toward Rachel wondering if the stories of madness were true after all, until she saw that Rachel had uncovered a bare human foot. Hannah stopped. She felt bile rise in her throat. She wanted to help, but found moving toward Rachel was like walking through quicksand. The last place she wanted to go was near the dead body of Low Queen Rebekkah. Then, Hannah realized the endless days of searching the woods had ended. Rebekkah's body had been found. Hannah could return to the theater. Rachel could have peace. Hannah found the strength she needed to inch toward Rachel and the body of her dead daughter.

Ava was roused from her unconscious state by a gentle tickle on her foot. At first, she did not know where she was. She must be home and had overslept for breakfast. She was hungry—hungrier than she had ever been before.

"Mother?" Ava asked, before the memory of her exile rushed back to her.

Both Rachel and Hannah heard the weak cry. Hannah stopped in her tracks. It was not possible for Rebekkah to have been found alive. Women and slaves frequently disappeared and were found dead in this forest. Their culture was rich with stories of the damage ghosts and evil spirits wrought. The goddesses were known to play cruel tricks upon mortals. What Rachel had found could not be huwoman. Hannah was terrified again.

Rachel had been wondering how she would get Hannah to return to the city without her. Now she had to. Her voice reverberated with urgency and authority that belied her disheveled appearance.

"Hannah, Rebekkah lives! Leave the paint pot and supplies and run quickly back to Evlantis. Bring a doctor and some slaves to carry her back to the city. Run as if your legs were the wind itself!"

Hannah needed no second prompt. She did not wish to be alone with Rachel and whatever she had found; not for one second. She ran with speed fueled by fear.

Left alone, Rachel worked frantically to clear the brush. Her mind raced. She could not tell if Rebekkah had chosen this place to hide or if someone else had hidden her here. Rachel's mind tumbled over scenarios of how Rebekkah could have survived these last four months in the wild, of why she had not returned to the city, and why she would have abandoned her Ring of Power. Nothing made sense to her. She hoped Hannah would bring help quickly.

The last four months had been hell for Rachel. Her plan to feign madness to cling to life and buy time had required her to act as if she believed Rebekkah was alive. So she had not allowed herself to mourn, not even in private.

As Rachel cleared the brush, she methodically checked the body for broken bones and other wounds. It was on Rebekkah's arms, which were crossed over her chest, where Rachel found the faint beast-claw scars, and at her heart she found the knife wound scar. Rebekkah's hands were tucked beneath her chin, and upon examining them, Rachel was shocked to see a raw scar circling the ring finger that the Ring of Power usually encircled. Rebekkah moaned in pain when Rachel examined it. It looked as if the finger had been cut from her. This would explain how the ring had been taken from her daughter, but there was no earthly explanation of how the finger had grown back on.

Rachel had the feeling something was wrong. She knew subconsciously that this was not her daughter's body, even though it was similar. It carried none of the familiar scars her daughter's body bore. It was thinner and less muscular. Yet her mind could not take in that it could be anyone other than Rebekkah. No one had been reported missing from the city, and womankind was alone in the world. Rebekkah's face was hidden. Rachel could not yet confirm the woman's identity.

Rachel used her fingertips to carefully feel the spine at the base of the girl's skull for more injuries. When Rachel was sure it was safe to move her, she supported the thin, lithe body at the waist and neck and slowly freed the head from a hollowed-out space in the log. Matted hair covered the face. The hair was thick, lush, long, and brown with a hint of red, exactly the color of her daughter's hair. Rachel took a deep breath, and with trembling hands that had never shaken in all the emotional duties she had had to perform in the past, she gently and lovingly moved the hair from Rebekkah's face.

Rachel stared in shock, and then she wept. Deep shuddering torrents shook her and tears ran freely, bathing the face of the stranger.

Ava was powerless to run, as she wanted to, from the woman who had found her, so she pretended to be asleep. Her initial contact with her stepsiblings had left her scarred, both physically and mentally. She now understood the seriousness of Archangel Michael's warning. She longed for home, for Paradise, and she was certain that living just outside its walls would be sweeter than living inside the walls of Evlantis with Rebekkah's people. Ava struggled with the decision of if, when, and how she would keep the promise she had made to the woman whose remains decomposed under the monument of rocks she had built up and embellished to help fill her time while she grew stronger.

Ava remembered the ravine that had been deep and narrow. The trees grew densely at the upper edges of the ravine. She had food and water but no direct sunlight. The light had teased her by dancing on the center of the stream a few hours a day, a place she could not reach. She knew her healing was not complete, but a day came when her boredom was so great and she missed the warmth and feel of the sun so much, she decided to climb up out of the ravine.

It was a difficult climb, but she persevered. Once she made it out, she basked in the warm sun on a rock and decided not to return. She could not know it had been a mistake to leave the stream. Her body needed water to complete the healing process. Without it, she grew weak again.

She had wandered in the forest becoming thirstier as each day passed. She could not find water. It was hard to think, and she was often confused. She spent long hours sleeping. Sometimes she became so cold she shook; other times, she was so hot she sweat. There came a day when she realized she was not alone in the forest. Not being sure of her welcome, she hid from the disheveled woman with the strangely lined face and the beautiful girl, keeping them in her sight as they went back to the city each day. There had come a day when she was so weak she could no longer follow them. She had chosen a hiding place where she hoped she would be safe to sleep and heal, but now she had been found.

Ava was still having difficulty thinking. The chills she had been experiencing for some time set in again. She let her thoughts drift to the present. She heard the woman crying over her and felt the drops of tears rain on her face. In the cries of the woman, she heard the pain she had caused her own grieving mother.

"Mother, I am sorry, forgive me," she said. Ava wept silently. Her body refused to give up water for tears.

Rachel heard the words the stranger said. Her heart was touched. Rachel held the stranger and they mourned together for a time, though each did not yet understand the other's grief. Once their tears had passed, Rachel tended to the stranger at her side, for she was compassionate, and the girl was dying. She had a fever. Her deadly wounds were infected.

Rachel rummaged through the pack Hannah had left behind to find the medical kit she always brought to the forest in case one of them was ever injured. There was also water for drinking, a small pouch of wine, and food for a snack as they returned to the city. There was outer clothing in case it became cold on their walk back at the end of the day.

Rachel used the medical kit to tend to the stranger as she slept. She worked silently, her agile mind spinning with questions and possibilities as she worked. She did not rise to her position of eminence in the city simply because of birth or favor, though she had both. Until this last contest with Sephora, she had beat her opponents again and again by out-foxing them. She hated to use this dying stranger, but Rachel was committed to undoing the damage Sephora had done.

The appearance of a stranger was shocking. From time immemorial, their civilization had been the only known one. Criminal and misfit women were sometimes banished. Scholars posited some may have survived, but since women could not reproduce without men, it was accepted as fact that the Evlantians were alone in the world.

There were the occasional deviants, sick perverts who thought slaves were equal to women, and from time to time, they ran with them, away from the safety and advantages of the city. Rachel wondered if enough had run away over the centuries for there to be a thriving settlement elsewhere. Here was a woman she did not know, who appeared to be in her early twenties. She was not any of the women Rachel had banished in her term. She had to be the child of someone sent away over twenty years ago. As soon as the stranger's wounds were bandaged and she was dressed in the warm outer clothing, Rachel gently dripped wine in the sleeping stranger's mouth to give her nourishment.

Rachel expected Hannah back just after sundown. Those coming to assist them would surely be riding horses, and they would have a litter to carry the girl—whom Hannah would surely report was Rebekkah—back to the city. Rachel laughed to herself at the thought of Sephora's surprise when Hannah returned claiming Rebekkah was alive.

Perhaps some good might come of this stranger's impending death. Rachel wondered if in some way this stranger's appearance could be linked to Rebekkah's disappearance. Rebekkah had disappeared over three months ago. No woman could have survived that long with the wounds this stranger had. Pushing her questions aside, she turned to look at the stranger and found brown eyes—the color of her own daughter's—open, sentient, and fixed upon her.

Rachel did not believe in honey-coating bad news. She held the stranger's penetrating gaze.

"Your wounds are fatal," she said, "but I will help you as best I can."

The stranger just blinked, but Rachel thought she saw amusement in those eyes.

"Can you speak?" asked Rachel. "Can you tell me what happened to you?"

The stranger shook her head, almost imperceptibly. Rachel realized she should have asked the questions separately, for now she did not know whether the stranger could not speak or whether she could not tell her what had happened.

Rachel paused to consider a different strategy, but decided it would be impossible to rally the women of the city to fight a threat of outsiders, a threat they surely would not believe based on the appearance of one stranger. No, her first idea was the best. She would use the women's natural superstition and belief in mystical experience to get her leadership back. It was how she had lost her crown, and it was fitting that she should win it back by using Sephora's methods against her. She would never get her daughter back, but she could rescue her beloved city from Sephora's destructive rule. If the outsiders' plan was to get their spy inside her city, their plan would work, but sadly, this woman would die there.

Rachel glanced up at the sky to estimate the time. Hannah should have arrived at the city gate by now. It would not be long before someone would come to either kill them or take them to Sephora. She thought it would be the latter, for Hannah could not enter the city unseen, and Sephora would be curious. Rachel turned back to the stranger.

"I am Rachel, the former High Queen of Evlantis. I have been pretending to be mad these last few months in order to buy time to outwit my enemy, the present High Queen Sephora. The girl who was with me, Hannah, has gone back to the city for help. Sephora will send someone who will either take us back to the city or kill us. I will do my best to protect both of us if the latter happens. Tell me, are there others with you?"

This time Rachel knew to phrase her questions separately. The stranger shook her head.

"Can you tell me your name?" Another wordless negative followed.

"I have a lot to say to you before they come for us. I think you must be the child of someone banished from the city before my rule, for I have ruled the city of Evlantis since before you were born. I spent my life protecting and nurturing my city. My people have held all knowledge, sacred and mundane, since the beginning of time. Our way is the only way. If you and your kin wish to challenge our way of life, then you are my enemy."

The stranger spoke for the first time.

"Not enemies," Ava said weakly, but clearly.

This revelation spawned many more questions than it answered, but answers had to wait. She could not use this stranger without her full knowledge and consent. Rachel smiled and spoke again.

"I am glad of that. Fate has brought you to me. Through you, I have a chance to save my city from the greatest threat it has ever faced: the rule of Sephora. I am an honorable woman. I will not use you without your permission. I will explain the events that have led up to this moment to tell you my plan, and if you are agreeable, I will enter a Pact of Honor with you. In our way of life, this is the most binding of all contracts. Listen well so that you may judge me, and if you find my cause worthy, be of some help to my people before you leave this world."

The stranger nodded her head, so Rachel began.

"My mother was Reged, a Royal of the Agriculture Sector. I was her only daughter, born late in the year 1467. I was gifted with a quick mind, a forgiving spirit, and an iron hand. To my mother's chagrin, I ruled our household from the time I was old enough to talk. Leadership came naturally to me, and at the age of thirteen, I became the youngest elected Low Queen of the Agriculture Sector.

"Motherhood did not come naturally to me, however. I was unlucky when it came to quickening and bearing children. I was unable to run for the office of High Queen in 1486 because I had not met the eligibility requirement of being a mother. I forced myself to go to my quickening appointments, but most months I was unfruitful. On two occasions I became pregnant, but while the babies were female, thank goddess, both were stillborn. On the very last occasion that I was eligible to visit the Quickening Chamber, in the spring of 1491, I became pregnant once more. I suffered terribly. The final three months I was ordered to stay in bed, but at the end of the year, I delivered a perfectly healthy and absolutely beautiful baby girl. I named her Rebekkah. A year and a half after her birth, I ran for the office of High Queen and won.

"I am an excellent student, and I studied the herstory of Evlantis so I could rule wisely. I implemented a policy Cleopas the Wise had tried in the year 402—that of growing crops in rotation so there would be no famine. This meant that teams of women would not need to hunt in distant places while babes died at home-hearth. Where Cleopas had failed, I succeeded, for instead of chanting to the cloud god for rain, I had the slaves dig trenches from the mountain springs a few miles away, and droughts have not decimated the crops as they used to. No one died of starvation during my reign.

"Once my people were fed, contention grew. Feuds have always been a problem in Evlantis, but prosperity brought increased bloodshed. I reinstated Wanda the Just's court system. I also made improvements to the army. I believe I have the best-disciplined and most skilled warriors in all herstory. I used my army to quell the occasional riots and to oversee the slaves. Since I shaped what was a rag-tag bunch of soldiers into an elite team, we have not had one rebellion or unplanned quickening in twenty years.

"Since I have mentioned the army, I must again mention my daughter, Rebekkah. She was extraordinary. She excelled at everything she did, especially any kind of physical activity. At the age of fifteen, she qualified for military training, and she quickly rose to the top of her class. She was an excellent tracker, markswoman, and fighter. She had never been beaten in hand-to-hand combat. She rose through the ranks quickly. When she was eighteen, she challenged Low Queen Gayla and won the right to be Low Queen of the Soldier Sector. She was elected to the post in 1523, and has ruled that Sector ever since. She has been missing for four months now.

"But, I'm getting ahead of myself. When Rebekkah turned six, Sephora began her rise in power. Sephora competed openly with me throughout her years in government, but seldom bested me. I knew Sephora was jealous, but I did not realize the extent of her hatred toward me until these last few months, after she defeated me in this year's election for the post of High Queen." Rachel glanced at Ava in concern. "Are you comfortable?"

Ava nodded her head. "Continue, I am listening," she whispered.

"I ruled Evlantis with a strict but fair hand. Sephora cares only for the trappings of power and personal gain. Since she wrested power from me, she has implemented policies that will lead to famine, unrest, and slave revolt. She has taken everything the men hold dear so they have nothing to lose by fighting. She has released her secret police, and now my people live in fear. We will soon return to the dark ages we suffered under Halfa the Shortsighted. The blood of good women murdered is flowing in our streets again. Sephora's enemies live in fear while her friends live lawlessly. All this came to pass because Sephora set a trap for me, and I fell into it. I underestimated her."

Rachel took a sip of water and continued.

"I do not believe the goddesses control our fate. I believe we forge our own destinies. Throughout our recorded herstory, a barren woman has been hung from the Sacrificial Tree each spring. I've always believed this is a horrible custom that only exists to appease the superstitions of the lower class.

"Rebekkah hated the custom even more than I do. She took it upon herself to come up with a plan to end the sacrifice. She began by studying the patterns of the Beast that killed the victims. Rebekkah discovered the Beast was an animal that hunts in that area during spring because it sleeps all winter and wakes hungry. Rebekkah tracked it and found others of its kind. She killed a small one to make certain they were mortal. A female among them became enraged and attacked her, and she engaged in hand-to-hand combat with it. That night she dined on beast meat! She said it was tough, but hearty. It sustained her on her trip home.

"Rebekkah believed the best way to end the sacrifice was to become the sacrificial victim and kill the beast. She even found a way to get down from the sacrificial tree. I forbade her in no uncertain terms. It was far too risky."

In her mind's eye, Ava remembered the way Rebekkah had grasped the tree branch with her thighs. She realized now that Rebekkah had not been playing a game, as Ava had believed. Rebekkah had been tied to the tree by the leather thong. Ava tuned in to Rachel's words once more.

"Then, this past winter, Sephora made several speeches in the Palace Hall about how offering the lowliest among us must be offensive to the goddesses. We should try offering one of the greatest among us. 'Imagine our rewards then', she said. This stirred up the people, common and noble alike. Fear increased among the Royals, who wondered who Sephora's target was. Each family petitioned Sephora with bribes to keep their family safe and to convince her to choose their rival.

"At last the day came to choose a sacrifice. Rebekkah came to me just before the session to tell me Sephora was going to suggest that she be the sacrifice and to beg me to support her. We entered the Hall together and I went to my throne on the stage while she went to hers on the floor. Each Low Queen was called upon to make a suggestion. The Low Queens sit on thrones arranged in a semi-circle around the Palace Hall stage. When the Queens are called upon to speak, they do so in order of the seating. However, the direction alternates so one Queen is not always called upon first. By chance, the calling order favored Sephora that day. When called upon, Sephora suggested Rebekkah.

"Pandemonium broke out in Palace Hall. After a dramatic pause, Rebekkah asked for the floor, though normal procedure was to have the proposal seconded so that it could be voted on later in the session.

"When the soldiers imposed order in the Hall, every eye was on my daughter except mine. I was watching Sephora. Rebekkah stood ramrod straight in a confident military pose as she turned her back to me to make her answer to the people. Her voice was clear and her tone confident.

"'It would be my honor to serve this city, as I hope I always have loyally and competently, by offering myself as a pleasing gift to the goddesses,' she said.

"Every eye was trained on me. I stood and walked the stage, as is my custom, scanning faces as I went. Sephora's features were composed, but for a second I saw a smug look pass over her face. It raised the hair on my neck. I felt I was missing something important. I walked the stage a second time, to give myself time. If I lost my daughter, a great deal of what gave me joy in life would be gone. But such a thing was unimaginable. Rebekkah was prepared to triumph, even if I did not want to risk it.

"I made a third circuit of the stage and stopped in front of Sephora. 'Low Queen Sephora', I said to her, 'you speak of offering the best among our daughters to the goddess instead of the least. I am honored you chose my daughter instead of one of your own'. There were snickers of amusement. Sephora blushed, but she made no comment.

"I completed my circuit, taking in what I could of the reactions. They were mixed. Some were shocked by the whole departure from tradition. Some grieved to be losing Rebekkah. Some expressed sympathy for me, and some showed rage against Sephora. Many faces showed relief that their families had been spared. I deduced all these things from their facial expressions and their comments as I finished my walk and stood in front of my daughter.

"Women began to cry out. 'Don't do it!' 'Not Rebekkah!' I happened to glance at Sephora, who had dropped something and picked it up. It must have been a signal, because a chant began in her Sector that overwhelmed the other comments. 'Give our best to the Beast!' I gave a hand signal to Rebekkah to silence the crowd, and she dispersed soldiers to key points in the room. They held their spears over their heads in the command for silence. The tide of noise subsided and ceased altogether as I began to speak. No one wanted to miss it.

"'Daughter,' I said to her, 'You are not only the daughter of my beloved city but the daughter of my womb. As a mother, can I allow what I love most to be given for the good of all? Is not this the dilemma one mother finds herself in each year during the spring sacrificial season? Those mothers have no choice and no say in the matter, while I have the right to refuse your service. You are not a child. You are a fully-grown woman, a Low Queen and Commander of the Armed Forces of Evlantis, and you have accepted this fate. I marvel at the fullness of love in your heart for all women. My daughter, I, with both grief and pride in my heart, accept this sacrifice you choose to make for our people.'

"The buzz in the hall rose to such a level that no one heard my last words. They were words every woman knew by heart. Caliphus spoke them each year during the religious rite the day of the sacrifice. 'May the sacrifice you make find favor with the goddesses so we may prosper and grow, have food at our hearths and daughters in our wombs, and find purpose and meaning in our existence.'"

Rachel paused here, lost in memories. She would continue soon; she had to before they ran out of time. Ava reached for Rachel's hand and held it weakly. Rachel's story explained so much. Of course, Ava knew how the sacrifice had ended.

Rachel was ready to speak again. She loosened the stranger's grip and gave her wine to sip. The young woman drank so well that Rachel gave her water. The woman swallowed greedily.

Rachel had spent many hours each week tending to the sick of her Queendom. It was common to see the dying refuse food and drink, as if the body knew it was shutting down. Rachel thought it odd the stranger had such a great thirst, but she had to get on with her narrative. She hoped to enter into a Pact of Honor with the stranger before others arrived.

"Rebekkah and I treasured the days before the sacrifice, not because we believed she would die, but because everyone else did. We did what was expected of us. We visited many of the people we held dear and lived life as if it were our last days. Now, I am so glad we did.

"The days of the sacrificial season came, and everything went as it was supposed to until the fourth day when the High Priestess brought me the Ring of Power from Rebekkah's finger. I was sure Rebekkah would come back to me."

Ava shuddered.

"Cold, are you? They should be here in less than an hour." Rachel arranged the extra cloak more securely around the woman before continuing her narrative.

"To make the story of the last three months short, Sephora won the election by a very small margin. Using my new status as a motherless woman against me, she stripped everything from me. I was sent to live in the Arts Sector to serve a family she had chosen there. I knew she was plotting to kill me.

"I came up with the plan you have unwittingly become part of. I pretended madness. I said I could hear my Rebekkah weeping for me in the wood, and I had to go to her. It suited Sephora to have me out of the city, and I needed time to think and plan beyond the scope of her watchful eye. I can count on four of the six Low Queens to be sympathetic to me. I believe they will support the claim I intend to make, if you help me.

"Sephora used the religious beliefs of the people shamelessly. She claimed the goddesses were so pleased with the sacrifice that they endorsed her as High Queen. With your help, I will fight fire with fire. I shall make the claim that you are my Rebekkah, returned to me by the goddesses. I will say you told me Sephora sent her minions to kill you, but the goddesses returned life to you and sent you back to me."

At this point, the stranger shuddered again and mumbled. Rachel bent low to hear her and asked her to repeat herself.

"Sephora sent some men to kill Rebekkah," said the stranger, more clearly.

Rachel corrected her, thinking the girl was trying to get her story straight.

"No, dear, not men. No one would ever believe slaves could kill my daughter. We will have to accuse her of sending women from her secret police force, a story that would have credibility.

"We need to account for the fact that while you could be mistaken for Rebekkah from a distance, anyone who really knows my daughter will know that you are not her. We will say the goddesses took pity on your injuries, and they were pleased that you volunteered to be the sacrifice so they gave you a new, glorified visage. The women of the city will love the story. I will demand a new election. I could even bring false charges of attempted murder against Sephora."

Rachel felt awkward saying this, knowing it would only be a matter of time until the stranger died and Sephora would be charged with murder.

"I must do something," said Rachel, feeling guilty for using the dying woman. "Sephora is doing great harm to my people.

"I don't think you have long to live, and I'm sorry for how you've been involved in this. But I promise to look after you, to ease your pain, to give you a peaceful death, and to live peacefully with your people if you back up my story with your dying breath. Will you help me?"

Ava's head was clearer now.

"You are High Queen Rachel?" Ava asked. "The mother of Rebekkah?"

"Yes," replied Rachel. Again, she asked, "Will you help me?"

"I will help you," Ava answered. "Sephora sent them to kill Rebekkah. They tried to kill me."

Rachel assumed the girl was parroting the story back to her.

"Thank you," Rachel said. "I will tend to you with a mother's love. You did well. We will make our pact, and after we complete it, you must remember that you are now Rebekkah. Our story will be that Sephora sent her henchwomen to kill you. Do you understand?"

Ava didn't have the energy to clarify once again that some men had killed Rebekkah. She realized if she had done Rebekkah's bidding and taken the Ring of Power to Rachel along with Tiburnus and Baraus, Sephora would not have won the election for High Queen. To assume Rebekkah's identity was a serious commitment. Rebekkah's dying words echoed in her head: "Carry on what I have begun." Adam's daughter spoke, her mind made up.

"I am Rebekkah, and Sephora sent henchwomen to kill me."

"Thank you," Rachel said again. She hoped the girl would live long enough to utter her statement to their rescuers. Then she could save the Queendom.

"Do you have any questions before we finalize our Pact of Honor?"

Ava looked up into Rachel's face and studied it. It was like her mother's face in many ways. There was one difference, and in the haze of her illness, she was curious without reservation.

"Only one," Ava's voice was weak. "How did you get those lines on your face? My mother does not have them."

"Lines on my face?"

The stranger reached up with her right hand and used her index finger to trace the concern lines on Rachel's forehead, the eagles' feet at the corners of her eyes, and the joy lines at the corners of her mouth. Rachel realized the young woman meant her folds-of-good-living and wondered again where she was from. Perhaps the women died young where she came from, or they were put to death in their youth. Rachel would have many occasions to dwell upon the oddities of this woman before the truth would come to her.

"These are folds of the skin that come with age. We look at them as signs of a full life lived well. They herald the beginning of the age of true wisdom and peace in a woman's life. The women of the Arts Sector resist their appearance with creams and other methods, but most women welcome them. Slaves get these signs of wisdom and maturity much later in life than women, and sometimes not at all. This is evidence of man's inferiority to women."

The stranger looked troubled. Rachel could tell she was struggling to stay awake. Rachel spoke with concern in her voice.

"I promise we will speak of whatever is troubling you later. I'm sure you have as many questions for me as I have for you. You must sleep if you hope to live long enough to help me save my city. It is the custom of the women of Evlantis to seal our Pacts of Honor with an embrace. Before you sleep we must seal our bargain."

The stranger nodded in agreement and opened her arms. Rachel bent over her, picked her up slightly, and gently held her in her arms. The stranger circled Rachel's back with her arms. The pact was sealed. Rachel lowered the stranger carefully back down upon her bed of leaves and grass.

Without thinking, Rachel began to sing a favorite lullaby. With the relationship between mother and daughter being the one most celebrated in Evlantis, the lullaby was the most popular musical genre in the Queendom. There were thousands of them. Rachel had always sung to Rebekkah as a child and to the babies she comforted on visits she made to her people as High Queen. The music was more effective at venting her feelings than the tears she shed.

Ava thought the music was beautiful. The tone was mournful as it expressed what was in Rachel's heart. Though Ava was tired, she listened, and then she sang along. The women's voices mingled beautifully, eerily out of place in the dusky forest. Soon, only one voice sang on as Ava, her body refueled by the water and wine, fell back into the sleep of healing.

Rachel rearranged the cloak around the stranger. She felt a need to stretch. She rose and did a battle stretch by placing her hands at her heart to harvest energy, and then she took a deep breath to refuel her body with oxygen. She stretched her hands above her head and then dipped her body into a full bend. She moved her head right and left in this position and heard the tension crackle in her joints. She breathed in deep and exhaled to remove the tension, and swept into an upright position, hands in front of heart. She took deep breaths steadily, in and out, until she felt centered and calm. Then, in spite of her fifty-three years, she nimbly climbed a nearby tree. She sat in the branches listening quietly, her eyes constantly scanning to search out any sign of an approaching party.

UNEXPECTED ALLIES

In a state of panic, Hannah ran through the forest. Everyone knew ghosts existed. Ghosts and evil spirits were common themes in theater plays. The ghost of the Great Mother had been seen many times at her gravesite. There were regular sightings of ghosts around Rowada's Swamp, where the unwanted babies were tossed.

Sweat formed on Hannah's forehead and ran into her eyes. She had to keep wiping it away so she could see the paint she had left on the trees to mark the way back. She was cold right down to the marrow of her bones, and it seemed to her that her heart was pounding in her neck instead of her chest. Terror drove her. When she couldn't run any longer, she slowed to a fast walk, but she kept moving as quickly as possible. At times, her breath was so ragged she thought she would pass out. Sometimes she fell, but she kept moving forward. She crawled on her hands and knees until her breathing was controlled enough to run again. She never stopped, would not stop, with Rachel in danger and the ghost-thing behind her.

She was no longer concerned about sleeping snakes or rodent holes. She hardly noticed the branches and brambles that tore at her face and arms. The only thing she cared about was keeping the marked trees within her sight. She did not want to get lost in the woods. She must get help for Rachel.

Hannah was crawling in the clearing at the perimeter outside the city gates when a soldier on the wall noticed her and called out a warning. A soldier patrolling on the ground ran toward her. The soldier reached Hannah and scooped her from the ground effortlessly. She carried her back to the wall, where the other guards waited.

"Oh my goddess!" said the sentry Sephora had posted to wait for her prisoners. "Is that Hannah? She returned without Rachel? Look at the girl! She is filthy! She is scratched and bleeding. Partouche, what should we do?"

They looked to Sephora's agent for direction. Sephora had assigned Partouche to supervise Rachel and Hannah. It was obvious Hannah was terrified. She was mumbling incoherently.

"We must take her to Sephora at once!" said Partouche. "Stay here and watch for Rachel, in case she appears. I will take Hannah to the High Queen myself."

"Should we go and look for Rachel?" asked a soldier.

"Under no circumstances should there be any effort made to search for Rachel. Stay here and guard the wall as you were ordered to. No one goes in or out. If Rachel shows up, take her into custody and escort her to the High Queen as quickly as possible."

They heard hoof beats and looked up to see Arrival approach them on Stealth. Partouche added one more instruction.

"Obey me, even if the Commander has a different opinion. You know I speak for the High Queen."

"What's going on?" Arrival asked as she slowed Stealth to join the group.

"Commander," said Partouche, pretending Arrival was her leader, "Hannah returned to the city without Rachel. We must get Hannah to the High Queen at once. You know Sephora will be quite interested in whatever Hannah has to say."

"Hannah only! My mother did not come back with her?"

"No. So far there has been no sign of her."

"I will go find her." Arrival feared she had failed Rebekkah and that now it was too late to tell their mother the secret.

"You will not."

Arrival looked around at the faces of the soldiers. She recognized them all as infiltrators to her Sector, assigned by Sephora herself. They were heavily armed and she was outnumbered. Arrival was no use to Rachel dead.

"You are right, Partouche, I will take Hannah to the High Queen."

Before Partouche could react, Arrival dismounted, scooped Hannah out of the arms of the soldier holding her, and slung the shaking, mumbling girl over the back of Stealth. She remounted and was galloping down the main road toward the Palace before any of the soldiers could challenge her.

"Remember my orders!" said Partouche, and then she whistled for her mount. Her horse had been grazing nearby. Partouche mounted quickly and galloped after Arrival.

Sephora was in the Royal Dressing Room trying on gowns for the Harvest Festival, the annual celebration that lasted a week and a day. Her three daughters and the High Priestess, Low Queen Caliphus, were in the next room waiting to join her. Once she had chosen the perfect gown for herself, she would choose theirs to compliment hers. Sephora loved to be at the center of a good show. Her predecessor had done her duty, but she had been bored by the ceremonial requirements. Rachel would rather have been examining the granaries, improving the irrigation system, inspecting the troops, or visiting the sick. Sephora thought those jobs too menial for the Ruler of the World and assigned minions to do them in her name.

Sephora had been in a good mood for months. She prided herself on her patience and intelligence, and now she was exactly where she had wanted to be, planned to be, and deserved to be for her entire life. Rachel had done all the hard work, and now Sephora would reap the benefits. Rachel still lived, but as soon as Sephora no longer took pleasure in observing the pain of her enemy, she would arrange for Rachel and Hannah to have an accident on one of their outings.

She gazed at her reflection in a mirror framed by candles. She was diminutive and looked at least ten years younger than her age. She had intelligence, patience, and vibrant beauty, but her greatest asset was her ability to manipulate others to get what she wanted. She had used whatever means necessary—charm, lies, threats, violence—and now she had it all. She lived in the palace and her every whim was catered to. The Low Queens and Royal citizens lived in fear of her. The poor loved her. The slaves were under her thumb.

Sephora's reverie was disturbed by Arrival, who barged in carrying a woman in her arms. Partouche was three steps behind her. There had been no time to send an advance messenger. Arrival had one of the fastest stallions in the army, and not even the speed of gossip could outpace it. Sephora vented her anger at the intrusion by scolding.

"See here, Low Queen Arrival, I am trying on dresses for the Harvest Festival. It is bad luck to see the dress before the ceremony. This one will have to be discarded now, and it was my favorite."

Arrival made no effort to answer her. Partouche, gasping for breath with the effort it had taken to keep up with Arrival, explained the situation to the High Queen.

"Beloved Sovereign, I ordered Arrival to bring Hannah to you. Hannah arrived at the city wall less than twenty minutes ago without the former High Queen Rachel. I thought it most urgent for you to see her immediately."

"What? Rachel did not return? What did Hannah say?"

Sephora's anger dissipated instantly and was replaced by hope. Perhaps a wild beast had done what she had not yet ordered. This was the best Harvest Festival present she could hope for.

"Nothing, High Queen," said Partouche. "Hannah was found crawling on her hands and knees, talking insensibly. Arrival wanted to search for Rachel, but I knew you would want to question Hannah before sending out search parties."

Sephora smiled.

"You were right, Partouche," said Sephora. "You serve the High Queen with your brawn and your brain. I will issue a commendation for you. Such insight is exactly what I am looking for from the Commander of the Soldier Sector. Perhaps you would consider challenging Arrival for the position one of these days. It would please me greatly." Sephora turned to Arrival with a frown.

"Arrival, why are you still standing there? Put Hannah in the most comfortable chair in the room, there." Sephora gestured, and then she launched into one of her stellar performances. If she hadn't lusted after the trappings of power, she could have been a famous actress as her mother Sepheera had been. Sephora went to Hannah and fawned over her.

"Hannah, darling, what have you been through? I should have never acquiesced to Rachel's request. You are shaking, dear one, and you are dirty and scratched. You tremble so."

Sephora knew Hannah well, since the girl belonged to such a prominent family in the Arts Sector. Sephora motioned for the servant who had been attending her during the gown fitting.

"Get the warmest fur blanket from the royal bedchamber. Send for the Palace physician, and bring back a good wine from the winery. Hurry!"

The serving girl flew from the room, no less afraid than Hannah had been on her journey through the forest. Everyone in the palace had quickly learned that when Sephora said to hurry she meant it.

Sephora knelt by Hannah and took her hand. She smoothed back the girl's disheveled hair.

"Hannah, dear, everything will be all right. No, don't try to speak, darling, wait until you calm down a bit."

Hannah's eyes were wild with terror, which piqued Sephora's interest. Other attendants in the room began making the sign of protection against evil. Sephora was certain there could be only one explanation for why Hannah had returned alone and in such a state. *Still*, Sephora thought, *better safe than sorry*.

There was a knock on the door. Sephora turned her head in time to see a soldier step into the room. The woman saluted Arrival and spoke to her in hushed tones. The soldier left again.

"What is this disturbance about?" asked Sephora. "Can't you see I'm trying to take care of poor Hannah?"

"Madam High Queen," Arrival said to Sephora, "a mob has gathered outside the Palace perimeter. News that Hannah has returned to the city without Rachel has spread. What are your orders?"

Sephora stood and struck a pose conveying the gravity of the situation, her head resting on her right fist and her brows furrowed.

"Arrival, I cannot leave dear Hannah now. She has been through some kind of shock, and I am worried about her. Have the crowd assemble below the west balcony. Inform them I will be out shortly to make an announcement. This room must be cleared so that when Hannah is able to speak, I can get the news without interruption. Then I will decide the best course of action to take. Everyone must leave—now!"

Arrival exited, her face a mask of duty. She had been hoping to stay. She, too, needed to hear whatever Hannah had to say to Sephora. On the ride to the palace, Arrival had been able to hear only three of Hannah's mumbled words: Rachel, ghost, and Rebekkah. Arrival had no idea what to make of them. Arrival hurried to carry out Sephora's orders so that she could take care of state business of her own.

The serving girl returned with the blanket, the wine, and the physician. Hannah was covered with a beautiful lion skin throw. The physician, who had been briefed by the serving girl on their way to the Royal Dressing Room, quickly examined Hannah. Sephora poured herself a glass of wine.

"This woman is in shock," said the physician. The doctor pulled an armchair from a corner of the room and placed it directly in front of Hannah, raised Hannah's legs, and rested them on the arms of the chair with pillows underneath for comfort. The doctor rummaged in her bag for a packet of chemicals, added them to a glass of water, and handed it to Hannah, who was looking around the room wide-eyed with shock.

"You will be fine if you drink this and rest," the doctor said to Hannah. She turned to Sephora and said, "Don't let your patient get too hot or too cold. The solution I gave her does not taste good, but she must drink it."

"Thank you, doctor; I will take excellent care of the patient. You may go."

Sephora was finally alone with Hannah. She gazed at Hannah with intense concentration.

"Hannah," Sephora said to her, "why have you returned to the city without the former High Queen? It was your duty to stay with her—to die with her if necessary."

Hannah felt dizzy, but knew it was important to explain clearly. She found her voice and said what Sephora did not anticipate.

"Queen Rachel commanded I come. She found something. I think it must have been a demon-ghost. She thinks it is Rebekkah. I heard the ghost call Rachel 'mother'. We need to go back and get them, or her, or..." Hannah glanced at Sephora and fell silent. The look on Sephora's face frightened her.

"Rachel is alive?" Sephora asked.

"When I left her, yes," answered Hannah. Unaware she had found the only words that would extend her life past this audience,

Hannah waited. She forced herself to drink the awful solution the doctor had prepared. It tasted like salt water, but Hannah knew that she needed to feel better quickly so she could help Rachel.

Sephora turned her back on Hannah and pondered the situation. Finally, Sephora spun back to face Hannah.

"Tell me everything that happened, from the time you left this morning to the time you returned here now. And be quick."

Hannah began her narrative. Her speech was slurred, but Sephora did not complain. In the beginning, Sephora paced. As Hannah finished, Sephora turned her back on Hannah again and spoke.

"Did you see this apparition?"

"High Queen, I saw only one foot," Hannah answered.

"Did you tell anyone?"

"No, High Queen, you are the first to know." Hannah answered as honestly as she could, though in truth she could not remember what she had said to the soldiers who found her.

Sephora was calm again. She had an amazing capacity to track details in her head. She was acutely aware that her daughters and the High Priestess awaited her summons in the next room. It was her remembrance of this detail in this moment of crisis that gave her inspiration. She turned back to Hannah.

"You are a fool, Hannah, a cowardly fool. No one leaves a woman who is soft in the head in the forest unattended. If those who are loyal to Rachel hear of this, surely they will kill you. You are lucky I do not kill you here and now for your disloyalty. I will protect you for now. I will send you to a place no one will think to look. I must repair the damage you have done. I will allow you to remain among the living, but know that you live because of my good grace alone. You may kneel and kiss my feet in gratitude." Sephora picked up the wine bottle as if she was going to pour herself another drink.

Hannah wasn't sure what had happened, but she knew something was very wrong. She lowered her feet and slipped off the chair. She dropped to her knees and crawled to Sephora to kiss her feet. She never saw the blow that rendered her unconscious.

Sephora set the wine bottle down and quickly pondered the options available to her. Clearly, Rachel had come up with some scheme to cause trouble for her. Sephora had risen in popularity by appealing to the religious idiosyncrasies of the city. She would now use this to remain in power. While dismembered body parts and entrails were signs from the goddesses, demon-ghosts were something to be truly feared. Legend claimed that male demons often powered ghostly apparitions—demons looking for bloodthirsty revenge. Their hatred against womankind was legendary. Sephora did not believe in them, but she knew she could manipulate the awaiting crowd into believing this myth.

With the help of the High Priestess, Sephora could put off the search for Rachel until morning. This would give her time to get rid of Rachel permanently. The only thing the searchers would find in the morning would be Rachel's body. Sephora herself would call for Hannah's execution, and this desperate attempt by Rachel to cause trouble for Sephora would fail miserably.

Sephora was enjoying herself again. She called her daughters and the High Priestess in from the waiting room.

From her hiding place, Arrival saw and heard everything that took place between Hannah and Sephora. The Royal Dressing Room was one of the Royals' favorite places to come to gossip. Many political alliances were formed there. It had been the second room where Rachel had a secret viewing area installed, and it had been the most useful.

When Sephora clubbed Hannah on the back of the head with the wine bottle and Hannah lay slumped on the floor, Arrival worried that it was time to move. Sephora had promised an announcement to the crowd. Arrival would have to be there at Sephora's side. Intuition told her to wait. She watched as Sephora ushered her three daughters into the room along with High Priestess-Low Queen Caliphus.

Within seconds, they were assembled. The High Priestess looked in surprise at Hannah lying prostrate on the floor. Sephora's daughters paid the body no mind. This was not the first time they had entered a room to find their mother in the presence of an incapacitated person.

"Hannah came back without Rachel," Sephora stated flatly. "What no ears but mine have heard is that Hannah claims Rebekkah is alive."

Her daughters gasped in horror. They loved the luxury and power their mother's status afforded them. If Rebekkah was alive, she could be a threat. Yet, they had learned to take their cues from their mother, and Sephora seemed calm. She continued.

"It is not possible, even for the almighty Rebekkah, to have survived in the forest for months with the blood loss we know she sustained at the sacrificial site. We must assume she is dead. Hannah reported to me before she succumbed to fright that she believes Rachel has found a ghost. A demon-ghost is a danger to the entire city, is it not?" Sephora turned to Caliphus. "Isn't there an ancient prescription about closing the gates to prevent demon-ghosts from entering the city?"

Behind the tapestry, Arrival gave a start. She did not need to hear more to know what Sephora had in mind. Sephora and Arrival had similar levels of education, and Arrival wasn't as easily duped as many of the other women were. Arrival realized Sephora was going to use Caliphus to shut the gates so that Rachel could not be rescued tonight. Arrival was certain Sephora would not leave Rachel's death to chance; Sephora would never just assume that a wild beast would take Rachel's life. Sephora was serious about killing Rachel, and she would make it happen. It was up to Arrival to save her mother. She came up with a plan of her own. It was risky, and she had little time to implement it before she had to stand beside Sephora on the balcony, but the time for action was now. She left the hidden chamber in haste.

Caliphus also realized what Sephora planned to do. Caliphus had enjoyed working with Rachel, but if Caliphus did not support Sephora, Sephora would find a way to replace her. Caliphus had spent thirty years trying to fulfill the secret mission of the High Priestess, which had been handed down to her by the former High Priestess on her deathbed. Caliphus had made more progress than any of her predecessors and thought she might live to see the mission fulfilled. Caliphus would not see hundreds of years of work accomplished by the Royal Religion line undone to save one, possibly two, women. Caliphus stilled an impulse to tap her foot. She drew a deep breath. She answered Sephora's question carefully.

"Yes, High Queen. There is such a ceremony. The Ancients believed people could come to harm, even be killed, by the souls of the dead seeking revenge against the living. It was said Great Mother herself was haunted by the demon-ghost of the man who quickened her with her twin sons. In those times, whenever these evil creatures were spotted, the villagers barricaded themselves in their homes from dusk until dawn, since it is said such spirits have no power when there is daylight in the air. This practice took the name of demon barring. After oil lamps were invented and lengthened the productivity of the day, the practice of demon barring fell away, as no harm came from the demon-ghosts people feared during the night hours. If you feel it is warranted, High Queen, I will enact the ancient practice of demon barring this night."

The High Queen addressed the Low Queen scathingly.

"I am only concerned about my citizens. The mad former High Queen Rachel may have unwittingly released a true danger to our city. It is not my desire to have gates closed. I would like nothing more than to rescue the former High Queen. Closing them will mean certain death for Rachel. You must do your duty and do what is best for the city. Do you understand, Caliphus?"

Caliphus understood. Sephora wished this to be on her shoulders alone. So be it. The priestess drew herself up and pretended to take offense. Sometimes dealing with Sephora required bravery one didn't feel. Sephora respected strength.

"I understand, my Queen. As Low Queen and High Priestess of the City of Evlantis, I exercise the authority vested in me to protect all citizens of the city by proclaiming demon barring is required tonight."

Sephora laughed.

"It will be as you have said. You understand your duty well. I am sure your goddesses will reward you mightily. Go and wait for me on the west balcony. Prepare the people, but make no formal announcement until I come and address them. After I have had my say, you will suggest demon barring. I will protest, but you will convince me it is best for the city. Is this clear?"

Caliphus knelt before the High Queen.

"Perfectly clear, my Queen. I will do as you command."

"Good," Sephora answered her. "I will join you soon."

Sephora turned to her daughters the moment the door closed behind the High Priestess.

"What do you make of all this?" she asked them.

"It must be a trick of Rachel's," answered Second Sephora.

"Obviously," said Sephora scathingly, "that is the only possibility."

"You seem so sure of yourself, High Queen Mother," said her eldest. "Why are you so certain Rebekkah is dead? She has survived in the wild far longer than three months. Perhaps Rachel has indeed found Rebekkah. If so, your days as Supreme Ruler of the World may be numbered. The populace, with the assistance of Rachel and Rebekkah, will see this as some kind of sign from the goddesses and riot to have a new election. Rachel and Rebekkah will rise to new heights amidst the glory of the legend they have built. Their names will go down in herstory, whereas yours will be forgotten before the year is out."

Sephora slapped her. Her eldest daughter had been surly and bitter since losing her challenge to Arrival. She was jealous of Third Sephora and felt it should have been she, First Sephora, who was given the throne of the Arts Sector. Sephora was angry at First, who she had counted on to take the Throne of the Soldier Sector. There was constant palpable tension between them.

Sephora answered her coldly.

"I know in my heart Rebekkah is dead. She would have died before losing the ring she earned and held dear as Low Queen and Commander of the Soldier Sector."

First's cheek was still red, but she challenged her mother again.

"Is it only your heart which tells you so? Don't forget both Second Sephora and I gave you an alibi for your absence the third night of the sacrifice. I am thinking perhaps a certain slave you used to be very close to, who has not been seen since that night, may have given you proof of Rebekkah's death."

"Bitch," Sephora said coldly, "if had I chosen to make you a confidant of mine, I would have done so by now. Perhaps you would be one if you had toppled Arrival from her throne as I asked you to do, but you failed at that, didn't you? Your insinuations mean nothing to me. You will know whatever I tell you, and nothing else."

"I must go and address the people. The gates will be closed in the demon barring ceremony, but I will not take chances. The three of you must find a way out of the city and find Rachel. You may find her dead, for better women than she have not survived a night in the forest. If you find her alive, kill her instantly. Leave her body where you find it. Hannah will take sole blame for leaving Rachel alone in the forest with a demon-ghost.

"Rachel may have an accomplice. Hannah testified she saw a human foot. You must kill her also, but before you do, you must learn her identity so I can punish her family in secret for her insubordination to the Crown. Use whatever methods necessary. Find a place to hide her body where it will never be found. Return in secret, before dawn, to the temple of Ephrea where I will spend the night.

"I will order the Soldier Sector to guard the city wall tonight. If Arrival's soldiers are too efficient and you are not able to get back into the city, return to my bedchamber after the gates are open. You must disguise yourselves, for I will have three women stand in for you in black hooded robes so no one will question your absence. Do you have any questions?"

The princesses shook their heads.

"One last thing," Sephora said. "If you fail me, do not bother to return."

"Mother!" said Third Sephora. "If we fail, where on earth would we go?"

"Why even speak of failing me, you ungrateful wench? Rachel is a woman in her fifties while you are in your teens and well trained in fighting. We do not know the identity of Rachel's accomplice, but I expect you to take them by surprise.

"If you fail in this simple task I give you, I don't care where you go. If you come back here, I will kill you myself. You are all replaceable. I bore three daughters, and I can do so again. Laws no longer burden me, and they certainly do not apply to me. Even now, I may be pregnant with Fourth Sephora.

"However, I prefer that you return. You are useful to me." Sephora became impatient. "I cannot delay my address to the populace any longer. Return to me before dawn with your task accomplished. At first light, we will travel to find the fruits of your labor this night. We will mourn in public and celebrate in private. Now go—goddess speed to you three."

Sephora left the room without even one last backward glance at her daughters.

Servus stood alone in the barracks. It was his practice to spend a few quiet minutes by himself before retiring each day. The men respected him as a leader of great vision and left him alone as he requested.

It was during this time that he practiced new fighting moves to teach the men, away from the eyes of the women. It was during this time when he planned strategies for his campaign for freedom and dreamed of what the world would be like when the men were free.

When Arrival came through the soldier entrance to his barracks unattended, Servus was shocked. He began to fall to his knees as protocol demanded. Arrival forbade him.

"King Servus, do not bend your knee to me. Today I come to you as an equal, Low Queen to Low King." Arrival spoke formally, and bent at the waist.

Servus, stunned, returned the bow in a similar fashion.

"King Servus," Arrival said, "I have a proposition for you. Have you heard that Hannah returned this evening without Rachel?"

"I heard." Servus replied curtly with a nod.

Arrival spoke more quickly, less formally.

"Good, that saves me time. I don't have a lot of it. I know you long for equality. Tonight I need you to enter a Pact of Honor with me.

"What no one but a handful of people know—and this won't be common knowledge after I share it with you—is that Rachel has found Rebekkah, perhaps alive. I believe Sephora plans to send someone to kill them. I want to save them, and I need an ally. I need your help."

Servus raised an eyebrow.

"What could you possibly offer me to convince me to help Rachel and Rebekkah?" he asked.

"I have two things in my power to trade for your service. First, I will allow two men of your choosing to escape tonight. The second thing I offer is knowledge. It involves a grave-secret I keep for

Rebekkah. I have been unable to share it with Rachel, but if she returns to the city unharmed, I will tell the secret to you. It is information that could change the course of herstory."

"What are you asking me to do?" asked Servus. He was intrigued.

"I need you to assign men you trust to guard all the exits of the city. Sephora will implement the ancient practice of demon barring tonight. She wants to keep Rachel and Rebekkah outside the city, and she will allow no one to leave to rescue them. I am certain she will send someone to kill them. I want to prevent her henchwomen from leaving the city. The men you assign as guards must come back in the morning, and to ensure that they do, I must hold the young boys hostage. I apologize for taking such drastic measures, but I'm sure you understand the position I am in."

"Yes, of course, but…" Servus fenced.

"I also need you to choose two men who have entered into illegal pacts of fidelity with women to leave the city with them and protect Rachel and Rebekkah until first light. I'm sure you have an excellent idea of whom to send. Send them out at first light. Upon my honor, I swear to you that if the couples you choose skirt Mount Great Mother and follow the first river they discover upstream, they will live and prosper for the rest of their lives. Will you accept, Servus?"

Servus wanted to accept instantly, but he negotiated.

"Queen Arrival, surely you must know I prefer Sephora as my enemy. It is much easier to rouse the men against the rule of Sephora than the rule of Rachel. My goal is nothing less than freedom for all of mankind. The freedom of two men is not enough reward to make this Pact of Honor with you."

"Do you have something else in mind?" Arrival had limited power to bargain with Servus and they both knew it. Arrival was in a hurry.

"As leader of the armed forces, when the slaves rise up in rebellion, you could choose to make decisions in battle that would lead to a slave victory with less bloodshed for either side."

Arrival let out a low groan.

"Servus, you ask too much. The slaves and soldiers live side by side. Many soldiers believe that men, though not equal to women, have much to offer society and that they should be treated more fairly. We do not hate or fear you, as some do, and since we are celibate, we do not use you for seed. But to ask me to betray my own gender in war is too much. I can however promise you this: when Rachel is made High Queen again, I will plead your cause of freedom to her. Once Rebekkah's secret is made known, it will strengthen your case in ways you cannot imagine."

Surely, Arrival was hinting that they were not the only people in the world. This, like the slave genealogies that they had learned indeed existed, was a common hope among the men. To suggest that the couples sent to protect Rachel and Rebekkah would live and prosper seemed to support this theory. Perhaps another city would provide assistance in their fight for freedom. The two men released tonight would serve as his ambassadors if another settlement existed. Freedom seemed much more attainable than it had a few minutes before. He must know the secret Arrival was keeping.

"Fine, Queen Arrival, I have asked for too much. If you want my help tonight, you cannot refuse my next request. It is not negotiable. If Rachel lives through the night and returns to the city, I will give you twenty-four hours to tell me the secret. If you do not, I will consider our Pact of Honor broken, and I will do everything in my power to set my hand against you and your family."

He would learn the secret eventually anyway, from the couples he would send on Arrival's mission. They both knew it.

Arrival had no choice. She would deal with the consequences later.

"I agree to enter a Pact of Honor with you on those terms, King Servus."

There was an awkward pause. Neither knew if the other was comfortable completing the pact. Finally, Servus stepped forward and opened his arms, challenging Arrival to treat him as an equal. Arrival, who had never embraced a man before, stepped forward, blushing. They hugged. Servus, remembering how pleasant it was to hold a woman in his arms, though it had been twenty years or more since he had done so, was loath to let go. Arrival, who had never embraced a man, felt her heart race at the contact, which was pleasant and unlike anything she had ever experienced.

A slave burst into the barracks, yelling.

"King Servus, the High Priestess has been speaking to the people…" his words trailed off as he took in the scene before him. The couple hastily separated. Servus, enjoying himself immensely, turned to the man who had entered.

"Kiertus, as your King, I have just entered into a Pact of Honor with Low Queen Arrival. Please finish what you came to say." Arrival's cheeks were still flushed.

Kiertus, rarely at a loss for words, stammered.

"Y-You asked to be kept abreast of developments. Caliphus is on the west Palace balcony addressing the women who are gathering below on the lawn. She has been giving a herstory lesson about the dangers of demon-ghosts. Wild rumors are spreading. Sephora is expected to appear at any moment."

"I must go now," Arrival said, and hurried back to the passage that led to the Palace, hoping she would beat Sephora to the balcony. Arrival was eager to get away from Servus, who she suddenly found unbearable for reasons she did not understand. Arrival made it to the balcony minutes before Sephora made her dramatic entrance.

Sephora was a classic study of a tragic heroine, one torn by a difficult decision and burdened with worry and grief. Arrival didn't admire much about Sephora except for her uncanny ability to project whatever she wished at any moment. Arrival wryly noticed Sephora still wore the elegant Harvest Festival gown she had been trying on when Arrival interrupted her. The way it emphasized her feminine curves enhanced the illusion of vulnerability. Arrival knew it must be exactly what Sephora intended; otherwise, she would have changed before appearing to the crowd.

Low Queen Caliphus had been speaking, but her words trailed off as the crowd below her knelt and then stood again at the appearance of the High Queen. Caliphus stepped back from the railing to let Sephora take her place. Sephora wasted no time.

"Good women of Evlantis," Sephora said, "tragedy has struck our fair city. The unthinkable has happened. Hannah has shown herself to be a traitor. She returned to the city gates a short time ago without our beloved, mad former High Queen Rachel."

The crowd was stunned. Even with High Priestess Caliphus's talk of demon-ghosts, they hadn't been expecting this. Some women began to weep. Some began to call out their willingness to find Rachel. Many owed her their lives; others had liked living in the peaceful city Rachel had cultivated, and even women who had disagreed with her respected her. Arrival gave hand signals to disperse soldiers into the crowd to keep peace.

Sephora allowed the crowd to murmur for a while as the news sank in. Then she stepped forward and raised her arms in supplication to the crowd.

"I wanted to go immediately to find Rachel. But the High Priestess, who happened to be attending to my needs of piety when the news came, stopped me. Let her tell you in her own words why."

Caliphus swallowed hard. Her foot began to tap and she did not even try to still it. She stepped up beside the diminutive High Queen and spoke words of betrayal to her friend and colleague, Rachel.

"What good Queen Sephora has said is true, but she left out the worst news. I do not want anyone to panic. I have been reviewing our knowledge of demon-ghosts in order to prepare you. I fear that dear ex-Queen Rachel stumbled upon one. Her madness made her a perfect victim for such a danger. Hannah saw the apparition and heard it speak. It was a fearsome sight."

Caliphus embellished the story to stoke fear in the people. Caliphus knew that if she failed Sephora she would be punished, perhaps even killed. Motivated by her desire to survive, Caliphus borrowed images from their legends to portray a terrifying creature.

"The demon-ghost stood seven feet tall and had sharp pointed teeth six inches long. Its skin was gray, the color of the most powerful demons in existence. It had deadly talons on its fingers and toes. Its eyes glowed red and it spoke gibberish."

Many women were weeping. A few were repeatedly making the sign against evil. Some began to chant prayers. Sephora interrupted Caliphus.

"Dear daughters," Sephora cried out, "Poor, mad Rachel called this beast Rebekkah and went to embrace it. Hannah, by her own admission, ran away, back to the city, never once trying to aid our dear former Queen."

Someone in the crowd yelled, "Death to Hannah! Hannah must die!" Sephora considered releasing Hannah to them now. She would be torn limb from limb by the crowd, a sight Sephora would enjoy. She held back for the simple reason that if her daughters failed her, she would have to convince Hannah to uphold the ridiculous story Caliphus had just spun. Sephora wished the High Priestess had not embellished so much, but recognized that many of the more impulsive among them who might be tempted to leave the city to search for Rachel might now be too afraid. Sephora held up her hands for silence.

"No matter how heinous the crime, every woman in Evlantis is allowed a fair trial," Sephora said. "I have put Hannah in a place of safekeeping. After the morrow, we will deal with her. May the goddesses protect our beloved, mad, former Queen. Let Low Queen Caliphus continue."

160

Behind them, Arrival made a sign to release more soldiers for crowd control. Soon they would have a riot on their hands. The emotions of the women ran high.

"Beloved sisters of Evlantis," Caliphus began, "not only can we not save Rachel tonight, but we are in great danger ourselves. It is written in ancient documents that such demons attacked and killed dozens of women in a single night. We must hurry and institute the ancient practice of demon barring at each gate of the city so it may not enter. I have dispatched priestesses, and they wait at all six gates of the great wall. At my signal, they will begin. Soldiers must guard the wall all night, and they must stand facing outward toward the forest instead of facing inward. No one will be allowed in or out until first light. I have spoken."

Caliphus stepped back, leaving Sephora alone at the rail of the balcony. Caliphus was tempted to push her over the edge and send every available priestess out in the night to rescue Rachel, but she did nothing.

"The safety of every woman and child of the city depends upon the success of this ceremony," Sephora said. "I am miserable. I cannot send anyone to save Rachel because this would put the entire city in danger. Her daughter sacrificed herself to save us, this may be Rachel's fate as well." Sephora was weeping again. Arrival marveled at her ability to deceive.

"But all may not be lost. I believe we must put this into the hands of the goddesses. I have sent my daughters to the temple of Ephrea to fast and pray in the inner chamber. I myself will join them until first light when we will open the city gates in the safety of dawn and make all haste to find Rachel. I suggest all of you pray as well. This, my dear people, is the darkest night in the herstory of the city of Evlantis.

"High Priestess-Low Queen Caliphus," Sephora's voice boomed out, "I command you to close the gates in demon barring, as you recommend. Attend to me in the temple of Ephrea when it is done."

Caliphus left the balcony in a hurry. Arrival had arranged for horses and an escort of soldiers to accompany the priestess to the main gate.

Darkness would fall on the city soon. The crowd understood the urgency, and the women parted on their own when Low Queen Caliphus appeared. Sephora and Arrival watched her gallop away.

Sephora's mention of prayer had dampened the violent mood of the crowd. Women began to make their way toward the Religion Sector. They were determined to do all they could to save Rachel. Sephora had suggested a peaceful outlet for their feelings. Sephora turned to Arrival and extended her arm as an invitation to walk together. Sephora smiled sweetly at her, knowing Arrival would try to rescue Rachel.

"Arrival," said Sephora, "you must accompany me to the temple. Believer or no, I want you at my side while I pray."

"Of course, High Queen," Arrival said. Arrival's face showed no sign of the relief she felt that she had already taken action.

After Servus contemplated how best to carry out Arrival's request, he implemented a daring plan. If he sent out only men he trusted, they would be missed and implicated after the fact, so he used every slave. Those tempted to gain Sephora's favor by informing would not be able to tell of the evening's activities without bringing her wrath upon their own heads too. Sephora could not afford to kill all the slaves. The women reviled them, but they could never live without them.

Unknown to Sephora and Arrival, Servus had placed a second barricade around the city. The soldiers standing watch around the wall were easily seen. Outside the city walls, hidden from the soldiers' view but within sight of each other, was a line of slaves. They were not watching for wraiths on their way in, but had orders to stop anyone on their way out of the city.

The slave compound was empty. All except a few soldiers were dispersed upon the wall. Servus considered having the men escape en masse, but Arrival had two methods of leverage. First, the few soldiers not guarding the wall held the boys hostage, along with some women Arrival suspected were slave sympathizers.

Second, Arrival was well aware of the Code of Slaves, which Servus rigorously followed. She knew Servus prided himself on honor and demanded it of his men before all else. As Arrival anticipated, Servus could not bring himself to break the first Pact of Honor entered between a woman and a slave.

Servus said a quick prayer as a petition for success. Unlike Sephora and Rachel, he was a true believer. The religion of the slaves was different from that of the women. The slaves attributed their lineage to the Great Mother, but according to the legends they believed, Great Mother had lived in equality with the Great Father until she disobeyed a Major Goddess. She had been sentenced to leave Great Father forever. Slavery was an unjust revenge against mankind because of her disobedience.

Servus had saved the job of guarding the entrance to the slave barracks for himself and his most trusted men, Kiertus and Justus. It would be the most logical place for Sephora's minions to exit from, as it was closest to the horse stables. Servus suspected the women Sephora sent to kill Rachel and Rebekkah would try to obtain horses. If they did, it would be almost impossible for the slaves holding the perimeter to stop them.

Servus and his men waited. They were dressed head to foot in black, and had blackened their faces with coal, removing all possibilities of recognition. They carried wooden, hand-carved shields and were armed with crudely made slings. They did not know who, when, or how many were coming. Servus realized he could be wrong about the women stopping for horses. They could choose to go on foot. The men in the line would detain them and send for him if that happened. Servus and his men stood tense and ready, hiding in shadows in the barracks.

Servus expected the door he guarded to open at any minute. He had lowered the shades on the windows to maximize the darkness. There was one candle lit by the entrance so that he and his men could see whom they were dealing with before their enemies could see them.

Servus stared in surprise as the door opened and the Three Sephoras entered the barracks. This changed everything. Now, Rachel must survive, or Arrival would not be able to protect him. Odd to find he now genuinely hoped Rachel would live. He shook his head in frustration.

The sisters were making their way silently down the center aisle, armed and ready to fight if they needed to.

"Something is wrong," First whispered. "The blinds are drawn and there is a candle lit at the door. This is not how the men usually leave the barracks."

"Perhaps Arrival had the slaves shackled in the common room this evening to free up soldiers, and she has closed the barracks for the night," said Third.

"Yes, perhaps," the eldest whispered. She halted. "Why is there a candle at the door, then? I think we are walking into a trap."

"Let's go back," said Second Sephora. "It is more important for us to live so that we may succeed rather than to fall into a trap and fail."

"No," said the eldest, "this is the best way. We need horses. Every minute we lose could spell disaster for mother and for us. We must go on, but we will not be ambushed."

She whirled with catlike agility and caught Kiertus in a stranglehold. Servus had sent him to circle behind them to guard the door to the passageway that led back to the palace. First Sephora pulled out one of her daggers and held it to his neck.

"The rest of you show yourselves, or he dies," she called out to the darkened room.

Servus could not see an advantage in waiting, so he stepped forward from his hiding place and motioned for Justus, who was positioned to guard the door leading outside, to do the same.

"What?!" First said. "Only three of you! Third was right—this is no trap!"

Servus knew if they couldn't stop the sisters, they must at least delay them. If the men at the line couldn't stop them, the couples he had sent to guard Rachel would have to do the dirty work. He chose to banter.

"We did not expect such august visitors this evening. To what do we owe the honor?" Servus put his hands on his hips, holding his shield behind his back, and blocked passage down the main aisle.

"King of Beasts," First Sephora said, "I don't know whom you were expecting or what is going on, and I don't care. Get down on all fours and crawl out of our way."

"I can't do that," said Servus. "We had a visitation this night from the Great Father himself. He said for the men to pray and fast in the men's temple. Great Father said our salvation would come through the palace door and we have been waiting for someone to come. Here you are. You must have some message for us, even if you do not understand it yourself. Please give us this message and then we will let you pass."

Servus noted Kiertus imperceptibly brace himself to make a quick move for freedom. They practiced such maneuvers regularly. Servus would only be able to keep this ruse up for a second more, but the odds would be better if Kiertus could fight with them instead of being stilled by First's dagger.

"The message is this! Get out of our way at once or this animal dies!" First Sephora screamed as she began a movement to slash Kiertus with the blade she held.

Kiertus moved. He balanced on one leg and hooked her support leg with his free foot, causing them both to fall. If Kiertus had been fighting any of the men in Servus's secret army, it would have been the end of him, for they had learned to deliver death strokes while falling, but the last thing First Sephora expected was to have Kiertus fight back. The blade clattered to the floor as they went down. Kiertus broke free and took cover, for the other princesses had loaded their bows. First was shaking with rage as she grabbed her dagger and regained her feet.

"What is the meaning of this?" she screamed.

Servus answered calmly.

"Just as you have orders to leave, we are under orders to keep you here."

An arrow flew past his head.

"You fool!" said First. You will die here tonight. How can three unarmed men overcome three armed women? Why, anyone of us unarmed could overcome ten men. As the saying goes, 'One woman at rest is worth a hundred men at their best.' Get out of the way, and we will see you die quickly, all but Kiertus, who is mine to torture as I see fit. This is not a request; it is an order."

Servus felt his anger kindle. An angry Servus was a dangerous foe. The words, pent up too long, tumbled from him, the sound filling the empty barracks.

"You have no idea of the power of men. To you we are beasts, lackeys, and a means to beget children. But we have our own power—a power you will learn tonight. It is you who are at our mercy, foolish woman. You are vain with your own pride, swollen with the luxuries the palace provides. You have the fear of your mother to motivate you, but we have centuries of mistreatment and abuse fueling our desire to live. We do not sit idle, but constantly develop the strength unique to men. We are not the savage animals you assume us to be. We are a brotherhood. We are simple yet complex, and we have our own Code of Honor. Tonight, for reasons you will never know, we stand against you, and we will prevail. If you have a favorite goddess, you should pray to her. Tonight is the night you will need her."

The sisters had been firing arrows, but so far had not managed to hit their targets because two were moving in the shadows. Servus remained in the center aisle and blocked them with his shield.

"Stop firing, fools," said First to her sisters. She was a skilled tactician herself. "We will run out of arrows, and they will use them as weapons against us. Engage in hand-to-hand combat; it is the quickest way. Ladies, pick your slave. I myself will take Servus and teach him to mind his manners." First ran directly at Servus, Third claimed Kiertus, and Second Sephora targeted Justus by default.

"Be quick," First Sephora commanded, "and kill them. We must hurry on our way."

Servus barked out orders as First Sephora rushed toward him.

"Use all your skills to subdue them, but kill them rather than let them get away."

First Sephora let out a bloodcurdling cry and lunged at him with her dagger. Servus deflected the knife with his shield and dropped. First fell over him. That might have been the end of the fight, for Servus threw away his shield to pin her to the floor, but First was so enraged she squirmed wildly. She managed to turn on her side. She still held the dagger in her hand. She used it to hack at him.

Servus backed off quickly knowing her rage would make her moves unpredictable. He must stay calm to win. He must wear her down. He jumped to the opposite side of the cot on his left and flung the bedding and mattress of straw on her.

With no time to see how the others were doing, Servus jumped back into the aisle in front of First Sephora and watched for an opening to attack as she struggled with the bedding. First coughed, trying to clear her lungs of the hay and dust the bedding had stirred up. She flailed her arms. Servus saw that she had drawn her second knife, another dagger, and was wielding both blades in the circular motion the Evlantian warriors favored.

She didn't expect the kick that sent the knife in her left hand flying. His maneuvers were about timing. He had never been sure his tactical fighting would have any benefit for him in his lifetime, so he was pleased to see them work so well.

Clear of the bedding, First Sephora got to her feet and readied the dagger she still held in her right hand. She expected another kick, so she readied her left hand to deflect it and lunged at him in a killing rage. Servus quickly dodged right, throwing a punch that landed on her jaw. She was momentarily stunned, both by the pain and his unpredictable tactics. He used the opportunity to grab her wrist and twist. She dropped the second knife and howled. She threw a punch to his kidney. In spite of the pain, he did the last thing she expected. He moved toward her, not away, and caught both her arms in a bear hug.

Her struggle to free herself caused them both to fall backwards. Servus resisted the impulse to break free and right himself. Instead, he fell with her and knocked the wind out of her upon impact with the floor. This gave him the opportunity he had been looking for. He flung her face down and completed the pin he had attempted at the beginning of their conflict. This time he planted both of his knees on her back and wrenched her arms securely behind her back. She spit in fury and gasped for breath.

He looked up to see how his men were doing and found them watching as if enjoying a spectator sport. Second and Third Sephoras were trussed like pigs with vines the men had gathered from their hiding place earlier. Kiertus threw him a coiled vine, and Servus tied up First Sephora, who had regained her breath and was cursing him.

"Need some help, Servus?" said Kiertus, laughing.

Servus raised an eyebrow and replied, "There is plenty of fight left in this one. I could free her and let you take your chances."

Kiertus smirked. "You could free her, but it wouldn't be me she would try to kill."

First began to threaten them loudly. Servus gave her a warning.

"You are my prisoner. Making noise will not set you free. The only attention you will attract will be the attention of slaves. Do you wish to be known throughout herstory as the princesses who were taken captive by three unarmed slaves? What would Sephora do?"

This silenced First, but Servus was taking no chances.

"Besides which, if you do not shut your mouth and allow me and my men to decide what to do with you, I will do to you and your sisters what is done to slaves who speak out of turn."

"You wouldn't dare," First Sephora hissed.

Though trussed, it hadn't yet fully sunk in to First Sephora that they were at the mercy of the slaves. Servus held the dagger he had taken from her to her lips. She turned her head from him in silence.

"I have seen good men choke to death on their blood after having their tongue cut out for imagined insults," Servus said. "To keep you quiet I will begin with the less intrusive method of putting a horse's bit between your lips and binding it there with a cloth. I will do whatever I have to do to keep you from making noise."

This silenced First. Sephora's other daughters had kept silent, transfixed with fear, and remained so. Third would lose her throne if this incident became known. Second kept quiet for a reason known only to her. Second had put up little resistance in the fight. She had seemed reluctant to risk injury.

Servus examined his thigh. First had nicked him lightly during their fight, and he was bleeding. He was relieved to find it was a superficial wound. It was painful, but pain was something the slaves had learned to deal with at a young age. The women beat them regularly and then offered them poppies for the pain. It kept the men subdued, passive, and dependent on the women for their relief. Servus and his men belonged to a sect of men who chose other avenues of pain management. They applied mind over matter practices and used repetitive prayers to the Creator of the Great Father to manage pain. Servus knew that if he were to be useful tonight, he would need to stop the bleeding. First's robes were cleaner than any of the bedding, so he used the knife to slit a hole in the fabric, and then he tore the bottom of her cloak off to wrap his leg. Wisely, she did not object.

"What now?" Justus asked as Servus finished wrapping his leg.

"We wait," answered Servus. "I never expected to catch these three in our trap. We need to see what the events of the night bring before I make my next decision."

"The High Queen will soon miss us," First said quietly. "Your vigil will end in your death when she finds us."

"You lie as badly as you fight," said Servus, baiting her. "I think you were trying to leave the city. No one is supposed to leave tonight, on pain of death, for the safety of the city. The way I see it, you owe us your lives. The High Queen may even reward us."

First stayed silent rather than confirm that Sephora had sent them.

"Where are the other slaves?" Third asked timidly. She wanted to know if other slaves would see them in their humiliating positions. Servus smiled broadly, correctly guessing her concern.

"For now your reputation is safe. As I said before, they were sent to the common area to pray for Rachel's safe return. They won't return before first light."

First smiled craftily.

"Fine, free us and take us there, and we will lead them in prayer."

Servus stretched out on the cot adjacent to where First was lying trussed on the floor.

"I think not, First Sephora. I think the six of us will do our praying right here while I decide what to do with you."

She hissed at him, and he could see she was furiously working to free herself. He would have to stay alert to make sure that didn't happen.

"Keep sharp, men, it is going to be a much longer night than we anticipated," Servus said.

ISOLATION

Deep in the forest, Rachel sat on her perch in the tree, staring blindly in the direction of the city. It was past sundown, and there was no sign anyone was coming for her and the strange young women she planned to pass off as Rebekkah. She estimated Hannah should have returned to the city at least an hour ago. If help had been sent, it would have arrived by now.

Something terrible could have happened to Hannah in the forest. Rachel regretted sending her back alone. It occurred to Rachel that "something terrible" could have been Sephora. Rachel marveled at the depth of the hatred Sephora nursed toward her. Sephora must have engineered a way to leave them in the forest overnight and perhaps forever.

Rachel hurried down out of the tree. In order to survive the night, she must build a fire and prepare to protect herself and the stranger against any danger, four legged or two, that came their way.

The fallen tree trunk she had found the stranger under made a perfect cover. It was a natural lean-to. She cleared out some brush and rocks to make space for herself, and then she placed fallen branches along the back for extra protection. The fire burned between them and the forest, a barrier to keep wild things away.

Rachel knew they had a good chance of surviving until morning. Her daughter had told her many stories of how she survived in the forest for long periods. Rebekkah had made it sound easy.

The certainty of Rebekkah's death finally sunk in. After the election passed without Rebekkah returning, Rachel had known in her deepest heart that her daughter was gone forever. She could not save Rebekkah, but she might be able to save her city.

Rachel noticed the stranger's eyes were open, so she gave her more wine and water. She left the stranger's wounds as they were. There was no sense checking them until morning. She could not see well enough to avoid causing the stranger unnecessary pain. She had promised the girl a peaceful death, and she would keep her promise. The stranger stared at the fire with a hint of a smile on her face. Rachel checked her vital signs and was surprised at their strength. But then, she had seen many mortally ill women seem to recover almost completely before their death, as if to take care of unfinished business and bid farewell to their kin before passing. Perhaps their Pact of Honor gave this stranger reason to hang on to life. Rachel was cheered at the thought.

For reasons she could not totally understand, she began to talk to the stranger about Rebekkah. She didn't care if the stranger listened or not. She needed a way to pass the time. She poured out her most precious memories as the hours wore on.

The inner sanctum of the largest temple in the heart of the Religion Sector was a vast square chamber with a high ceiling. Icons adorned the walls, and alcoves harbored statues in various positions of repose. There were goddesses for every imaginable illness, pain, and desire. The popularity of each goddess waned and waxed in accord with the needs of the people. In times of famine, the goddess of the harvest was called on most often. In times of plenty, the goddess of pleasure was the most popular. But the popularity of the goddess portrayed by a giant sculpture in the inner sanctum never waned. Ephrea was the goddess of life—the goddess of fertility. The most common portrayal of her showed her cradling a very pregnant Great Mother in her arms.

Sephora entered the inner sanctum of the temple with Arrival and knelt to pray. She joined the mysterious three women in black shawls and black hoods who had arrived before her. The acolytes were startled to see the High Queen. They went about their duties in the temple as best they could, but they were clearly distracted by the presence of the High Queen and the three dressed in black that they assumed must be Sephora's daughters.

Sephora chose to kneel before the fertility goddess. She had been here before, of course, but only when custom required her presence. She peered out from behind her hands at an icon on the wall of Great Mother giving birth to her twin sons. Both myth and religion were unclear about how the earth was populated. Sephora pondered these things as she bent in an attitude of prayer, making sure she looked pious enough. That was the problem with religion. It left too much unexplained. Why all the mystery on the part of the goddesses? She could not understand why a whole Sector of the city was devoted to such imaginative practices. As High Queen, she now had access to the forbidden room of the great library, but she doubted she would learn anything of importance in the boring scrolls of ancient herstory. The acolytes bustled about, disturbing Sephora's thoughts as the High Priestess entered.

"Thank you, girls, you are dismissed," Caliphus said to the acolytes. "I will attend to the needs of the High Queen and pray with her myself. The High Queen has called the women of the town to fast and pray. You will be busy tonight keeping order in the temples and teaching those who do not come here frequently the ways of supplication to the goddesses. No one is to disturb us until an hour before first light. That is when we will begin preparations to see if our valiant effort at prayer led by Queen Sephora to spare the life of our former leader Rachel has been met with favor by the goddesses. Is that clear?"

The senior acolyte among them nodded her head and spoke.

"It is clear, High Priestess. We will obey you as if you were Great Mother herself." They filed out silently.

Sephora waited until the door was closed behind them before moving from her spot. She greeted Caliphus as a friend.

"You have exceeded my expectations, High Priestess and Low Queen of the Religion Sector. I am well pleased. Now, I say this with no disrespect to the goddesses, but I am tired of praying. I have no doubt what the morning will bring. Come, Arrival, come girls, and you yourself High Priestess, join me in a merry hand of cards. Though I must warn you, I am as good at games as I am at ruling our city."

The High Priestess willed her features not to show the shock she felt at games of chance being played in the inner sanctum.

"I must beg you to allow me to pray in your stead, good Queen," Caliphus answered. "As High Priestess, I have little time for cards, and I am afraid you would find my playing boring and predictable."

Sephora's laughter rang out.

"Well said, Priestess. You may pray. But the girls and I will gamble. Arrival, I insist you join us. I would like to win back some of the money the city pays for your salary. I need new shoes to go with my Harvest Festival dresses. There is nothing your mother left behind that suits the office of High Queen. Come now, you four join me."

The High Priestess again calmed every nerve in her body not to show the jolt she felt when the three, whom she presumed to be Sephora's daughters dressed in black head to foot, their faces hidden by hoods, flung off their outer dressings. They were not the Three Sephoras, but were Salla, Meerta, and Tyvaal, Captains in Sephora's secret police force. The Priestess quickly took Sephora's place in front of the statue to hide the growing alarm she felt and to pray in earnest for the state of the city. Both her feet and hands tapped out a rhythm to the desperate pleas she made to the goddesses.

Arrival would have preferred to join the High Priestess. Now that Arrival was idle, she realized what a huge chance she had taken by putting her trust in Servus. Arrival played card games badly and lost often, though she was certain at times that it was because Sephora was cheating. Arrival did not care about losing at cards. She was afraid of losing her mother, and especially of being burdened with the unfulfilled grave-secret of her sister for the rest of her life.

Rachel tended the fire, feeling weary. A deep sadness had fallen on her. She felt as though any movement she produced was directed from far away, and her limbs seemed weighted down. Her body resisted the impulses of her mind.

She had used a small travel ax from the pack to cut forearm-sized pieces of wood from several fallen tree branches that she found on the forest floor. The stranger appeared to be sleeping again. Rachel envied the peace that was bestowed on her, and the peace beyond which waited for her. Rachel had to carry on against all odds without the one dearest to her in the world.

The fire gave off a crackling brilliance. She had laid up many good size logs to use as the night wore on, but not enough to last until morning. She knew that in order to stay awake, she would need the exercise that chopping wood gave her, so she purposely did not cut as many as she was able. She sat down to rest feeling melancholy and alone.

Rachel listened to the sounds of the forest. Wolves howled in the distance—a chilling sound. Things rustled in the underbrush around them, and every now and then an owl hooted. When the wind blew, there was a shushing sound. The forest looked livelier during the day, but at night, it sounded much more alive. By day,

Rachel had found solitude in the woods. By night, there was no peace, only wariness and a constant, desperate assessment of the sounds.

Rachel reclined, looking at the fire and tracking the progress of wolves by their calls. Thus mesmerized, a cloud of depression dulled her senses. Her eyes slipped lower until, against every intention she had, she slept deeply.

In the temple, Sephora grew bored.

"I am tired of playing cards. Give me your cloaks so that I can sleep comfortably." The High Queen made a makeshift bed on the floor. Salla, Meerta, and Tyvaal lay down near her, fawning over her and tending to her comfort.

Arrival knelt next to Caliphus and prayed. Like Rachel, Arrival believed women shaped their own destinies, and if there were goddesses, they mainly stayed aloof from the troubles of womankind. But to cover all possibilities, Arrival prayed in earnest. She prayed for the safety of Rachel and Rebekkah, and she prayed for the goddesses to grant Servus wisdom to carry out his part of their Pact. She prayed for the goddesses to deliver her from the unholy attraction she realized she felt for Servus. At times, Arrival dozed while kneeling. She accepted sleep when it came so that she would be rested and ready for whatever the morning would bring.

The night was brightly lit by an almost-full moon. In the forest, the two couples assigned by Servus to protect Rachel and Rebekkah traveled slowly. Yarr was in his forties. He and Calena had met in the Quickening Chamber when she was just fourteen. They had fallen deeply in love. Most of the forbidden attractions begun in the Quickening Chamber did not stand the test of time, but Calena and Yarr had seen all the difficulties through, and had continued their love affair secretly for over twenty years. Their only child together, a daughter, was now a woman with a daughter of her own. She lived her life oblivious of her mother's sick obsession with her father. Calena and Yarr were afraid of the consequences to their daughter and granddaughter if they were discovered, especially with Sephora ruling as High Queen. It would be a blessing to their children if the couple's disappearance would be put down to a demon-ghost instead of the fact that they loved each other and had run away.

The other couple was in their teens, and had recently fallen in love. Titus was young, hot-tempered, and idealistic. Raysa had no family to speak of, and was little better than a slave herself. They had met in the palace dungeon where she served, and where he was being disciplined. They met secretly to talk for hours, declaring themselves soul mates, but had never been together intimately. This was the only chance they would ever have for both freedom and love.

Calena was a trained scout from the Livestock Sector. She spent a great deal of time cross training in the Soldier Sector to hone her tracking skills. She had packed provisions to last on their journey and provided them with arms. She and Titus led the way. He kept the path clear while she followed the marks on the tree and Hannah's tracks. Raysa followed with Yarr. They kept the other two within their sight, but surveyed the path behind them, covering tracks they left behind as best they could, and watched for predators, both animal and huwoman.

Calena motioned for her group to stop.

"I think we have finally found them! I see a low burning fire ahead."

"Do you see Rachel or Rebekkah?" asked Raysa.

"No, I do not see any sign of huwoman life," Calena answered. "I am going on alone from here. I will be in touch."

Calena listened for a minute, and then she held a finger up that she had licked to determine the direction of the wind. She walked eastward away from the camp. Yarr lost sight of her quickly as she effortlessly blended into the trees.

"What did she mean she will keep in touch?" asked Titus.

"The two of you," Yarr smiled and waved a hand at Titus and Raysa who stood arm-in-arm, "have had it much easier than the rest of us! While you were having private meetings in the dungeon, the rest of us criminals had to sneak around and develop other ways to communicate. It won't be long until you have the answer to the question you just asked me."

"Look!" Raysa said, and pointed at the camp. They had moved closer in order to see more clearly.

They watched Calena feed wood into the fire with stealth they never dreamed possible. Calena straightened for a minute, and then she merged with the shadows at the tree line of the small clearing. Yarr thought he saw her climb a tree, but he couldn't be sure. Finally, Yarr heard the noises he had been waiting for. There was an owl hoot, followed by the sound of a howling wolf.

"That was Calena. She told me there are wolves stalking the camp."

Yarr made a hollow chamber with his hands and then pressed his thumbs to his lips and blew puffs of air into them. The sounds that resulted mimicked a pigeon's call.

"I've asked her how many," Yarr explained. "Hurry, we must join her to protect Rachel and Rebekkah."

The group heard an answering call.

"She thinks there are eight in this pack. Let's move."

A wren trilled.

"That means hurry," said Yarr. "Draw your bows and be ready."

Raysa and Titus looked at each other, afraid. There was no mistaking the urgency and fear in Yarr's voice. They hurried.

Ava was wide-awake. She had been listening to the wolves move closer for a while. She planned to stay where she was and kill them with Rachel's weapons as they came into range. She did not feel confident of staying on her feet, though she was feeling better now. The chills had all but subsided. Her head was clear enough to realize the healing process had stopped when she left the ravine and the stream from which she drank fresh water. Now, with the wine and water Rachel provided, healing had resumed.

Ava had seen Calena approach, and she had watched as she stoked the fire, climbed the tree, and spoke in code. The answering sounds, out of place in the still of the night, let her know the woman was not alone. Ava waited to see what would happen next to determine if the people who had come were Rachel's friends or enemies.

The woman in the tree took aim and shot a small spear using a crude propelling device. The spear was much smaller than the one she had seen Rebekkah use to kill the beast. She heard a wolf yelp in pain. It should have scared the pack off, but it did not. *The animals must be very hungry to take on humans*, Ava thought. She wondered if she could stand on her feet long enough to be of assistance. She inched away from Rachel and slowly rose to her full height. She was dizzy and weak, but she was able to take a few steps forward. She directed her full attention to the newcomers, who were killing the wolves.

"That's number eight," said a man's voice softly. Ava could hear them congratulating each other. They thought they were safe. They must not be aware there were nine. She picked up a knife from beside Rachel and slowly made her way forward.

"What do we do now? Did you find out if Rachel is alive?" asked Raysa.

Calena did not answer because suddenly a woman appeared before them, seemingly out of nowhere. Calena had not heard her approach. None of the four had ever seen Rebekkah close up, but when the ninth wolf lunged at Raysa, and the woman knocked the girl out of the way and hurled a concealed knife directly into its heart to kill it, none of them doubted it was Rebekkah who stood before them. They fell to their knees before her. Calena knew Rebekkah was a bigger threat to them than the wolves.

"Rebekkah, daughter of Rachel, Low Queen and Commander of the Soldier Sector, we greet you in gladness," said Calena. "We were sent to find and protect Rachel until first light. Is she with you?"

"Yes, my mother sleeps beside the fire," Ava answered.

Ava said nothing during the short silence. She would take her cue from whatever this woman told her next. She had a Pact to fulfill. She sensed their fear of her, and it puzzled her. She attributed it to the high station of Rebekkah, whose place she was taking. Ava began to understand that on this side of Eden, some people were held in higher esteem than others were. It made her sad, and she looked grim. Calena had been studying Ava's face from her position on the ground. Calena misinterpreted the look and spoke before the princess standing before them could pass judgment on them.

"My lady, I am Calena, daughter of Nuen, of the Livestock Sector. I beg you for mercy. I confess to the unnatural crime of loving the slave Yarr. You have saved Raysa's life, she who loves Titus. Before you came to our aid, we killed eight of your four legged enemies. Two legged ones may be on their way as we speak.

"Let me tell you how things stand in the city. Hannah came back without Rachel and Sephora had the High Priestess close the city gates using the ancient proscription of demon barring. We were told Sephora had sent someone to kill Rachel. We were told to find Rachel and guard her with our lives. If first light comes and Rachel is unharmed, we are free to travel on and leave the city and its ways behind us. I have loved Yarr for twenty years. Our families will be told we were victims of the demon-ghosts so they won't try to follow us. We would rather die together than live without each other. If you must kill us, be merciful and kill us quickly, please. Don't let our families be shamed, I beg you."

There were mysteries here that Ava did not understand. She could not imagine what slaves were, or why love between man and woman was a crime. If she asked them, they would suspect she was not Rebekkah. She needed time to figure this out. She was getting tired. She needed more healing sleep. If she let these matters go, these people would keep Rachel and herself safe. They could sleep all night in peace.

"You have begged for mercy. I grant it to you. A bargain made honestly must be kept," she said. "You were sent to guard us, so do so, and disappear at first light. I give you my blessing, and I thank you for your protection. It is welcome."

She turned away from them as they profusely, but quietly, thanked her. She thought of something and turned back. She felt a lump rise in her throat. The women and men were on their feet, embracing each other with tears of joy glistening in their eyes.

"Tell me one thing," Ava said. "Who sent you to guard Rachel?"

The four looked at each other uneasily. Ava thought she might understand why.

"I give you my word this person will come to no harm," Ava reassured them.

"We do not want his blood on our consciences," Raysa said.

The others glared at her. While dozens of women might have sent them, there was only one man who had the power to give orders to slaves.

The forest around Ava was spinning slowly. Ava wanted nothing more than to lie down, but she and her brothers and sisters had spent days engaging in elaborate strategy games, and she felt this to be a key piece of information for survival in this land. Ava tried a desperate strategy to get the name.

"Of course there is only one man who could have sent you," said Ava. "I want to have you speak his name to me. By sending you, he has saved the life of my mother and me. I am in his debt.

I will find a way to reward him. I give you my solemn oath that no harm will come to him."

Ava knew she would not be able to remain on her feet much longer. She felt horrible. She hoped she sounded more confident than she felt. Calena feared, from the look on Rebekkah's face and the stance she had taken, that Rebekkah was about to change her mind about letting them live.

"It was Servus, King of Slaves!" Calena said, cursing herself inwardly, but she had not received the promise of freedom to live with her true love only to lose it again. "Who gave him the authority to act, we do not know."

Rebekkah's reaction surprised her.

"Servus, of course," said Ava with a smile. She was relieved she could at last return to Rachel and lie down. "Thank you for the courage you showed when you spoke his name. I will sleep now. Guard us until first light as you have promised to do, and I will say nothing of your presence here, not even to my mother."

Ava summoned the strength to return to her makeshift bed. She fell deeply to sleep as soon as her head touched her pillow of leaves. She did not hear Calena give orders to defend the perimeter of the camp.

There was also a task Calena gave to Yarr. The slaves had developed covert communication systems using many different mediums. They used hand signals, beats tapped out, and animal noises. For long distances in darkness, they used light. She sent him to climb a tree with a torch to deliver a pre-arranged signal to a slave sentry waiting in another tree near the city.

A runner burst into the slave barracks from the main entrance. "Servus! Servus! I bring news!"

Servus sat upright quickly, and then stood erect in spite of his wound. Servus did not want him to enter far enough to see the princesses bound on the floor. He commanded the man to stop by holding up one hand. The man stopped in his tracks. Servus's men were as well trained as the women's army.

"Has there been a vision during prayer?" he asked the messenger.

The mood in the barracks was tense. He and his men had to constantly check the knots on the vines and make adjustments. The messenger realized Servus, Kiertus, and Justus were not alone, though he saw no prisoners. The messenger understood the cue Servus had given.

"Yes," said the man, "there has been a mighty vision during prayer. The goddess has shown us Rachel and Rebekkah alive. There are friendly spirits guarding them—spirits who will leave at first light."

Servus let out a sigh of relief. Arrival would keep her word. Rebekkah alive was an unexpected development. In spite of Arrival's confidence, he had not believed Rebekkah would be found alive. He wondered if Rachel and Rebekkah would support the actions Arrival had taken tonight.

"Thank you for coming to tell me of this vision," Servus said to the messenger. "Go and tell the men to sing songs of thanksgiving to the goddesses until an hour before first light; then they may return to the barracks to get an hour of rest before going about their duties."

"Yes, Servus."

The man exited quickly.

Servus surveyed his prisoners. This news meant he would have to detain them for as long as he could, but how? First and Third looked furious, and had resumed struggling against their bonds. Second had begun to cry silently. It was Kiertus who came up with a solution.

"King Servus, may I make a suggestion?"

"Speak freely."

"It is in our best interests to keep the princesses indefinitely, yet we have limited resources for doing so. There is a place we would have access to tonight, though, a place where the Three Sephoras would be well out of the way, and three more men could go and find freedom. The answer requires deep thought."

Justus understood instantly and laughed aloud. It took Servus a minute more. When he understood what Kiertus meant, Servus grinned.

"Kiertus, you are brilliant," he said. "Justus, go and get a cart for us to pull. We are taking the princesses for a ride."

It took them over an hour to pull the princesses to the place Kiertus had referred to. They had to keep stopping to make sure the women were not untying each other's bonds. In addition to being trussed, the three were now blindfolded and gagged, though Servus had used more cloth torn from First Sephora's cloak and not the horses' bits as he had threatened earlier.

The men unloaded the princesses at their destination and untied the cloth from their eyes. Their mouths were left gagged. It took the women a minute to get oriented to their surroundings. First and Third began cursing, while Second resumed her quiet weeping.

Along the road, which led outside the city between the soldiers' training grounds and the pastures for the city's herds of animals, there were pits dug into the ground. These pits descended twenty feet or more into the earth. They were six feet long by four feet wide. There was a slab of slate beside each pit upon which was written symbols denoting the occupant of that pit and his crime.

The pits were the form of punishment the slaves hated most. Slaves found guilty of crimes were sentenced to time in these holes. They were given limited food and water, barely enough to last until their sentence was up. Sometimes the pits were covered day and night so the prisoners were deprived of light and a sense of time. Servus had been sentenced twice, both for one-week terms. He didn't mind going hungry, but he didn't like the lack of company, the confined space, and the constant chill of the damp under-ground. It was like being imprisoned in a coffin.

The pits were a controversial form of punishment. Many women thought the punishment too brutal and extreme. They argued that a beating or even death was preferable to the torture of the pit; no animal deserved such a fate. They argued that other beasts, such as goats, dogs, or sheep, were never punished in the pits, so why were the slaves? The pits were usually watched from towers to ensure no one tried to sneak extra food to those being punished, but tonight the soldiers who guarded the pits had been reassigned to guard the perimeter from demon-ghosts, thanks to Sephora's edict.

No one used the punishment of the pits more often than Sephora and the women of the Arts Sector. Servus did not think these pampered beauties would do well in the place they loved to send the slaves, but no one would think to look for them there. As Kiertus pointed out, three more men could go free tonight.

"Justus, who occupies these three pits now?" asked Servus for the benefit of the women. "What Sector sentenced them here?" Servus knew full well who was here, and why. Justus played the game.

"There's Caaros, in for the crime of disobedience, sentenced in the Arts Sector. There is Leged in for the crime of spending time with the boy known to be his son, sentenced in the Arts Sector. And then, let me think a little...yes, I believe Satrun is in for the crime of displeasing a princess in the Quickening Chamber, sentenced in the Arts Sector."

The slaves glared at First Sephora, who glared back. Satrun was a merry soul. He had a quick wit, was very handsome, and had a gentle way about him that made him popular in the Quickening Chamber. He never seemed to resent his slavery or his duty, but took life as it came. He was easy going, and got along well with the women and men alike. He had a fine sense of humor, and was always laughing and making others laugh. The oldest Princess had him imprisoned after spending one night with him in a Quickening Chamber. He waited two and a half months in the Arts Sector prison for a trial, at which he was sentenced to a month in a pit. No one could imagine what he could have done to deserve such a fate, but Sephora was High Queen by the time of Satrun's trial, and no one dared question the punishment.

Many women were displeased at the loss of Satrun. They gossiped constantly about what First could have asked Satrun to do that he couldn't satisfy. Satrun would not talk about what happened, not even at his sentencing. Slaves were never allowed to speak in their own defense. They were allowed to speak for one minute before being handed their sentence. Often they said their good-byes to their comrades. To everyone's surprise and dismay, Satrun had let his minute go by in angry silence.

Servus nodded to Kiertus, who moved the wooden cover off the top of the pit Satrun had been put in.

"Hey, down there, Satrun, how are you?" Servus called into the pit.

"Servus, is that you? Is my time up already?" The voice of Satrun rose from the earth.

"You've earned time for good behavior, and the ladies miss you, so come out!"

Each stone slab anchored a rope ladder. Kiertus flung the ladder down into the pit.

"Sorry we didn't bring any light but that of the moon; you'll have to feel around for the ladder."

"It might take me a while to find it in my spacious abode, but I'll find a way to make it up." Satrun joked and made good his words. He soon appeared, unkempt, smelling rank, but in his usual fine spirits. Each man embraced him, happy to see him. The other two pits were twenty and forty yards away, respectively. Servus sent Kiertus and Justus to free the other two men.

Satrun looked around, bemused.

"What is this? What is going on? Why are you here in the middle of the night?"

"This is a momentous night, my friend," replied Servus. "The High Queen invoked the ancient order of demon barring and closed the city gates to make sure nothing got in. We were called upon to make sure nothing got out. Look what we caught trying to leave the city." Servus made a flourishing gesture to the ground where the princesses lay. Satrun gasped. Servus continued.

"The boys and I were looking for a place to keep our catch safe, so we thought we might borrow a few of these pits and put real criminals in them for a change."

"Servus," said Satrun, his tone turning unusually serious, "Sephora will kill you if you put the princesses down there."

"Friend," Servus said, "we were guaranteed a death sentence the minute we attacked the Three Sephoras. No one will think to look in the pits, so it buys us time. I plan to complete preparations to wage war for our freedom. If I fail, I will have the benefit of dying knowing that I set three good men free in the process."

"Free?" asked Satrun, stunned. It hadn't occurred to him that he would have to make a run for it. "Servus, I don't think I'm right for living a solitary life in the wild. Put me back in the pit and let me serve my sentence so that I can go back to my life. I never minded slavery the way you do. This is the way things have always been. Your idea that men should be on an equal level with women is controversial. Everyone knows women are smarter. They get the better of us every time. The balance of power will always be in favor of the women."

"Satrun, you are wrong. Men and women were meant to live in equality. We are the same race, just different sexes. You will not be alone. Four others were released from the city tonight; you can travel with them."

Satrun did not look convinced. He remained quiet, lost in his thoughts. It was a rare moment for a man who took nothing, not even the pits, seriously. Servus was discouraged that Satrun asked to remain enslaved.

In the distance, Justus returned from the farthest pit alone. Caaros must be dead. Leged appeared at the opening of the middle pit, and Kiertus helped him to ground level. They walked quickly toward their King, his prisoners, and Satrun.

When Leged reached them, Servus gave instructions to Leged and Satrun, neither of whom seemed very eager for freedom.

"Follow the markers left by Rachel's girl, Hannah. Four preceded you." He did not give the names since the princesses could hear them. "If you don't find the four by first light, you'll have to track them until you catch up with them. With six of you there will be an even better chance of survival." Leged was shaking his head in disagreement.

"What now?" Servus asked.

"I will not leave without my son," Leged answered.

Servus realized he should have anticipated Leged's reaction. When Leged was finally discovered missing, his son would be held and tortured as incentive for him to return. The boy would be killed if Leged did not show up.

Most of the men were not lucky enough to know which of the boys who were chosen to live and brought to the nursery were theirs. Leged, in his quickening duties, had been favored by one of the Royals. She had carried his male child to full term, and she was the only woman to deliver a boy at the end of the month of Octo. That particular year, all male children were allowed to live to replace aging slaves. Only one boy, who was brought to the nursery after the three-month weaning period during the month of Un, could be the son Leged had fathered with the Royal woman. Leged had been as father and mother to the child since the day the boy was brought to the nursery. Their bond rivaled the famous bond between mother and daughter that the women fostered.

Servus often wondered if he had fathered any of the young men he worked alongside of every day. A few resembled him in features, personality, and mindset, but no one could ever know for sure unless, as in Leged's case, the mother was well known and the birth was a well-published singular event. What bothered Servus even more was wondering how many of his sons had been thrown into the Swamp of Lost Innocents to die. But he had learned not to dwell on these matters for long. Many slaves had brooded themselves into a tortuous dance with a mood so black that they became useless, and were put to death by the women they served. Servus turned his thoughts to the matter at hand.

"Leged, the boys are being held hostage tonight, but even if I had the power to let your son go free, it would end badly. If your boy is discovered missing this morning, the soldiers will immediately go to pull you from the pit to hold you as a hostage and torture you against his return. When you are not found, they might check the other pits as well and find the princesses. It will lead to immediate and widespread torture and slaughter of all slaves, boys, and men. In a few days' time, I will have the men ready for war. Wouldn't it be better for the men to die fighting than at the hands of Sephora's torture squads? If we win, then your son will be able to live his whole life in freedom."

Leged had not thought this through. His face fell, for he wished to fight with the men so his son could live in freedom.

"I must go back into the pit. It is the only way. I can't leave without my son, and I can't take him with me. If things don't go as you plan and I am found missing at the end of my sentence, they will torture and kill him. It's a chance I can't take." Leged gripped Servus's arm. "You must win this war, Servus, so both my son and I can live in freedom. My only regret is that I can't fight beside you."

Servus sighed. "Leged, truly, in your place I would do the same. Go back into the earth with my blessing."

Leged turned to Kiertus. "Walk with me, Kiertus, and help me back into my pit. If I never come out again, tell my son how much I love him." The men were solemn as Kiertus and Leged walked away from them.

Servus was more than a little discouraged. He had hoped to be able to give three more men their freedom this night. He turned to Satrun and asked, "Do you refuse to give up your freedom too? And if so, will you share your pit with the princesses?"

Though Servus was cruel when he had to be, he could not put the women in the pit with the body of Caaros. Leged's sentence was up sooner than Satrun's, who had two weeks to go. Servus thought he could begin the war to end slavery within a week's time, but felt better knowing he had two weeks before the princesses would be found.

Satrun gave his answer.

"Servus, I am not cut out for life on the run. I will endure the hardships I know rather than face those I do not. Sharing my pit with three princesses won't be too bad. I promise to be a most gracious host."

Servus shook his head in resignation and turned his attention to the princesses.

"I can't think of a better place for you to spend your time than where you are going now. Before you are lowered into the pits, we will extend to you the same courtesy you extend to us, for I wish to treat you as my equal. You deserve the same consideration given the slaves and not one iota more." He had the full attention of the princesses now. He smiled at them. His grin was not pleasant. "You may each have exactly one minute to speak. Satrun, you count out the seconds silently and call out when the minute has passed. Justus, take off this woman's gag so that she may speak."

Servus walked to where First Sephora lay and nudged her with his foot. She struggled ineptly to lash back at him. She tried to bite Justus as he removed her gag. She spent her minute spewing a stream of curses and threats at the men who were her captors. After Satrun called out the time when her minute was up, it took both Satrun and Justus to hold her down to replace the gag in her mouth. Servus paid no more attention to her.

"Now this one," Servus said as he walked to Third Sephora who happened to lay closest to First. She lay very still as Justus untied her gag. She spoke calmly.

"Gentlemen, I too believe men should live in freedom. I support your cause. As Low Queen of the Arts Sector, I can and will give you immunity from all the crimes you have committed against the High Throne tonight; just let us go now. Even better, put First Sephora and Second Sephora in the pit. They are not trustworthy. Return me to my throne and I will keep your secret. You can go with me to my Palace and live in luxury for the rest of your lives. I will give you anything you desire, and together we will work tirelessly to end slavery."

At the signal Satrun gave, Servus held up his hand for her to stop speaking. He chose to address her, though he had not spoken to First.

"Your words are good to hear, Third Sephora. It is wonderful to know we have an ally in one of the Low Queens. As King of Slaves, I accept your offer of friendship with the following condition: You must suffer as the men have suffered. Once your term in the pit is over, I look forward to a long and productive alliance with you."

He bowed to her. She cursed him as the gag was replaced and the men laughed.

Second Sephora was last. Justus removed her gag and she surprised them all.

"Please," she begged, "do not throw me into the pit with the others. All these years I was thought to be barren, but the truth is that I am pregnant with Satrun's child! I want to be a mother to this child, whether it is a girl or a boy. Nothing else matters to me. I am little more than a slave to my mother and sisters, anyway. I beg you to let me take the freedom you offered Satrun. Or, if he will go free for the sake of his child, I will accompany him and be his slave for as long as he allows me to live. I will forsake my homeland and my family. At least allow me to live until the child is born, and then, if Satrun wishes, he may kill me. My child has little chance in the pit. Should the babe survive the pit, my mother and sisters will never let me keep it. Let me go, only so my child may live."

Satrun was so shocked he lost count of the seconds. He stood with his mouth open.

"What kind of trick is this?" said Servus. "Everyone knows Satrun was with First Sephora, not you. How could you be carrying Satrun's child?"

Satrun walked to where Second Sephora lay. He smoothed the hair from her face, cupped her head gently in his hands, and moved her head from side to side studying it in the moonlight. He then pulled up her cloak and gown up to her ribs and revealed a gently swollen belly. She did not resist. He covered her again and looked grave. Somehow, First's gag had come loose and she screamed.

"Do not say another word, you delusional fool. You would betray us just to avoid the pit. Do not listen to her. Every word she speaks is a lie."

Satrun looked up at Servus.

"I am sure this is the princess I met in the Quickening Chamber. Which one do you say is First Sephora?"

Servus stepped to where First Sephora lay and couldn't resist kicking her slightly as he answered.

"This pile of dung."

Satrun walked over and knelt by First. He tried to examine her features, but First began to thrash wildly. Kiertus had returned, so Servus, Justus, and Kiertus held First Sephora still while Satrun examined her features. Even so, she spat at him all the while.

"Servus," Satrun said, "upon the life of my unknown father I swear I was with this woman." He walked back to where Second

Sephora lay and pointed to her. "Her belly was flat, concave almost. Now it is swollen. You say this is not First Sephora?"

Servus frowned.

"No, this one here is First Sephora. I have met her in hand-to-hand combat many times. But what purpose was served by the switch?"

"I can tell you," said Second Sephora, but First Sephora began to scream to prevent her sister from being heard. Servus had had enough of all three princesses.

"Enough of this. Silence First Sephora and put them all in the pit," he ordered.

Second Sephora began to cry. She knew what she had to do to avoid the pit and to save the life of the unborn child within her. She swallowed her pride and pleaded.

"Please, Uncle Servus, I beg you for mercy. You have a blood tie with the baby I carry, since I am your niece. Please!"

The men had been preparing the ropes to lower the princesses, one by one, into the pit. All activity stopped as they gaped in astonishment.

"Are you related to this princess, Servus?" asked Justus.

"Whether she speaks truly or not, I cannot say, but at the audience Sephora called me to when she became High Queen, Sephora Prime asked First to read the name of my mother from the Genealogy of the Slaves. First seemed genuinely surprised to read Sepheera of the Arts as the name recorded there."

"It is the truth. Servus is my mother's brother. He is related to all three of us. Please, Uncle Servus, I would rather live as the slave of a slave and as an outcast than be a princess in this royal family of vipers one minute more."

Satrun, who had looked troubled since the announcement, suddenly looked like a man of resolve. He stood up straight and addressed his King.

"Servus, if it is not too late, I would like to accept your generous offer of freedom. I petition you to allow me to take Second Sephora and my unborn child with me."

Servus stared at him in disbelief.

"Are you mad? This is one of Sephora's daughters. You would be hunted for the rest of your life. A swollen belly is not proof of pregnancy."

Satrun again looked doubtful. Second Sephora, still crying, saw she was losing support. She gave out the last bit of information she had, desperate to save the life of her child.

"The third night of the sacrifice—the night after which Rebekkah was presumed dead—my mother left the city. First looks most like her and often takes her place dressed in veils. This way, my mother comes and goes as she pleases; the restrictions of duty do not apply to her. Since First Sephora was providing mother with an alibi, First could not be at the Quickening Chamber as the schedule demanded. I was chosen to go in her place. I had never conceived before and had stopped going to the Quickening Chamber, so it was thought there would be no complications as a result of that night.

"After the night had passed, Satrun was not sent back to the slave quarters because mother worried he might realize he had been with me and not First Sephora. We brought false charges against him. I am sorry for the part I played in punishing an innocent man. I am ashamed because that night was special. Never before had I been with a man so thoughtful and caring. Satrun was gentle and kind. He touched my heart. In return, I betrayed him. I do not deserve to go free. In truth, I deserve the pit. I do not ask for freedom for myself, but only for the sake of Satrun's child. Please Uncle, let me go so I may give birth to your niece or nephew. Satrun, please forgive me long enough to allow me to bear your child; then, if I have not served you to your liking, dispose of me as you wish, but let our child live!"

Servus could never say if it was the show of respect or the power of the ancient word uncle, but he was moved. He still did not trust her, though. This would have to be Satrun's decision.

"Satrun," said Servus, "I again urge you to escape; take freedom for yourself. You may also take this woman who claims to be pregnant with your child if you promise to keep her from doing damage to our cause. Do you take responsibility for this woman, and if she speaks truly, your child?"

Satrun looked stunned. He was the first slave in their knowledge to be entrusted with the care of a woman and child. Satrun made his mind up.

"King Servus," he said, "I will take the freedom you offer me. I will take this woman with me. I take full responsibility for her."

"Go, then, with my blessing, and live in peace and freedom. Raise my great niece or nephew well."

"Thank you, brother. May we meet again in the land of our unnamed Father," Satrun replied.

Satrun untied his woman. She clung to him weeping in gratitude and covering him with kisses. The display shocked them all. Servus needed to give instructions to the couple. He moved them away from Third Sephora and spoke quietly so she could not hear him. First had already been lowered into the pit by Kiertus and Justus.

"You will need to stay out of sight of the soldiers on the wall. There are slaves guarding the perimeter beyond the soldiers' sight. The password you will need to pass our line is 'beast's throat.' Tell them it is safe to come back in, but they must do so carefully so they are not seen by the soldiers on the wall."

"There are slaves guarding the perimeter?" Satrun was astonished.

"There is no time to explain. You need to catch up with Yarr, Calena, Titus, and Raysa. They will tell you the whole story. Go now."

Satrun took Second Sephora's hand in his and they hurriedly made their way toward the tree line in the distance. Servus stood and watched them until they disappeared from sight. When he turned back, he found Justus and Kiertus had completed the task of lowering Third Sephora into the pit. They replaced the cover and eradicated the signs of their presence there.

"Come, men," said Servus, "we must get everyone safely back in the barracks before the demon barring is over." The three men hurried back silently the way they came, each one occupied with his thoughts.

Hannah woke up and groaned. The back of her head ached with a sharp searing pain. It was dark and cold where she was. Her eyes adjusted to the gloom, and she saw the bars. She was in the palace dungeon. She felt despair. Sephora had lied. She was not here for her protection. She was here to die.

Despair and fear left Hannah as raw emotion that had been pent up inside for years engulfed her. She felt anger over having been displaced in her family by her younger sister, anger that once she had found happiness she had been pulled from her job to take care of Sephora's enemy. She felt anger because doing her duty was going to cost her life. As she reviewed her grievances, she felt a just rage rise up in her. She vowed to fight. The cell Hannah was in had debris of all sorts in it. Hannah began to sift through the filth to find something that would help her survive.

INCLUSION

Caliphus roused Sephora an hour before first light. Sephora sprang up energetically. She had preparations to make. Once they found Rachel's body, she would throw the biggest, most elaborate state funeral the city had ever seen. Then she would celebrate in secret. With Rachel dead, her future as dictator for life was secure. She would manipulate succession to one of her daughters, and in her dotage, she would enjoy the benefits of palace life surrounded by daughters, granddaughters, servants, and slaves to fulfill her every whim. Everything she had worked for these many long years would come to fruition.

She commanded Caliphus and Arrival to be at the main gate at first light to begin some kind of showy rite to open the city gate. Sephora went to the palace to get ready. Her three faux daughters, dressed from head to foot in long, black, hooded cloaks, accompanied her.

Sephora wasn't unduly worried when she discovered her daughters were not waiting in her quarters. She turned to the doppelgangers.

"You will have to stay in my quarters until the Three Sephoras return. I have no choice but to go without them this morning."

In her room, she took a sponge bath, dressed in funereal black, and had her hair and make-up done in stately fashion. She wished to look every inch a queen in mourning today. She loved the drama. It was unfortunate that the Three Sephoras were missing, but she was certain they had gotten stuck outside the gates and would make their way back inside once the gates were open.

Sephora made it to the gates with her retinue a quarter-hour before first light. The priestess was waiting, as were many members of the city Royals on horseback, and hundreds of civilians on foot. At first, Sephora was annoyed, but she soon realized she should have anticipated this horde. Indeed, she began to enjoy herself when the sea of people parted silently to allow her to pass through. Sephora nodded solemnly left and right, acknowledging her subjects. At last, she reached the priestess at the gate.

"First light is approaching, Low Queen Caliphus. Call upon the goddesses to keep us safe as we venture forth from the city Great Mother gave to us in her wisdom."

The High Priestess muttered prayers and incantations and waved a staff that burned incense. As first light filled the sky, it caused formerly hidden clouds to appear purple on the horizon. Caliphus let out a great cry and signaled the soldiers Arrival had standing ready to open the gates. Twenty soldiers stood shoulder to shoulder in pairs, one pair for each gate, and upon receiving the signal, they moved into place and pushed on the massive doors. The doors swung open slowly with a great deal of creaking, for they were not shut often.

"I will lead the way with Arrival at one side and our good Priestess on the other," Sephora's voice boomed out. "Everyone is welcome to follow behind us."

"Where are the Three Sephoras?" someone in the crowd yelled.

"I did not wish to risk the entire Royal Family in the forest, so I have asked the princesses to stay behind and pray."

A murmur went through the crowd, and Sephora couldn't tell if it was in approval or not. She did not care. Sephora was eager to get on with the work at hand. Without further ceremony, she spurred her horse forward.

"To Rachel, may she yet live!" she yelled, and galloped across the clearing toward the first marked tree.

Rachel awoke with a start. First light was breaking. She had slept! She jumped up, breathing in the new day deeply. Her bones were stiff, and she gingerly approached the fire that still burned. That was impossible. She eyed the injured woman, who was either dead or sleeping. Her need to know who had fed the fire led her on a search of the perimeter. Rachel found dead wolves and signs that people had been there.

Someone must have been sent to protect them. If so, where were they now? And who had sent them? Assassins had thus far never made it to her camp, or if they had, their bodies had been disposed of. She and the stranger had lived through the night, but Rachel knew they were not out of danger.

She walked the stiffness out of her bones before she returned to where the fire burned. It was time to find out if the young woman was still among the land of the living. Before Rachel could check for breath, the stranger's eyes flew open and their eyes met. Neither spoke. Rachel had nothing left to say. Ava kept silent about the events of the night. She did not want to endanger the lives of the four who had guarded theirs.

Rachel let Ava drink some sips of wine for nourishment and then some water. Rachel felt the girl's head and was surprised to find the fever had left. She would have changed the dressings on her wounds, but Ava pushed her hands away. Rachel broke the silence.

"As you wish; I will leave your dressings as they are for now. We should be back in the city in a few hours, and if you survive the trip, I will have better supplies for tending to you there.

"First light has come and gone. I expect people from the city are on their way to find us. It will most likely be High Queen Sephora and some of her cronies. Do you remember everything of last night? Our pact? If you help me, I will tend to you gently with my own hands and ease you into death as painlessly as I am able. If you do not help me, most likely we will both die a hideous death at the hands of Sephora's torture squad. Their skills are legendary. Sephora always had a streak of cruelty. I should have challenged her more over the years, but I never dreamt it would come to this."

Rachel shook her head sadly and mused, "I have paid too high a price for turning my head from the truth. Our democratic government leaves too much room for the abuse of freedom."

With more urgency now, Rachel said to Ava, "If you live long enough, you must claim to be Rebekkah in a new form that the goddesses have granted you, a testament to their satisfaction with you as a sacrifice. And you must swear that Sephora tried to kill you."

Ava answered Rachel, her voice much clearer and stronger than the day before.

"I remember everything, and I understand. I will do my best to bring honor to the memory of your daughter, and I will fill her footsteps well as long as I am able. I will help you in your fight. I want you to know my name. It is A...."

"No!" said Rachel. "Do not tell me! Our success hinges on you claiming to be Rebekkah. If I know your real name I might make a mistake."

Ava looked sad. Rachel's heart went out to the girl who was dying so far from home. To die without her own name suddenly seemed cruel to Rachel.

"I'm sorry," Rachel said. "I am all too huwoman and have been making a lot of mistakes lately. I must insist you not tell me your name, but I did hear you make the 'A' sound. When Rebekkah was little I often called her Bekka. When we are alone, I will call you Abekka. Even if someone hears me I doubt it will raise suspicion. It is the best I can do to honor the importance of you having your own name. It that acceptable to you?"

"Acceptable? I like it!" said Ava. "You are thoughtful and kind. Thank you." She smiled at Rachel, and Rachel's heart was touched by her sincerity. She smiled at Ava and then turned to the large knapsack Hannah had packed the previous morning. It seemed such a long time ago. She took the second extra cloak out of Hannah's abandoned pack and changed out of the dirty, smoke-tinged robe she had slept in. Adept at all forms of arts cultivated in the Agriculture Sector, she mischievously wove wild flowers into garlands to wear around her head and neck. She would now pre-tend her mourning was over. She had extra flowers, so she arranged them around the stranger, who had fallen back into a fitful sleep. Rachel fed herself day-old bread and cheese, untangled her hair with her fingers, cleaned her teeth as best she could, and sat in a faint spot of waxing sunlight to warm up while she waited.

Sephora had no difficulty following the marks on the trees. The trip was much easier by daylight and on horseback than it was at night and on foot. If Sephora had looked for them, she would have seen signs indicating others had come this way recently.

Arrival saw them, but doubted anyone else would spot the broken branches or tracks along the way they followed. The sea of people trailing behind would destroy the trail markings, mak-ing it impossible to tell if Sephora's agents, or hers, had been this way before. Arrival hoped her luck would hold. There had been no chance to check with Servus before heading out with Sephora.

Within the hour, they reached Rachel's camp. Though Sephora led the way, it was the High Priestess who saw the dead wolf.

Caliphus scrambled off her horse and ran to it to read it for messages from the goddesses. Arrival noted the dead wolf and looked beyond. There was a small clearing ahead. Sephora saw it too, left the Priestess where she was, and spurred her horse for speed. Arrival fell in behind her. As they were in the densest parts of the forest, they could only ride one or two abreast. The city Royals straggled close behind. Sephora entered the clearing and came to a stop. Arrival reined in beside her. The sight before them caused mixed reactions in the two women. One looked on in horror while the other looked on in suppressed elation, because there was Rachel, dressed in a clean robe garnished with flowers, tending to a young woman lying prostrate and covered at the other side of the clearing.

Arrival stayed where she was at Sephora's side. There was a physician with them, and she started forward across the clearing. Caliphus was reading messages from the goddesses in the wolf very carefully so as not to be part of whatever drama was unfolding ahead. The next person into the clearing turned back to the person behind her to give the news that Rachel had survived. The news trickled through the crowd in waves, and Sephora knew it would travel back to the city long before they returned.

Sephora cursed herself for involving religion. It had allowed her to win the election, but it left her vulnerable this time. And what had happened to her daughters? This was their fault. Rachel should be dead. She glanced with seething hatred at Arrival standing at attention next to her. Arrival, as Commander of the Armed Forces, was duty bound to stay at the High Queen's side. Sephora knew every fiber of Arrival's being must want to cross the clearing and give obeisance to Rachel. Sephora realized the picture she had painted for herself as dictator for life of the city of Evlantis was now in jeopardy. She did not know what Rachel had planned, but Rachel was a formidable foe.

The clearing was filling up. It was time for Sephora to start the show. She sprang lightly down from her horse and hurried to Rachel, who stood to meet her. Sephora would have preferred Rachel to kneel. Sephora knew now was not the time to press the issue.

"Dear Rachel," Sephora began, deliberately omitting the honorary title of Queen, "I have been up all night praying for your safety. I am grateful the goddesses have granted our petitions. And to find you with…" Sephora paused and gestured toward Ava, who was covered from head to toe.

Rachel stalled for time because the clearing was not as full as Rachel would have liked. Both women agreed on one point, though: this was a show. Rachel needed a large and sympathetic audience. Rachel did not address the unspoken question, but raised a different issue instead.

"Thank you, good queen, for your sleepless night full of prayers for me. The goddesses have indeed answered your prayers. Thankfully, you are an obedient and pious queen, for your words have reached the ears of the highest goddess herself."

Arrival willed herself not to smile. Standing still at Sephora's side, her face remained a mask.

"The whole city prayed, High Queen Rachel," a voice cried out from the crowd.

Rachel bit back a smile as Sephora's head swiveled to take in whom it was who dared to call Rachel High Queen in her presence. This gave Rachel an opening to delay further. Rachel turned toward the owner of the voice. It was a young girl of nine or ten years old. She stood beside her mother, who looked horrified.

"Sephora is High Queen now," her mother whispered loudly.

"No harm done," Sephora said dismissively, and turned back to Rachel. She intended to learn who or what was under the blankets, but Rachel spoke to the child.

"Thank you for your prayers, dear one. What is your name?"

"It is Rachella," said the child.

Rachel was flattered. It was common to give children names that were derivatives of the names of family members, great actresses, or queens.

"You look familiar. Do I know you?" Rachel asked Rachella's mother.

The mother, wishing a hole would open up in the ground and swallow her, replied, "We have never met, honored leader, but my sister served under your daughter. On one occasion, Rebekkah saved her life during a city skirmish. Rebekkah was the greatest warrior who ever lived. My mother was Quenta, of the Livestock Sector."

"Of course," Rachel said. "I know your sister Quertha. How is she?"

The mother bowed her head and spoke quietly.

"My sister has been assigned to the post of border guarding in the outer portion of the Agriculture Sector."

Rachel could not stop a sharp retort.

"We will petition the goddesses who helped me live through the night to have your sister re-assigned to a post of glory. She has earned no less by her valiant service in the past."

Rachel hoped Sephora would be drawn into defending her actions, but Sephora turned the conversation back to Rachel's unidentified companion.

"Rachel," Sephora said, "we expected to find only you here, but there is another with you. Is this the ghost Hannah spoke of?" In saying this, Sephora had given Rachel another opening to delay. The clearing was packed with women, and some had begun to climb the trees to get a better view. Arrival posted the few soldiers present in strategic places to keep space in the clearing and the women in order.

"Where is Hannah?" Rachel asked. "When she didn't come back last night, I worried that harm had come to her."

There were too many witnesses to deflect the question. Sephora cursed Rachel inwardly for her shrewdness. She was glad she had withheld her rage and spared Hannah's life.

"Hannah came back terrified and talking about a demon-ghost. I was afraid the citizens would harm Hannah after they found out she had abandoned you. I put her under my own personal protection. She is safe and unharmed, but not knowing what we would find this morning, I kept her in hidden in the city."

Caliphus pushed her way into the inner circle aided by a soldier. She did not glance at Rachel, but instead looked only at Sephora. Rachel began to worry. She would need limited cooperation from Caliphus.

"High Queen, may I have leave to speak?" Caliphus asked.

Sephora only wanted to know the identity of the stranger, but she could not be rude to the priestess in front of so many women.

"Speak, but make it brief. I am sure Rachel and her companion," Sephora waved vaguely at the bundle, "would like to get back to the city after their harrowing night."

The priestess bowed.

"This indeed has been a mysterious and miraculous night. There are nine dead wolves, but the weapons used to kill them are missing. The bodies of the predators come no closer than a hundred feet of the camp. It is as if the invisible hand of the mightiest goddess herself stopped these killers in their tracks. This is a holy place, and it should be deemed so. A chapel should be erected on this spot."

"Thank you, Priestess. That will be taken under consideration."

Sephora wondered if her daughters had turned on her and had protected Rachel. She turned to Rachel.

"We must get you back to the city. I have brought a litter to carry you."

Rachel realized it was a funeral litter and that Sephora had hoped to carry back her dead body. Rachel had the opening she was looking for. The clearing couldn't hold any more witnesses safely. She projected her voice and spoke clearly to address everyone present.

"Thank you for your concern. I am unharmed. I slept through the night peacefully. The High Priestess spoke truly. This is a holy place. A miracle happened last night. I willingly accept use of the litter to return to the city. But I ask you, Your Highness, to allow the litter to carry Rebekkah back. For I have found her. The goddesses have given her back to me. She lives." Rachel swept her hand dramatically toward the stranger.

Many women hadn't realized there was another woman in the clearing. There was a collective gasp followed by silence, then pandemonium. One woman fell out of a tree and began screaming. The crowd surged forward, but Arrival's small ring of soldiers held them back.

Sephora was unhappy at this turn of events.

"Women, come to order!" Her words went unheeded. Everyone wanted to see Rebekkah.

"Arrival, get these people in order."

Arrival gave commands to her soldiers, but it was not enough for Sephora. She grunted in frustration, unhitched the whip at her waist, and began to lash those who tried to break through the line. She whipped soldiers and citizens alike. When women realized what was happening, their frenzy subsided. Injured women sobbed quietly as Sephora lectured them.

"We are women of Evlantis, not slaves who lack self-control. I will have order."

The clearing became silent.

"Let me see Rebekkah," said Sephora, "and I shall be the first to welcome her back. Arrival, your position as head of the army is in jeopardy."

"I will gladly return command back to Rebekkah," said Arrival, smiling.

"I'm afraid that will not happen," said Rachel, sadly. "Rebekkah is very ill, perhaps even mortally so. All this time I heard her calling to me, but I found her only now. I may not have found her in time to enjoy the gift the goddesses have given me. I wish to take my daughter back to the city so that she may die in peace among her friends and loved ones."

Sephora felt a rush of joy. This was a setback, but Rachel without Rebekkah was a threat she could contain. As for seeing Rebekkah, she would be denied no longer. She walked to Rebekkah, knelt in front of the witnesses, and pushed back the hood from Ava's face. Those who could see Sephora did not understand the look of confusion on her face until she stood and spoke.

"Rachel, I do not mean to be disrespectful, but this is not Rebekkah."

Rachel was ready.

"Good Queen, look again. This is my daughter. I would have you all take a good look."

Rachel nodded to Arrival, trying to signal her with her eyes for Arrival to follow her lead, and motioning Arrival to assist her. Together they moved the stranger free of the fallen tree so all could see her. Rachel, tending to the stranger as a mother would, gently smoothed her hair and moved the outer cloak away to reveal the bloody bandages underneath. Ava seemed to be unconscious, but she was actually listening to everything that was said. She kept her eyes closed as she was being moved. Those who had known Rebekkah intimately knew that this was not she. Those who had not known her believed it was.

Rachel addressed the crowd.

"As you all know, mothers are given a special intuition regarding the needs of their daughters. I have known for these long weeks that my Rebekkah was alive. High Queen Sephora generously allowed me to search for her. Though her cries grew weaker and weaker in my heart, I did not give up, and yesterday I found her."

Rachel saw some of the women crying. She thought she had cried out herself, but their tears touched her, and she began to weep again. The tears streamed down her face. She did not wipe them away. The public had never seen this, not in the long weeks since Rebekkah was presumed dead. She continued.

"I do not wish to speak for the goddesses, which is the job of the Priestess, but I can speak as a healer and as a mother. I found my daughter barely alive. She had wounds from beasts, and other wounds that I will tell you about later. While her form has stayed the same, her visage has changed. This must be a whim of the goddesses. They are capricious, as we all know. But I stand here as your former ruler and as an equal citizen, and I proclaim to you that this woman lying here is indeed my beloved Rebekkah."

Even as she said it, Rachel felt a chill down her back, and knew by intuition many of the others felt the same. Finding a stranger in the woods was unheard of. Who else could it be after all? She saw movement from the corner of her eye and turned to see women kneeling before the form on the ground. As if choreographed, the women in the clearing knelt also, then the ones behind them, and the ones behind them. The women in the trees bowed their heads in silence. The only ones standing, as far as the eye could see, were Sephora, Rachel, and Caliphus. Sephora's hard eyes glittered. She may have lost this round to Rachel, but Rachel had said the wounds of the stranger were fatal. Sephora tried one last gambit to regain control from Rachel.

"Priestess, can you tell us if the goddesses have granted life in new form to Rebekkah?"

Caliphus went to the figure on the ground. She took her time, thinking of the position of the wolves. There was a miracle at work here. Did she trust the goddesses enough to spare her life if she took Rachel's side against Sephora's? She gently turned the stranger's head back and forth to examine it. She pried one eye open to check its color. She paid special attention to Rebekkah's hands, particularly the one with the scar on the finger where the Ring of Power used to sit. This gave Caliphus an idea and she turned to Rachel.

"Do you have the warrior Ring of Power which I brought to you when you were told Rebekkah was dead?"

Without a word, Rachel pulled a chain from around her neck. On it, she had kept the ring close to her heart. The ring was warm. Caliphus took it and gently slid it on Ava's finger. It fit perfectly.

Ava had been waiting for a chance to take stock of the situation. Listening only gave her part of the picture. She needed to know what the key players looked like. The moment she felt the ring settle on her finger, she opened her eyes. She pretended to struggle to sit up and gasp for breath. She looked around her slowly.

The woman holding her hand must be the priestess. Rachel was standing to her right. The woman kneeling must be Arrival. The stranger met her eyes for a long moment. Then Ava turned her gaze on the other woman standing in the clearing, and their eyes met. The stranger was shocked by the look in her eyes. She knew this woman dressed in black with the long shiny black hair marked her for annihilation, and she felt fear. Then she deliberately and slowly met as many eyes around the clearing as she could. It was overwhelming. She had never imagined so many people in the world. They were all shapes, sizes, and colors. Many had faces lined with the folds-of-good-living Rachel had taught her about. Some girls were short and had none. She realized these must be young girls. Ava had never seen anyone younger than herself except in the pictures her parents and siblings had drawn to preserve the memories of their youth. Once she had gazed at every face in the crowd that was visible, she pretended to faint, and was laid gently upon the ground.

Caliphus stood. She needed no more hints from the goddesses about which direction to take. If this led to her death, she walked to it knowing she followed the path the goddess Ephrea had led her on. She must trust that the goddesses would use another to carry on the secret mission of the priestesses.

She drew herself to her full height and raised the ceremonial scepter she carried on her royal belt. This indicated that she spoke as High Priestess, and not as a woman. Her words were simple.

"This is Rebekkah."

The soldiers could not hold the crowd back any longer. People pressed forward, straining to see Rachel and Rebekkah. Arrival had anticipated this and had waved what Sephora had hoped would be a funeral bier forward. Eager hands reached out to help put Rebekkah and Rachel in it. Not even the shrill voice of Sephora could stem the tide of action. Arrival wondered if she could prevent Sephora from being crushed to death. Arrival surreptitiously began a chant.

"Carry her home."

She commanded her soldiers to push the bier over the heads of the women. The women in the crowd caught on, and the platform was propelled overhead by dozens of hands in the direction of the city. This would keep Rachel and the stranger safe for now.

The pressure around them lessened, and Arrival made her way to Sephora's side to guard and guide her back to the city. Their horses had been swept up in the throng returning to Evlantis. Arrival knew that if she signaled Stealth with a special whistle, he would return to her, but she also knew Sephora would commandeer him.

Arrival had been relieved to see Rachel in full possession of her wits, and she wondered how long that wise woman had been planning this maneuver. She knew it would help Rachel if Sephora remained in the forest as long as possible, though Arrival wanted to return to Rachel quickly and tell her the secret she had carried too long. Arrival chose to travel back on foot, leaving Stealth to return on his own, and thus delaying the High Queen's reentry to the city.

Sephora was seething on the inside, but emanated joy to those around her. She commanded Arrival to clear her way and get her back to the city as fast as possible. On her way, she chatted gaily with people, playing politics as she did so well. In public, she must show nothing but happiness. She must do all in her power to keep Rachel and the impostor close to her until she figured out exactly what Rachel was up to and how to counteract it.

Rachel and Rebekkah were carried by the people, not just to the city line, but all the way to the Palace. There was no one to deny Rachel entrance. She commanded the palace staff to set her up in a room on the northwest side, the side that bordered the Soldier Sector. The staff had missed her, and happily carried out her requests.

Two days prior, Rachel had been an outcast, a pariah. To be seen with her was politically unwise. Many thought her mad. Now she had returned in triumph, her status immediately elevated to one of unprecedented glory. Her claim that Rebekkah was alive was treated as fact. For the moment, until Sephora returned to the city, Rachel was in charge. Rachel wished Arrival had returned with her, but she understood why Arrival had to stay with the High Queen.

Rachel wondered where the Three Sephoras were and when they would appear and cause trouble. Rachel knew she had supporters. Someone had definitely worked behind the scenes in her behalf during the night. It would be helpful to know who it had been, but that would have to wait. In her many years as High Queen, she had learned the value of waiting. Solutions to problems and answers to questions often revealed themselves in their own time.

For now, there was work to be done. She needed to find a physician to examine the stranger, lie about the prognosis, and confirm that this indeed was Rebekkah. There was a midwife in the city she had assisted hundreds of times. They had a strong respect for each other. With the royal physician trapped in the forest with Sephora, she thought she could count on Ahmilia for just the right help. She sent for her.

For now, Rachel chatted gaily with the women surrounding her; she was a happy mother reunited with her long lost daughter. This was a familiar theme in their literature, art, and music. The bond between mother and daughter was a fierce and tremendous one. Nothing was more complicated and infuriating, yet at the same time more precious than that bond.

Rachel washed and towel-dried Ava's beautiful auburn hair gently and requested a steady stream of visitors be allowed in to share in this sweet return. There were many people left behind in the city, especially the elderly and mothers of young babes, who wanted to see Rachel and Rebekkah with their own eyes. The line formed quickly and wound through Palace corridors and outside to the grounds as women returned from the forest.

When Ahmilia entered, Rachel had the room cleared so that it was just the three of them.

"My daughter has returned to us," Rachel said.

"So I have heard," Ahmilia answered. "Why have you called for this humble old midwife instead of waiting for the palace physician? She is much better able to take care of the injured than I."

Ahmilia was shrewd and liked to steer clear of politics, but Rachel needed her.

"Ahmilia, I will speak plainly. Sephora set out to ruin me, and she almost succeeded. You see the steps she has taken in the city. She will weaken, perhaps even destroy, what many good leaders have built up over the years. I need to take the city back and depose Sephora. However, I need time. I found my daughter in the forest, but her wounds are fatal. I ask that you would examine her and say that she might get better, just to give me time, because we are old friends. Please, Ahmilia. You are a woman in your older years who has served the city well. Sephora would not dare to harm you or your family for your part in this."

"She could harm many who are not family but who are dear to me nonetheless," Ahmilia said with venomous anger. "I do not wish to see anyone I love suffer the way you have. Just by summoning me you have put people I love in danger. What does Sephora care whether I answered the summons or not? It will only matter to her that she could use me against you."

"True, Ahmilia, but the difference between Sephora and me is that I care, and I will do everything in my power to protect you, to win the city back, and to put all of Sephora's enemies out of harm's way. It is time to choose a side, Ahmilia. In the meantime, my only daughter lies there dying. Will you help me?"

Ahmilia walked to the only window in the room and looked out. The perimeter of the castle was lined with women waiting for a chance to greet Rachel and Rebekkah. Ahmilia saw makeshift tents and cooking fires. Some of the women had never returned home the night before, nor had they gone to the Religion Sector, but had opted to stay out all night. All around them, slaves went about their duties as usual. Ahmilia knew Rachel was right, but she resented being forced to take a side.

"Where is Sephora?" Ahmilia asked.

"Sephora is on her way. Please, do the examination for me now."

Ahmilia moved to the bed where Ava lay. When she got close enough to see Ava's face, she stopped, and then turned her head slowly to look directly at Rachel.

"This is not Rebekkah."

"I know. I found her in the forest. I don't know who she is. Herstory teaches that the leaders of Evlantis, in the twentieth year after its founding, sent out parties to search for any missing descendants of Mother Eve. Every family was accounted for and absorbed into the city or wiped out. If isolated pockets have sprung up from the occasional escaped slave or exiled woman, we will have to ferret them out and then decide what to do with them. This woman is no one I recognize, and I have been acutely aware of every woman banished or missing for the last twenty-five years. She looks to be under thirty. She could be the child of a survivor who was perhaps

215

unknowingly pregnant, just as the Great Mother was when the first man abandoned her. In the meantime, Sephora has been claiming a religious mandate. I have borrowed that torch from her and fanned it into a bonfire. I suspect that the same people who elected her believing she was speaking for the goddesses can be manipulated to demand I be returned to my throne when they believe the goddesses granted my daughter new life. I have spoken to the stranger. I have promised her a peaceful death. I would like her to hang on to life as long as possible. Every minute will help me gain momentum to remove Sephora from power. If you proclaim that Rebekkah has been granted new life, you will strengthen my position."

"May I speak freely?" Ahmilia asked as she stepped away from the body. Rachel motioned for Ahmilia to join her at the window. They talked in whispers.

"Speak," said Rachel.

"You will not like what I have to say," answered Ahmilia.

Rachel gazed at Ahmilia steadily and said, "I have had many shocks these last three months. Whatever you have to say I can handle."

"Rachel," said Ahmilia, "I can say this woman is Rebekkah, but Sephora will not believe it. I must burden you with knowledge that I thought you were too fragile to handle. There is no concrete evidence; Sephora is too long practiced at covering her tracks for that, but after Rebekkah was presumed dead, First Sephora was rumored to have been drinking in elite taverns in the Arts Sector, bragging that her mother had arranged for Rebekkah never to return from the sacrifice. Sephora heard about it and spoke with First Sephora, who had a black eye and a total change of attitude afterwards.

"I kept my eyes and ears open. I discovered the night of Rebekkah's death that two slaves who resided at the Low Palace of the Arts had disappeared. I know a young woman who was, shall we say, close to one of the men. He simply vanished, along with another slave named Tiburnus."

"Are you suggesting two slaves killed my daughter? That is preposterous!" said Rachel.

"Rachel, do you truly believe the beast could have killed your daughter? And do you believe she would have left her ring and spear behind and followed an old custom, denying you proof she was gone? Would your beloved daughter have followed a tradition of pride and denied you the comfort of providing full burial ceremonies?"

Rachel had no answer for these questions. Ahmilia continued.

"Rachel, what if Sephora armed those slaves? What if they attacked Rebekkah while she was tethered to the tree? What if the slaves themselves took Rebekkah's spear and killed the beast? Sephora would have to make those men disappear. She would have been charged with the serious crime of giving weapons to slaves, and worse, for the crime of murdering your daughter."

Rachel gasped, then attempted to control her reaction; they were standing in front of a second-story window and women were watching. She remembered what the stranger had said—that some men had killed Rebekkah. Had she been there? Rachel looked troubled.

"You should have told me this months ago."

Ahmilia sighed. "What good would it have done? The outcome is the same. Killed by beast or killed by Sephora's slaves, Rebekkah is dead just the same. At least you could picture her dying an honorable death instead of being murdered."

"Then this must work. Do the examination, Ahmilia. You owe me. Tend to her gently. It is not only a matter of righting the damage Sephora has done to the city, but of avenging my daughter's murder."

"You are going through with your plan then? It will not bring Rebekkah back." Ahmilia was hoping to dissuade Rachel because she did not want to incur Sephora's wrath.

Rachel drew herself up to her full height and spoke haughtily.

"I have entered into a Pact of Honor. I am a woman of my word, and I will fulfill it. Ahmilia, you must choose a side now. No one knows better than I do how important it is for a physician to remain apart from political alliances, but this is more than politics. It is about saving the Queendom and bringing a murderer to justice."

Ahmilia sighed deeply and nodded. As her answer, she turned away and tended to the woman lying on the bed. Her examination was thorough, but Ava did not seem to be conscious for any of it. Ahmilia, though a mid-wife, had wrapped every kind of wound in her day and knew anatomy just as well as the Palace physician did. She worked quickly and gently, changing the bloody bandages and replacing them with new ones. She frowned throughout as if troubled by something, but she didn't speak until she was done. She turned to Rachel.

"This daughter of yours will live."

Rachel bowed to Ahmilia.

"Thank you. I will provide protection to you and your loved ones. Send a list to Arrival of anyone who is vulnerable to being harmed by Sephora and her minions. Now, go and spread the good news that Rebekkah lives."

Ahmilia left, still scowling.

The news that Rebekkah may have been murdered unsettled Rachel. She tried hard to hang on to her objectivity and reason. Before this, she simply wanted to do what was best for the city. Now this intent was mixed with a desire to hurt Sephora as much as she could.

Rachel mused on this a bit, waiting for Sephora to return to the city. She wondered at the mystery of the dead wolves, and the fact that the three princesses had not put in an appearance. If they had been further back in the procession, surely they would have appeared at the castle by now. They had not been with their mother. Where were they?

Rachel called for the reception line to resume. She put aside her musings and chatted happily with each woman who entered, sharing Ahmilia's false good news.

The doctor's hands upon Ava's skin had been gentle and effective, and her wounds hurt less. For three months, they had been as a constant fire burning upon her body: the knife wound at her heart, the beast claw wounds across her arms and trunk, and the scar around her finger. She knew she would not die, but she had sometimes wished she could. Her first encounter with her stepsiblings had been a rude awakening to the ruthlessness and cruelty of life outside the Garden.

She was stuck in the middle of a power struggle in a strange land among strange people. She had thought the gathering of women in the forest was immense, but their number was nothing compared to the throng outside the palace windows and those streaming through the room in a steady line. In her wildest dreams, she had never pictured so many people on the earth.

She observed that the women controlled everything while the men stood back and waited to be commanded. She saw many girl children and babies. The babies were precious, and she longed to hold one.

This place was like nothing she had ever imagined during the years she spent traveling, looking for her stepsiblings. This whole situation seemed to be what Michael had warned her of: a situation that demanded some kind of correct decision on her part lest she lose any chance of returning to her loved ones. She had never felt the way she did now—full of terror and curiosity at the same time. Not being sure of how to proceed, she continued to feign unconsciousness, though she took in everything going on around her through barely closed eyes.

She had the ability to retain everything around her perfectly, and to move whatever she chose from short-term to long-term memory. As the line of women wound its way into the room and

Rachel chatted with each one, Ava stared through lowered lashes and committed names, faces, and facts to memory. She thought the best way to start taking Rebekkah's place was to get as much information as possible.

There was another visitation going on. As each woman, child, and baby passed through the room, she brought with her centuries' worth of germs, bacteria, viruses, and other assorted hosts of contaminants. Where Ava came from, illness did not exist. Her immune system kicked into high gear at the exposure of so many unfamiliar invaders. Soon she was running a fever again. Rachel was not surprised when the fever returned. Had not the girl been covered from head to toe, Rachel would have been surprised to see measles spots come, and then disappear, rashes appear and then fade away, and a host of other symptoms do the same. The stranger's immune system was much stronger than when Rachel found her, but it could not keep up with the sheer magnitude of what she was being exposed to. Though Ava tried to stay awake, another healing sleep claimed her.

REVELATIONS

As soon as Arrival returned to the city, she delegated orders to her generals. Arrival informed her troops that she would get cleaned up, then take respite in the reflection room before returning to duty. Arrival took a shower as quickly as possible and entered the reflection room, but she did not stay, though she longed to. She had no time for such luxuries. She used a door at the other end and took the passageway to the Palace. Arrival knew right where to go to find Servus on any given day. It was his day to do maintenance in the Palace Petting Zoo.

Due to the presence of a soldier she did not trust, Arrival sized up the situation for a moment before she spoke imperiously to Servus. Sweat glistened on his arms and face as he wielded a shovel, cleaning away pony dung. Even though it was morning, he looked exhausted.

"Servus, I must speak with you."

Arrival turned to the soldier on duty, intuitively cautious. Partouche was relatively new to the Soldier Sector. There were rumors about her that suggested she was a high-ranking member of Sephora's secret police sent to spy on them.

"Partouche, some strange things went on last night. I need to talk to this self-proclaimed leader of slaves to see if he has any knowledge of the events. I'm sure our Queen would be interested to know if he does."

Partouche smirked. "What Queen would that be?"

"Sephora, of course," Arrival said. "You will address me as Commander, soldier. I was in the reflection room thinking about how best to proceed when I realized I should question this slave leader."

With Partouche openly questioning Arrival's loyalty, Arrival knew she should not risk questioning Servus in private right now. She hoped he was every bit as quick as the intelligence reports claimed.

"Servus," said Arrival, "are you aware of anything unusual last night that I should report to our High Queen?"

"It is odd you should ask," Servus said. "Last night, we slaves heard the ancient rite of demon barring was instituted. Being more susceptible to demon-ghosts, a few of my men and I guarded the barracks. Around three in the morning, we saw seven rabbits— three black and four white—grazing on the common lawn. We were amazed to see three eagles swoop down out of the night sky and catch the three black rabbits in their talons. There was no hope for them. The four white rabbits got away. Other than that, the time passed slowly and day came as usual.

"No guard came to do a count, and I fear perhaps the demon-ghost came and took some of my men. No one has seen Yarr or Titus. They have disappeared without a trace. Perhaps the demon-ghost put me and my men in a deep sleep and took them."

Partouche scoffed.

Arrival turned to her.

"Is it true no morning count was done?"

"It may be true, Commander. It was an unusual day and the count is tedious; many say it is even superfluous."

Arrival didn't like Partouche's snide tone. "I was with High Queen Sephora all night. Would you like to be the one to tell her the count was not done and there may be slaves missing?"

Partouche blanched. She came to full attention and for the first time resembled a soldier of the army.

"No, Commander. I apologize for the error. I will check the roster and report the soldiers whose duty it was. I will call all the slaves back to the barracks and begin a count at once."

"Good. If there are slaves missing, dispatch the trackers to find them."

"Yes, Commander." Partouche turned to Servus. "Hi, there! Back to the barracks, you animal!" Partouche was livid at Arrival's rebuke, and in her wrath she gave Servus a blow that sent him sprawling. Partouche smiled in satisfaction.

Arrival shook her head in disapproval of Partouche's cruelty. Soldiers were sometimes called on to do disagreeable things to slaves to keep them in line, but she preferred her soldiers not to enjoy them, and never to lash out in anger. She would deal with Partouche later, not wanting to bring further misplaced retribution on Servus.

Partouche had her back to Arrival. Arrival shot Servus a grim look, darting her eyes at Partouche and shaking her head to show her disapproval of that soldier. Servus just shrugged his shoulders as if to say, 'What can I do?' Arrival held up two fingers in the gesture of a pact made and kept. Servus nodded slightly and got up to leave, breathing a deep sigh of relief.

When Arrival had appeared, he had entertained the thought that she had come to kill him. Such things had been known to happen to those who trusted women. He was glad to be alive, for circumstances were perfect for rebellion. He would wait for Arrival to do her part in honoring their pact; meanwhile, he would see how the power struggle played out between Sephora and Rachel. Then the men would make their move.

Arrival found herself admiring Servus's cunning. He had managed to tell her he had stopped the Three Sephoras and that they would not be a problem. The four she sent to protect Rachel had gotten away. Had he and his men killed the princesses? If so, it might be difficult for Arrival to keep her promise to protect him from harm if this became known. *One problem at a time*, Arrival mused to herself.

Arrival's thoughts then went in another direction. Love between a man and a woman was taboo. The women spent their days in the company of other women. Arrival found it tedious and often wondered what it would be like to find an equal, a counterpart, among the men. Herstory taught them that men were treacherous and untrustworthy. But she wondered what it would be like to daily spar with a man whose intelligence equaled her own. She knew many women had secret agreements with slaves, and many had their hearts broken. But others seemed to find the forbidden love so sweet as to be a gift from the goddesses themselves. Arrival had often watched Servus from a distance, admiring the lines of his body as he worked. He was thought to be seditious and dangerous, and was frequently given backbreaking tasks to wear out his body and sap the strength of his spirit. Nothing had broken him. If ever a man was her equal, it was Servus. She wondered what he thought of her.

Then she caught herself. It was silly to be thinking of such foolish things when she could not even be sure of seeing the sunset this evening. If Sephora came out on top of this power struggle, there was no hope for her. Arrival knew better than anyone that the woman whom Rachel claimed was Rebekkah was no such woman. Arrival and Rebekkah had always been close, and there had been no sign of recognition in the stranger's eyes. Arrival had chosen Rachel's side in the clearing, and she would not waver from that stance. She had been waiting for a chance to show her fidelity to Rachel short of resigning her post, and this was it. What was her mother thinking? Where did the girl come from? It was time to jump back into the thick of things. Arrival strode away pushing all thoughts of Servus out of her mind.

There was never a break in the stream of visitors flowing through the room Rachel had chosen for the Evlantian women to greet her and the stranger. In a city of six thousand women, Rachel could not know every visitor, but they all knew her. Rachel stood at the sleeping stranger's head and gently tended to her as the line filed by. Women talked in hushed, reverent tones, and no one was at a loss for words. Rachel greeted women frequently with a phrase she hoped would be repeated and remembered.

"I welcome you joyfully. The daughter who was lost is now found. This mother's happiness is complete. Come share in the happiness of Rebekkah's return."

As women left, Rachel could hear them commenting on how indeed the figure on the bed was Rebekkah, and how this was a time of great miracles. Momentum was in her favor. The knowledge that her daughter may truly have been murdered by Sephora was a dull ache within her.

Rachel was genuinely glad when Arrival hurried in and knelt at her feet.

"Arrival, Arrival, daughter of my heart, stand and greet me properly with a hug and a kiss," Rachel said.

Arrival did so immediately, glad of the chance to whisper in her ear so she could not be overheard.

"The Three Sephoras were sent to kill you. They are being secretly detained."

As Rachel squelched the reaction that rippled across her face, Arrival said loudly enough to be heard by all, "Mother of my heart, I rejoice with you at the return of my sister. How is she?"

"Your sister sleeps. Ahmilia has examined her and has said she will live," said Rachel.

"Yes, it was a night of miracles," said Arrival. "The goddesses protected you and blessed you all at once. I was with Queen Sephora, who should reach the palace any time now. She prayed for your safe return, and goddesses be praised, here you both are."

"Yes, I owe all my recent fortune to Sephora," Rachel said wryly. "I have much to repay her for. And you, daughter of my heart, are also Commander of the Armed Forces of Evlantis. I do not wish to keep you from your duties. Thank you for stopping to see this humble citizen in her hour of joy."

Arrival nodded, knowing Rachel was right, but not wanting to leave. She still needed to tell Rachel the secret Rebekkah had told her so she could keep her pact with Servus. With all the people streaming through, now was not the time. There were plenty of other things to be done. She turned to leave.

"I will return to you and my sister as soon as I am able."

Before Arrival could make her exit there was a commotion in the receiving line. Sephora swept majestically into the room.

She smiled brightly and spoke loudly.

"I hope the Palace staff has filled my orders to make you comfortable. If there is anything else you need, do not hesitate to call for it. The entire staff is at your disposal. This is a great day. I insist that you stay here and enjoy my hospitality."

Rachel would not challenge Sephora now, but she felt hatred well up inside her. She had always looked at Sephora with distain, but now she loathed the woman with every fiber of her being. Rachel believed in doing nothing in anger. Anger in a woman was a fearsome thing when unleashed. It did nothing but cause harm. Rachel needed to focus on undoing harm. Her first goal was to undo the damage Sephora had done to Evlantis. After her city was safe, Rachel would make Sephora accountable for the murder of Rebekkah.

Rachel willed herself to speak civilly.

"I am grateful to your majesty for allowing us use of the palace."

Sephora gave Rachel a sharp glance.

"Is something wrong, Rachel?"

"High Queen, it is nothing but the overwhelming joy I feel at knowing the fate of my daughter. I am basking in the glow of this reunion. I am weary from my night in the forest, but I wish to share my happiness with as many women of Evlantis as possible."

"I cannot permit you to exhaust yourself, Rachel. Arrival, clear the room and then attend to me in my private chambers."

Her voice carried outside the room and the women who had been waiting in line groaned in disappointment.

"High Queen, do not forget I am also Commander of the Army and Low Queen of the Soldier Sector," Arrival said. "I have neglected my duties long enough. The Harvest Festival begins tomorrow. I will send General Portia to attend you."

Sephora stopped and turned, narrowing her eyes.

"Fine. There is no need to send Portia to me. I will use soldiers I have trained from my own Sector."

The unspoken communication was clear. Lines were being drawn. Civil war was just a spear throw away, and Arrival suspected Servus might view civil war as an ideal opportunity for the slaves to begin a war for freedom. Never in the herstory of Evlantis had the slaves fought against a divided Queendom, but Arrival would serve Sephora no longer. The question Arrival had was, would her soldiers follow her or Sephora?

Rachel spoke again, this time as loudly as Sephora so that she too would be heard outside of the room. She had an unreasonable urge to disagree with Sephora, and she gave in to it.

"I will be fine, High Queen. I have the rest of my life to be with my daughter, but only these few hours to share her homecoming with the people. Let no one else be added to the line, but allow those who have been waiting to come through."

A cheer went up.

"That will take hours!" Sephora said.

"I have no duties to attend to other than the care of my daughter. Now that I am no longer High Queen, the cares of state do not burden me. You, however, have much work to do. I remember the pressing duties of Festival time well. It is a good thing you have three daughters whose help you can rely on."

Rachel could not help adding this last jibe. Arrival withheld laughter.

Sephora was cornered.

"Very well," said Sephora. "Let it be as you wish. I will not have it said that I am a difficult hostess. However, I insist on having a private dinner with Rachel and…" for a split second Sephora stopped speaking as she waved an arm in the direction of the stranger. Sephora would not call her Rebekkah. "I will see you then."

Arrival and Sephora left the room together but went separate ways. Arrival had things to attend to in the Soldier Sector before she could return to Rachel and tell her the secret she had kept for too long.

Sephora went to her quarters fuming, where Salla, Tyvaal, and Meerta were still waiting. Her daughters had not returned. She had told them not to come back if they couldn't kill Rachel, but now Sephora wondered if harm had come to them. It upset Sephora to see Rachel installed in the Palace. In addition, Arrival had disobeyed a direct order of the High Queen.

Sephora called for Pirna, her poison mistress. Before the day was out Sephora would remove the poser. Then she would make Rachel her prisoner and remove Arrival from power. As soon as Pirna entered, Sephora wasted no time. She spoke to the captains first.

"I have assignments for you. Whoever completes their task first will replace Arrival as head of the Army. I will forcibly remove her from power as soon as one of you proves yourself to me.

"Captain Tyvaal, you must bring Hannah to me. After I have spoken with her, you will use whatever means necessary to convince her to back up the story the High Priestess told last night.

Hannah may be reticent to support me, but I'm sure you have methods that will effectively change her mind."

Tyvaal smiled and nodded. She was pleased to have such a simple task.

"Captain Meerta, you must find my daughters. They could be anywhere, but search the forest first. Tell them they may approach me for forgiveness, and that I will be merciful. They will understand."

Meerta smiled grimly, but also nodded. She was jealous, for hers was not as easy a task as Tyvaal's.

"Captain Salla, your task is to discover the identity of the woman Rachel claims is her daughter. There is not one woman among us whose lineage is unknown. There are no strangers in Evlantis."

Salla saluted. She didn't think she had much chance to beat Tyvaal, but she would try. Besides, Sephora was ridiculously generous when she was pleased. There would be something in it for her if she finished her task quickly, even if she didn't finish first.

"One way or another, we will foil Rachel's plot before she can take it any further. Go, goddess speed to you three."

The secret policewomen left in a hurry, each eager to be the first to return. Sephora was left with Pirna. She smiled brightly at her poison mistress.

"I have a very special task for you. Come close enough for me to whisper in your ear."

Captain Tyvaal opened the door to Sephora's quarters with confidence, certain that she would be the next Low Queen of the Soldier Sector. It had taken her all of thirty minutes to bring the prisoner up from the dungeon. Pirna had left by the time she returned. Tyvaal did not know Hannah, but she knew her background and thought a girl raised in the Arts Sector who worked in the theater section would be very pliable once subjected to Tyvaal's favorite methods of torture. Tyvaal presented the prisoner, who was bound and gagged, to Sephora with a flourish, forcing Hannah to her knees.

Sephora did not look pleased.

"Who is this, Tyvaal?" she asked.

"This is the woman I found in Hannah's cell. Isn't this Hannah?" asked Tyvaal with an uneasy feeling.

"This is not Hannah. Take off her gag so she can tell us where Hannah is."

As soon as she was able, the woman spoke in a voice that quavered with fear.

"I am Certa. I am new to service in the dungeon. On my rounds, I saw Hannah in her cell, bloody and non-responsive. I opened the cell door to check on her and then..." her voice faltered, but she quickly recovered and continued. "She viciously attacked me. I woke up bound and gagged and wearing the cloak that was hers. Have mercy on me, High Queen, I am your humble servant."

The jailer was no more than a child, but Sephora was furious.

"Obviously you are not fit for your duties. Tyvaal, reassign this woman to duty in the outermost fields in the Agriculture Sector."

The Agriculture Sector thrived because of slave labor, but women were assigned to work in the fields farthest from Evlantis. The lowest of the low of the Queendom had to live outside the city walls in mere shacks to provide labor for the fields and to make certain that no slaves escaped through that Sector. Among the many hardships those women endured was the loss of their right to visit the Quickening Chamber. Pregnancy would interfere with their required duties.

The girl sobbed.

"Please, no, it would break my mother's heart. I am her only daughter, and I am scheduled for my first quickening visit next month. I am her only hope to continue our line."

Sephora did not care.

"Be quiet and get out," she said. "I have things to talk to the Captain about. Working in the Palace in any capacity is a privilege, and you have failed me. Get out before I decide to make your mother childless."

Certa, having been threatened with worse punishment than the hard labor of the outermost gardens, left Sephora and Tyvaal alone. She had not gotten fifteen feet from the door when it opened again and Tyvaal flew past her. All Sephora had said to her was "Bring Hannah to me before sundown, or you will join Certa."

Arrival sat at the plain wooden table that served as the Commander's desk and tended to some routine duties of office while she waited for word that she could return to Rachel in private. She had assigned soldiers to guard the end of the line and to keep the line moving. She ordered another soldier to report to her when the last woman in line was ushered into the room. Arrival had also scheduled a meeting with her generals after the dinner hour. Plans were taking shape in her head. She wanted to make sure the soldiers would be with her.

It was many hours later, almost time for dinner, when Arrival finally found herself alone with Rachel. Ava still slept, though it was a more peaceful sleep than earlier. Her immune system had almost finished creating antibodies to kill each of the microscopic invaders she had been exposed to throughout the day, though Rachel interpreted the deeper, more peaceful sleep as a sign that the girl was closer to the everlasting sleep of death.

Rachel was tired, but glad to see Arrival. She realized that when she lost Rebekkah, she had abandoned Arrival.

"Arrival, I love you, and I have missed you," said Rachel. "I owe you an apology. You have had a horrible time defending your position these last three months. I am sorry I was not there for you."

"My queen and mother of my heart, no apology is necessary. Your actions were understandable, and I don't doubt your love for me. However, now you must listen to me. I have carried the burden of the secret entrusted to me by Rebekkah before she went to sacrifice too long. I think you should sit."

"Yes, I will hear you now. I received news from Ahmilia that I will share with you." Rachel had no idea that Arrival's news would change her profoundly.

"I don't care what Ahmilia said. It is irrelevant. I have to get back to my soldiers quickly. If Sephora has her way, there will be civil war. I also believe the slaves are preparing for rebellion. You must hear me now."

Rachel looked grim.

"Perhaps I should not challenge Sephora now; perhaps I should wait until you deal with the slaves."

Arrival, usually patient, became frustrated.

"Mother! There is no time for second-guessing! You have finally begun what needed to be done three months ago. Right now there is no time for me to do anything but tell you the secret so I can prepare my soldiers to save the Queendom. Just listen.

"Rebekkah came to me with shocking news right before her death. There is a village where others...."

"There must be," said Rachel, interrupting again, "I wanted to question...."

Arrival's voice rang out, the secret finally bursting forth.

"Mother! Listen! You have grandchildren! Rebekkah has children among the others!"

Relief washed over Arrival. She felt renewed and invigorated. She was free now to follow her own course. She hadn't realized what a heavy toll keeping Rebekkah's secret had taken on her. Now that she was free of this responsibility, her life was hers to do with as she wished. She could live and die for the cause she chose as Low Queen and Commander of the Soldier Sector. For the first time she felt the power of her position and knew exactly how she would use it.

Rachel was speechless. She felt her knees go weak and her eyes water. Arrival was suddenly at her side to help her into a chair.

"What? How? When?"

Arrival took a softer tone with Rachel.

"I didn't want to tell you so abruptly. You left me no choice, Mother. Rebekkah found a settlement of people on one of her early searches for a building site for constructing a second city. Men and women live as equals there. They contract in monogamous relationships and raise children together, both male and female children. When the settlement gets too crowded, some leave and settle elsewhere. Sometimes they go off before it is too crowded. They have learned that man has a natural restlessness and a thirst for adventure.

"It is a wide world, and there are many more people in it then just Evlantians, though Rebekkah did say she thinks we still out-number them. Because they are outcasts, they hide themselves from us. They consider themselves superior to us, though they do not have the comforts we enjoy because we hate men and control our population by killing our children. Their religion is radically different from ours.

"When she discovered them six years ago, Rebekkah could not fight and kill them all. They took her prisoner. She begged them to allow her to return to us, but they denied her. You know Rebekkah—she did not rest until they came up with a compromise. Rebekkah was told that she must keep their secret by becoming one of them. If she wished to return to us, she had to contract in marriage with a man of their city, and she would not be allowed to leave until she was pregnant. She came back to us for three months and left again. She delivered a healthy baby boy in their settlement. For six years, she has kept their secret and lived two lives, Mother. She bore children every two years. She spoke of them with love and pride. Your firstborn grandchild's name is Jarod, named for his father. After Jarod, Rebekkah bore two daughters; she named one Rachel and the other Arrival."

Arrival, the hardened soldier, felt tears prick her eyes.

"Your daughter, my sister, lives on in her children."

"This changes everything." Rachel said softly. "I had thought to win my Queenship back and wage war on the outsiders, but now I realize that to do so I would endanger the lives of my own flesh."

Rachel had lived her whole life believing Evlantis was the only civilization in the world. Discovering Abekka changed that. Now everything changed again as she realized her daughter lived on in children being raised by those she had thought to conquer. She had long ago made peace that her line would die out with her daughter. Now her matriarchal legacy would continue. This knowledge brought her peace and joy, and a sense of wonder that she thought she would never experience again.

After her initial reaction, she felt the prejudice she had been raised with flood her being. Rachel jumped up in alarm.

"My goddess! I must leave at once," Rachel said. "My granddaughters are being raised by a man! I must find them and bring them here!"

"Mother, stay focused!" said Arrival. "In order to be of any use to your grandchildren, you must remove Sephora from power. If she knew they existed she would seek Rebekkah's children out and flay the skin from their bodies while you watched. She hates you, and she will do anything to remain in power.

"It is why Rebekkah needed to become the sacrificial victim, so she could challenge our ways slowly. She needed to challenge our religious beliefs and have the village where her children live discovered naturally as we expanded our boundaries. There is no quick fix here, as much as you might want one."

"I suppose I see your point…" Rachel murmured.

"Mother, I have to leave. I have urgent things to attend to. Don't leave the city now. You will lead our enemies right to Rebekkah's children if you do. Can I trust you to stay?"

"Yes. I do not understand why she felt she could not tell me, but I understand how heavily this has weighed on you. Thank you for doing your duty. I know you must go, Arrival, but please know how much I love you for carrying this burden and giving me this joyous news. You are the best daughter a mother could ask for."

Arrival nodded and wiped tears from her eyes at the recognition she had longed for. She left quickly. Arrival hurried back to the Soldier Sector a free woman at last.

Rachel moved to where Ava lay, picked up a brush, and began brushing the young woman's hair gently, lost in her thoughts.

"Mother, if everything I have heard is right, then Arrival spoke truly."

Rachel jumped when Ava spoke. She had not expected her to regain consciousness again.

"Welcome back to the land of the living," she greeted her new foster daughter, and then added, "Are you in pain, Abekka? Can I get you anything?"

"I am hungry and thirsty, but I feel much better, thank you."

Rachel's eyes filled with tears.

"You are a brave young woman. I won't leave you, Abekka. I will wait until our pact is fulfilled. Afterwards, why should I wait to rescue my granddaughters?"

"Because they are not in danger. My father was wonderful with children. My childhood memories are happy ones. But your grandchildren do need you. They will need you to comfort them and to keep their mother alive in their memories with your stories—stories their father does not know, but first you have a Queendom to save. Once our work is done here, perhaps we can travel there together."

"Do you know my grandchildren?" Rachel didn't have the heart to tell Abekka her traveling days were over.

"No, I'm sorry. I come from a different settlement than the one Rebekkah joined."

"How can children be safe with their father? Men know nothing of child care."

"A father's love is not inferior to a mother's. It is merely different. Men and women have different strengths and different perspectives. A child needs both loves. You are wrong to think men are inferior. You are wrong to keep them enslaved. Your world has been shifting since you met me. Allow it to shift a little more. Let go of the lies you have spent your life believing."

Rachel was unconvinced.

"Your ways and mine are different. How can you be so sure my way is the not the right way?"

"Because," Ava said with a joyful smile, "I know the One who created man. A man who walks in truth is a marvelous creation, one that is only a little lower than the angels; he is a force to be respected and treasured...."

Rachel was intrigued and longed to hear more. She believed every woman could sense truth if she allowed herself to. She put no trust in the goddesses, but valued her own intuition. Though this sounded crazy, she heard the small still voice of truth in Abekka's words.

Ava would have continued, but Sephora entered.

Arrival returned to the Soldier Sector headquarters and called a meeting with her Generals. She questioned them on the state of mind of the women of the armed forces. She needed them to be prepared for a two-pronged war, woman against woman as the Queendom divided in civil war, and women against slaves. The soldiers who served under her had come to respect her during the past three months as she defended her Low Throne against Sephora. In the matriarchal society they lived in, it brought them a sense of comfort that the sister of their beloved Commander ruled in Rebekkah's place. The Generals assured her the soldiers would follow her no matter which Queen she commanded them to support.

Sephora had been infiltrating their ranks with her secret police, and these women did not ingratiate themselves with those who had chosen the army for life. Indeed, a soldier's highest calling was celibacy, and those women visited the Quickening Chamber illegally whenever they took a whim to. The women of the Arts saw the Quickening Chamber as another avenue of self-expression, not just for duty alone. The privileges these women took for themselves angered the regular army.

Once war began, the first order of business would be to turn on the members of Sephora's secret police who had infiltrated their ranks and immobilize them until the fighting was over. One of the Generals suggested they be held as hostages, but it was generally acknowledged that Sephora would not yield anything to spare their lives, and true soldiers only shed the blood of womankind when it was absolutely necessary.

Arrival left the meeting feeling pleased. She had given her Generals orders to arm all soldiers to the maximum and begin drills on the training grounds. Since the week of Harvest Festival opened tomorrow night, everyone would think they were preparing for the Festival displays hosted by the Soldier Sector. The stage was set for her to complete her pact with Servus. She would be expected to question him.

Arrival dispatched an armed escort to bring Servus to an interrogation room. She made sure the room was secure, and then she waited in the reflection room until the escort came to get her. It didn't take more than half an hour for the escort to return.

"Servus is in interrogation room six as you ordered, Commander and Low Queen."

"Very good, soldier. I will question him immediately. This should not take long. Please accompany me and stand guard outside. Let no one disturb me. Then you may take him back to his work while I visit our sisters on the training field."

The soldier saluted and followed Arrival as she went to complete the Pact of Honor she had entered with Servus. Arrival waited until the door closed behind them and bowed to Servus at the waist.

"King Servus, you have conducted yourself admirably and held up your end of our bargain as well as any woman could have done."

Servus returned the bow.

"Queen Arrival, it was a delight to enter this Pact of Honor with you. Have you called me here to keep your end of our bargain?"

"I have. I recently returned from unburdening myself of Rebekkah's grave-secret, and I may now tell you." Arrival told him the secret she had shared with Rachel. Servus grasped the implications at once.

"Rachel will not dare attack the others, not with Rebekkah's flesh and blood among them."

Arrival nodded her head in agreement.

"You are correct. Besides, Rachel has enough to keep her busy in the attempt to regain her throne. Sephora will not leave quietly. Servus, may I have your word the slaves will not rebel until this civil dispute between Sephora and Rachel is settled?"

"What kind of King would I be if I let this opportunity go by, Arrival? As a commander, what would you do?"

Arrival shook her head sadly.

"Servus, it has given me great pleasure to join forces with you. I don't want to fight you."

They stood face to face. He took a step closer to her and she did not back away.

"The pleasure has been all mine Arrival."

Arrival felt a slow blush begin, and so she turned to business.

"What happened to the Three Sephoras?"

Servus grinned.

238

"I will tell you what it is safe for you to know. Two of them remain in the area but will not resurface for at least a few weeks. Second Sephora has made a permanent break with her family and for freedom."

Servus grew serious and changed the subject.

"You say the men and women contract in monogamous relationships and raise children together as equals. Rebekkah herself contracted in such a union. How do you feel about that, Arrival?"

He took another step toward her and she could feel his breath on her lips. She was a tall woman, but Servus matched her in height. Thoughts she had been trying to put out of her mind flooded her senses. Her heart pounded, but she was a warrior and would not back down from what Servus had started.

"If such a practice became adopted here in the Queendom, I would not need to travel outside these walls to find a man who I felt was worthy to share myself with. What do you say to that, Servus?"

His answer was to take her in his arms and kiss her. He was out of practice, and she had never kissed a man. Passion and respect guided them. Both sensed it was a sacred moment.

When they broke apart, Servus spoke gruffly.

"Arrival, join me in my fight to free the slaves. Then I may court you in a manner you are worthy of."

"I told you before; I will not betray my gender! I am Low Queen and Commander of the Soldier Sector. For goddess's sake, Servus, you are asking me to betray the thousand who serve beneath me to satisfy my own longing! If I did, I would be no better than Sephora, who serves only Sephora. I live for duty and honor."

"Arrival, I withdraw my request," Servus said. "And I apologize. If you betrayed your throne for my sake, I would love you less."

"Love?" Arrival gasped.

"Yes, love. I have watched you from afar since you were a child. I was glad when you chose the life of a soldier so I would not have to think of you in the arms of another man. You are honest, brave, and loyal, all traits I value highly. I find you to be the most beautiful woman in the Queendom. I would think of only you when I had to fulfill my duty in the Quickening Chamber. Women seem to sense when your thoughts are not with them. My duty there did not last long. I have been planning the war to win men's freedom for a long time, and no small part of my motivation is so I can present myself to you as an equal. I have always hoped I could win your respect and perhaps your love. I do not wish to fight you, but I have no choice. I felt that a goddess brought you to me to arrange a Pact of Honor. That same goddess is now having her revenge for the sweet pleasure of being your equal for a little while."

Arrival held her head up high.

"Servus, I wish we did not have to be enemies. Duty and tradition force us to live separate lives. If fate allows, and if we both live through the coming war, I will accept your attentions with pleasure."

Servus nodded. His eyes expressed the sadness he felt. Arrival spun from him and left the room quickly. The choice had not been easy. For over four months, Arrival had been tempted by the vision of having a mate and bearing children as Rebekkah had. She was attracted to Servus in a way she had never felt before, and it frightened her. She wondered what Rachel would think of her now.

The guard outside the room saluted her.

"Escort Servus back to his work," said Arrival. "If I am needed I will be on the training fields."

"Yes, Commander," the guard answered, and entered the room.

Arrival whistled for Stealth, who was grazing nearby. By the time the guard left the interrogation room with Servus, Arrival was already galloping away.

The son Leged had chosen to sacrifice his own freedom for was called Lyal. The men had called the boy after Leged at first, but as children often do, the boy mispronounced his name and Lyal had stuck. Lyal had a pleasing visage and form. He would be old enough to begin quickening duty in a few weeks. It was clear the women who supervised the rooms had their eye on him, so he had his mind on one thing only. Becoming a man was one duty all slaves looked forward to.

It was Lyal's day to stock hay in the second story of the mule barn. It had to be rotated so that the fresh hay went in last and the older bales were moved up front. It was backbreaking work, but it gave Lyal an outlet for his energy, and he daydreamed about quickening duty as he worked. Perhaps he would even be lucky enough to father a son who would be chosen to live, and he could present his loving father with a grandson! It was the least he could do for the man who did so much for him.

When Lyal moved a hay bale and saw the vision of beauty hiding there, he thought he was merely dreaming. Lyal was used to seeing the older women who tended the boys' barracks, and of course, the soldiers. Many of the soldiers resembled men. All were muscular and fit. This beauty had flaxen hair and blue eyes, and though she was fit, she had no bulging muscles. She instead had gentle curves barely hidden under a flimsy shift. Instead of the self-confident presence the soldiers commanded, this lovely mirage trembled in fear. Lyal thought this was a vision from a goddess portending an omen for his upcoming duty.

He knelt before her.

"Goddess, speak to me. Your servant is listening."

"Please," the vision whispered in terror, "do not hurt me, and do not turn me in to Sephora, I beg you."

Lyal looked around to make sure there was no one else in the barn. They were alone. He was often left alone to do his duties as this barn was small and he could do the work himself easily. A soldier came around periodically to check on him, but Lyal didn't expect her until later.

He crept closer to her.

"I will not hurt you," he said, "and I will make sure no one else does either. You are beautiful. Are you a goddess in flesh come to give me a message?"

She looked even more terrified at his closeness, but his words made her smile.

"I am no goddess. I am Hannah. I am a prisoner of Sephora's. Protecting me will surely get you killed, but I beg you not to turn me in. I have nothing to offer you in return for helping me."

She dissolved into tears. Lyal felt powerless yet strong at the same time. Lyal gave her the strongest oath a slave could give.

"You do not need to give me anything. I swear on my father's life that I will help you. Tell me your story so I will know best how to help you. I am Lyal, son of Leged, who is a good friend of King Servus. I will use my connection to protect you. Servus will be happy to help an enemy of Sephora's."

Hannah began to relax for the first time since attacking the girl who had checked on her in the dungeon cell. Adrenaline and anger had carried her through her attack on the young guard. The weeks in the forest had made her much more physically fit than she had been before. She had found enough debris on the floor to set up a pile of garbage that hid from view the hole left by stones she had dug up out of the floor using a wooden comb she had found. With the rocks she had killed several of the rats that ran boldly through the cell and were easy to catch. She had smeared their blood over herself. When the guard had checked on her, she had lifted her foot over the garbage on the ground, and when her foot landed in the hole, she lost her balance and fell.

Hannah had been waiting for that opportunity. She knocked the guard unconscious with one of the stones. She took the guard's outer cloak and dressed the girl in her own. She ripped her outer dress into strips and bound and gagged the guard with them. In the confusion of the night, she was able to move freely through the palace by staying in the shadows. She found an empty wash closet to cleanse herself in and made it outside to the mule stable before hearing voices. That was when she had hidden in the loft, moving a few bales of hay to create a pocket to hide her from view.

The rage she felt had diminished, leaving her terrified. She could not, and would not, go back to the forest, but she wasn't safe in the city. She had no idea what she would do, and she was worried about Rachel.

In her relief and gratitude, she reached for Lyal's hands and held them in her own. Her eyes shown with hope, which lit her face up like the sun. The course of Lyal's life was set in that moment. Her beauty dazzled him, and her confidence in his ability to help her made a lump rise in his throat. All thoughts of the joys of quickening duty left his mind. He wanted nothing more than to champion this beauty for the rest of his life. He would protect her or die trying.

"My name is Hannah," she began in hushed tones. "This is my story." She poured out the heartache of her life to the boy who listened raptly, never once interrupting. He was shocked at the coldness of her mother all but abandoning her when she did not conceive a child. No matter what Lyal did, he knew his father would love him always. He grew angry when she spoke of Sephora's abuse of her. She concluded with her attack on the guard and her flight to the hayloft.

When she finished her narrative, she said, "Tell me, do you know what happened to Rachel? Does she live? I have been sick with worry. For all her troubles, she has never once been unkind to me. I am afraid I have caused her death, as Sephora said I would."

Every slave knew of the recent events, even the boys who had been held hostage, as Lyal had been.

"Rachel returned to the city in safety, and Rebekkah is with her," he said.

"Oh, Lyal, thank you for telling me this good news."

This time Hannah flung herself into his arms, sobbing quietly in relief, and he sat transfixed by feelings he had never felt in his life. That moment he became a man, for he understood that this sharing of himself—his strengths, his courage, and his time—determined manhood, not the act that took place in the Quickening Chamber.

Rachel was not prepared for the wave of anger that welled up in her when Sephora entered the room. She forced herself to breathe deeply and center her thoughts. Losing control and venting her feelings would gain nothing. She longed to confront Sephora, but confrontation must wait until Sephora was no longer a threat to everything she held dear. Years of practicing self-control saved her. She pushed the hatred away and forced herself to see Sephora merely as an opponent that she must beat in an intricate game. Because Rachel was so fixated on her inner sensations, she never saw the profound change that came over Ava's face as she observed Sephora.

Sephora was all smiles. She stood in the doorway for a dramatic pause and then swept into the room. She wore a simple pale peach sheath. Her long black hair swung loose and shone brilliantly. Her green eyes, lined in kohl, seemed to burn like emeralds in her face. For all the simplicity of her outfit, she had chosen the largest and most ornamental crowns of the Queendom to sit upon her head.

Sephora walked to Rachel and hugged her warmly. Rachel returned the hug enthusiastically. Both women greeted each other like long-lost friends as the serving girls laid out a feast fit for queens.

No one paid the least bit of attention to Ava, who was staring in a state of shock at the general vicinity where Sephora stood. In Ava's homeland, angels came and went freely. Sometimes they would appear as if made of flesh and bone. Sometimes they took their own form. They were Spirit in nature, but the air around

244

them shimmered. In full daylight, they were impossible to detect by the human eye, though many times sweet scents surrounding them gave away their presence. By other lights, she and her family had no difficulty seeing the change in the air, the shimmer and shifting of light that heralded an angel's presence.

For this reason, Ava had no doubt of what she was seeing, though it made no sense to her. Around Sephora hovered at least a dozen angels. The light was perfect for detecting them. The sun had set and oil lamps were casting tall shadows around the room.

This presented a paradox to Ava. These were the first angels she had seen since her conversation with Michael almost three years ago. How could it be that Rachel, who seemed to embody goodness and truth, had no such heavenly escorts, but Sephora, who by all accounts wrought terrible chaos, was accompanied by so many? Ava did not recognize any of them, and they took no notice of her.

Ava began to worry that she had made too hasty a pact with Rachel. Perhaps Sephora should have her support. She would have to re-evaluate everything she had learned much more carefully before she did any damage to her soul. She would not immediately abandon Rachel and her plan, but she would pretend to be sicker than she was and observe the women carefully.

The serving girls, with downcast eyes and trembling hands, had finished setting up the repast. They had brought in two feasting couches and set them up near the bed where Ava lay. The couches had a back to recline against and an arm on one side. It was the women's practice to recline on their left side while eating with their right hand. In front of each guest, the girls had placed a small table. Each table had a place setting that included a large bowl, several smaller ones, a medium sized plate, a goblet, woven napkins, and a fork, spoon, and knife. In the center of the smaller tables was a large low table laden with food. It was a simple feast, but it contained all the foods Sephora was known to love: fruits, stews, rice, breads, and nuts. Also on the table were several bottles of wine.

The serving girls lined up in fear to wait for Sephora's judgment of their work. Sephora had insisted everything be perfect, and she was famous for never being totally pleased with anything. She walked around the feasting tables and eyed them critically. True to form, Sephora found something that displeased her.

"This spoon is out of alignment with the fork and knife." Sephora gestured to a place setting. Rachel could see nothing wrong with it, but did not interfere.

"Who set this place?" Sephora demanded.

To avoid the wrath of Sephora was to pay a heavier punishment later, so one of the girls stepped forward. Tears had already begun to make their way down her face. She fell at Sephora's feet and kissed them.

"I am sorry, High Queen, for displeasing you. Please punish me so I may do my job better next time," she answered.

Sephora frowned. "This is a very important dinner. You have let me down and embarrassed me in front of Rachel and her guest. You have earned your punishment."

Rachel raised an eyebrow. Sephora was steadfastly refusing to acknowledge Ava as her daughter. Rachel understood why.

Sephora continued to threaten the girl prostrate before her.

"Was it your eye that caused you to make the error or your hand?"

Rachel shook her head sadly. This fit the rumors Rachel had heard, that Sephora would make her victims choose their own punishments. No one ever brought a complaint before the High Throne, and a Low Queen's rule was absolute in her Sector. Rachel had not thought such barbaric behavior possible, but for the first time, she gave credence to the rumors she had heard. If all the worst accounts of Sephora were true, then this girl was being asked to choose between losing an eye or a finger. Rachel would not allow this to continue.

Ava knew none of the dark secrets Rachel had heard whispered about Sephora and never guessed Sephora's intentions toward the girl.

"This servant is a mere child," said Rachel. "I ask your Highness for mercy. This is a night for celebration, a night to extend pardon."

This insolence of Rachel's was what Sephora had been hoping for. She knew that Rachel expected to be in total control of the Queendom again in the morning. She would have this girl's right pinky finger cut off and her right eye gauged out while Rachel watched.

Sephora smiled, truly happy.

"Of course, you are right. I will fix the spoon myself and we will pretend this never happened."

Sephora reached down and moved the spoon a hair's width toward the fork.

"You are all dismissed," she said, "so that I and my guests may feast in private. I will serve the meal myself."

The weeping girl stood, wiped her tears away, and thanked Sephora profusely. All the girls filed out glad to be relieved of the responsibility of serving Sephora.

The minute the door shut behind them, Sephora spoke.

"Now we will feast! I have brought a meal fit for Queens. It is too bad there is only one present."

Rachel longed to assault Sephora. With anger fueling her, she might be able to kill the younger woman before she was able to react.

Rachel glanced at the bread knife, sharpened to a fine blade to render the thin slices Sephora preferred. Rachel rejected the thought at once, though she would regret it later. She chose a verbal assault instead.

"Now it is your Highness who is in error," said Rachel. "As the saying goes, 'Once a Queen always a Queen'. There are clearly three Queens present."

Rachel chose the couch closest to Ava and reclined without being invited. "Was it your mind or your tongue that caused the error?"

"Rachel, both your eyes and mind deceive you. If I must count the mad former High Queens among us, then I grudgingly agree there are two Queens present, but not three," Sephora answered.

"You seem so certain Rebekkah has not been returned to me. Do you have some knowledge I do not?" Rachel asked.

"Though I am younger, I would say I have much knowledge that you do not. What is it exactly you are hinting at?" Sephora answered with a smile. She remained standing to serve the meal.

Rachel too smiled. Sephora had much more practice at this double-edged talk than she did. Rachel did not wish to endanger the life of Ahmilia. She longed to hint that Arrival had told her Sephora's daughters would not be available to help their mother, but she did not want to put Arrival in more danger than she was already in. Nothing restrained Sephora's behavior, yet Rachel's concern for the safety of those she loved forced her to keep her own counsel. She backed down from veiled threats and resorted to insult.

"Perhaps I hint at nothing. Perhaps hunger causes me to question your disbelief. I believe you said you would serve the meal, or is this one of your famous tortures?"

This struck home. Sephora stopped smiling. Rachel had insulted her hospitality and challenged her about something that had been overlooked in the past.

"I alone of all your Low Queens ruled without any help from you for years. You never truly appreciated me, and now you insult my hospitality. I shall not wait one minute more to feed you, you ungrateful harpy. What would you like, Rachel?" she asked.

"My daughter Rebekkah and I will eat whatever you eat and drink whatever you drink."

Rachel decided to give heed to all the rumors she had dismissed over the years about Sephora. Chief among them was the rumor of the many poisonings she commissioned.

"It is a good decision you make, for it is fitting and proper to emulate the High Queen. Let us feast."

Ava stirred. She had been alert to the goings on, but felt there was subtext she was missing. She moved to get a better view of Sephora. Rachel addressed her foster daughter lovingly.

"Rebekkah, the High Queen has come with a feast of celebration. Will you eat a few bites with us?"

In truth, Ava was hungry. She nodded weakly. She still did not know what to make of the angels that attended Sephora. She could still see them clearly, though they took no notice of her.

"Perhaps your daughter would like to have some bread spread with strawberry preserves?" Sephora cut a piece of bread and spread the fruit on it as she spoke. Ava refused by shaking her head. She recalled every word Rachel had said to her in the forest the night before and remembered Rebekkah was allergic to strawberries.

"Have you forgotten my daughter gets hives when she eats those berries, Sephora?" Rachel asked.

"No, Rachel, I have not forgotten. I see you have coached this girl well. Good job."

"When could I have coached her, Sephora?"

"How could I know how long you have been planning this usurpation of my power? Whatever you are up to will not work."

"Open your eyes! This is my daughter!"

Sephora did not show the irritation she felt. She spoke as if she were humoring a child.

"Fine. Whatever you say. I hope there is no objection to stew, then?"

Sephora offered her stew. It looked to be full of vegetables in some kind of thick broth, so Ava smiled at Rachel, who nodded in approval. Sephora served herself first, then the others. She put grapes and apple slices on her smaller plate and then served the same to the others. She repeated the ritual with a sampling of breads. She poured wine from one bottle into all three chalices, beginning with her own. Then she sat and began to pick at her fruit, letting the stew cool.

There was a tense silence while Sephora served them. Rachel watched Sephora carefully and only began eating when Sephora had swallowed a bite. Ava followed Rachel's lead. Rachel's distrust of Sephora was insultingly obvious. Sephora paid it no heed and took great pain to savor each bite.

The fruits and breads did Ava a world of good. She had eaten so little for three months that she was soon sated. She was full by the time Sephora ate her first spoonful of stew.

Rachel had stew. Being certain it was not poisoned, she took a spoonful from Ava's bowl to feed her. Ava was full and would have refused the stew, but was distracted by the angels who quivered in anticipation of what would happen next.

The spoonful went into her mouth. The flavor was good, but slightly bitter. The angels stared at her, and she swallowed. Ava began to feel odd. There was a burning in her esophagus and stomach, and she began to feel sleepy. She thought the illness had returned. She spoke in front of Sephora for the first time.

"Mother, I think I shall go back to sleep. Thank you, High Queen, for your kindness to me and to my mother. Please, Mother, eat to keep your strength up for my sake. I will sleep a little while. May I have some water first?"

"Of course, Rebekkah. Here."

Rachel was not unduly concerned. Ava drank heartily and lay back. She tried to stay awake to hear what her foster mother and Sephora talked about, but she could not. She fell into a deep sleep, which mercifully blocked out the fiery pain in her intestines.

The stew was excellent, and Rachel ate heartily. She had saved her wine for last. She had observed Sephora drinking liberally, so she felt confident she could drink the wine as freely as Sephora did. She picked up her chalice and held it.

"I propose a toast," Rachel said. "May the best woman for the Queendom sit upon the High Throne."

"Yes," said Sephora, smiling in agreement. "I will drink to that."

Both women raised their chalices and finished the wine at once. Sephora filled both chalices and raised hers in return.

"It is my turn to toast," Sephora said. If Ava had been awake, she would have seen the angels quivering in mirth and excitement again. Rachel was feeling a bit tired, a bit numb. She had been through a lot. She assumed the food was making her sleepy until Sephora raised her glass and finished her toast.

"May I finish this night what I began when I took the High Throne from you."

Sephora drained her glass.

Rachel looked horrified.

"What have you done?" Rachel asked.

"I have done nothing but foil your stupid plot before you could bring it to fruition. I deserve the power of the High Throne, and I have earned it. Were you thinking I would sit idly by while you had some pretender help you steal what is mine? It is just a matter of time until I discover her identity. She will be beyond the reach of my revenge by then, but her family will suffer in her stead.

"I have given you nothing but a strong sedative. You will sleep soundly all night and wake in the morning. But this woman you claim as your daughter will not survive the night. It is such a shame. Once she is gone, any accusations you make will be your word against mine."

"Why not kill me, too?" Rachel asked. She found that speaking was difficult, and she could barely keep her eyes open.

"People can say what they want when the impostor dies. Her health is questionable anyway. Some women believe your story and some do not, but with her dead it will not matter. I can't let you both die on the same night, however, because everyone would know I was behind it.

"With you gone, I doubt anyone would challenge me, but it's not worth taking a chance. Arrival might take the law into her own hands. Even now, the soldiers are armed and drilling on the fields. With Harvest Festival about to begin, I can do nothing to stop her, and she knows it.

"With you still alive, Arrival will have no real cause to challenge me. Indeed, she may resist the impulse to rebel on the strength of the fact that I will own you from this night forward."

"I will never give my support to your rule. You murdered my daughter."

Rachel was fighting to stay awake. It didn't suit Sephora's purposes to have her fall asleep immediately. She went to where Rachel reclined on her dining couch, pulled her up by her collar, and slapped her repeatedly on the face.

"What did you just say?" asked Sephora. She grinned evilly into Rachel's eyes.

Rachel was tired, but not so doped up that she didn't realize her mistake. She covered it instantly.

"My daughter, Rebekkah, who lies here beside me. You have poisoned her. You are her murderer. I will find a way to avenge her death."

"Once again you underestimate me. It was always your biggest failing. Come the morning and ever after, I will drug you by day and torture you by night. You will beg me for death in a week's time. You thought you suffered before, but you know nothing of suffering. I will teach you, yes I will. Sweet dreams, bitch."

Sephora released Rachel, who fell back against the couch and did not even try to resist the effect of the drugs any longer. Briefly, the room swam before her eyes and then all was dark.

The spirits Ava had seen were noiselessly howling with glee. The show had been a good one. They could always depend on Sephora for entertainment.

Rachel's eyes closed. Sephora did two things before she summoned servants to clean up the meal. First, she knocked over

Rachel's wine chalice, breaking it and spilling the wine. Second, she took the bowl of soup the stranger had eaten from and placed it in the ornate crown on her head, where it fit perfectly. No one would know she had left with the bowl.

Then Sephora swept out to attend to other duties. The Harvest Festival would begin the following night. She still had to pick out a dress and inspect the preparations in each Sector. She hoped her henchwomen hurried back with their assignments complete. She wished to be done with the ridiculous distraction Rachel had strewn in her path. Enough was enough. It was time to get back to the good life.

MASQUERADES AND MISCONCEPTIONS

*L*yal requested to see Servus during the time he used for reflection. Servus assumed the boy was worried about his father, so he agreed to speak with him. Servus wished he could tell the boy of his father's sacrifice, but he could not burden him with so big a secret. Lyal entered and knelt before his King. Servus was shocked when Lyal told him about Hannah and begged him to help her.

"Where is the girl now?" Servus asked when Lyal had finished telling him about finding Hannah.

"She is still in the hayloft, but I arranged the bales so she is hidden more thoroughly."

"What do you want me to do?" Servus was bemused.

"Find a way to help Hannah hide from Sephora. I know you can do it, King Servus. I will do anything for her. I ask you to do it for my sake."

If Servus had not recently had his own brush with romance, he might have used Hannah in a bargain with Sephora. As things were, he found he could not deny the boy. He sighed and sat on a bunk, deep in thought. Lyal remained kneeling. He had complete confidence in his ruler.

Servus stood, smiling.

"Lyal, I can and will help your Hannah."

Servus retrieved one of the blades he had taken from the Three Sephoras and handed it to Lyal.

Lyal looked horrified.

"King Servus, please, I cannot hurt her."

Servus laughed,

"This is for her hair. If she wishes to remain hidden, she must cut it. She is going to masquerade as a slave. No one will look for her here."

"You are brilliant, King Servus."

Servus had to agree. Everything was going to work out perfectly. Hannah would masquerade as a slave, and with one of the robes he had taken from the Three Sephoras, he would masquerade as a woman. Tonight he would find and kill Rebekkah with the dagger studded with First Sephora's symbol. With First Sephora implicated in the killing, the Queendom would dissolve into chaos. It was the perfect way to begin their war for freedom. Servus gave Lyal specific instructions to carry out along with the supplies the boy needed, and then he watched as the boy scurried across the compound to the mule barn. He dispatched two of his men to find Justus and Kiertus and give them the message to meet him in the men's temple.

Lyal climbed the ladder to the hayloft and walked to where Hannah was hidden. He tapped out the beats they agreed would signal his return. Hannah did not answer, and for a minute, he thought he had imagined seeing her here. He moved the hay and was relieved to see her curled up and fast asleep. He called her name, but she did not wake up. With his heart pounding in his chest, he reached out and touched her gently. Her eyes fluttered open and he snatched his hand back.

"Lyal!" said Hannah, stretching. "What did your King say? Can he help me?"

"Hannah, King Servus has a solution to your problem. You are to hide among the slaves. We will cut your hair, and you can dress in an extra set of clothes I have brought for you."

Hannah laughed softly.

"It will be like playing a part in the theater. If I hadn't enjoyed sewing so much, I would have loved to be an actress. I can stay in the city and hide from Sephora. Your King is a genius."

"He is! But his help comes with a price. He has a job for you to do, Hannah. He has an errand to run tonight. Since you will be dressed as a slave, he will be dressed as a woman. He will use your hair to make a hairpiece for himself. He will dress in women's robes. He needs you to accompany him to complete the illusion that he is a woman traveling in the company of a young slave. Will you do it?" he asked her. He did not like to pressure her, but Servus had made it clear this was the only way he would agree to hide her.

Hannah agreed quickly.

"Of course, Lyal. This is sure to work. I owe you my life, and it will be the most fun I've had in months. I've hated being exiled in the forest. But how will we cut my hair?"

Lyal showed her the dagger. Hannah gasped, but said nothing. The dagger told her two things. First, Lyal could easily have killed her; second, the dagger bore the crest of the royal line of Sephora. Hannah recognized it immediately. There was more going on here than Lyal knew. He was just a boy, though a handsome and compassionate one. She was almost a woman of twenty. Hannah decided that if she was going to oppose Sephora, she might as well do so completely.

"Let's get started. I'm eager to assume my new identity and to begin my service to your King," said Hannah.

Since Servus needed her hair, first she braided it tightly and bound it with a piece of cord at the top and bottom of the long braid. She showed Lyal where to cut and asked him to do it for her. The sharp blade sliced through the hair, and Hannah's waist-length hair hung from Lyal's fist. He had never touched anything so soft before. Hannah turned to him, took the blade from his hand, and began to hack off chunks of her hair near her scalp. When she was done, her hair was closely cropped in uneven sections, just as many of the slaves wore theirs.

"How do I look?" Hannah asked Lyal, who still grasped the braid.

"You are beautiful," he said, staring with his mouth wide open.

She would have laughed, but she saw he spoke from his heart so she thanked him instead.

"Let's see the clothes."

They were too big for her, but using the blade, she shortened the trousers and tunic. No one had thought to take Hannah's waist purse away from her in the dungeon, and from it she withdrew a needle and thread she kept with her at all times. She took the clothes in at the sides. The simple alterations took no time at all for Hannah to complete. She fashioned a makeshift belt to keep the trousers up, and took a strip of extra cloth to bind her breasts so they would not move beneath the tunic and give away her gender. Lyal turned his back as she dressed. He turned around when she bid him to, and he stared in shock at the transformation.

"Hannah, you could attend Sephora herself and she would not know you."

"Lyal, how can I hope to repay you for championing me, and for giving me hope?" she asked.

He blushed. "You do not need to repay me. It is a pleasure to help you. Just be safe, and live."

"That I will certainly try to do. Now please take me to your King. I can at least pay my debt to him."

258

They made their way without difficulty to the men's temple where Servus awaited them accompanied by Kiertus and Justus. The temple, though scrutinized carefully, was the only place the men could meet privately. Servus could not stock weapons there, however, because the soldiers searched every inch of it meticulously and daily, but it would serve as the perfect meeting place tonight. He was committed to doing everything in his power to keep Sephora on her throne because he knew it would motivate the men to fight for their freedom from her iron-fisted rule.

When he saw Lyal enter with another slave, he was disappointed.

"Would she not agree to help, Lyal?" Servus asked.

The boy grinned as the pair got closer.

"Look carefully King Servus. She did agree."

Within three feet of Servus, Lyal stopped and kneeled. Hannah followed his example.

"Lyal's King is my King," she said. "Lyal's people are my people. I owe him my life."

Her voice removed all doubt about her gender.

"Rise, Hannah of the Arts Sector," Servus said, smiling.

Hannah rose obediently. Servus walked around Hannah inspecting every inch.

"You have surpassed my wildest expectations. If I can be half the woman that you are a slave, victory will be mine tonight. Rise, Lyal, son of Leged. You have served me well."

Lyal rose, his heart swelling with pride.

"King Servus, Hannah has made this transformation herself. I am confident she can help you with yours."

Servus's eyes sparkled.

"Let it be."

Servus flung his outer robes off to reveal First Sephora's cloak underneath. She had worn a simple dark cloak instead of one with a royal crest. Hannah giggled at the sight of the King of the Slaves dressed in women's clothing.

"What do you find funny?" he asked gruffly.

"You are missing a few essential things you need to be a convincing woman," she said. "I can help you with that."

Actresses had often asked Hannah to sew padded inserts for their costumes. Using the copious scraps she had saved from the alterations to her slave clothing, she fashioned padding for Servus to wear on his chest and hips. His body took on a feminine shape. Kiertus and Justus whistled in appreciation. Servus gave them a glance that stifled the whistles.

"With my hood up and your hair upon my head I should be ready to go," he said. "You have done well, Hannah."

"I am not done yet, King Servus."

From the cord around her waist, she brought out her supplies. Most women in the Queendom never went anywhere without a waist-pouch containing items the women considered essential. For a woman raised in the Arts Sector, that included powders and creams in many colors to enhance one's natural beauty. Each Sector had its priorities. In the Arts Sector, personal beauty was almost a cult.

"None of you must see what I do to your King until I am done. I respectfully ask you to stand behind him, there."

Hannah was careful to phrase her directions as requests, not orders, keeping in mind that they were equals now. The men moved to stand where Hannah bid them.

"King Servus, I respectfully ask you to sit. Trust me as I have trusted you."

Servus sat. Hannah worked for ten minutes applying powders and creams here and there. By the time she was done, every inch of his face was caked with something. He felt as if he were looking through a mask. Finally, Hannah took the thick braid of hair and worked magic with it. When she had time, she often helped the girls at the theater with such duties. When she finished, she stepped back and surveyed her work with pleasure. She slipped the hood onto Servus's head and bid him to stand. Theatrically, she spun him to the men waiting behind them, and then she took her place at his left side, two paces behind him, with her head and eyes downcast in the same manner that a personal slave would stand.

There were no whistles in jest now. The men stood awed. No one would suspect Servus and Hannah were anyone other than a woman and her slave. Without thinking, Lyal and Justus made the sign against evil, so uncanny was the transformation.

It was Kiertus who broke the silence.

"King Servus, it is the perfect disguise except for one thing, which, if not taken care of, will be the undoing of you both."

"Speak Kiertus, quickly, for we must hurry."

But Kiertus did not speak. Instead, he rolled up his sleeve and bared his forearm, revealing the numbers tattooed there. They all gasped. To forget to put slave-markings on Hannah would have been a fatal error. The marks on the arm of Servus were covered, but both of Hannah's forearms were bare.

"This will have to do for now," Hannah said, drawing out her waist-pouch again. She took some sticky black resin and asked to see Lyal's mark. She copied it, almost identically, varying one mark.

"Good job, Hannah. That was fast thinking, Kiertus. I thank you. Come, Hannah, we have to hurry. We must get to the palace and find Rachel and Rebekkah. Once we find the room they are in, you must find an excuse to get Rachel out of the room so I can speak alone with Rebekkah."

Servus wanted the murder to be on his head only. He would not reveal to Lyal and Hannah what his real plan was, though of course Kiertus and Justus knew. They had orders to begin the war on Festival Eve, even if something went wrong and he did not return.

Without another word, Servus headed for the door with Hannah two steps behind him. It was an exhilarating feeling. The most dangerous part of their journey was getting to the horse stable, but they made it without incident. Once there, they left boldly, as if they had just been inspecting a horse for sale. They made their way to the Palace, and Hannah, disguising her voice, asked a palace slave for directions to the room Rachel was staying in. Hannah had no difficulty finding her way to the room. Before Tilda eclipsed her place in their family, Hannah was a regular visitor to the Palace. It was tricky leading Servus from two paces behind, but they had worked out a code. A sniffle meant turn right, a cough meant turn left. When they reached the room, Servus was surprised to see there were no soldiers on duty at the door. He and Hannah entered. There were no guards inside the room, either.

The mystery was cleared up when they tried to wake Rachel. She was sleeping so soundly they could not rouse her.

"She has been drugged," Servus said to Hannah.

"No!" Hannah said, crestfallen. "I wanted to apologize for leaving her in the forest, to make sure she was all right. Who do you think drugged her? Do you think she will be okay?"

"I heard she dined with Sephora this evening," answered Servus, "so there is no mystery concerning who drugged her. We must assume Rebekkah has been drugged too. I must try to rouse her. Go keep watch outside the door. Warn me if someone comes."

Their voices woke Ava. Her immune system was back to normal now that the basic nutritional needs of her body had been met. The exposure to the many diseases had made it more efficient at creating antibodies to fight foreign substances. The deadly poison was identified and encapsulated almost instantly after she had consumed it, though the sedative had made her sleepy. Ava looked forward to having a conversation with a male from this city. She lay quietly and waited for him to approach her.

The door closed behind Hannah as she left. Servus removed the blade from its hiding place beneath his tunic. Moonlight from a window glanced off its blade. He strode to the figure on the bed and evaluated his options. Ava's long auburn hair covered her face. She lay on her side. Her arms and a blanket protected her vital organs in front, but her back, which faced the fireplace, was partially exposed. Servus liked the imagery of her being stabbed in the back with First Sephora's dagger. He smirked at the uproar Rebekkah's murder would cause. Servus moved to stand behind her. He raised the dagger high and brought down his killing stroke.

Arrival had been meditating in the reflection room. She had felt the warning tickle of intuition since dinnertime and had finally found time to sit quietly. Her mind, body, and emotions were distracted by every sound. It had taken longer than usual to achieve the trance-like state necessary to be in tune with the sixth sense she possessed. Finally, she achieved the state necessary to understand that her mother and the new Rebekkah were in danger. Arrival jumped up. There was a knot of fear in her belly. Calling for Stealth would take too long. Somehow, Arrival knew she was too late. She sprinted toward the Palace anyway, hoping there was something she could do to help her mother.

Rebekkah had always been fast; she had always beaten Servus in battle exercises, but the speed with which the figure on the bed turned and grabbed his wrist mid-thrust astounded him. Ava sat up and looked into his eyes.

"Why are the men here always trying to kill me?" she asked. The musical voice was unfamiliar to him.

"I don't know you," Servus said.

"No one here does," said Ava, sadly.

Her eyes took him in more fully, and they widened in surprise.

"I heard your voice when you entered. I peeked and saw the light reflect from your blade as you crossed the room. I assumed you were a man! Are you a man?" Ava asked timidly.

"I am indeed a man." Servus blushed, a rare thing for him. "I had to put on a disguise to travel in freedom. Where is Rebekkah? I came to kill her. I have no dispute with you. I apologize for my rash action."

He could not understand why they were conversing. She should have called for soldiers to take him away and have him killed. There were so many laws that he was breaking that any of the mock trials the women usually put slaves through would not be necessary. Instead of calling for soldiers, she smiled at him with a twinkle in her eye.

"My name is Rebekkah. But before you try to kill me again, tell me, what is your name?"

"I am Servus, King of Slaves."

"Servus! I have heard your name before!" Ava stood up and clapped with happiness. Then, with a flourish, she bowed to him. "I owe you a debt of gratitude. You sent four people to guard Rachel and me in the forest. Are you now trying to take that gift of life back? And, tell me, please, what are these slaves I keep hearing about?"

Servus was genuinely confused.

"You were with Rachel in the forest?"

The situation he found himself in was surreal. He was conversing on equal terms with a woman who should have been Rebekkah, but he knew she was not. He wondered if he was dreaming or drugged.

"I was. The four you sent to save me—Yarr, Calena, Titus, and Raysa—earned their freedom." She could see that he was going to ask her more questions, so she forestalled him. She stomped one foot impatiently.

"Ask me no more questions until you have answered one of mine. Please, what is this slavery that everyone seems to know about but me? And Servus..." her voice trailed off timidly.

"Yes?" he said. He tried to grasp something about the situation that made sense and found nothing. She was talking and acting almost like a child, but she was clearly a fully grown, intelligent woman.

"Would it be an imposition to ask you to remove your disguise?"

In spite of himself, he laughed and answered by removing the cloak and hood, the padding underneath, and the hair Hannah had arranged upon his head. He walked to the washbasin to remove the makeup. Ava watched in amazement as the real Servus appeared to her. As he shed his disguise, he answered her question about slavery.

"All of mankind is enslaved to the women," said Servus. "They are our masters. We must do what they say and when they say it. We have no property. The clothes we wear, the food we eat, the work we do, and even the time we have to live is allotted to us by the women.

"We have no mothers and no fathers. Very few of us know who our sons are, and none of us know our daughters. Indeed, these words indicating male familial relationships are taboo and denied to us by our masters." Servus spoke passionately. He began to pace. He was aware of how out of place he was in the opulent, feminine, and tastefully decorated room that Rachel had chosen for herself upon her return to the city. He felt like a bull trying to navigate through a crockery kiosk.

"We are punished at whim, anything from a beating to death. There is no justice for us. Many women don't consider us huwoman. We are looked upon as mere animals, beasts of burden. They do not allow us to learn, to read, or to write. Whether we live or die is determined by how many of us the women can manage at a time. Newborn boys who are not needed as slaves are thrown into

Rowada's Swamp to die. We call it the Swamp of Innocents. Those of us too old or sick to work are often used for target practice or surgical experiments."

He glanced at her and his words trailed off. As angry as he was, she seemed ten times so. She was shaking with rage.

"You lie. No human can be capable of such cruelty against another," she said.

"I swear to you I am not lying."

He showed her his forearm with the tattooed numbers on it.

"The males who are allowed to live are given identification numbers. All living men have these. Have you seen these on the women?"

Ava thought hard. "I have not, and the women do speak often of slaves. I have observed that there are many more women than men."

"Where are you from that you don't know this? Arrival told me there were others. I thought they would be those who had survived banishment from our city. Those survivors would know about slavery."

Ava looked troubled.

"It suits me for now to have the few people who know there are others outside of Evlantis to think I am from such a settlement, but I am not. I come from Eden. Will you keep my secret? I will tell you about where I come from and give you my promise I will not leave this city until I bring an end to this slavery."

Servus nodded his head solemnly. It would only help his cause to have a woman fight beside them. He thought Hannah might be open to joining their rebellion, too. He stopped pacing and gave her his full attention.

Ava continued.

"I come from a place where I too have a Master. But where yours are many, mine is One. Yours determines the course of your life and the number of your years. Mine gives freedom and unlimited possibilities. Your Masters revile and curse you. My Master treasures me. Your masters punish; mine rewards.

"Where I am from, men and women live as complements to each other. We bring to each undertaking a fresh perspective seen from two different ways of thinking. Where I come from, we are valued because we were created in the image of the Master. We walk with Him proudly, almost as equals."

"Please, take me there," Servus said. "Take all the men. We will leave at once."

Tears formed in Ava's eyes.

"There is nothing I would like more, but I can't. I have been banned from my home. I disobeyed the Master. It was an accident, but it was disobedience all the same. He was more than fair to punish me. All the same, I miss my home, my mother, my father, and my siblings. It is so different here in so many ways, and many of them are bad."

She began to cry. He was at a loss for what to do. To touch a woman without her permission was punishable by death, but she was not from here. He was a man of great drive, but also of great compassion. With a sigh, he put his arms around her to comfort her. He held her quietly, not knowing what else he could do.

"Thank you for your kindness," she said after her tears subsided. "This water from the eyes which accompanies great sadness is new to me since leaving my homeland. The pain in my heart because of the separation is quite intense. Does this mean you no longer want to kill me?"

"I don't want to kill you, no," said Servus with a smile. "But, please explain to me how it is you are sleeping where I expected to find Rebekkah. Where is she?"

They were talking comfortably. Not since she had met Rebekkah had Ava felt completely at ease with anyone from this part of the world. She was frank with him.

"Rebekkah is dead. I entered into a Pact of Honor with Rachel. My part of the Pact is to pretend to be Rebekkah, who was injured by Sephora's henchwomen in the forest the third night of the sacrifice. Rachel feels this is the only way to rescue her city from Sephora."

Servus let out a low whistle.

"How is she explaining the difference in appearance?"

The twinkle appeared in Ava's eye again.

"The goddesses took pity on me for my grievous injuries and healed me, giving me a new form in the process. Rachel's part of the pact was to give me peaceful passage into death. It is a promise I do not intend for her to be able to keep."

Ava looked wistful, and though Servus thought she was going to speak, she kept her peace. The mood passed quickly.

"Why did you come to kill Rebekkah?" she asked him.

"I want to lead the men in a war for our freedom. I planned to stab Rebekkah in the back with Sephora's eldest daughter's dagger. The murder would have divided the Queendom and created chaos. With the women at war with each other, I planned to lead the men in a campaign to end slavery. Would you consider fighting with us? If you went to war on our side, we would have a greater chance of winning."

"No, Servus. Slavery is horrible and must be ended, but I will not fight and kill others to do so. I held Rebekkah as she was dying. I saw a man named Baraus die. I hate death."

Servus looked crestfallen. He would not kill this woman. He would have to wait longer to set his plan in action. She seemed to read his mind.

"You are disappointed."

"I can't deny it. For a moment I felt that freedom was within mankind's reach."

"If you kill me, though I am not Rebekkah, it would have the same effect."

"I cannot kill you. I live by a Code of Honor. You are as innocent of any offense against mankind as any of the babes thrown into the Swamp of Innocents. Unjustified murder is not an acceptable means to the end I have in mind."

"I am glad to hear you say that, Servus. It saves both of us time and aggravation. A man named Tiburnus tried to kill me once already. He stuck a knife in my heart. It healed, but the healing took many months, and I became ill, something that does not occur among my people. It was painful and I have better use for the time my Master has given me. You have told me many things I needed to know, things I cannot ask others who think that I am the reincarnation of Rebekkah. I am sure there is much more you can tell me. Enter into a Pact of Honor with me. Protect me any way that you can and give me more information, and in return I will use my identity as Rebekkah to help you end slavery without bloodshed."

Servus laughed.

"I will help you, but without a pact. You are powerless to end slavery by yourself!"

A change came over Ava. She stood straighter and lifted her chin. Her being radiated power and majesty. Servus wanted to kneel before her, but he stood his ground.

"Servus, King of Slaves, hear me," said Ava. "There was no one among my family who was more stubborn than I. Whatever I set my mind to, I accomplish. If I choose to end slavery single-handedly, it will be done." She looked stern. Suddenly a smile lit her features making her look mischievous. "But, it would be better to have help with this. How binding are these Pacts of Honor?"

"They are non-retractable," answered Servus to the enigma that stood before him. "Only death breaks them, and sometimes pacts are handed down from one generation to the next."

"Is each party responsible to fulfill the pact?"

"Yes, of course."

"If Rachel wishes me to remain Rebekkah, then, by virtue of the fact that she cannot tend my dying, she will owe me something."

"You would ask her to free the slaves? To give men equal rights with women?"

"When the time comes, I will. I give you my word."

She held open her arms, and he embraced her. Servus thought it was pleasant, but it lacked the fire of passion of the embrace he had shared with Arrival.

"You remind me of one of my brothers," said Ava. "His name is Seth."

It struck Servus that this was what it would be like to have a sister he respected. He would gladly trade Sephora for this Rebekkah.

"We will be as brother and sister then," said Servus.

The door opened and Hannah entered the room. She meant to tell them Arrival was coming, but she was speechless at the sight of Servus and Rebekkah in each other's arms. Hannah found her voice and cleared her throat again to speak, but lost it again in astonishment, as a stranger, the woman she had presumed was Rebekkah, turned her head to face her. Hannah knew it would only be seconds before Arrival entered. Without a word, Hannah knelt on the ground before the impostor. She hoped they would understand. Servus did, but not in time to untangle himself from Ava's embrace.

Arrival, out of breath and out of her mind with worry for Rachel, entered the room. She thought she would find her mother dead or in danger. Instead, she discovered Servus in the arms of another woman. Upon her entry, they parted, clearly startled. Arrival was distracted by unfamiliar feelings this roused in her. She glanced at the other slave in the room. He looked familiar, but she could not recall his name or number. Arrival did not notice how glad Servus and the stranger were to see her.

Arrival knew she should kill Servus immediately. To touch a woman outside the Quickening Chamber was punishable by death. That she was required by law to kill him when he kissed her earlier had never occurred to her. She noticed Servus was smiling warmly at her. She glanced away. She would not look the traitor in the eye.

"What are you doing here?" Arrival asked gruffly.

"I came to begin my war by killing Rebekkah," answered Servus. "But I have changed my mind. We are allies now." Servus was merely giving information. He had no agenda, no hidden message. He respected Arrival's decision to remain on the opposite side of the war.

Arrival heard something entirely different. She thought he was saying Rebekkah had chosen his side, whereas Arrival had not. She thought he had lied to her about his love for her in order to cloud her feelings and sway her to his side so that he could win his war. Now he had used the same tactics with this stranger and won her over.

Soldiers were aware they could have strong emotion and strong passion that could carry them out of the moment. They were taught to resist such feelings, that feelings sometimes lie, and determining truth was necessary before action was taken. Arrival was aware she was having such a moment now. She would not be hasty. She would be justified in killing Servus and the unknown slave. Finding Servus in the stranger's arms felt like a betrayal. Though she wished to kill him, it was her desire to spill his blood that stayed her hand. In her moment of jealous rage and anger, she did nothing.

None of the others in the room were aware of the state Arrival was in. The last three months had taught her to hide her feelings well. She was unaware at this moment that she was as good an actress as Sephora was.

"Come," she said gruffly, "I don't know how you got here, but we must get you and your friend back to the slave barracks quickly. It is almost time for the night count."

Hannah went to Servus and helped him quickly back into his disguise. Arrival watched in amazement at the transformation.

"That would explain it," she said. She stood, shook her head, and smiled, even though she was still hurt.

Servus gave her First Sephora's dagger.

"I cannot be found with this, and you may be able to plant it somewhere as a distraction. I understand Sephora has her secret police looking for her daughters."

Where she wanted to plant it was in Servus's cold heart. She took the dagger from him and nodded in confirmation. Her sources had told her the same thing.

"Could you walk with us outside to the horse stables?" Servus asked. "We will be able to make it from there without any trouble."

He tried to meet her eye, but she was not responding to him. He was puzzled.

"I can do better than that," she said. "I can take you through the palace. Then you will have time to spare before the evening head count."

She had not addressed Rebekkah. She did so now.

"How nice to see you up and about, Sister. How is it Rachel was not awakened by your visitors?"

Arrival strode to Rachel feeling edgy and distracted while Ava answered.

"Thank you. I am much better. Our foster mother sleeps soundly. Servus said she was drugged."

Arrival answered Ava more sharply than she had intended.

"You must watch your tongue carefully. Rachel is foster mother to me, yes. To you she is birth mother."

Ava hung her head.

"Yes, Sister," she said, chastened. She thought of all she needed to learn and saw a way it could be accomplished.

"Arrival, I would like to keep this slave as a personal servant for Rachel and me," Ava said as she waved a hand at Hannah, who Arrival still did not recognize.

Arrival felt guilty for snapping at her and replied in a kinder tone.

"Certainly you may. You are each entitled to a personal attendant. You are lucky Sephora has not yet thought to assign two slaves of her choosing. I will inform Palace Security you have chosen a slave to act in this capacity. But Servus must go back to the barracks, and the sooner, the better."

"Rebekkah," said Servus, "for your second personal slave, request a young boy named Lyal." So far, Hannah had fooled Arrival, but another slave would figure out Hannah's ruse quickly. He must pair Hannah with someone he could trust, someone who would coach her in her duties.

"Thank you, I will," Ava replied.

"Consider it done," said Arrival. She sensed there was something here she was not being told and she resented being left out. "He will attend you in the morning."

Servus was glad. Before he could thank Arrival, she strode to the door, opened it, and walked into the hall, still avoiding eye contact with him, though she glanced at the second slave again. Arrival could not understand how he could be close to Servus and yet had previously escaped her attention.

Servus hurried after her, quickly. It was his right to walk beside her and he intended to enjoy every minute of it until he had to resume the role of slave once again. The door shut behind them. Ava and Hannah stared awkwardly at each other.

"You do not believe I am Rebekkah," said Ava.

"No," said Hannah, "and I am not a slave any more than Servus is a woman or you are Rebekkah. I am Hannah, daughter of Nebo of the Arts Sector. I owe my life to Servus, who has granted me sanctuary and hidden me from Sephora."

"Hannah, anyone who is friends with Rachel and Servus is my friend too. I need your help. I need to know everything you can tell me about this land, your people, and how I can fool everyone into thinking I am a princess. Rachel told me about the life of her daughter, but I know nothing of your laws and customs."

Deep in thought, Hannah walked to where Rachel was sleeping. Without thinking, Hannah began to tend to Rachel. Ava joined her, and together they made her as comfortable as the dining couch would allow. Ava's kindness to Rachel helped Hannah make up her mind.

"I will help you," said Hannah. "I will tell you everything you need to know. Let's get comfortable. This will take a while."

Neither Arrival nor Servus spoke on their way back to the horse barn. Arrival was furious with herself. She could not believe she had been fooled by him and allowed him to kiss her.

Servus had too much on his mind to chance speaking with her on their walk. He had left the slave quarters intending to become a murderer and had returned with a powerful ally. He needed to speak with Kiertus and Justus as soon as possible to prevent the start of war. They were housed in different barracks, and he had to get back to his own barracks before the next head count. He would have to wait until morning after breakfast.

Safely inside the barn, Servus turned to Arrival with a smile. They were alone. He wanted to talk to her, to use any excuse to be near her. He was disappointed when she turned from him without a word and strode quickly away. As he watched her go, a feeling of misgiving washed over him. Something was wrong, but he did not know what it was. He quickly washed the make-up off in the trough, removed his women's clothing, and made his way stealthily to his barracks.

FESTIVAL EVE

R achel awoke in the morning disoriented. Her mouth was dry, and her head ached. She felt as if she were looking at the world through a fog. She couldn't remember where she was or what day it was. She tried to sit, and the world spun around her. She felt as if something urgent needed to be attended to, so, in spite of the pervasive dizziness that lingered, she sat up. The room did not look familiar. She moved her head slowly to take in her surroundings.

When she saw the long auburn hair spilling out from beneath the covers on the bed across the room, it all came back to her. She gave a low moan and felt tears well up in her eyes. She willed her body to stand, and she made her way slowly to the body of her foster daughter.

"Abekka, I am sorry. I meant to protect you from Sephora. I don't know how she managed to poison us. I took great pains to see that we ate only what she did. I have failed you and broken our Pact of Honor. I did not tend you gently into death."

Bitter tears coursed down her face. Rachel was certain Ava was dead, so when Ava opened her eyes and spoke to her, Rachel jumped back in shock.

"Kind mother, it is time you learn you will have many years to keep your promise. Had I been well enough when you found me,

275

I would have told you then. I think I may have gotten the better of the bargain, for you are a good woman. Rebekkah was blessed to call you mother."

"What do you mean?" Rachel put her hand on her head. "Am I dead? Dreaming?"

"You are among the living and are fully conscious. I will not die. My wounds have healed. I cannot explain how. I can only assure you it is true."

Ava tore away the bandages at her heart and on her arms to reveal fully healed skin beneath.

"Your wounds were fatal. How can this be?" Rachel asked as she stared in shock.

Ava was troubled. She wanted to tell Rachel the truth, but could not fathom how the Master's angels attended Sephora, who seemed the antithesis to all He stood for, while this humble woman, who was so kind and loving, seemed to have none of His blessings for all her labors of love, only pain and trouble. There was a deep mystery here that she did not understand, so she kept her secret to herself for the time being.

"There may be a time when I will be able to explain everything to you. For now, I must keep my own counsel." She sat and reached for Rachel's hands and held them. "Sit next to me. I have some news to share that will cheer you."

Rachel was too confused and groggy from the drugs to argue. She sat, and Ava's arm encircled her. Rachel was comforted by the gesture.

"We had some visitors last night. You slept so soundly that you did not awaken. One of them was Hannah. She is in hiding from Sephora, who is searching frantically for her, but Hannah will not be found."

Rachel met Ava's eyes, which sparkled in mirth as she continued.

"Hannah has taken on a disguise that will not fail. She was worried about you so she came to check on you. She declares her loyalty to you."

"I am so glad to hear that. I have been worried about her. Why, though, would she choose my side? She and her family are from the Arts Sector."

"Why don't you ask her yourself?" asked Ava.

"May I? Where is she? When can we go to her?" asked Rachel.

She looked around the room seeing no one. She didn't give the young slave in the room more than a passing glance. It shocked Rachel when the slave stepped forward, unbidden, and spoke.

"I will tell you why. You could have made my service to you unbearable, but you didn't. You showed me kindness and respect. I have always felt empathetic toward you. I am barren, and you lost your only womb-born daughter. Sephora wants us both dead. You may be sure of my loyalty."

"Hannah?" Rachel said, aghast.

"Yes," Hannah replied. "When I returned from the forest the night before last, Sephora said I was a coward for leaving you in the forest alone with a demon-ghost. She assaulted me and had me thrown in the palace dungeon. I escaped and hid in the mule stable. A young slave found me there and took me to Servus, King of Slaves, who protected me and brought me here to you. I am here to serve you."

"Hannah, this is a dangerous position you are taking. Aren't you worried Sephora will recognize you?" Rachel asked.

"You did not recognize me, and you have had much more contact with me than Sephora. Arrival was here last night, and she did not recognize me. Let me stay, Queen Rachel. I will take my chances with you. I would rather die serving you than die serving Sephora. I choose death rather than the forest, which is my only other option."

"Hannah, I do not wish to put you in further danger, but I am in no position to refuse your help. Your valor and loyalty move me deeply."

"Thank you. You will not regret allowing me to serve you."

"It is I who thank you. I promise that if we come through this alive, I will find a way to show proper appreciation for your service to me."

Rachel embraced Hannah. They parted a moment before Sephora entered. She was fully armed with daggers and a sword, and accompanied by four members of her secret police. She was ready and eager to make Rachel's life a living hell.

Sephora stared in disbelief at Rebekkah. The slave in the room faded into the background. Sephora barely glanced at him.

"What trick is this?" Sephora asked, looking from Rachel to Ava, who she couldn't believe was alive after what she had done to her the night before.

Morning light streamed through the windows. In this light, the immortal could not see if angels still accompanied Sephora.

Ava gave a small bow and said, "Good morning, High Queen. Mother has inspected my wounds. She tells me I am fully healed. Is this not wonderful news?"

Rachel did not bow to the High Queen.

"The goddesses have healed my daughter a second time," said Rachel. "We should celebrate again, though I insist this time I will provide the meal."

Sephora narrowed her eyes. She pivoted and left the room without a word. She could not touch Rachel and get away with it while the impostor lived; not yet, anyway.

The door slammed shut behind her. Rachel could not help herself. She laughed for the first time since her daughter died. Deep belly-wrenching guffaws echoed from her and shook away the tension and sadness. Hannah laughed with her. Rachel thought she heard music and looked for the source. She found that Ava had joined in, her voice a beautiful, almost musical tone.

Back in her quarters, Sephora paced. Someone had to pay for this most recent setback. She would punish Pirna, her poison-mistress.

Sephora had removed the bowl of stew herself the night before so that no tests could show there had ever been poison in it. It was still hidden in the crown she had worn. She summoned Pirna, whose quarters were adjacent to her own. Since it was early, Pirna was still at the Palace. It did not take long for her to arrive.

"The impostor lives," said Sephora when Pirna shut the door behind her. "Your punishment is that you will eat this stew."

Sephora handed the bowl to her. Pirna inspected it. She had coated this one with poisons, air-drying the bowl carefully so the residue was distributed evenly and not noticeable. She had marked it with a small x scratched into rim, noticeable only to one who looked carefully for it, as the serving girl had been instructed to. At the High Queen's request, Pirna had been experimenting with coating dishes with poisons so that meals could be served to a group, but only the target would die. The experiments had been successful on the slaves. Pirna turned white with fear.

"High Queen, what madness is this? I will die. The dose is lethal."

Sephora drew her sword, incensed.

"You dare call me mad? Eat or I will disembowel you here and now. Besides which, you stupid cow, you will sicken, but you will not die. Rachel's accomplice, the woman your poison was supposed to kill, is alive! This lesson will teach you not to fail me next time."

Pirna wondered how many women had died because of her work. She had always suspected to suffer retribution for it eventually. Her day of reckoning had come. She had chosen a life of ease and privilege while serving death to others through herbs and deadly plants. She had chosen to serve Sephora, whom she loved with all her heart.

"High Queen, I apologize for my rash words. To eat this stew is a death sentence. Even the smallest bite passing through the throat will kill. Are you certain the impostor ate from this bowl?"

"Yes," said Sephora, "the girl swallowed one full spoonful from the dish in your hand. She refused to eat more and fell into a deep sleep. This morning she was sitting up chatting gaily and fully healed of all her wounds. Now eat. You are lucky all you will suffer is a similar fate. You may thank me later."

Pirna hesitated.

"Eat!" Sephora held the sword against Pirna's lower abdomen to make the first cut should she disobey.

"I will obey you in this, as I have always obeyed you, mistress," said Pirna. "Hear me first. I have always told you that I would die for you, not knowing that you would be the instrument of my death. Remember, after I am gone, I do not blame you. I forgive you. You will never find another woman who will love you and serve you the way I do. I will wait for you in the afterlife. Good-bye, my love."

"Your love failed me when your poison did," Sephora was not moved by Pirna's words. "Drink and suffer. Then, someday, I might forgive you, bitch."

Pirna held the edge of the bowl up to her lips. She tipped the bowl slowly, knowing the more poison her first swallow contained, the easier her death would be. She drank deeply from the bowl, swallowing the chunks of meat and vegetables in gravy whole. Before it was half-gone, she fell to the floor writhing in pain. The bowl shattered, and chunks of stew spattered the floor.

"Goddess, help me!" Pirna cried out. It was one long minute before the sedative she had mixed in brought merciful relief.

Sephora watched as Pirna writhed in pain. At first, she was satisfied thinking that at least the impostor had suffered, even though she had somehow lived to see another day. Her satisfaction turned to disbelief as the aroma of feces filled the air when Pirna's bowels and bladder voided at her death. She checked for Pirna's life signs and found none. Sephora howled in anger. How was it possible that the impostor had lived when Pirna had just died from the same poison?

Everything seemed to be going against her. Sephora felt as if every step she took was impeded by quicksand. Her daughters were missing, and yet Rachel's substitute daughter lived. Her secret police told her the mood of the populace was ripe with sympathy for Rachel. Hannah remained at large, and now her poison mistress, the most talented woman she had ever prepared for the job, was dead. All this was Rachel's fault.

An image flashed briefly through her head of the festival preparations she had inspected the night before. The fanny dancers, slaves who danced for the erotic entertainment of the women, were in especially fine form. An idea occurred to her. She could vent her rage and humiliate one of her enemies at the same time.

A palace page girl had been cowering outside her door in fear. She heard Sephora's scream of rage. Action usually followed one of Sephora's temper tantrums, which were becoming more and more frequent. The page girl was not surprised when the High Queen opened the door, but she was relieved to see Sephora perfectly composed. The High Queen was famous for her labile moods.

"Send the King of Slaves to me," Sephora commanded the page girl. "I will be in the throne room."

"Oh," Sephora said as an afterthought, "Pirna miscalculated one of her doses. It is a shame, but accidents happen. There is a mess to clean up in here. Assign some slaves to the work at once."

This time, when Servus was called before Sephora, he was not afraid; he was impatient. He had not yet had a chance to tell Justus and Kiertus about the change of plans. He knelt instantly when he entered the room, forehead to the floor.

Sephora dismissed everyone from the room.

"On your feet, vermin," Sephora said.

He stood impassively, forgetting that last time his lack of emotion had kept her needling him. He showed no reaction as she circled him, examining him as she had done three months ago. She pulled her dagger and held it to his heart, leaning against him, drawing a bead of blood.

"Look me in the eye," Sephora said. Her voice sounded calm, but it was sheer fury he saw when he obeyed her command.

"I need a scapegoat today, and since my daughters are gone, Hannah is missing, and I cannot yet destroy Rachel, the honor falls upon you. I know you would give your life for freedom. I have something else for you to give me."

She withdrew the pressure she exerted on his chest and moved the dagger down to his groin. At first, he was confused. Surely, she was not asking him to sleep with her. According to rumor, he was far too old for her taste, and besides, she knew they were brother and sister. She observed his confusion and laughed.

"I do not intend to use your manhood; I intend to take it from you. How many of the slaves will follow a King who has no… courage?"

At first, Servus had no idea what his sister meant. Her smile was evil. When she made a slashing motion with the dagger, he finally understood. He gasped.

"High Queen," said Servus, "castration was discontinued centuries ago! The virgin priestesses decided it was inhumane to make eunuchs of the slaves that served them, and they chose to do all the menial tasks themselves, offering their labors up to the goddesses."

"You are a student of herstory, are you?" Sephora said. "Then you should also know that what a High Queen commands is done."

Servus swallowed hard. It was true there were no laws binding the High Queen, unless the Low Queens outvoted her. As a slave, he would not even be granted a trial.

"When?" Servus asked her.

He desperately needed time to tell Kiertus and Justus of the stranger's pledge to help them. Kiertus and Justus were set to begin the war tonight at the start of the Harvest Festival unless he could get word to them. The first prong of the attack was to take as many girl children as possible hostage. He did not know if he could count on the new Rebekkah's help if she thought he had broken their Pact of Honor.

"It will happen tonight after the fanny dancers perform as the Festival Eve entertainment."

Servus was relieved. That would give him time to figure out how to avoid his fate.

"You will be among them," Sephora said.

"What?" Servus asked. His alarm was unmistakable.

Sephora gloated. She clapped her hands and Octovin, the fanny-dance trainer, left his hiding place behind the decorative curtains against the back wall. Servus only knew of the man by reputation because Octovin had lived in the Arts Sector longer than Servus had been alive. Octovin was a graceful, distinguished looking older slave. He had been quite beautiful in his youth. His blue eyes, which he was famous for, had lost none of their brightness, and though his hair had turned silver, he still made women's hearts pound in admiration. He walked with the aid of a cane that he used with his left hand. He was missing two fingers on his right hand.

Octovin circled Servus, looking him over as Sephora had done. Servus was shocked to hear him address Sephora as an equal.

"Sephora, darling, when I told you last night it would be fun to add something different to the Festival Eve fanny dance, this was not what I had in mind. He's too old. Look at these scars; they are not aesthetic in the least. Even if I could make it work, I'd need more time than a few hours to get him ready."

As shocked as he had been at Octovin's tone to Sephora, he was even more surprised by Sephora's answer.

"Octovin, if anyone can make this work, you can."

Octovin narrowed his eyes and tapped a finger on his lips, deep in thought.

Servus watched in disbelief as Sephora came up behind Octovin and began to knead his shoulders, whispering in his ear.

"Hmm…that could work," Octovin murmured. "You don't say? Really!"

Servus reddened as Octovin glanced down at his groin. Sephora must have revealed what would happen after the dance.

"Well then," he said, his smile matching hers, "I think I can guarantee a very different and very entertaining Festival Eve fanny dance. What did you say his name is?"

"S-S-S-Servus," Sephora hissed the name and spat in hatred.

"Ooh, the famous Servus, King of Slaves? Maybe this will be fun after all. Come along, S-S-S-Servus," Octovin said, laughing. "We have work to do."

"There is a full contingent of my secret police waiting outside to escort you back to the theater. This one can be dangerous, Octovin. Take precautions; the Queendom cannot afford to lose your talents. I have already lost Pirna today, thanks to some trick of Rachel's."

Octovin was visibly dismayed by the news.

"High Queen, please accept my condolences for your loss. I know how useful Pirna was to you and how much you depended on her."

"Thank you, Octovin," Sephora said. "I don't think the loss has truly sunk in yet."

Octovin held out his arms and Sephora went into his embrace. Servus could hear her muffled words.

"I may need you to fill in some of the duties I had assigned to Pirna until I find a suitable replacement."

Servus believed the initial reaction of the old man was disgust, but Octovin was a consummate politician.

"Whatever you need, my Queen, I will do my best to satisfy, though the talents Pirna had were especially suited to your needs."

"Octovin," said Sephora, stepping back and taking his three-fingered right hand in her own, "I know your devotion to me is

284

every bit as strong as Pirna's was. You will best be able to serve me by keeping yourself safe in these troubled times." Sephora kissed each of Octovin's three fingers.

"Give me your permission to leave, High Queen," said Octovin, in response to Sephora's veiled threat. "I have a lot of work to do in order to earn your blessing for tonight's fanny dance performance."

"Go then," said Sephora as she smiled. "I value slaves who understand their priorities, as you always do."

Octovin wasted no time in leaving the High Queen. He prodded Servus with his cane. Servus thought his best option would be to try to escape while he was en route to the Arts Sector. When the two slaves reached the door to the throne room, Octovin tapped on it. The door swung open to reveal twenty heavily armed members of Sephora's secret police. They shackled his arms and legs with chains, the long ends of which were secured on not one, but two guards' armor. Sephora had ensured it was impossible for Servus to escape during transit.

Octovin walked beside Servus. The contempt Servus felt for Octovin grew. The slaves who followed the men's Code of Honor had always looked down upon the fanny dancers because they were chosen on looks alone, and though it took grace and talent to dance, Servus thought its only purpose was to entertain the women. Servus thought it was demeaning to the very ideal of manhood, which he believed was to live honorably, to keep one's word, and to be self-sufficient, as far as their lot would allow. Servus knew that if men were unshackled from the rule of women, they could accomplish great things. The world was waiting to be discovered and tamed by the hands of men.

Pandering to the whims of womankind seemed to him a double form of slavery. Fanny dancers lived luxuriously, being valued for their looks and the skills of their bodies. They eagerly and salaciously competed for the favors of women while being entirely dependent on them for every comfort they received. Now he would be one of them. The thought occurred to him that if he danced well enough, perhaps he could inspire a powerful woman to beg Sephora to allow him to keep what she wanted cut from him. He shook his head in frustration. There had to be a way out of this without depending on a woman. He had survived the pits, beatings, and hand-to-hand combat practice with ferocious soldiers. He was sure he could figure out a way to circumvent Sephora's threat.

Octovin's voice interrupted his train of thought.

"Have you ever been in the Arts Sector before?"

"No," replied Servus. "I have primarily been called to do hard labor on the grounds of the People's Palace and in the Livestock Sector." Servus looked around him. They were in the marketplace of the Arts Sector. The marketplace for each Sector was sand-wiched between the property of the palace and the Sector Proper. The marketplace of the Arts Sector had different wares for sale than the Livestock Sector, but the arrangement and design of the buildings was the same. It was a busy day, and if he weren't so heavily guarded, the conditions would have been ideal for escape. Servus sighed in frustration.

"You will be amazed by what you see there. I have been in every Sector except for the Religion Sector. I couldn't care less about seeing the schools and temples, but I regret never being able to see the Great Library."

"Why? Can you read?" asked Servus.

"Oh, yes, Sephora taught me how to read years ago. She hates the paperwork that comes with administrative duty, so I do some of it for her. It is easier to motivate the loyalty of slaves than the loy-alty of freewomen sometimes." Octovin waved his three-fingered hand and winked at Servus. Octovin continued speaking as if he were conducting a tour.

"The difference between the Sectors constantly amazes me, and I think it is a key to understanding the women, as much as it is possible for slaves to grasp the complex natures of the mistresses whom it is our privilege to serve. The soldiers live the simplest life."

"Yes, I've been there too. The Soldier Sector is luxurious compared to the Slave Barracks."

Octovin shuddered. "Don't remind me. I left there when I was a boy and vowed never to return. Let me tell you about the other Sectors then; it will help you appreciate what you are about to see in the Arts Sector even more.

"The Agriculture Sector is a step up from the Soldier Sector. Each building is constructed for function and basic comfort. Women there don't live as simply as the soldiers, and they hold task completion above all other ways of life. If a thing does not have function, it has no value in their Sector.

"The Livestock Sector, where you spend your time, is more ornate. The women there are the most nurturing of the Queendom. Their buildings reflect their beliefs, which is that life is good and is meant to be cherished and enjoyed. In addition to caring for animals, fashion is their domain. They spin and knit yarn, weave fabrics, and harvest animal skins from animals that have passed away by natural causes to use as trim."

"Yes, it is a messy job, and one I have done many times," Servus replied.

Another thing Servus knew about the Livestock Sector was how sympathetic the women were to the plight of the slaves. He was treated much more huwomanely in the Livestock Sector than on the Palace Grounds. Many of his men, including Kiertus, lingered in that Sector when duty allowed. He would have done this himself if there weren't a greater chance for him to see Arrival on the Palace grounds.

"So then," said Octovin, "let me tell you about the Government Sector. The administrative arm of the land likes to live well. It is made up of a rag-tag collection of buildings from different eras of the herstory of Evlantis. Instead of re-building, they refit the old while adding new. The effect is quaint, and no luxury is denied to the bean counters and the law-scribes of the land.

"Keep all this in mind as you enter the Arts Sector, for this Sector is the greatest of them all. It is the Sector with the most creature comforts. It is said the greatest achievements, and the worst, are generated in this one Sector. It is the one with the bitterest feuds. More women die in this sector from murder than in any other. The women of the Arts are famous for love potions, beaded fashions, written arts, painting, music, and sculpting."

Octovin, with his flair for drama, had timed the end of his litany to coincide with their arrival at the Arts Sector.

"Here we are at last," said Octovin. "Home sweet home. Look, and be amazed!"

The buildings Servus observed for the first time were impressively designed with carved edifices and beams. He had never seen anything so beautiful as the decorative plots of flowers and grasses in front of each immaculate house. There were statues everywhere, and many of the sides of the houses and businesses were decorated with spectacular murals. The women on the streets all looked like theater stars. Small pets, dogs dressed up in fine clothing, and brilliantly colored birds that perched on their shoulders accompanied many of the women. The women had their hair done elaborately. Their figures were set off to full advantage by their clothing, and they were in full make up—darkened eyes and red lips over a pale, powdered foundation. Servus had worn that look recently, and in spite of his current difficulties, he smiled at the memory.

Sephora was happy again. She hummed as she threw herself into Festival preparations. This would be the first year she presided over the eight-day festival as High Queen, and she wanted it to be the best festival ever, something no woman would ever forget.

Each Sector hosted a presentation during festival week. Festival Eve always began with the Arts presentation. The Arts Sector flirted most heavily with the sacrilegious, so the Arts presentation fell outside the official week. The religious services took up the entire last day of the festival. The Agriculture Sector and Livestock Sector got two days of presentation. Agriculture took one day for culinary presentation and one day to inform the public about advances in medicine. Livestock used two days, one for fashion presentations, and the other for animal exhibits. The Government Sector used its day for presentations in citizenship. They gave out coveted awards, including the Woman of the Year award. The Soldier Sector hosted drills on the practice fields and held contests of skill by fighting with each other and against slaves.

Sephora remembered that she needed to inform Low Queen Arrival that Servus, a festival favorite in the Soldier Sector contests, would need to be replaced. With the plans she had for him, he would be in no condition to fight. She laughed aloud as she went to find Arrival.

She would tell Arrival of her plan to punish Servus, but no one else. She would send out the word on her gossip network that there was a surprise attraction in the Fanny Dances this evening and that all the Low Queens, as well as Rachel, would be required to attend. This would ensure the Arts Sector Fanny Dance would be the best-attended event of the whole week. If only Third Sephora was found in time to preside, it would be perfect.

Rachel could tell something was bothering Abekka. Though Rachel had tried, she couldn't make the stranger tell her what it was. Instead of waiting in the palace, making themselves easy targets for Sephora, Rachel suggested they keep busy. Rachel thought that if she could show Abekka the marvels of Evlantis, she could give the girl more information about the city, and in the process, find out what was troubling her. She sent her new slaves, Hannah and Lyal, to procure a cart, horse, and driver. They would spend the day touring the market places of each of the Sectors, sightseeing, shopping, and visiting with the people.

As the day progressed, Servus found fanny dancing to be the hardest skill he ever had to master. The movements required muscles that he was not used to using, and though his mind was agile, remembering the steps seemed impossible. The other dancers mocked his clumsiness. It wasn't long before Servus found himself covered in sweat and out of breath.

Octovin would not allow him to stop. While other dancers got breaks, Octovin made him do the routines over and over. Servus stubbornly refused to ask for a breather. He just worked harder. Around mid-day, Octovin took a break.

"Keep practicing," Octovin said to Servus. "I am going to have my lunch. I only hope I can keep it down after watching you massacre my choreography."

The Fanny Dancers laughed. No one had any doubt of the enmity between Servus and Octovin. Servus was glad to see the back of the eight-fingered dance master, and did not stop practicing. Not because Octovin had ordered him not to, but because he was determined to succeed where everyone expected him to fail.

Octovin hurried back to his private chambers. His mind never stopped working. He was a brilliant man who had weathered many political changes and managed to hang on to his position. He knew how to handle both women and men. Though he gave the impression that he loathed Servus, he respected him. He had two chances to help Servus. The first was to turn the man into a polished dancer so that Servus could tell the story of the horrors of slavery with his body. Octovin could tell he had it in him, and drove him hard.

He would foster that second chance now. Very few in the Queendom knew of the power Octovin possessed. He had used the men under him that he had handpicked very carefully to earn favor and position for himself. His dancing boys lived well. He saw to it that they never complained or wanted for anything, but his own lifestyle rivaled that of the High Queen.

In addition to being the Fanny Dance master, he was the best choreographer in the Queendom. He was often sought to consult at the Amphitheater of the Arts. The shows he worked on won awards. The girls he mentored became stars. This helped his rise to power, though his work went unrecognized.

Octovin had many women who were willing to serve him. He sent for one now. She was one of the youngest actresses at the theater. He knew she secretly longed for him. He could trust her to do what he asked. She arrived quickly and out of breath, looking pleased to have been called by him.

"Asheia, I want you to bring me my lunch. However, lunch is only the pretense I have called you for. After you have brought it, I have a very important and dangerous mission for you, if you will accept it. I believe I can trust you, and I think you are the right person for this errand."

Asheia blushed with pleasure.

"Yes, sir. You know I would do anything for you."

"If you get caught, it will be death for me and severe punishment to you. Do you understand?"

Her face sobered.

"I do not wish to do anything that would lead to your death."

"Asheia, I would not ask you to risk my life and your position if this were not important. Will you accept?"

The girl looked unhappy, so Octovin walked to her and took her in his arms. The blush turned into sunburn. He stroked her hair with his five-fingered hand.

"Please," he said.

Asheia was weak in the knees. She cursed the blush that betrayed her, not knowing a hundred signs and signals had long ago shown him how she felt about the handsome, older man.

"I accept." It was all she trusted herself to say.

Octovin was relieved, and he showed it. He whispered to her.

"Sephora is planning on having Servus castrated after the Fanny Dances tonight. You must get word to either Kiertus or Justus for me as soon as you can. Tell one of them and no one else. You are a clever girl. You will think of a way to do this. If you succeed, I will choreograph a dance for you in your next play that will make you a star. Do you understand?"

Asheia did understand. She cared less that she was betraying Sephora than she did that she was putting Octovin's life in danger. But this seemed important to him.

"I only ask you one thing, Dance Master," she said reverently. "How will you know if I succeed?"

The question pleased Octovin.

"I will know, Asheia," said Octovin. "Everyone will know. Now I am hungry. Get my lunch and hurry. Between the two of us, I have the more difficult task to accomplish and must get back to it at once. I must make Servus a great dancer."

Partouche had hinted to Sephora that there was more than met the eye going on between Arrival and Servus. Sephora suspected it had more to do with the trick Rachel was trying to pull than some kind of illicit relationship, but Sephora watched Arrival carefully when she tracked her down. Sephora found Arrival drilling her troops on the practice fields.

"Arrival, I have been searching for you for over an hour," said the High Queen. "Goddess, you look terrible. You look more like a field hand than a Queen. Are you ill?"

Arrival had spent the remainder of the night sleepless, and in the reflection room. She now knew what the Great Mother had felt when man betrayed her. Surely, women were indeed better off with men as slaves, rather than enduring the pain of rejection. She tried desperately to fight the sickening waves of emotion, sorrow, grief, anger, and loss. Through it all, what disturbed her most was the knowledge that seeing Servus in another woman's arms did nothing to stop her ridiculous desire to be with him. She still wanted to believe he loved her.

"I am not ill, High Queen," replied Arrival. "I have been overtaxed drilling the troops for the Festival Entertainment since Rebekkah is still recovering from her wounds. I am sorry if you were inconvenienced by your search."

"It looks like it will be quite a show," said Sephora. "Every soldier in the Queendom must be here, and fully armed too."

"Yes, High Queen, Rebekkah and I intend it to be a show no one ever forgets." Arrival kept her tone neutral. Sephora smiled back and launched her weapon.

"I have come to tell you that if you were planning on using Servus in any of your presentations, you must make a substitution for him. He will be in no condition to fight."

"Very well." Arrival would not ask Sephora directly what she had in mind. She tried to draw her out in another way. "It is a shame, though. I was going to fight him myself, kill him, and present his head to your Highness as a gift."

Arrival lied. As angry as she was, she found she did not want Sephora to harm Servus. He was driven by a goal. Arrival was foolish to have believed the things he had said to her, but her shame did not change the feelings he had stirred up in her, and she did not forget his service to her. If not for Servus, Rachel would be dead.

Sephora raised her eyebrows.

"Is that so? What a lovely trophy it would have made. However, I have decided to give myself a present. Instead of taking the head of Servus, I will take his manhood."

Sephora was deliberately misleading.

Arrival was confused, thinking Sephora wished to take him as a lover. She felt jealousy, but sensed Sephora was testing her in some way. She remembered the soldier who had been present yesterday morning when she had spoken to Servus.

"Do what you like with him. He is no concern of mine," Arrival heard herself say.

"I will, Arrival," Sephora became imperious. "Servus is going to star in the Fanny Dances tonight. I am ordering all Low Queens to attend. You may sit with Rachel and the woman who calls herself Rebekkah; they are also required to be there. I will have a special box ready for you. If Servus does not excel, the trophy I will require of him will be the organ of life."

"You are going to castrate Servus?" Arrival was shocked, but as soon as she had blurted out the words, Arrival sensed it was important that she pretend not to care. She continued. "Brilliant, High Queen! Though such a practice has not been used in five generations, it is the perfect way to take the wind out of Servus's sails without making a martyr of him. I kneel in awe of your superior leadership."

Arrival knelt, so she could hide her emotions from Sephora. Arrival found her feelings for Servus were far from under her control. Though Servus had betrayed her with the stranger, the thought of such a cruel fate horrified her. Arrival must find a way to wrest the Queendom from Sephora's grasp before she could harm Servus.

"Mm," said Sephora, narrowing her eyes. "I have a lot to do. In addition to my duties of High Queen, I must also help Third Sephora with her duties in the Arts Sector. She has not been feeling well and has taken to her bed.

"I've learned your mother has taken her newly adopted daughter…."

"Rebekkah," Arrival interrupted.

"Whatever," said Sephora. "I heard she has taken the girl on a tour of the city. I will rely on you to find them and give them my order that they must attend the Fanny Dances this evening. I will see you there."

Sephora and her attendants left the training field. Arrival watched them go, her face inscrutable to the generals that attended her. At last, she turned back to her soldiers.

"I will find my mother and sister at the dinner hour. I think I know where they will dine. Until then we practice."

"Can the soldiers lay down some of their arms? The women are beginning to tire."

"No," answered Commander Arrival. "Tell them they can rest when I leave, but not to disarm. I want every soldier in full body armor from this point on."

The hours of the day passed very quickly for the former High Queen. Ava's mood had lifted a little once they left the Palace. The sights, sounds, and smells of the city were a distraction to her, as Rachel suspected they would be.

Ava enjoyed herself on the tour. She did not have to question the meaning of the angels attending Sephora and wonder whether she had chosen the right side in this struggle. Just for this day, she also put from her mind the quandary of how she was going to end slavery.

The companionship of Rachel was wonderful. The citizens of the city welcomed her among them with open arms. Rachel had explained it was customary for mothers of infants to approach famous soldiers and ask for a blessing for their baby. To Ava's great delight, she was solicited many times during the day to give the Soldier's Blessing. She got to hold the babies, trace a circle on their forehead, and say the words, "Daughter, may you grow strong, aim true, and live long serving the goddesses of Rule and Community."

Ava loved holding the little bundles because it was like holding hope. She sensed that each tiny person had the potential to usher in a brighter future for humankind.

They were eating dinner at a kiosk in the Agriculture Sector's marketplace when Arrival found them. Ava had been holding a group of women spellbound with the story of how the beast had been killed the third night of the sacrifice. Rachel listened and wondered again if Ava had some connection with her daughter because the story sounded so like Rebekkah. When the time was right, Rachel would ask her.

Rachel was surprised when Arrival interrupted Rebekkah's story rudely and delivered the High Queen's order that they must attend the fanny dances that evening. Rachel watched as the mention of Sephora's name turned Ava pensive again. Rachel broke the party up quickly.

"I wasn't planning on attending the dances, but now we must go," she said. "It would not be wise, at this point, to refuse a direct order of the High Queen. We will need to return to the Palace to get ready for the big event."

Ava politely excused herself from the group of women who had gathered around her and accompanied Rachel back to the cart where their slaves, Lyal and Hannah, waited to pull them to their next destination. She pondered her dilemma on the ride to the Palace.

As night fell and women from all Sectors of the Queendom made their way to the Arts Sector, Kiertus and Justus called an assembly of the men in their temple. Excitement was building among them. Many men were ready to fight for freedom.

Kiertus and Justus stood on the platform. They had agreed Kiertus should do the talking. Justus stood beside him with his arms crossed in front of his chest. As soon as the temple was full, Kiertus began to speak.

"We have called you all here to talk to you about the difficult times we live in and the suffering we have endured these past few months."

The men nodded and grumbled. An old man yelled from the back of the room.

"Suffering is part of life, Kiertus; even the women are not exempt."

"Of course suffering is part of life," Kiertus continued. "No one escapes it. But there is a big difference between the suffering from sorrow that life brings and the suffering inflicted upon us by women who call themselves our masters. They say they are superior, but they treat mankind shamefully."

"Life wasn't so bad under Rachel," someone else yelled. Kiertus expected objections and was ready for them.

"Rachel is no longer High Queen," he responded.

Another old man spoke up.

"She is back now; may she reclaim her throne. Hail Rachel!"

Men all over the temple began to yell "Hail Rachel!"

Kiertus silenced them quickly.

"Do you wish to bring retribution from Sephora upon your heads? Stop immediately!"

The men quieted and looked around them fearfully. Kiertus continued.

"I know some of you wish to see the status quo continue, but it cannot. Men and women were meant to live in equality with one another. Women will never give us our due voluntarily. We must fight for our freedom.

"You know Servus has been training men to fight. For your own safety you have not been told who, or how many. Now I tell you that a full third of us are prepared to battle the women. Weapon parts have been stockpiled. Last night many of those parts were brought in and hidden inside the complex. I need every available man to assemble the weapons and act as support to those who will fight. Every one of us must be ready. Tonight we begin the war that will end slavery for mankind forever!"

The young men were on their feet, cheering, ready for action. The middle-aged and old sat, still not convinced.

"Where is Servus? If this is so important to him, why isn't he here?" one of the old timers challenged.

The timing was perfect. Kiertus responded using the information given to him by the girl who had sought him out along his delivery route.

"Sephora has taken Servus prisoner. I have it on good authority that Sephora intends to re-institute the ancient punishment of castration after tonight's Festival Eve fanny dance, and she will make Servus the first victim."

The mood changed perceptibly from hesitance to anger. Protests rang out. Even the oldest men among them were on their feet now. Kiertus hammered home his call to fight, his voice raised to war-cry pitch.

"Tonight we fight back—for freedom, and for Servus!"

"For freedom! For Servus!" the men chanted.

Their enthusiasm was palpable. Kiertus and Justus quickly organized the men under generals whom Servus had previously designated and they outlined the plan Servus had given to them before he had been taken from them. Their first strike against womankind would take place within the hour.

QUEENS RISE

*T*he populace was stirred up on Festival Eve. Never had such portentous events taken place within the walls of the city of Evlantis. Rachel, who had been thought to be insane, was now claiming to have been doing the bidding of the goddesses. Rebekkah was back in a new form. No one had seen Hannah or the Three Sephoras in two days and there was speculation they were dead. There was also much speculation about what Sephora had planned for the fanny dance.

As night fell, privileged mothers of underage daughters left their children at Care Centers in the Queendom and made their way to the Amphitheater of the Arts. The air of excitement was palpable. The fanny dances, always a salacious form of entertainment, had never before been so well attended. This evening, every seat was taken in the Amphitheater of the Arts, and the galleries were full of women standing.

Every Low Queen was present. As Sephora had instructed, they had been seated in luxury boxes in the front row. Rachel, Arrival, and Ava, with their personal slaves in attendance, shared a box. Sephora sat alone, in the center box, attended only by Octovin.

Octovin watched the wings of the stage carefully from where he stood behind his master. When he could see everything was ready, he whispered in Sephora's ear. Sephora stood and gave a signal. The curtain rose. The hall quieted as women prepared to be entertained. Smoke rose from a hole in the middle of the stage. Over the hole was a cage. A solitary figure straddled the hole with his back to the audience. It was impossible to tell who it was.

The musicians began to play their instruments. Scales with halftones and quartertones set the mood of the first act and gave it an eerie ambiance. The dancers came onto the stage in pairs. Each wore only a thong with a pouch to cover and anchor their most private of parts.

There were exclamations of surprise from the audience at seeing such nakedness. The dance was done in three parts, and disrobing was normally part of the third act. Whispers temporarily disturbed the quiet as seasoned attendees shared the opinion with their neighbors that there must be something very good coming for this element to be eliminated from the dance.

Eight pairs of dancers took the stage. One dancer of each pair carried a whip; the other carried a beautiful fan made of feathers. Smoke continued to billow out of the hole in the floor center stage, obscuring the motionless figure in the cage as the dancing commenced. The dancers ignored the cage as they did elaborate gymnastic routines to the music, incorporating the whips and fans in graceful movements.

The regular dancers' oiled bodies undulated in time to the music. Their muscles rippled. It was erotic and very beautiful to behold. The gymnastics of the routine, along with the music, had an almost hypnotic effect. Women oohed and aahed as marvelous flips and feats were performed. The dancing went on for fifteen minutes, each stunt more graceful and incredible than the one that preceded it.

The music changed. Eerie became sinister, and the dancers moved like the walking dead, all suddenly fixated on the cage. Two circles formed and rotated around the cage. The dancers with whips approached the cage, and in time to the beat began to whip the figure inside. In time to a cacophony of drumbeats, the dancers with whips fell down as if they had been struck dead. The poses they fell into suggested pain. Sephora squirmed in her seat, remembering the way Pirna had writhed in death. She glanced at Octovin, wondering if he was mocking her in some way. He seemed unaware of her. He was fixated on the stage, counting beats under his breath. Sephora turned her attention back to the stage, dismissing her thought as paranoia.

The dancers with fans moved to the beat as they formed a circle and fanned the smoke into the audience. People coughed. When the smoke cleared, the fan dancers pretended to swoon on the floor, and the figure in the cage was standing, now clearly visible, for the smoke had ceased to billow from the floor. His back was still toward the audience, and he remained in the same position as before. His body glistened with sweat. Lash marks stood out upon his back, arms, and legs in vivid red. Abruptly, the music stopped and the curtain descended. Act One was finished.

The traditional bottles of new wine were dispersed down the rows. Each woman had brought a small piece of crockery for imbibing the wine. Sephora had given orders to let the wine flow freely.

In their luxury box, Rachel helped herself to the wine, but Arrival and Ava refused. Arrival knew who the figure in the cage was. Drinking was unthinkable with the bile rising in her throat. Arrival wondered if they had opened Servus's old wounds to make him bleed. She didn't know that Octovin had ordered the makeup artists to outline all of Servus's scars with red paint, as it was impossible to tell the difference from her vantage point in the audience.

"Do you know who that is?" Arrival asked Ava quietly so that Rachel would not hear. "Do you recognize the figure in the cage?"

"No," answered Ava. "I have no idea who any of the men are."

"Slaves," said Arrival. "You must remember to call them slaves. To call them men puts them on nearly equal footing with women.

People will begin to question your identity. Didn't you enter into a Pact of Honor with my mother?" Arrival's tone was a little sharper than she intended.

"Arrival, " whispered Ava, "Do you know the slave in the middle of the cage?"

"Yes, and I will tell you who he is so that you do not give yourself away when his identity is revealed. It is Servus."

"I didn't know he could dance!" said Ava with a smile.

"He can't," said Arrival. "He has only lived in extreme hardship. He doesn't know the first thing about dancing."

"What are you two whispering about?" asked Rachel.

"Nothing, Mother," Arrival said tersely.

"You are wound up like a tightly coiled spring. Maybe you should have a glass of wine. It is excellent."

"The lights should have dimmed by now," Arrival said. "That wine you are drinking is flowing very freely."

Rachel looked around her. "You are right." She glanced at Sephora, who sat back in her seat with a glass of wine in hand looking very contented as Octovin massaged her shoulders.

"Sephora wants the women drunk tonight," said Arrival. Ava looked at Arrival intently, but said nothing as the musicians finally began to tune their instruments in preparation for the second act. It seemed to Arrival that everything moved in slow motion. She sat as still as possible, willing her features to look dispassionate as the curtain rose. Something was missing. Arrival realized the curtain had gone up in silence. Why was there no music? An odd hush descended.

The second act was Servus's solo. It was so quiet that he could hear the pulleys creaking as the cage was lifted above him, leaving him free to move at last. Servus knew they all expected him to fail, and to embarrass himself. For that reason alone, he intended to succeed. At first, during practice it had seemed impossible, but once he committed the movements to memory, he began to feel the dance with his whole body.

There was much more to dance than he had ever expected. It was a way to communicate and to express oneself through movement. The story Octovin had given him to tell was of a bound and fettered man yearning to be free. It was his story.

A single note was played. It was Servus's signal to begin. He turned to face the women, and there were shouts of recognition. Every woman sat on the edge of her seat in anticipation. Sephora's surprise had not disappointed them.

The melody started. Servus put his heart and soul into the movements of the dance, and to the surprise of everyone he moved nimbly and confidently. The steps were elaborate, and they required him to move gracefully over the slaves positioned on the floor, in time to music that welled up and spoke of secret desires of the heart. It was a beautiful, haunting melody, one that would never be forgotten, not in all of huwoman herstory.

Servus's movements expressed pent-up power, rage, despair and longing for freedom. The fanny dancers usually gave salacious performances, but Servus refused to give merely a titillating performance, though he allowed his body to exude a sexual presence. His performance was breathtakingly and achingly beautiful. He made no mistakes and forgot none of the steps. Almost every woman present was swept up in his passion and charisma, and could feel the aching longing for freedom Servus emoted. When the music ended, there was a moment of silence before thunderous applause began and every woman in the building, except his sister Sephora, rose to give him a standing ovation.

Arrival had watched, first in anger, then in pride. Though she had learned he did not love her, she could not help but admire him. She could not imagine respecting a man as much as she did Servus.

Rachel watched with an open mind. His performance touched her heart. She had already begun to question beliefs taught to her from birth, beliefs about the non-huwoman essence of man.

Servus's performance solidified and strengthened Ava's arguments, which she had spiritedly made the night before about the error of slavery. Rachel found her mind spinning with the possibilities of a new and vibrant world populated with many cities where women and men lived as equals.

Ava watched in delight, entering into the spirit of the dance. She and her family loved to dance, but never had she seen such pathos expressed in the medium before. By the end of Servus's dance, tears ran freely and unashamedly down her face, and she was the first woman on her feet, though everyone rose because the occasion called for it, and not because they copied her. Indeed, no one had paid any attention to anyone but Servus.

Sephora alone was not delighted. She was angry. Always an angry and strident woman, she found little relief from the constant anger recent events had generated. She leaned back and whispered to Octovin.

"You promised me he would fail."

Octovin whispered his placating response.

"This was a surprise you sprang on me at the last minute. How was I supposed to know he could dance? And it hurts me to have you doubt me. The third act has not even begun. Watch and see. By the end of it, women will shed tears of laughter. It is the third act they will remember and gossip about. Trust me."

"It had better be as you say, Octovin, or the third act will end with me taking another finger from your right hand, as I promised."

Octovin leaned back satisfied. He was not worried in the least. Servus had performed exactly as Octovin had hoped. It was too bad Octovin had to spoil Servus's big moment, but he knew Sephora too well to allow Servus's triumph to last. While he respected Servus, respect was not reason enough for him to lose another finger.

Wine flowed freely again after the triumph of the second act. The second break did not go as long as the first because Sephora was eager to see her brother shamed. Very quickly, the curtain went up.

At the start of the third act, the music changed again, and the dancers lying on the stage floor rose. The entire ensemble danced together. Octovin had made last-minute changes with the regular dancers, and had instructed them to make Servus look as bad as possible. A few minutes into the dance, the ambush was obvious to Servus.

Though Servus tried his best to adapt to the changes, he was constantly out of step and in the wrong place. At first, there were snickers from the crowd, but soon raucous laughter rang out. Servus felt his face burn in shame, but he refused to quit. Though he tried his best, it was not good enough. It was impossible for him to anticipate what his next move should be. Toward the end, he found the dance had not been changed as much, and with relief, he fell into his place in one of two can-can lines. With only ten measures of the dance left to go, it became apparent why he had been allowed to find his place. There was a transition in the can-can lines that required him and every other man in his line to move forward to the front row. Servus began the movement with confidence, only to be surreptitiously tripped by a dancer beside him. Servus flailed his arms and reached for purchase on the first thing he came in contact with on his way down, which happened to be the thong of a man in front of him.

Off came the thong. The man shrieked as if wounded, drawing as much attention to his nakedness as possible. The thong was still in Servus's hand as he hit the ground and rolled sideways, knocking down four men in his path. Several of the dancers burst into tears and left the stage, including the naked dancer. Those who remained on stage scrambled to get into their end poses, though the dance was completely ruined.

Servus got to his feet and tried to help others up, but they shunned his help disdainfully, making it painfully clear they blamed him, though both he and they knew he had been shamelessly sabotaged. Servus tried to get into place, but the men blocked him from doing so. He stood alone.

The mood of the women had changed, as Octovin predicted. The same women who had cheered for him a scant fifteen minutes ago now laughed, hissed, and booed. Finally, someone threw a rotten tomato and hit Servus on the chest. This started a steady stream of rotten food and wine crocks flying at Servus. Servus merely stood erect, still as a statue. With his eyes, he searched for Sephora's face and met her gaze, trying to give her the message that, though she had succeeded in publicly humiliating him, she had not crushed his spirit.

Arrival's cheeks burned with shame at what the King of Slaves had been reduced to. Even more serious was that the false Rebekkah seemed to have no desire to take action against Sephora as she had promised. The stranger must take a stand against Sephora soon, or worse things would happen.

High Queen Sephora motioned for her secret police to hold Servus fast as she hurried onto the stage. Her moment had come. The real entertainment would begin soon. The women stopped hurling things at Servus when they saw her, and the amphitheater quieted.

"Good citizens," Sephora began, "I stand before you in shame at the travesty the self-proclaimed King of Slaves has brought to the festival dances. I promise you, by the power vested in me as your devoted High Queen, this mongrel shall be punished. I will go and consult with the Low Queen of the Arts Sector who could not be here tonight because of illness. Everyone is invited to the Palace Hall to hear the punishment of this animal that has desecrated the Festival Eve fanny dances. I will have the bells rung to invite everyone in the city to hear his fate. Tell our sisters who could not attend tonight to join us there." Sephora's voice boomed out loudly as she made her final pronouncement. "By Ephrea's name, I swear to you this slave will be punished before the clock strikes midnight. Bind him in chains and bring him to me in the fitting room quarters in the Palace."

The crowd broke into cheers. Sephora motioned for her secret police as she swept majestically from the stage.

"Bind him in chains and bring him to me," Sephora ordered. "I will be in the Royal Dressing Room at the People's Palace." Sephora made her way to the exit, cheered by the women of Evlantis.

Arrival, once again, watched Sephora from behind the secret viewing area to the palace dressing room. This time, she was not alone. Rachel, Hannah, Lyal, and the stranger were with her. *Let Sephora show her true colors*, Arrival prayed silently. *Let the stranger be roused from her apathy.*

Rachel and Arrival had agreed this was the best way to help the stranger understand the gravity of the situation. If she could see Sephora at her worst, perhaps the girl would finally embrace the role of Rebekkah fully and challenge Sephora in an outright effort to topple her from the throne. Arrival knew the stranger had feelings for Servus. Arrival hoped the threat to him would rouse her to action. Arrival would rather see Servus live as a complete man with her new sister Rebekkah than see him maimed.

Servus's hands and feet were bound in chains. He could only take small shuffling steps. In spite of the humiliation he had endured, he had an air of dignity that moved Arrival. She wondered what gave him strength in the face of such adversity. Not many women could take the abuse he had endured and still be able to stand erect without weeping.

Sephora began the interview.

"Have you forgotten your insignificant place in the world? Kneel to me, slave."

Servus remained upright as he responded.

"I am done kneeling to you, Sister. Kill me, or suffer me to stand in your presence. It is your choice."

Everyone behind the wall was shocked at the word sister. Sephora validated Servus's words with her next statements.

"Fine, remain standing. Do I care if dogs bow down before me? Slaves are less than animals. If we could find a way to quicken without your kind, I would have you all killed. And, as for you referring to me as sister, that has no meaning for me other than my mother was defective for bearing a son. It reflects poorly on her. It means nothing to me."

Arrival felt the stranger stiffen beside her. Arrival did not know the stranger could see the angels in the room with Sephora. Ava knew something was very wrong. The angels seemed to be taking joy in the very things that distressed Ava the most.

"Beg me for mercy," Sephora said to her brother.

"I will beg you for nothing," Servus replied. "Do you think I haven't heard stories of how you demand those you torture to do as you say, to thank you for your punishments, and then you destroy them anyway? I don't know how it is we came from the same womb. I would never commit the acts of cruelty you indulge in."

"You pretend to be better than me?" asked Sephora. "I have heard that you discipline the men under you as you see fit. And do you not think if you had the chance you would choke the breath from my body?"

"I use punishment to discipline my men to make them stronger," Servus countered. "You use it to increase fear of you. My goal is freedom for mankind. Yours is the satisfaction of your own desires. You would maim me for sport. I would raise my hand against you only to save the Queendom."

"Pretty words, beast, pretty noises," said Sephora. "The truth is you can speak all you want to, but it will not now nor ever change the fact that women are superior to men and will rule over them as their masters forever. You bore me with your endless prattle. If you won't play my game my way, then go and sulk in the holding cell until we finish this little drama in the Palace Hall. To help pass the time I will order the guards to beat you. Maybe it will make you stronger! Enjoy your last minutes as a complete man."

Sephora laughed and called the guards to escort Servus from her presence. She gave the order to have him beaten and gagged.

She demanded a certain dress and makeup artist brought to her at once. As she did, the group in the secret viewing area filed into another passageway to talk in secret. As Sephora prepared herself for the next act of her drama, Arrival made an impassioned plea to Ava.

"You must help us now! Forget for a minute that Sephora is bad for the Queendom. Do you understand fully what she is going to do to Servus? I thought you and he had a special understanding. You looked quite at ease with him when I walked in on you the other night." Rachel and Hannah detected the bitterness in Arrival's tone and exchanged surprised glances.

Ava looked miserable.

"You don't understand…" she began and then stopped.

Arrival lost patience with her.

"Explain it to me! I don't want to lose the best the man in this Queendom because you have trouble gripping the severity of the situation. If you don't act, and act fast, Servus will be a shadow of the man he is now."

Ava began to weep.

Arrival stamped her foot impatiently.

"Speak to me! What stops you from filling your Pact of Honor with Rachel and standing with us against Sephora?"

Ava continued weeping. Arrival grabbed Ava by the shoulders and shook her.

"For goddess's sake, you ninny! Don't just stand there crying like a child while the best man in the Queendom is butchered like an ornery bull."

Ava had never been handled so, and Arrival's passion and urgency loosened her tongue. Ava's words tumbled over each other. Arrival had trouble understanding, especially since much of what Ava said was incomprehensible. As Arrival listened, it felt as though the world she had known was slipping away from her. Rachel watched Arrival's face with sympathetic understanding. She knew those feelings well.

"I am lost Arrival," Ava said. "I don't fit in here. I think it may have been a mistake to come here. I was turned out of my home. I had to leave my family. It took years to get here, and everything is so different here from what I am used to at home. My people are different from yours. There is no death where I come from. Men and women are co-partners. We have made greater strides than you have in all aspects of living. Men and women alike answer to one Master, the Creator. I miss Him most of all. It was His rule I broke. I crossed the Wall separating our Garden from this harsh and cruel world. What is going to become of me? The Archangel Michael said I could not return. He said that perhaps the Master could use me here. His voice should be a whisper, but no matter how hard I try, I cannot hear Him."

Ava began to hyperventilate.

"This Master of yours sounds cruel," said Arrival. "To deny you home hearth is horrible. Perhaps you are better off without him."

Ava was shocked. She calmed her breath, smiled, and spoke again, this time more slowly. Tears continued to run down her face.

"No, Arrival, you do not understand. Here in Evlantis I feel a constant ache inside, a loss that never leaves. There was no ache in Eden. In the Master's Garden, we are all complete. He is love. He is life. I would do anything to see Him again, to walk beside Him again; to tell Him how sorry I am and how much I love Him."

Rachel intervened. She thought that she might finally understand where the girl came from. It would explain so much. When she was High Queen, she'd had access to every part of the great library of Evlantis. She had spent many quiet hours in the forbidden section of the Great Library reading ancient manuscripts. There was a myth in that section the others could not have heard: a myth, the unknown author claimed, that allegedly originated from the deathbed confession of the Great Mother.

"Child, we can debate the merits of your Creator later. I think I understand where you have come from. The matter at hand now is this: What is preventing you from taking a stand against Sephora and fulfilling the pact you made with me? I was sure you meant to help us, until after the dinner we had with Sephora. What has changed since then?"

"I saw angels. They are spirit beings that tend the Master. I did not recognize any of them, and they didn't seem to recognize me, but they were with Sephora last night when she brought us dinner. They were with her again just now when she was speaking with Servus. I have been questioning ever since I saw them whether I have chosen the right side in this struggle."

A look of shock crossed Rachel's face, but she remained silent. Ava continued.

"Even now, I am uncertain, Rachel. Please forgive me, but I can't help think perhaps I have already chosen evil by siding with you, and I did not know it. Perhaps I will never be of use to the Master again. This ache may never leave me!" Ava beat at her breast with her fists and her tears became a torrent again.

Rachel would have spoken again. She alone had the answer the stranger was looking for, but Arrival, in her desperation to help Servus, spoke first. There was one aspect of the stranger's condition she recognized. Arrival grabbed Ava's fists to still them and spoke heatedly.

"You are afraid, and fear is holding you back," Arrival said. "It is causing you to stand still when you should be taking action. Fear can be a hesitation that prevents you from trying something new, or it can be a force with the power to paralyze a warrior during an

311

oncoming attack. At the very least, it prevents enjoyment of life. At the most, it causes death. You said your Master is love. The wisest women have identified fear as an obstacle to love. You must walk through your fear. You must move. You must choose a side. Choose Rachel or choose Sephora, but choose. To stand still is to let fear win and to lose everything."

Ava had been listening with her head cocked to one side. As Arrival spoke, understanding dawned on Ava's face. Arrival had not realized how beautiful she could be, and her heart sank. Of course Servus would prefer this woman to her. Any man would.

"Arrival, you speak the truth. Michael said there would be times when not to make a choice would be evil. This must be one of those times...." Her voice trailed off and the troubled look returned. "I still do not know what to do. Have you never seen the heavenly spirits that surround Sephora?"

"I believe I can explain," Rachel said. She chose her words carefully. "There are those among us who sometimes see spirits; it is not unheard of. But did you not know there are two kinds of spirits? There are good ones and evil ones. In the forbidden section of the Library of Evlantis, there is an ancient document that explains this. It has been suppressed because it challenges all our beliefs. Among other things, it states a spirit underling once challenged the Creator of all Life. The Creator bested the underling in battle, but did not kill it. The underling and those who follow it go about the earth causing chaos, destruction, and other types of mischief. The good spirits do not interfere as much as the bad. We are supposed to rely on our own strength and goodness to overcome evil, and when that fails us, as it often does, we are to rely on the help of the Creator.

"The Great Mother was supposed to have talked face to face with an evil spirit in the form of a serpent. The serpent tempted her to eat of the tree of the knowledge of good and evil. She did so, but the man with her would not eat. She was banished from her home hearth forever.

"I do not know if this is true, but what every school child in Evlantis knows is that until her dying day, Eve cursed all serpents and destroyed them whenever they crossed her path."

Ava's eyes were wide. Her tears had finally stopped. She reached out to grip Rachel's arm tightly.

"What kind of beast is this serpent?" she asked.

Rachel didn't understand why that was important and hesitated to answer. Ava spoke with an urgency that seemed out of place for such an insignificant detail.

"Answer me!" Ava said with intensity.

Ava listened as Rachel described the reptile that had startled her as she sat upon the branch years ago while playing a strategy game with her brothers and sisters. She realized it was a spirit opposed to her Master who had tricked her into breaking the second rule. She needed no small voice to tell her the enemies of her Master were her enemies. She knew now that the spirits she had not recognized—the spirits that accompanied Sephora—must be evil. Ava was free now to do everything in her power to oppose Sephora.

The others watched Ava's demeanor change. Gone was the indecision and sadness. It was replaced by resolve and purpose. For the first time in a long time, Arrival felt hope for Servus, for Rachel, for the city, and even for herself. Ava's next question surprised everyone.

"Arrival, why do you care so much about the fate of Servus?"

This question penetrated the armor Arrival thought she kept around her heart. Arrival gave no answer, but a blush betrayed her. Ava gave her a knowing glance.

"Servus could not ask for a better partner than you, Arrival. I see, though, that you will have to face some fears of your own before this is all over. We will leave that for later. As for now, my first order of business is to dress the part I must play to save Servus and the Queendom. I rely on you, Arrival, to assist me."

Ava's eyes sparkled with good humor. Arrival wondered what she had in mind. Rachel asked outright.

"So you have made your choice and you will help me challenge Sephora?" asked Rachel.

"Mother," Ava called Rachel by the name she would use for the rest of Rachel's life, "I have a plan that will leave Sephora powerless, but at what you may perceive as a high price to the Queendom. All of you gather around me and listen. Then say whether you will help me or not. For I have two pacts I must fulfill, and with all of you to help me, I will accomplish them both tonight."

Lyal and Hannah had been quiet, letting Rachel and Arrival take charge. Ava indicated she needed them too. They stood in a small circle and listened intently to Ava's plan. As she spoke, each of the four faces around her took on a look of disbelief.

"Are you with me?" Ava asked when she finished, looking at each one in turn.

Lyal spoke first.

"To the death, Low Queen Rebekkah."

He knelt.

Hannah looked dazed at her part, and turned to Rachel with a question.

"High Queen, does this meet with your approval?"

Rachel answered with a smile.

"If Abekka's plan works, you will have to stop calling me that. But yes, dear Hannah, you have my blessing. I myself could not have thought of a better way to repay you for your service to me."

Hannah then echoed Lyal's words, though in a whisper, still dazed at the change this would bring in her life.

"To the death, I am with you." She knelt beside Lyal. He took her hand and squeezed it. She squeezed back, grateful for his support.

Rachel spoke next.

"It is a sure way to beat Sephora. I agree to it. I am with you, to the death."

Arrival was the last. Everyone looked at her.

"I am with you even to death," said Arrival. "Thank you for agreeing to save Servus."

"We must part for now," Ava said. "Each of us has work to do, but know this: No matter what happens, I will be able to fulfill my role. Trust me. I will see you all in the Palace Hall after Sephora begins her proceedings. Just remember to call me Rebekkah!" she added to lighten the mood.

They left to prepare for the coming showdown. Rachel went with Hannah and Lyal back to the secret viewing area of the Royal Dressing Room so they could take possession of it as soon as Sephora left. Ava accompanied Arrival to the soldier's barracks in haste. All the items she required were in Arrival's possession.

Sephora waited impatiently in the anteroom off the main hall as the bells were rung to signal the start of a session at the Palace Hall. She primped as she waited, and posed in front of the mirror to make sure the gown she wore gave the desired effect. She wore a silver sheath. Regal and strong, it was ornate, yet showed enough skin to show her oiled muscles off to good effect. Her make-up was feminine and included brilliant eye shadows and liner, pink lip color, and blush. Her black hair swung free, and the ornate crown was secured firmly on her head. She also adorned herself with a belt from which hung a collection of throwing knives, and she chose a spear to carry. Everyone would know that she viewed the recent events as battle worthy. She was done being patient. She would begin by making an example of Servus, and then she would challenge the fake Rebekkah and put an end to Rachel's ridiculous claim. Sephora had tired of playing cat and mouse and would see to it that everything went in her favor tonight.

She was concerned that Meerta, Tyvaal, and Salla had not reported back to her, which could only mean they had not been able to carry out their missions successfully. Her daughters and Hannah were still missing, and the stranger's identity was unknown. She should dispatch her police to bring Rachel and the stranger to the meeting. Someone at the gathering would be able to identify her as a citizen of Evlantis. Sephora was certain Rachel and the stranger would not come to the meeting willingly. She would send for them as soon as she had dispensed her special brand of justice to Servus.

Under the cover of darkness, the company of slaves led by Kiertus and Justus raided, and took control of, the Care Center on the Palace Grounds that housed the girls who were too young to attend the fanny dances with their mothers. The slave soldiers had been instructed not to harm anyone. They waited for the mothers of their hostages to appear so they could take them captive also. When they heard the Palace bells being rung, they knew the mothers would not be returning soon.

"It looks like we will have to improvise a little," Kiertus said. He was in fine spirits. The day they had planned for was here. The war had begun. He would win his freedom and his right to be with Ariana and his daughter, who had come into the world after he had broken up with her, or he would die trying.

"You have an idea?" asked Justus. He almost added the word son. He thought Kiertus knew how he felt. When there was more time, he would tell the young man why he had chosen to mentor him.

"Yes," answered Kiertus confidently. "How would you feel about us taking some of the young ladies in our care for a walk to the Palace Hall to trade them for our King?"

"What an excellent idea, Kiertus. After the streets clear we will put your plan into action."

"Agreed. Send a messenger to the armed men in the barracks to advise them of the change. They must hold off phase two of the war until they learn Servus is back among us. Order the men guarding the rest of the girls to treat them gently. Remind them every girl could be their daughter. Tell the men to save their anger to vent it on their mothers."

Forty-five minutes had passed since the bells had rung. Sephora waited in a room behind the stage. Partouche was among the loyal soldiers who accompanied her.

"Is the hall full yet?" Sephora asked Partouche.

"Give me a moment, High Queen. I will see."

Partouche left the anteroom and returned seconds later.

"Not only is every seat in the Hall full, but the hall is packed with women standing, too. The soldiers tell me there are plenty of women on the step of the hall, and at the windows also. If you wait, more women will come, but there will be no place for them to view the proceedings."

"Excellent. It is time. Let us get this over with. I am tired of placating slaves and mad women."

The soldiers with her laughed. Sephora, a silver spark, both stately and savage, swept into the hall. She held her head high as she walked, and the masses cheered her. Sephora wasted no time. She banged the shaft of the spear on the floor then raised it above her head.

"My fellow citizens and Low Queens of Evlantis, I thank you all for gathering quickly. I have urgent city business that needs to be attended to. The city has been in a state of unrest since the events that unfolded two short days ago. We must end the speculation now and return to our peaceful way of life. Rachel…" Sephora was interrupted by calls of "High Queen Rachel" but she ignored them and continued.

"Rachel has made an atrocious claim that Rebekkah has found favor with the goddesses and been given a new life, complete with new visage. Ex-queen Rachel…" Sephora maliciously emphasized the *ex* and she brought her spear down with a thud for emphasis, "…was examined months ago and proclaimed to be mad. Everyone must keep that in mind."

A murmur rippled through the crowd.

"I, more than anyone, would welcome Rebekkah back with open arms. Remember, it was because of my suggestion she was sacrificed to the goddesses. I would love to be expiated of the guilt I feel that such a young and vibrant woman of our city had to die, but the goddesses were pleased by her sacrifice. They allowed the death of the beast and our crops have flourished. The goddesses have shown in many ways they were pleased with our gift. They did not return the gift we gave, but kept it.

"The woman who was found in the woods is not Rebekkah. Rachel remains mad. The disruptions in our city must stop. We will deal with that later this evening. For now I wish to mete out punishment to the slave who desecrated the Festival Eve fanny dance."

The women began to cheer. To see how Sephora dealt with Servus was the reason they had come. Sephora's voice rang out.

"Bring out the prisoner!"

Sephora turned in a dramatic fashion toward the holding room door. As she did, she realized Arrival stood at the left side of the High Queen's throne instead of sitting on the Low Throne in the Soldier Sector. It was an unusual choice. Sephora realized something else was amiss, but she could not identify what it was. Sephora glanced at the Low Throne in the Soldier Sector. It was empty.

Two of her secret policewomen brought Servus in. They stopped just inside the doorway. He was shackled and gagged. He had been beaten, and blood mingled with the filth that had been thrown at him earlier. One eye was swollen and bruised.

He wore only the ridiculous dancing thong, yet he stood straight and proud, and in spite of the circumstances, looked calm and dignified. He had not given up hope, but if hope betrayed him, he would meet death unafraid. His bearing showed all this.

The women tittered nervously.

Sephora turned back to the crowd and rotated to the other side of the auditorium to face the Government Sector.

"By the authority vested in me, I call upon a proctor from the Government Sector to oversee the proceedings, that they may be sanctioned by the Sector to comply with the laws of Evlantis. The proctor whose turn it is for duty may take her place at the podium on the stage."

Liava, a middle-aged woman who had taken the oath of Proctor five months ago, and who took the position a little too seriously for Sephora's taste, stood slowly. Every eye was upon Liava as she left her seat, climbed the stairs to the stage, and walked to the dais to the right of the throne. Liava looked grim.

Sephora wished Arrival were sitting on the Low Throne of the Soldier Sector so Sephora could continue to face the crowd, but she would send Arrival to her place later. She turned sideways and addressed Arrival.

"Commander of the Armed forces of Evlantis, I order you to present the prisoner to me for the official reading of his crimes and pronouncement of his punishment."

Arrival did not move. Sephora was shocked at Arrival's insubordination but kept calm.

"Arrival, Low Queen and Commander of the Armed forces of Evlantis, present the prisoner to me, or you will be charged with disrespect to the High Throne and taken into custody."

Arrival responded according to the plan Ava had outlined to their small band of rebels.

"High Queen Sephora, I mean no disrespect, but it is not for me to do this duty. I appear here today as your personal guard only.

Another has filled the office you referred to, a woman far more qualified than I."

Sephora realized what she had missed. Arrival did not wear the crown woven of laurel leaves that the commander of the Army wore to official Palace functions. Before Sephora could respond, the crowd let out a collective gasp. Sephora turned to see the impostor decked out in Rebekkah's formal clothing, the crown of leaves upon her head, striding onto the stage behind her to greet her. She entered from the same doorway Sephora had, which was the opposite side of the platform where Servus stood. To weak cheers of the audience, Ava strode across the stage waving and smiling. She crossed behind Sephora. She chose very carefully the point on the stage where she stopped: directly between Sephora and Servus.

Ava smiled.

"High Queen Sephora, I must apologize for my tardiness. I had duties, long neglected, to attend to before I was able to present myself to you."

Sephora narrowed her eyes. She would not play this game.

"Who are you?" Sephora asked.

Loudly and clearly, so all could hear her words, Ava made her proclamation.

"I am Low Queen Rebekkah of the Soldier Sector. I am Commander of the Armed Forces of Evlantis. I am a Royal Princess of the city of Evlantis. I am the daughter of Rachel of the Agriculture Sector, former High Queen of Evlantis."

Exuberant cheers from the crowd were quickly hushed as Sephora scoffed.

"You have been among us for almost two days," Sephora said, "silent and unresponsive. Why now do you take up the story of the addled madwoman Rachel? What has she promised you?"

Sephora hadn't expected to deal with this right away, but she welcomed it.

"Until this morning," Ava replied, "my wounds had not fully healed, and I lay sick with a fever. But the goddesses have mercifully restored full health to me so I may be of aid to the Queendom tonight. I assure you I am Rebekkah. You may put me to any test you choose."

"Stranger, your identity will be tested, and you will be shown for the impostor you are. First, let us finish the task at hand. Until you are tested, Arrival is Commander of the Army. Arrival, present the prisoner to me!"

Arrival silently held her post.

"Fine; if you persist with this stubbornness, we will depart from custom and I will dispense justice as I see fit. It is the right of the High Queen."

Sephora launched the spear she carried at Servus. Ava was ready. She had been watching Sephora carefully. Ava gracefully flipped head over heels, and using her legs, she knocked the spear from the air in mid-flight. The crowd applauded.

"What insolence is this?" Sephora was red with fury. "How dare you!"

Sephora could take no further action because the crowd rose and cheered at a commotion behind her. Sephora turned to find that Rachel had entered from the doorway the stranger had entered a moment before. Rachel was garbed royally and was attended by two slaves.

Rachel had never looked better. During the months of searching the forest, she had shed middle-aged pounds. Hannah had worked magic with her hair and make-up, and had chosen a rich ruby gown that complemented her skin tone. Rachel wore elegant jewels, including a simple crown, which was the right of a former High Queen to wear in public. For the first time in their many years of political challenges, Rachel's beauty far outshone Sephora's, whose face was ugly with rage, while Rachel looked at peace. Mere moments ago Sephora had looked exquisite. Compared to

Rachel's understated regal elegance, she now looked gaudy. Rachel approached Sephora and embraced her, which drew more cheers from the crowd.

Rachel took the opportunity to whisper to her rival.

"Tonight you will lose what is most dear to you. Tonight I exact retribution from you for the murder of my daughter." For a millisecond, Sephora felt fear. Then it left her and her confidence returned.

The crowd forgot Servus as Ava joined Rachel at her right-hand side and Arrival left her position at the dais to stand at her left. Sephora fumed and waited for the crowd to quiet down so she could try to foil whatever Rachel had planned.

"Speech! Speech!" cried the crowd.

Rachel held up her hands and the crowd quieted.

"Good citizens of Evlantis, I hail you on this Festival Eve. I thank each and every one of you for your prayers, for they have reached the ears of the goddesses and brought my daughter back to me, for this is indeed Rebekkah, my beloved womb-born daughter.

"Our High Queen wishes to proceed with punitive action tonight against the man Servus. But perhaps she has not been High Queen long enough to know that she needs every Low Throne assigned before she can proceed. Arrival has abdicated her position to my daughter, yet High Queen Sephora still refuses to accept the gift the goddesses have given to the Queendom by returning Rebekkah to us. Since confirming the identity of my daughter is essential to determining whether it is Rebekkah or Arrival who will possess the Low Throne of the Soldier Sector, we must first remove all doubt that this is truly my daughter who stands before you.

"High Queen Sephora casts aspersions on the word of Low Queen Caliphus who proclaimed Rebekkah lives in this new form. Let High Queen Sephora choose three challenges for my daughter so that she may proceed with action against the man Servus."

Rachel was careful to refer to him as a man and not a slave, as Ava had asked her to do.

After a slight pause, Rachel said, "All in favor please rise."

At Rachel's invitation, every woman in the building stood. She had their support now, but for the most important vote that would come later, she would lose many of them, she knew.

"This is foolish," Sephora said. "There is no way this woman can be Rebekkah. I will grant unlimited privileges to any woman who can tell me who this woman really is."

There was a stir as the women reacted to the generous proposal Sephora had thrown out to them, but then a hush settled on the hall as it became clear no one could say who this young woman claiming to be Rebekkah really was.

For the first time it occurred to Sephora that perhaps the woman helping Rachel was not from the Queendom. This unsettled her. But it also gave Sephora a strategy. She became calm.

"The fact no one wishes to claim this woman as a relative is completely understandable, for she has taken a position of high treason against the throne. I will play this game of Rachel's to prove to my citizens once and for all that she is duping them. I will name three challenges for the impostor. When she fails, Arrival will take the Low Throne and I will proclaim Servus's punishment. All who agree to this, rise!"

Again, every woman in the Hall stood.

They sat again when Ava spoke.

"I am Rebekkah. Give me these challenges so that all will see and believe."

Sephora knew that to get the audience back on her side she would need to find three challenges the stranger would fail. It only took her seconds to think of the first one. Assuming this woman was not Rebekkah and not even from Evlantis, she would fail this very first challenge.

"Name every woman in the first row of the Palace Hall." Sephora grinned. It might even have been difficult for Rachel to do, for in the first row sat the Low Queens and two members of Royal families from each Sector. Sephora had made some court changes to her benefit since Rachel had pretended madness and wandered in the woods. There were eighteen seats in the front row. Two thrones were empty, the thrones of the Soldier and the Arts Sector. The impostor would have to name sixteen women.

Rachel's heart sank. She had thought Sephora's first challenge would be combat, which the stranger assured her little band of rebels she would win. Ava showed no sign they were in trouble. She walked to the first chair, smiled, and began calling out names with a flourish of her arm toward each member of the court as she announced her name and title.

"Arva of the Soldier Sector." The next chair was empty. "This, of course, is my seat."

This drew a laugh from the crowd. At the third seat, Ava spoke clearly again.

"Diana of the Soldier Sector."

Ava walked to the next Sector, where Ariana sat suckling her six-week old infant daughter.

"Lea of the Livestock Sector and Low Queen Ariana of the Livestock Sector." Ava stopped to give the Soldier's Blessing to the infant. It was vintage Rebekkah. Ava then walked the length of the first row and named every woman correctly.

Rachel willed her features not to show amazement. How did the girl know all the names? All the women of the front row had presented themselves in the reception line two days ago, but Rachel had been sure the girl had been unconscious. She remembered telling the young woman that the Sectors of the Palace Hall were arranged in the same order as the city sectors: Soldier, Livestock, Arts, Religion, Agriculture, and Government. It must be how she was getting each woman's Sector correct. The stranger had already reached the empty chair of the Low Queen of the Arts. Ava turned to Sephora with a look of sadness.

"This is the throne of the Low Queen of the Arts, your daughter, who remains nameless." Ava then moved on to correctly name the next woman.

Rachel marveled at the woman's cleverness. Had someone told her the princesses did not have names? Or had she been covering that she did not know the name? Ava reached the end of the first row and turned to Sephora.

"I have successfully completed the first challenge. Would you like me to go on to the second row?"

Before Sephora could answer, Ava turned to the first woman in the second row and greeted her by name, asking her about the health of her three-month-old daughter.

Sephora scowled.

"It will not be necessary to continue. The fact that you have a good memory for names and faces proves nothing. You must still pass two more challenges."

Ava was relieved, for she did not know all the names of the women in the second row. She had been bluffing. It was another skill she had learned from her eleven brothers and sisters. She was finding being the youngest of twelve immortals made her well suited to deal with her stepsiblings.

"Your next challenge," Sephora said, gloating, "will be to fight three of the Queendom's best fighters at once, unarmed."

The crowd roared. Such a fight was only done in punishment of slaves. It always ended in death for the slave.

"I accept," Ava said jauntily, and again showed full knowledge of their customs. "With the stipulation only daggers are used against me. Here in the Palace it is too dangerous to use weapons that sail through the air…unless you would like to move the entire assembly to the Arena in the Soldier Sector."

"Of course not," said Sephora, "though that was a clever attempt to delay the next challenge. We will stay here. But I will choose the challengers."

"I wouldn't have it any other way," Ava put some bite in her voice. "When I beat my opponents fairly in this next challenge, I do not wish to be accused of winning by another trick."

The Royals of the city had been divided in their opinions about whether the woman was indeed Rebekkah. Now, even the most skeptical among them was starting to wonder. Rebekkah had never backed down from a challenge and had never been afraid to confront authority.

Sephora's voice rang out.

"I call Partouche, Belaina, and Grebella."

The women Sephora called were the most vicious of Sephora's secret police. They were all present in the Hall, and it took them only a few minutes to assemble on the stage. Arrival signaled her soldiers to chalk off the combat circle.

If Arrival hadn't seen Ava knock the spear out of mid-air, she would be a lot more worried than she was. She stole a glance at Servus, to see how he was faring the challenges being put to his new girl friend, but she saw that he was looking directly at her. Her heart pounded, and she felt disgust for herself for her weakness evidenced by the effect this man had on her.

Ava consulted with Rachel, who was still standing on the stage flanked by her slaves.

"They are known for fighting dirty," Rachel said.

"Don't worry," Ava replied. "We expected this challenge."

"Yes, but I thought she would choose one challenger, not three."

"It changes nothing except that I will fight three times as hard and be three times as clever," Ava said with a grin.

Rachel felt a chill go up her spine, for it was exactly what Rebekkah would have said in the same circumstances.

Ava readied herself for the fight. She removed her ornate outer cloak to reveal armor underneath. Sephora noted this and realized she had played right into the stranger's hands. She began to wonder if the girl could beat three of her best fighters. If the doppelganger survived this challenge, Sephora would only have one more chance to make sure she failed. Sephora must come up with a fail-proof challenge. Sephora consulted with her fighters.

"Draw this out as long as possible to give me time to come up with an unbeatable third challenge."

"You don't imagine we are going to lose?" asked Partouche, amazed.

"Look at her. She came prepared for a fight. She has some trick ready. Be careful. If you can, kill her."

Sephora signaled the four fighters to take their place at equally distant points on the chalked circle, which measured thirty feet across. Arrival called out the rules of engagement.

"Each fighter must remain in the circle. No weapon may be thrown. To step or to fall out of the circle is to forfeit. The drawing of blood eliminates the injured party, and she must leave the circle. To surrender one must kneel, forehead touching the ground."

Ava had already chosen her strategy. Torches set in niches on the walls illuminated the Palace Hall. Most of the light for the stage came from the wall behind them. Each person on the stage cast shadows in four directions, but the longest shadows stretched toward the back of the room.

Arrival gave a signal, and two cymbals were crashed together to start the combat.

The crowd roared as Ava's first move was a complete surprise. She leapt into the circle and ran to stand with her back to the audience, facing the stage. The usual strategy was to vie for a position in the center of the circle.

Rachel and Arrival's hearts sank at Ava's mistake. They watched in horror as all three challengers put blades in both hands and rushed toward Ava, all arms churning in a circular motion.

Ava looked at the floor and watched the shadows carefully to determine the timing of her first move. At the right second, with perfect timing, she tucked herself into a ball and somersaulted at Partouche.

Partouche went down, her arms flailing. One of her blades nicked Belaina as she fell. Grebella barely stopped herself from leaving the circle, and spun to chase Ava.

"Belaina, eliminated!" announced Arrival.

Sephora glared at Belaina in anger as she left the circle, her head bowed low in shame. Ava and Partouche jumped to their feet. The three competitors stalked each other cautiously.

Grebella hissed at Partouche.

"Put your knives away and hold her for me. I will kill her."

Grebella outranked Partouche, so Partouche did as she was told. She began to lunge at Ava who was prancing lightly on her feet to defend herself against Grebella's parries and Partouche's attempt to grab her. On the fourth lunge, Partouche managed to grab an ornamental ring on Ava's armor. She pulled Ava to her and spun her around, grasping Ava around the waist and pulling her head back by her hair to expose Ava's neck. Grebella rushed to her, clearly aiming a killing blow to her neck. Ava raised both feet and kicked with a powerful strike.

Ava's legs were longer than Grebella's arms. The force of the kick, which landed high on Grebella's chest, knocked her on her back. One hand landed outside of the circle.

"Grebella, eliminated!" Arrival's voice rang out.

Women cheered and laughed in relief. No one wanted to witness a murder, and it had been clear Grebella would have slit the girl's throat. Cries of "Hail, Rebekkah!" rang out. Grebella left the circle coughing and sputtering for breath, clearly furious.

Partouche had lurched, but managed to remain on her feet. Ava, without any difficulty, moved her weight forward, flipped Partouche over her shoulder, and broke free of her. With only one challenger against her, Ava decided to have some fun. She let Partouche regain her feet to continue the fight. It was clear to the whole assembly that the woman who claimed to be Rebekkah was toying with Partouche. It was vintage Rebekkah. The assembly took to their feet and chanted.

"Re-bek-kah! Re-bek-kah!"

Partouche grew angry and rushed at Ava making wild hacking gestures at her face. Ava decided she was done playing.

Ava dodged the blows and caught Partouche around the waist and spun her, and now it was Ava who held Partouche the way Partouche had held her, pulling her head back and baring her neck as if waiting for someone to cut her throat. Then, Ava did something no one anticipated. She knocked Partouche's knees out from under her. Partouche fell into a kneeling position. Ava landed hard, on top of her. Ava grabbed both of Partouche's wrists and held them behind her back.

Partouche howled furiously as she realized her opponent's next move would be to force her forehead to the floor. The women in the Hall also anticipated the move and they began to laugh. Partouche was no match for Ava. Though Partouche fought, Ava used her weight to force Partouche's forehead to the ground.

Arrival, enjoying herself immensely, yelled, "Partouche surrenders!"

Every woman in the hall cheered. Sephora sat quiet and still. Though the outcome was not what she had hoped, the delay of the fight had given Sephora the time she needed to decide upon the third challenge. As soon as the hall quieted down, Sephora stood up and stepped forward.

"This only proves you are a better fighter than Rebekkah ever was."

The crowd began to boo her, and she gave a menacing look that silenced the jeers.

"Third Challenge," Sephora announced. "Sing the lullaby Rachel sang every night to Rebekkah when she was dying of the lung disease in her sixth year."

There were thousands of such love songs that the women of Evlantis sang their precious babies to sleep with every night. Only a handful of people present knew which of the thousands of lullabies Sephora referred to.

Rachel breathed a sigh of relief. She had sung that very song to Ava in the forest when she had reminisced about her daughter, not knowing or caring if the girl was listening. It was the song Ava had joined her in singing as though she already knew it by heart. Ava glanced at Rachel as she took her place center stage, and Rachel nodded encouragement almost imperceptibly. The arena was perfectly silent as Ava's voice rose in song. It was a beautiful, pure sound. No one present had heard anything as lovely, ever. Each word was heard clearly. The melody was haunting, and Ava sang it mournfully, as she had heard Rachel sing it.

"As night draws near,
Mama's babe must leave for a while,
Leave in sleep,
To travel in dreams.

If Mama could,
She would go with you.
To make sure you stay safe
And guide you through dreamland.

When morning comes and you return
Back from distant lands, bring Mama a smile
A souvenir of safe passage
Through the long hours that parted us."

Many in the hall had tears in their eyes, for too many of their daughters died in infancy. This lullaby was a gentle pleading for a child to wake safely in the morning. That Rachel had sung it to her daughter when she was near death in her childhood touched every heart.

Ahmilia, the mid-wife, stood crying openly.

"That was the one," she said.

Low Queen Dawna of the Government Sector and Low Queen Questar of the Agriculture Sector stood also.

"We were there. That was the lullaby," said Dawna, the older of the pair. Questar nodded her head in agreement.

All four of the Low Queens went to Ava, now acknowledged as Rebekkah, to greet her. Each of them ceremoniously bowed the half-bow of one Low Queen to another. She returned the bow in kind. Every woman was cheered. Sephora and Servus were forgotten.

It took twenty minutes for the excitement to die down. Sephora returned to her throne and sat. She waited quietly until she could command their attention again. It had occurred to her she had chosen the wrong challenge. Rachel could not have had this stranger waiting in the wings to help her any longer than the three months she was out of office. Surely, in such a short time, she could not have taught the girl to read fluently. She should have handed her the heaviest law book in the Queendom and had her read a page of text. She thought she could manage to bring her point home. She would prove this young woman was an impostor yet.

As soon as the room quieted, Sephora rose and spoke.

"I agreed that if the girl could pass three challenges, I would accept her as Rebekkah. Please take your seats everyone. We still have business to attend to. I have promised this day will not pass without punishing Servus for his desecration of the fanny dance."

The Low Queens took their places. Sephora had to wait again as applause broke out when Rebekkah took her place on the Low Queen's throne in the Soldier Sector.

With imperious decisiveness, Sephora took the scroll upon which the crimes of Servus had been inscribed and held it out to Rebekkah.

"I demand you read the crimes this slave is accused of for everyone to hear," she said.

There were four people in the hall whose hearts seemed to stop at this statement. Everything had been going so well. Here was something none of them had thought of. Ava never hesitated. She answered back cheekily.

"High Queen, is this another challenge? I know my place is to present the prisoner. I am not a lawyer from the Government Sector. I am a simple soldier. I am unsure whether you are casting doubt on my knowledge of Queendom policies or my ability to read. Yet," she continued slyly, "if you wish me to show I can read, I would be happy to read a page or two from the slave genealogies."

Sephora's heart skipped a beat. She had thought conspiracy was between Rachel and Rebekkah. This veiled threat showed either her missing daughters or Servus were aligned with the impostor. Sephora smiled broadly.

"You are right. It was another test. I apologize if I still seem unconvinced. But as High Queen it is my duty to be ever vigilant of the safety of the Queendom.

"We have more pressing business at hand. Commander, present the prisoner. Liava of the Government Sector, step forward to read the crimes against him."

Ava left her throne and strode to where Servus stood to escort him to Sephora. Ava was relieved to be beside him so she could protect him. She motioned for him to kneel, and he did. He landed heavily upon his knees since his hands were chained behind his back. Even on his knees, he emanated power and dignity. The women hushed as he took his position to be sentenced.

Liava opened the scroll and read.

"High Queen Sephora proclaims these crimes against the slave number 293326, also known as Servus, King of Slaves. First crime, Treason: setting himself up as a ruler opposing the High Queen; second crime, Rebellion: stirring up other slaves; Third crime, Blasphemy: purposefully and willfully bringing shame to the Queendom by ruining the opening night fanny dances. What is your punishment for this slave, High Queen?"

Sephora stood.

"He is beyond quickening duty and to kill him would make a martyr of him. As your High Queen, I say there is only one punishment worthy of his crimes. For his punishment I demand castration."

A low buzz echoed in the Hall as women began to debate the merits of the sentence, which had been banned long ago.

Ava had planned to object, but High Priestess Caliphus stood and shouted to be heard above the noise.

"Castration is illegal. This cannot be allowed! A hundred years ago the priestesses rallied to have the punishment banned from our Law. Thousands of priestesses chose to take on the labors of men to eradicate this brutal custom. It would desecrate the sacrifice we made for our brothers!" Caliphus shook with rage. Her foot tapped incessantly. She willed herself to stop. Further loss of self-control would not help the situation.

"I am High Queen! I am the Law!" Sephora yelled. She would have her way on this.

Rachel, standing to Liava's left, spoke clearly and dispassionately.

"To re-establish an illegal punishment is not a matter of opinion or the High Queen's will. It requires a majority vote of the Low Queens."

Liava glanced at the elders of the Government Sector, who were nodding in agreement with Rachel.

"The former High Queen speaks truly," said Liava. "A vote must be taken."

"Fine," said Sephora, calm again. "Liava, call the names of the Queens for the vote."

"Again, I must correct the High Queen," said Rachel. "No one should blame Sephora for her ignorance of protocol. She has only been in office for a few months. However, the vote cannot begin until all the Low Queens are present. Where is Low Queen Third Sephora of the Arts Sector?"

"She is ill," Sephora said, "so ill that she is not able to leave her bed."

"I am sorry to hear that," said Rachel. "I know what it is to worry about a daughter. I hope she is able to return to her duties soon, but if she cannot fulfill her duty tonight, then we will have to replace her temporarily until she is well enough to take up the mantle of her office again. That is, if you wish to have this matter decided tonight."

"I do. Let it be," Sephora answered, unaffected.

"I have a suggestion for her replacement," Rachel said. "Arrival of the Soldier Sector has leadership experience and would make an excellent substitute until such time as your daughter is well."

The women of the Arts Sector began to boo. Rachel had known they would. Sephora quickly made the correction.

"Rachel, surely in the time you have been out of office you have not forgotten that a Low Queen must be a lifelong resident of the Sector she is Queen of. Arrival has been a soldier her entire adult life. She cannot serve as Low Queen of the Arts Sector."

"But, I am merely following your inspired example," said Rachel. "The precedent was set by you when you opened the Throne of the Soldier Sector to anyone in the Queendom."

"That was different!" said Sephora. "The Soldier Sector's Queen must be the best fighter in the Queendom. The Low Queen of the Arts Sector must be an artist, not a soldier."

"I don't see the distinction as clearly as you do," said Rachel dryly. "That being said, is this so important to you that the matter cannot wait until Third Sephora is better?"

"It is that important to me, yes," Sephora said. "Surely there is someone from a royal family in the Arts Sector who could do the job."

"I can think of one," said Rachel. "She is the woman whose name would have been on the ballot for the special election if she had not been assigned to serve me in the forest as I searched for my daughter. May I suggest Hannah, daughter of Nebo, of the Arts Sector?"

Exclamations of excitement were heard in the Arts Sector. Many women had been disappointed Hannah had not been able to run in the election. Sephora summoned the disgraced Partouche to ask her a question.

"Why does she mention Hannah's name?" Sephora hissed in a loud whisper. "Has she been found?"

"No, my Queen," said Partouche. "I can assure you Hannah is not anywhere within the Queendom walls. Captain Meerta has extended her search to the forest. So far there is no sign of her."

Sephora addressed Rachel.

"If you can produce Hannah, then I deem her an acceptable substitute for the duration of my daughter's illness. You have three minutes to bring her here."

Sephora was already searching the faces in the Royal Sector of the Arts seating area for the woman she would replace her daughter with, someone who would do her bidding.

"I will not need that much time," Rachel said. Every occupant of the Hall watched as Rachel turned to the slave who stood two steps behind her and to the right.

"Hannah, you have heard the High Queen speak. You are Low Queen of the Arts Sector until Third Sephora is able to fulfill her duties again."

The women roared in shock as Hannah shed her disguise. Off came the baggy slave clothes. Underneath she was wearing a form-fitting white sheath, a popular style in the Arts Sector, which left no doubt in anyone's mind she was a woman. Lyal handed her the damp towel he had hidden under his tunic. Hannah rubbed the slave mark off her forearm and scrubbed her hands and face clean.

Lastly, she took a comb and smoothed her short, wild tresses as best she could. To the cheers of her Sector, she strode confidently to the chair of the Low Queen of the Arts. Hannah was no longer a mouse and a pawn. She was now a force to be reckoned with, and barren or not, there was royal blood in her veins. It showed in her face and bearing.

There was nothing the women loved better than drama, and this was drama at its finest. Hannah's mother and sister were seated a few rows back, and they wailed in joy as they made their way down to the throne to greet Hannah. Many women dissolved into tears at the reunion of mother and daughter, sister and sister. Sephora was helpless to take any action against Hannah. Sephora inwardly cursed herself for walking right into Rachel's trap.

"Speech! Speech!" cried the women of all the Sectors. They longed to know how Hannah had ended up at Rachel's side disguised as a slave. Sephora held up her hands and the room became silent.

"I'm sure Hannah has plenty to say. For now, she has a duty. She has been appointed to serve the people. The people's business for now is to punish the King of Slaves."

Again, the crowd had forgotten Servus. Ava had hustled him off to Sephora's right during the distraction. He stood between Arrival and Ava. Arrival had never felt more uncomfortable. Arrival leaned across Servus and whispered to her new sister.

"You should return to your throne. I will assign two soldiers loyal to us to guard Servus and take him back to the side of the stage. It will be safer for him there."

Ava nodded and stealthily made her way across the stage. She hoped she would not attract the attention of Sephora. Ava did want to get Rachel's attention, however, and was able to. Their eyes met, and Ava nodded. It was time.

INSURRECTION

"I challenge the High Queen's authority to punish this man," Rachel said. She was not certain this was the best thing for the Queendom, but it was time to fulfill the Pact of Honor she had made with the woman she had found in the woods.

"Thank goddess!" said Caliphus. "Finally, a voice of reason! Please continue!"

Sephora would have objected, but Liava silenced her with a look.

"Slavery is a crime against mankind," Rachel spoke the words Ava required of her, using the talking points Ava had given her. "It was a weakness of Great Mother Eve that she could not forgive the sin of her son. What is woman without man? How long could we survive without them? It takes both a woman and a man to create life."

A ripple of murmurs coursed through the crowd, but they remained hushed and listening. This was boldness at its finest.

"The strengths of womankind are legendary," Rachel continued confidently, "yet we sap the strength of those we should be calling our equals, our mates, our partners. We dance upon the backs of mankind and break those backs so we do not have to bend our own in labor. Shame on us! Where would we be without the strengths of

337

man? We harness him for labor but deny him the fruits of his work. It is stealing. Shame on us!

"The resources of our city are strained to the breaking point. For years I have begged the Low Queens to establish a sister city. My daughter," here she nodded at Ava, "has been hunting for ideal sites for us to cultivate a second city. But we women would rather see the fruit of our loins drown in Rowada's swamp than to give up the comforts of our home hearths. Shame on us!

"Look at this slave at my side. Do you know who he is? Look well. This is the son of the late great Riadha, Royal Matron of the Government Sector, and the slave Leged, who rots in a pit for the crime of trying to be a father to the boy. Riadha lives on in a daughter and a son, but the daughter is cherished while the son is an outcast. Shame on us!

"We are shadows of what we could be. We are controlling, stubborn, close-minded fools. We must change, and change must begin tonight."

Rachel paused before delivering the points that would pierce directly into the women's hearts.

"Many of you have loved men. This is not a crime. This is a blessing. Those who have opened their hearts to men must teach the rest of us how to see men, how to respect men, and how to live alongside them so that this city, and others we will build, will prosper in integrity. Not only do I repudiate Sephora's right to castrate Servus, I demand retribution for all men! I demand a vote of the Low Queens to end slavery forever and to establish a Seventh Sector in the city, a Mankind Sector, with Servus appointed to rule as Low King!"

Rachel's voice had risen in pitch and volume as she spoke until the last words were as loud as if a goddess had spoken from heaven. Her words echoed in the hall.

Sephora, normally careful to control every reaction, had a stunned look in her eyes. She stood in shock with her mouth hanging open. All this time she had thought Rachel would be fighting to get her throne back. This move would effectively make the position of High Queen superfluous. The High Queen would no longer be the deciding policy maker, since no vote would ever again end in a tie. The Low Queens would have the power to veto the orders of the High Queen, as they were attempting to do now.

High Priestess-Low Queen Caliphus stepped forward. This was her moment, the moment she had lived for since receiving the mission from her predecessor. She raised the staff to show that she was speaking as High Priestess, and she spoke with obvious passion.

"Goddess be praised for the wisdom coming from Queen Rachel's mouth! We women of the Religion Sector have long deplored the state our brothers live in. They are huwoman, as we are huwoman. They are our fathers, brothers, uncles, and sons. They contribute far more to our city by the sweat of their backs than many women do. We have kept their bodies and minds in chains too long. Free them! Educate them! Let us not move backwards to a time when we removed the essence of manhood from our brothers, but forward to a time when the best of manhood is incorporated freely into our city.

"As we all know, proposals for votes must come from the Queens only. With the authority vested in me as Low Queen and High Priestess of the Religion Sector, I propose a vote to free mankind from slavery, and I proclaim that the slave grounds be henceforth known as the Freeman Sector, and for Servus to be named Low King of that Sector."

From her post beside Sephora, Arrival surveyed the crowd. The women of the Religion Sector stood cheering enthusiastically, while the women of the Agriculture and Government Sectors hissed and booed. The three other Sectors—the Arts, Livestock, and Soldier Sectors—were clearly divided on the issue. Arrival left her post on the dais beside Sephora to confer with Ava.

"Commander Rebekkah," said Arrival when she reached her, "soldiers should be dispersed into the crowd to keep peace. Do you want to give the orders, or do you want me to do it?"

"You do it," said Ava. "I will stay here to vote."

"Of course," said Arrival, always the good soldier. She began the task of dispersing soldiers to keep order in the Hall.

Meanwhile, Sephora questioned Liava.

"Can this be done?" she asked.

"This certainly can be, and has been, done."

"Is there nothing I can do to stop this?" Sephora whined. "This will make a mockery of the High Queenship."

"I would say it is you who have made a mockery of the High Queenship," Liava retorted sharply. "In the past months you have done more harm to the Queendom than any ruler in the herstory of the city. You should be thanking the goddesses Rachel isn't trying to depose you, or worse, bring charges against you. I believe this is a valid vote. However, to be certain that it cannot be questioned later, I will consult with the elders of the Government Sector and the books of law and return promptly."

The soldiers took their places in the crowd and their presence calmed the women. This left empty seats in the Soldier Sector, and women who had been standing moved to sit in them. More women filed into the Hall from outside. The Hall was filled beyond its capacity. Liava returned to the podium next to Sephora and spoke. The women quieted to hear her proclamation.

"I have conferred with the elders and the decision has been made. While this is shocking, there is nothing in our constitution that prevents us from freeing the slaves. The proposal of Caliphus will be presented for a vote as soon as it has been seconded."

"I second the motion," said Hannah.

Liava wasted no time.

"The motion to set the men free and make Servus Low King has been seconded. The vote begins now. We will go in the opposite order of the last vote taken. Queen Dawna of the Government Sector how do you vote?"

Dawna stood.

"This is ridiculous," she said. "Men are not huwoman; they are animals, beasts of burden. To go against the wisdom of the Great Mother is foolish. I vote against."

The women of the Government and Agriculture Sectors cheered. When the cheers tapered off, Liava called for the next vote.

"Queen Questar of the Agriculture Sector."

Questar stood confidently. She had had a little more time to think about what she would say.

"The Agriculture Sector is the main source of food and medicine for the Queendom. Are you women willing to go out and work in the fields and orchards so we can have grain, vegetables, fruits, and herbs? Will free men consent to perform such backbreaking labor? This will not only end life as we know it, but without slave labor, we will starve. For the good of every woman and girl of the Queendom, I vote no."

More cheers from Questar and Dawna's sectors slowed the proceedings down. Sephora began to relax. She only needed one more Low Queen to vote no, and then she could cast the vote to break the tie in favor of keeping the men enslaved.

Liava's voice rang out again as soon as the cheers subsided.

"Queen Caliphus."

Caliphus had already made her speech. She kept her answer simple.

"I vote yes, to free the slaves and make Servus King of the Seventh Sector." Caliphus turned dramatically to face her people. "All those in support of my vote, rise in silence."

Every woman in her Sector stood. Caliphus turned back to face the stage, smiling widely. Liava continued.

"Queen Hannah of the Arts Sector."

Hannah was ready. She stood and turned to face the women of the Arts Sector to indicate she would speak to them. The background noises in the hall ceased. Every woman present wanted to hear what Hannah had to say.

"When I came forward a little while ago, you called out for me to speak. I will do so now. Bear with me while I tell my story and explain where I have been and why I have been in hiding. You all know me. I am Hannah of the Arts, firstborn daughter of Nebo of the Arts, sister of Tilda. You watched me grow. As with every precious daughter of Evlantis, I had a wonderful childhood. Every major development was celebrated, including every birthday anniversary, the day I chose my Sector, and the first time I visited the Quickening Chamber.

"When it was discovered I was barren, everything changed. Though I rejoiced because our family line would continue with the birth of my sister Tilda, I slowly became little more than an outcast." Hannah noticed some women in every Sector nodded their heads in a show of empathy. She had never realized so many had suffered the way she had.

"I found peace in my honorable work at the theater. I had purpose and a new family. I had joy in my life until the day Sephora pulled me from my place to tend to Rachel in the woods. Never one to shirk duty, I attended Rachel to the best of my ability. I hated every day I spent in the forest, but I did what the High Queen commanded.

"Two days ago, when Rachel found Rebekkah, she commanded me to go back to the city alone for help. Again, I did nothing but my duty. I reported to the High Queen and only to the High Queen. Sephora called me a coward. Then she bludgeoned me and had me taken to the palace prison. I believe it was her intention to kill me. I did not wish to give my life for the heinous crime of serving the High Queen, so I escaped.

"I could not go back into the forest, but I did not know where I could go to be safe. I made it to the mule barn, where I collapsed and hid in fear. A slave boy discovered me there. He listened to my story and promised to keep me safe. He pleaded my case to King Servus.

"King Servus had no reason to help me, and may have even benefited by turning me in. But he showed me mercy and helped me find a disguise to keep me from Sephora who has been hunting me.

"For a full day I have been hiding in plain sight, serving High Queen Rachel as her slave. Not one of you recognized me, though I stood here in front of all of you. Look inside your hearts, good women; what does this tell you about us? We have become cold and callous to those who do the most for us. After our children, the men are the Queendom's most valuable resource, but the men who serve us have become invisible to us. We take them for granted and abuse them, when we should be grateful for the labors they extend on our behalf.

"That sums up my journey of the last few days and what I have learned from it. Now, let me talk to you about the issue at hand. I know many of you engage in illicit relationships with men, hiding your feelings by day and hiding in the forest at night with your lovers. Let's not pretend to be shocked by what everyone knows is true. I have heard that those of you who love men often have lives that are better, richer, and fuller than those of us who abide by the law. Some hearts have been broken, but daughters often break their mothers' hearts. Women who partner with women have their hearts broken, too. Perhaps hurt is just as much a risk in any kind of love as the benefits.

"Some men may leave us once they are free. Can we blame them if they do? But I think many will stay. I have been among them. Most want to be fathers to their children, brothers to their brothers and sisters, and uncles to their nephews and nieces. Their code glorifies such relationships, as it does honor, self-control, and self-reliance. These are qualities that will make our all lives richer.

"Now, women of Evlantis, hear my vote: for the sake of every woman throughout our herstory who has loved a man and been slighted for it, and to repay the debt I owe him, I vote yes to free the slaves and to make Servus King."

Again, there was a mixed reaction. Some women cheered and some booed, though the cheers were becoming stronger.

"Low Queen Ariana of the Livestock Sector," Liava called for the next vote.

The mood in the room grew tense. Ariana was the fifth queen, and since the vote was now two for the proposal and two against, hers was the most crucial vote, because everyone guessed Rebekkah would vote to free the slaves. They had seen enough maneuvers between mother and daughter over their lifetimes to know they were acting as a unit. Once Ariana voted, the deed was done. By the laws of Evlantis, the issue could not be re-visited for seven years. Ariana stood, but before she could speak, screams were heard from the back of the room.

All eyes went to the rear of the building. A dozen slaves armed with spears entered the hall with twelve young daughters of the highest-ranking women of Evlantis. Kiertus and Justus led them. Sephora could see what was going on and felt relief.

"Here come the barbarians with our daughters as their captives," Sephora said loudly for all to hear. "You want to free them? We will see such sights daily and worse. Setting men free will make slaves of us women! Do you think they are above retribution, they who are closer to the beasts than to womankind? They will repay our discipline to them a hundred times over. They will rape and kill our daughters while we are forced to watch. They will bring us to subjection under them, for if they are not held back they will develop the superior strength their frames are capable of.

"If we educate them, they will challenge us. We will have to endure their foolish notions of a Great Father. We will no longer have the final say.

"Most of all, if we set them free, they will leave us, as the man left Mother Eve. They will abandon us and we will starve, not tomorrow, but in time. Our granddaughters and great granddaughters will die of starvation upon the steps of their home hearths, holding their dead babies to their breasts, cursing the generation who betrayed them, cursing us with their dying breaths."

"Be silent, High Queen. Be silent, everyone. Soldiers, calm the women."

Ava's voice rose above the noise in the room. The room quieted except for the quiet sobbing of the mothers whose daughters were held hostage and the murmurings of those nearby, comforting them. Ava thought quickly, for she too had seen immediately what was going on. It was risky, but she could see only one course of action.

Servus also had a clear view. Though he was glad his men were trying to rescue him, he had never felt so fettered before. He had borne his suffering honorably and with dignity. He had not given up hope, and his spirits had risen as Rebekkah orchestrated a vote for freedom for the men. When Kiertus and Justus appeared, he felt a rare wave of despair. He had not been able to get word to them, and just as slavery had been about to end without bloodshed, his men had begun the first stage of the war they had planned.

Gagged as he was, he could not command them to stand down now. They had no idea what they were walking into. He met Kiertus's eyes and shook his head no. Kiertus look confused, and then even more so as the new Rebekkah strode up the stairway toward him with a big smile on her face and her arms open wide.

"You brought the children; thank you. You have done well. Now let them go to their mothers as we agreed."

Kiertus looked again at Servus, who was bound and gagged on the stage, but he managed to nod his head at Kiertus nonetheless. Ava took the steps up to Kiertus and Justus two at a time. She addressed the assembly.

"I asked these men to bring some children to witness their fathers, brothers, and uncles being emancipated. Gentleman, come with me and stand with your King."

Servus was still nodding his head. The scene before Kiertus was surreal. Both Sephora and Rachel were dressed as High Queen and on the stage at the front of the hall. Servus was gagged and bound. There was a complete stranger dressed as Rebekkah standing before him and giving him orders. Everything in him told him to keep the girls and continue with the war. It was only his great regard for his King's will that led him to turn to the men who were with him and issue a new command.

"Release the girls. We have done our job and brought them here as the Low Queen requested."

Sephora did not want to see this end peacefully.

"Now it is Rebekkah who does not seem to know the law!" screamed Sephora. "Does she forget children are not allowed in the Hall? Or perhaps it is something this woman never knew. Open your eyes, women, see what is right before you. Centuries of progress are about to be eliminated by a total stranger."

Women's heads swiveled back to the stage as Liava answered her furiously.

"High Queen, it is you who are out of line. I warned you before. Rebekkah's identity has been established to the satisfaction of the Queendom. You reveal your ignorance and your love of chaos with your statements. Children are welcomed on momentous occasions such as this. Rebekkah was not out of line when she sent for them. It was unorthodox to use slaves to bring them, but she is a Low Queen. She may command them as she sees fit. We have business to attend to. If you have one more outburst, I will have you removed from the Hall."

"But those slaves are armed!" Sephora continued outraged. "They should be put to death at once, as should the person who put weapons in their hands."

"It was you who armed them," Ava said from the back of the hall. Heads swiveled to the rear of the building. "Your handling of the men made them desperate. They feared for their lives. They were being poisoned at meal times and punished for the least of offenses while you increased their quotas and decreased their resting time. Not since the rule of Ferrata the Vain have men been treated with such cruelty. When Rachel found me in the forest, King Servus, thinking Rachel might reclaim her throne, and not wanting to bring retribution down upon their heads, went to Commander Arrival to turn in the weapons.

"When I was able to resume my duties, Arrival briefed me on them. I insisted the men be given the spears they carry tonight for two reasons. First, because I could spare no soldier to bring the children here tonight and I was afraid the women watching the children would be loath to let them go; second, because I wanted every person in the Queendom to know what risk your cruel policies put them at."

Sephora scoffed.

"Your story has as much worth as broken crockery. If it is as you say, why are the children still captive?"

"We are not captives. We are here of our own free will." It was a child's voice—the voice of Rachella, the young girl Rachel had spoken with the forest. Kiertus looked at Justus, surprised.

"It is true, Kiertus," whispered Justus to Kiertus. "When I went to gather some children to bring with us, these girls begged us to take them."

One of the younger girls tugged at Rachella's tunic.

"I want my mommy," she said, tears in her eyes.

"Go then, Suetina," said Rachella, who was clearly the leader. "All of you who wish to, go. Show our mothers, aunts, sisters, and queens we are free to move about as we choose."

Kiertus nodded to the men holding the children as three of the girls left the group and made their way to where their mothers were seated.

"What is the meaning of this?" yelled Sephora. "Are you feverish, child? Have they drugged you? Get away while you can!"

"I, and those with me, do not wish to go," Rachella answered clearly. "Any one of these men could be my father, my brother, or my uncle. The horses in the stables and the pigs in their pens are treated with more respect than they are. I want things in our Queendom to be right and just. It can't be so with one portion of the population enslaved to another."

Rachella addressed Justus, her eyes sparkling in excitement.

"Low Queen Rebekkah says they are voting to make you free. Let us do as she asked, and join your King on the stage."

Rachella put her hand in his and tugged at him. Justus's last remaining doubts had been removed by her words. He glanced at Kiertus, who nodded the affirmative, and motioned for their companions to follow. Ava walked with them down the aisle to the stage.

"Caliphus!" Sephora spoke calmly so Liava would not be tempted to make good on her threat to have her removed from the Hall. "What lies have you been teaching these children? We send our children to be educated in your Sector, not to fill their heads with idiocy!"

Caliphus sat on her throne, smiling. She was proud of her students. Her life's mission had been to improve the life of the slaves in any way possible. She had done so by teaching the children the wrongs of slavery. If the proposal passed tonight, she would be the first priestess in centuries to complete the secret mission.

"If you wish to question me on the curriculum of the elementary schools," said Caliphus to Sephora, "now is not the time. I will be happy to meet with you after Festival Week is over. For the good of the Queendom we need to finish this vote here and now.

"As for the child's words, they only show even a child can see the truth of the matter. We grown women need to pay heed to the words of this young one and question the wisdom of those who went before us. Sephora, please have Liava continue the vote."

Sephora was desperate to stop the proceedings. She knew Ariana was the swing vote. Rebekkah would vote to free the slaves. If Ariana voted to free the men, the thing was done. Total submission of men to the women had taken them a long time to master. Sephora looked to where Ariana sat, debating the merits of continuing. Her eyes opened wide as she watched Ariana take her infant baby out of the arms of the Royal Nanny and hurry up the steps from her Sector to the stage and over to the group of slaves and children who had finished climbing the steps of the center aisle to the stage.

"Kiertus, Kiertus," Ariana said as she reached him. Tears streamed down her face. "Here is your daughter...our daughter. Take her...take me. Whatever happens from now on happens to us both."

Ariana's back was to Sephora. Kiertus could see the hatred on Sephora's face. There was no doubt in Sephora's mind anymore which way Ariana would vote.

"Ariana, you must return to your throne quickly," Kiertus whispered to her. "You must vote for my freedom—for our freedom. Then we can be together." He tried to push her away, but she would not be moved.

"Don't you love me anymore? Please, Kiertus, take our daughter. Take me in your arms. Let everyone see how much we love each other." Ariana began to shout. "He was my quickening partner and is the father of my infant girl!"

Kiertus could see what was coming as clearly as he could see the face of the woman he loved and the infant girl who was born from their love. He took the child quickly and passed it to Justus. He gathered Ariana in his arms, spun her around, and pushed her to the side quickly, just as the spear Sephora threw pierced his back.

"Kiertus!" Ariana screamed his name and threw herself on the floor beside him, sobbing. The Hall fell silent. More than half the women present had clearly seen Kiertus give his life for Ariana and her child. The sound of Liava banging her gavel rang out over the frightened cries of the children present.

"High Queen Sephora," said Liava, "I warned you repeatedly about your conduct! You put the lives of those children, including a baby, in danger just now. This Queendom is a Republic, ruled by the people. The position of High Queen is one of leadership. When you took the oath of office, you promised to keep peace in the city, but just as you did in your own Sector for years, you are spreading nothing but chaos. You are making judgments out of turn. I will not suggest formal charges be brought against you tonight, but I will make good on my threat."

Liava then called out, "Soldiers, remove the High Queen from the stage."

Arrival left Sephora's side and summoned soldiers to help her carry out Liava's command.

"I will die before I let you remove me from the proceeding, Liava!" said Sephora.

Sephora gave a signal and a half a dozen of her secret police-women were at her side, their weapons drawn.

"This is rebellion," Sephora said to them. "For every enemy soldier you kill you will be rewarded generously."

"You've heard the High Queen," said Arrival, giving her soldiers orders. "She ordered her women to kill. Put away your anger and your hatred. Be strong and fight for what is right. Aim true. If you must take the life of a sister to preserve your own, then let it be. Now, warriors, give your best."

Fighting began on the stage.

Ava would have liked to stay and help fight, but she knew she must get the group of men and children to safety. Justus was immobile. He stared in shock at Kiertus, dead on the floor, with Ariana weeping over him. Justus was still holding the baby, the daughter of Kiertus. The children, including Rachella, were weeping. Ava gently took the baby from Justus.

"Can you carry Kiertus off the stage?" Ava asked him. "I would like to get you all to safety. Fighting has begun. You are all in great danger."

"I can carry him," said Justus. He stooped and put a hand on Ariana's shoulder, a crime punishable by death. Justus no longer cared.

"Lady, we must go. We must get you and his daughter to safety."

"I will not leave him," said Ariana.

"You do not have to leave him. I will carry him."

"I will help you," she said. Together they lifted the body of Kiertus. Ava felt relief.

"Rachella, we must get you safely off the stage."

"I want to go to Servus," Rachella said, stubbornly. "I want to help him."

"You cannot help him if you are dead," replied Ava.

Ariana looked around her and realized the gravity of the situation.

"There is a back way to the other side of the stage," she said. "Let's leave by this exit and we will re-enter by the other. Then we will be able to help Servus."

"Why should I trust you?" asked Rachella.

"I swear on my love for this man, it is the truth. A hallway connects all the anterooms. Come with me, and live."

"Queen Rebekkah? Is it true?" Rachella asked.

"Yes, of course it is true," said Ava, hoping it was. "Ariana will lead you, and I will follow behind to protect you." Ariana glanced at Ava and nodded. If Rachel and Arrival had thrown their lots in with the stranger, she would too. Especially since the woman was helping her honor Kiertus.

"Thank you, Low Queen. You are a good friend to me." Ariana did not stay to see the grateful look Ava gave her, but headed toward the nearest exit from the stage to the connecting anterooms.

The fighting was fierce, but Ava was able to defend the group from the few attackers that left the knot of warriors concentrated on the stage near Sephora. They made it through the exit safely.

On the stage, blood flowed freely as wounds were inflicted. Sephora's soldiers fought wildly. Self-discipline had never been their strong suit. Arrival's soldiers followed her orders to the letter. Their faces were emotionless masks. They used all the skills they possessed to find their opponent's weakness, exploit it, and gain the advantage. It was a game of skill to them, of risk, and they operated as a strategic unit. They proudly remembered why they were warriors, and they began to overcome Sephora's women.

Arrival found herself fighting Partouche. Partouche leered at her and mocked her.

"You are fighting to save your boyfriend, aren't you, you filthy man lover!"

Arrival willed herself not to hear the words; not to react. She saw herself not as a woman who preferred men, but as a woman who valued each person present in the Hall. Partouche's words could not distract her.

"I couldn't beat the demon-ghost your bitch mother brought among us, but I will kill you."

Partouche continued her verbal battle not realizing Arrival was beyond caring what words left Partouche's mouth. Arrival fought on, parrying each thrust efficiently and evaluating Partouche for a weakness.

Partouche drew first blood. Arrival noticed she favored a knife stroke given with her left hand but which fell too high to do any major damage. Arrival stepped into the way of a stroke purposefully to make Partouche overconfident.

"Go to the land of doomed warriors!" said Partouche, as she withdrew her left blade from the flesh of Arrival's right arm and raised her right for a killing stroke.

Arrival was ready. Partouche never saw the blade Arrival drove into her midsection. Arrival dropped her right blade and used her right hand to drive the blade up. Partouche opened her mouth, but no sound came out. She slipped on a pool of blood under her feet and went down. What Arrival had planned to be a disabling flesh wound became fatal.

Arrival had no time to recuperate. Sephora immediately replaced Partouche, fighting in her place. Sephora circled Arrival, taunting her as Partouche had done.

"You are wounded, rebel. I should kill you here and now, but I would like to see you hang for your crime of insurrection against the High Throne."

Arrival remained distant, and sharpened her senses. She was fighting wounded. Sephora was known to be an apt opponent. Though Arrival had no qualms about killing Sephora, she knew the Queendom would be better off if the High Queen did not die upon the floor of the Palace Hall stage. Partouche's death had been an accident. If she had not slipped, she would have been badly injured, but alive.

Sephora made quick darting movements with the daggers in her hands. Her fighting style was much different from the wide swinging arcs Partouche and the others used. Arrival's right hand remained empty while she parried thrusts with the bloody blade that had killed Partouche. Arrival first thought she would put a small shield in her right hand, and then thought better of it. As she and Sephora circled each other around the fallen Partouche, Arrival reached into her tunic for the weapon she had hidden there. She drew it out. Instead of freeing it from its leather scabbard, she held it by the blade end, still sheathed, and flicked it back and forth with her wrist to use the handle to deflect Sephora's thrusts.

Sephora laughed merrily.

"Have you lost so much blood you have forgotten how to hold a weapon?" Sephora asked.

Arrival smiled and continued to defend herself. Sephora doubled her efforts upon the right side, forcing Arrival to use the knife handle to deflect most of her blows. Arrival waited patiently for Sephora to recognize the dagger. A minute later she did.

"You bitch!" hissed Sephora. "You have my daughters! I will..." but her threat trailed off. For at the moment of recognition,

Sephora had hesitated in her strikes. Arrival had dropped the blade she held in her left hand and unsheathed First Sephora's dagger in one fluid motion. Arrival grabbed the front of Sephora's glistering silver gown to hold her in place while she held the blade of First Sephora's dagger to Sephora's neck.

"Drop your weapons and order your women to stop fighting. Do it now, or I will kill you."

Sephora looked into Arrival's eyes and saw nothing but cold purpose in them. Sephora felt a chill roll up her spine. Arrival was not bluffing. No one had ever threatened to kill her before. She was afraid.

"Soldiers of the High Queen, lay down your arms!" said Sephora. "I surrender." Sephora dropped her weapons, and her lackeys followed suit.

Liava was quick to take control of the situation.

"Arrival, Second in Command of the Armed Forces, I commend you on your service to the Queendom. Please escort the High Queen to a comfortable waiting area in the Palace and make sure she is secure until we either require her to break a tie vote or the proceedings here have finished."

Sephora knew no good would come out of resisting now. She would bide her time and strike back when she was able. She left the stage to muted cheers, which died the moment she turned back to see who dared celebrate her exit.

Rachel had watched in disgust as Sephora behaved like a spoiled child throughout the meeting. It was time to restore some normalcy to the events.

"Liava," Rachel's familiar voice rang out, "I have been standing all this while. May I have your permission to sit?"

Rachel gestured at the empty throne center stage.

Liava smiled. "I give you my permission and my blessing. Though you may only take this seat temporarily, it would do this heart good to see you sit upon it one more time." Liava held her hands to her heart.

Rachel approached the High Throne, and with as much drama as possible, sat down. Women cheered. When the noise subsided, Rachel turned to Liava to continue the vote, but there was a disturbance as Ava and her group re-entered the stage behind Servus, who still stood in place, all but forgotten.

"No! Oh, no!" It was the voice of Rachella wailing in distress. "What have they done to you? You poor man!"

The women of the city protected the children from the gory sight of punished slaves. It was the first time Rachella and her companions had seen anyone in such a deplorable condition. Added to the trauma of seeing Kiertus killed, the children were quite upset.

Instead of continuing the vote, Rachel discreetly gave orders to have the stage floor cleaned up by attendants and to have Partouche, the only fatality of the fight, covered with a white sheet and carried out of the hall.

"Queen Rachel," said Rachella, turning to the throne, "please tell the soldiers to take the chains off this man. Allow me to have some clean water from the attendants so I may wash his wounds."

The former High Queen nodded.

"Let it be. It is said the reward for compassion is service. This child is wise for her age."

An attendant brought Rachella the water she had asked for. The child untied her headdress. She dipped it in the bucket of clean water, and weeping, began to clean Servus's wounds. Tears flowed freely down her face as she worked. The sight was a moving one. Some of the women in the hall began to cry also. Rachel noted the pencils of the Royal illustrators were busy sketching the scene. Out of all the outrageous things that had happened tonight, Rachella washing the wounds of Servus was the most moving.

Rachel thought it was the perfect time to continue the vote, but from the Arts Sector there was another outburst. A very pregnant woman tried to climb onto the stage. She babbled and cried at the same time. Arrival's soldiers held her back.

Rachel, frustrated at another distraction, stood and called out. "What does that woman want?"

The woman answered for herself, still sobbing.

"The child is right. What they have done to Servus is terrible. I want to help her tend to him. Let me go to him, I beg you."

The women of Evlantis had a name for the hormonal swings that made women irrational during pregnancy: pregandemonium. The woman was obviously in the throes of it. Rachel sighed.

"Woman, Servus is being tended to. It is obvious to all of us here you should be thinking of your unborn child. Go back to your seat. Do not risk the life you carry needlessly. Calm yourself."

"You do not understand," the pregnant woman said. She continued to struggle with the soldiers. "I am a friend of the High Queen's missing daughter, First Sephora. Almost three months ago she told me her mother had opened the slave genealogies, and she learned that Servus is my father."

Another collective gasp went up from the crowd. Rachel felt as if the fabric of their culture was unraveling far too quickly, but she knew that whatever weakened Sephora's reign would be best for the Queendom in the long run.

"Go to him," Rachel said. The soldiers stopped struggling with the woman and escorted her up the stairs and across the stage.

Physically, Servus was weak from hunger, the exertion of the dance, loss of blood, and the death of Kiertus. Mentally, he felt strong, surrounded by Justus and his men and cared for by the child. At this newest revelation, Servus, King of Slaves, felt water rise up in his eyes. He was finally free of his gag, but found he was speechless. As soon as the very pregnant woman was ensconced within the group of Servus' supporters, Rachel was finally able to turn to Liava.

"Liava, please continue with the vote at hand."

"Queen Ariana must abstain from the vote," said Liava. "She has just witnessed the death of her quickening partner and has demonstrated behavior that may or may not be indicative of illegal activity. The vote for the Livestock Sector must proceed to the twelve Royal Matrons in that Sector."

Rachel anticipated further outbursts, so she stood with her arms outstretched in the signal for silence. Rachella had finished her work but was still crying bitterly. Because of the acoustics in the hall and the women's obedience of Rachel's signal for silence, most women could hear the child weeping. Rachella's sorrow reminded many of them of the first time they had seen a slave punished severely and had been shocked by it. Somehow, each had overcome her shock and pity and had grown callous to the suffering of the men over the years. Ariana cupped the child's face in her hands and tried to comfort her.

"Child, you have been true to your heart and shown mercy where it was needed. Why do you still cry?"

"I cut my finger once, chopping onions for Grandma's stew," answered Rachella. "It hurt for days. How much more must this man hurt? I have cleaned his wounds but I cannot stop his pain. I can only hurt for him."

"Child, you must look further than the pain. This man's suffering is like the pains of childbirth. No woman can bear that burden for another. I have great hope his suffering will usher in an end to slavery and new life for the men and the women of the Queendom. Stop crying and stand bravely with him."

Rachella did as the Queen asked. Hope replaced the look of abject sorrow. Ariana, obeying an instinct she did not understand, stood next to Justus. The older man was moved. Kiertus was gone, but he had held his daughter and now the woman Kiertus had loved stood beside him. Justus put his arm around her and Ariana leaned against him.

Servus's wounds were bandaged. Rachella waited with him patiently, holding his hand, but his daughter was still fussing over him. She had seen to it he was seated in a comfortable chair. She had sent a slave to fetch it from the palace. In this way a slave in attendance at the Hall was able to give word to a palace slave there was a vote going on to free them. Word would spread quickly. Servus knew it would reach his soldiers in time to prevent them from carrying out any more steps of his campaign for war.

Arrival had slipped back into the hall quietly as Ariana was speaking. She had taken up her post beside Rachel and was giving crowd control signals to her soldiers who were still in place from the last outburst. It was clear Servus had everything he ever wanted: a woman to champion him, a daughter, and a grandchild on the way.

With some semblance of order restored, Liava was determined to finish the session as quickly as possible.

"Royal Matrons of the Livestock Sector, you now know the position of your Queen and why I cannot allow her to vote. All those in favor of Caliphus's motion to free the slaves and make Servus King of a Seventh Sector, please rise. You have three minutes to decide. The gong will sound when your time is up."

Three women stood immediately. Two women stood after a minute. Two more minutes passed slowly, and as the mallet for the gong was being swung to end the vote, one more woman, her face troubled, rose to her feet.

"Six votes for the motion," said Liava. "You may be seated. All those against Caliphus's motion to free the slaves and make Servus King of a Seventh Sector, please rise. You will have three minutes to decide. Again, the gong will sound when time is up."

One woman stood immediately. The five women who had not yet voted were good friends of hers. When she stood, they stood. The three minutes crept by. None of the women who had voted yes changed their vote, though they had the right to. The gong sounded.

"Six have voted against the motion. The vote in the Livestock Sector is tied, six for and six against. Ariana must remain in abstention and cannot break the tie. The Low Queens' vote remains tied at two for and two against. We must again break to consult the elders and the law books to see what the correct procedure is."

Before the crowd could react, Rachel stood and addressed the women.

"Women of Evlantis, I command you to use this time for silent contemplation. These moments will be a time of introspection for all. Whether the slaves are freed or not, we can never go back to our old way of dealing with them. Think well on all you have seen and heard tonight."

Order was maintained as Liava left the podium to consult with the Royal Matrons of the Government Sector, who had already begun poring over the scrolls of law.

Rachel sat on the throne, radiating peace. She knew what the outcome would be. She had ruled the women for over forty years and knew the law far better than Liava did, whose turn had simply come up to serve as moderator. She reflected this would be the last time she sat on the throne in the Palace Hall. Sephora would remain High Queen no matter which way the vote went. Rachel doubted Sephora would be re-elected once her seven-year term was completed. Rachel mentally allowed herself to let go of the leadership of Queendom. This was her last great service to Evlantis. After this, she would prepare for the very important journey to find her grandchildren.

Arrival, too, was at peace. She had chosen the life of a soldier and a soldier she would remain. She anticipated Ava would step down from her throne to have a life with Servus. Arrival would take up the post of Commander and Queen again, and be fulfilled by it. Servus would be a King, a father, and a grandfather. Arrival was pleased at the part she had played in keeping him whole, and helping to free the slaves. She found her happiness for him soothed the ache in her own heart.

Rachel and Arrival's demeanors were calming to the people. Barriers had been broken. They all waited patiently, reflecting in silence. Liava approached the podium. She gave no preamble. Everyone had waited long enough.

"The law is clear. The Livestock sector vote will remain tied. There is no requirement for it to be broken. That leaves the decisive vote to Low Queen Rebekkah, Commander of the Soldier Sector."

Ava had returned to the Throne of the Soldier Sector after escorting the children to the stage. She stood slowly, savoring the moment. Over the last few months, she had learned the meaning of suffering. Her soul had been to a dark place where it could not hear the Master's voice. For the first time since leaving the Garden, Ava felt the joy of being with Him though she could not see Him beside her. She felt she would bear the suffering again to have this sweet moment of certainty that she was doing His will. She smiled.

"It is my great privilege to give the Queendom the greatest gift in recent herstory," she said. "I vote yes to the proposal. Free the slaves, and make Servus the King of the Seventh Sector, which will henceforth be called the Freeman Sector."

Liava nodded.

"It is done. From this moment on, the slaves are free. All men are officially members of the Seventh Sector of the Queendom. Servus is Low King."

Rachel walked to where Servus stood, took the simple circlet from her head, and placed it on his. More women than not started cheering. Most shed tears. The men on stage, and those who were serving in the Palace Hall, could not contain their jubilation.

Servus, Low King of the Freeman Sector, stood proudly with his little band of former slaves and children celebrating around him, tears of joy running down his face.

A retinue of priestesses led by Caliphus approached Ava. She turned briefly toward the stage and managed to catch Servus's eye, and then she winked at him. The priestesses lifted Ava up on their shoulders to carry her around the Hall in a Procession of Triumph, but not before Ava had the chance to mouth the words of a message to Servus. Servus read her lips clearly.

"I told you so!" was the message that accompanied the wink she had given him.

Servus surveyed the hall until he found Arrival. She was in motion, busily giving orders to the soldiers. It looked as if it might be a while before they would be able to meet in private, but he could wait. Now that he was free, nothing would prevent him from courting her. He was free to pursue Arrival, the woman he loved more than life itself.

End of Book One

EPILOGUE

*A*rrival had secured Sephora in the Royal Dressing Room where she raged while she waited to be told the outcome of the vote. How things had gone so wrong just when she had achieved everything she had worked for so patiently was a mystery to her. Now she had to start over. As she vented her rage in a vile string of abusive words, she paced and threw things. And she schemed. If she couldn't have the power she always dreamed of, she would have revenge.

Made in the USA
Charleston, SC
05 December 2012